Other Works by Fern Brady

Short Stories and Poems in the following Anthologies:

From Inklings Publishing:
Eclectically Carnal
Eclectically Criminal
Eclectically Heroic
Eclectically Magical

From other Publishers:
In the Questions
Waves of Passion
Short Stories by Texas Authors Vol. 2

Graphic Novel in collaboration with illustrator Rosamaria Garza:
Mr. Landen's Library Volume 1: The Heir

Under her Pen Name: Lady Nefari Ydarb

Short stories and poems in anthologies:
Perceptions: Bullying
Perceptions: Friendship

Picture books in collaboration with illustrator Araceli Casas
Smiley Face Blatoon
Picture Day, Ella!

UNITED VIDDEN

FERN BRADY

www.inklingspublishing.com

Houston, TX

UNITED VIDDEN

First U.S. Edition
Houston, TX

Development Editing by Max Regan of Hollowdeck Press
and Kelly Lynn Colby of Cursed Dragon Ship Publishing
Copy Editing by Amy Megill
Cover Art by Verstandt
Formatting by Manon Lavoie
Maps by Araceli Casas

ISBN: 978-1-944428-37-2 Print Book
ISBN: 978-1-944428-38-9 Ebook
by Inklings Publishing
http://inklingspublishing.com

Printed in the United States of America
20 19 18 17 16   1 2 3 4 5

DEDICATION

This novel is dedicated to the students who passed through my classroom during my 15 year tenure as a public school teacher. Thank you for joining me on the adventure of writing and making up worlds for characters to inhabit. Thyrein's Galactic Wall was born there and I will be forever grateful to have worked and known all of you—yes, even you troublemakers—you know who you are!

ACKNOWLEDGMENTS

Writing is a team sport.

Though at first glance it seems a lonely, isolated profession, upon closer inspection, it is done in the warmth of a beautiful and supportive community. My journey began when Cristina Kindred introduced me to the Houston Writers Guild. There I met Julian Kindred and Pamela Fagan Hutchins. They sparked a fire to return to my first love and pursue it in earnest. All my life, I have been a writer, and, in the welcoming cushion of the guild, I found the strength to seek it out as a profession. Andrea Sanchez, the current CEO of HWG, has been a longtime friend and I'm glad she took on the organization and is leading it in new directions.

While we are on the topic of communities and organizations that support authors, here are some of the organizations that have been a lifeline for me as I move along the path of my life as a working author: Authorology, headed by JoAnna Jordan and Greg Kelso; Authors Marketing Guild, headed by B Alan Bourgeois; and Writers In the Schools, with whom I had the pleasure of working.

As I took each tentative and frightening step forward, I found amazing authors turned friends who gave me help and encouragement. In no particular order, I want to honor here the ones who have most saliently been my rocks of support: Manon Lavoie, Karina Winbigler, Russell Little, Leroy Ussery, Alicia Richardson, Dorothy Tinker, Kelly Lynn Colby, Verstandt and Jennifer Shelton, Felicia 'Mack' Little, Billy Steed, Kyle McKee, Pamela Lombana, Araceli Casas, Rosamaria Garza, Raul Herrera, Frank Chambers, Connie Gillen, Landy Reed, and other wonderful writers from various retreats and critique groups who helped shape my messy drafts along their way to publication.

Speaking of messy drafts, the most important people in the production of this finished novel, that is now readable and coherent, were the team of professionals who shaped it and polished it with me. Here they are, these miracle workers and loving support team: Max Regan, of Hollowdeck Press, who took me on and became my writing coach; Kelly Lynn Colby, of Cursed Dragon Ship Publishing, who developmentally edited this book; Amy Megill, who copyedited the final draft to make sure it complied with quality standards of English use; Manon Lavoie, who formatted the interior and made it look amazing; and Verstandt, who created the kickass cover that caught your eye and helped lure you into purchasing and reading this book. Without these amazing people, this book would still be on my flash drive, a hodge-podge of crazy thoughts about some princess that runs away. A special thanks to Karina Winbigler and Sandy Lawrence, along with her amazing team, who help create promotional materials and spread the word about this book so readers can be lured into buying it and reading it.

The inner circle of the writing community that helped me along this path was supported by an outer circle of friends and family. In this sphere of love and disbelief that I was actually crazy enough to pursue writing as an actual job are the people I love with all my heart: Mike Brady, my ex-husband who gave me the freedom to quit my day job and became my number one fan even after I killed him off in a short story (which was not the reason for the divorce); my parents, Ramon and Lourdes Del Villar, who think everything I write is absolutely perfect and have taught me to be the strong, independent, and badass woman I've become (see how humble I am); and my brother and his wife, Ramon Jr and Mariely Matos, who make me laugh and let me train their dogs to later undo the effort.

Mental health is incredibly important for an author, whose sensitive and creative nature can easily become despondent or self-critical. The beings who have been here for me when I get depressed are not human, but they are still incredible people. Their fuzzy ears and cold noses have pulled me back to the happiness of living time and time again. Some are now gone, and I will see them again when my time comes to transcend to the next level. Some new ones are always added. Here are the fur babies that have been my best friends and psychological support as this book is brought into the world: Georgina, a Netherlands dwarf bunny; Twinkle, a Chilean Rose Hair tarantula; Arwen, a German-Shepherd/Lab mix princess (aka Smoochie); Ella, her litter mate sister who my brother adopted (aka Peluchie); Grace, a blonde German Shepherd who I adopted and gifted to Mike Brady even though he said he wasn't ready (of course, men don't really know when they are ready so I took care of the matter—also not the reason for the divorce, in case you were wondering); Merlin, a Great Dane/Lab plus other mix boy who is the sweetest least elegant and dignified dog I have ever known; Coco and Misty (aka the Minis) my brother's current babies who are absolutely the epitome of mischief and love; and Arya, my husky and the most talkative dog I have ever met.

Of course, the most important person to thank and acknowledge is the Great I Am. He knew me from before the beginning of time and created me for His purposes. He has called me to be a woman that encompasses a man and I look forward to making the destiny He has for me a reality. In His love, I walk with wisdom and understanding and try to do good wherever I go. Thank you, Abba, for creating me and making me the wonderfully complicated and completely eclectic person I am.

Well, now that I have mentioned all the people who have been instrumental in getting this novel out here into the world, and probably forgotten some names that should be here, I welcome you to enter into the world of Thyrein's Galactic Wall. I hope you enjoy the story and the universe it's set in. Please consider leaving a review for the book and, if you wish to learn more about the universe these characters live in, check out my website: www.fernbrady.com

Maps of
United Vidden

Dramatic Personae

Kingdom of Dravidia

King Dekkyle
Princess Verena
Eldor, Earl of Sarnac
Sir Eriq Seller, Lord High Marshal
Countess of Cartul
Lady Margy
Lady Geld
Duchess of Fen
General Oldan
Col. Folgero, REIS team leader
Helen, Garinquel servant
Sir Grahan Sorma, Lord Chamberlain
Lady Soane
Mrs. Denip, Hudroid
Count of Tor
Jolyon, Viscount Tor

Principality of Aulden

Prince Amiel ra Aulden
Figor, Duke of Aul
Sabred, Earl of Udeep, the Dragonslayer
General Nataya, Countess of Udeep
Godar, Nijar Lord (Viscount Pembra)
Lord Uld
Lord Ydarb
Sir Andross Draneg

Rajin Order

Rajin Master, Lord Horsef
Rajin Master, Lady Vivelda
Rajin Master, Lord Bral
Lord Orloff, Prophet of the order of Resord

Elmalin Order

Dova Elmalin, Lady Jafra
Misrim Elmalin, Lady Nomri
Misrim Elmalin, Lady Andiera
Lady Daria

CHAPTER 1

COMING OF AGE

CLAD IN SIM-ARMOR, Princess Verena prepared for the battle intended to prove her worth as a ruler. Her heart rate quickened. On this, the morning of her twenty-first birthday, she would fight a virtual represent-tation of a venladon queen, the most dreaded beast in the entire known universe. Thanks to the digital fibers embedded in her suit, she would feel the full effects of the monster's attacks. She thought of the bruises she'd be sure to have by the time her party started tonight and was glad the dress she'd chosen would cover most of them. She pulled her long auburn hair into a tight bun. Her emerald eyes took in the elegantly attired guests from the fifty-one planets of Thyrein's Galactic Wall.

For past heirs, many noble families had skipped the coming-of-age ritual. After all, the outcome was assured: The heir to the throne always died. The contest was about stamina, critical thinking, and endurance. It measured how long the warrior lasted and how much damage he inflicted upon the one monster that could not be killed by the hand of man.

But today, every person of importance in the Intergalactic Alliance turned out to witness her demise. The dynamic interface software, gathering signals from the sim-armor, would record the hits the animal made on her, just as it would those she managed to inflict on it. The DSI would calculate when she'd lost enough virtual blood, or received a deathblow, and declare the battle over, the heir to the kingdom dead.

Verena noticed the speculative stares directed at her and the excited chatter filling the room. The question in their eyes: How long would the first female successor to the throne of the Kingdom of Dravidia last against a venladon queen? Verena straightened and squared her shoulders.

The taut hide of the arena stretched out before her. Verena looked down at herself. The protective gear she wore, like that of the elite knights, was made of honrol. The unique metal interacted with her body's energy, making it malleable to allow for her fluid movements. Yet it was strong enough to guard against all manner of weapons. Verena enjoyed how it hugged her hourglass figure like a second skin.

Tall and slender, Grahan Sorma, Lord Chamberlain, came forward. He had donned his formal suit of office; its silver sash crossed his double-breasted coat bearing the royal insignia. Verena's eyes fell upon her family crest. Courage enveloped her as she considered the legendary sword, Marama, depicted in silver thread, outspread dragon wings sprouting from its hand guard, emblazoned on a field of purple. Her house had forged the Intergalactic Alliance through her ancestor, Thyrein, who'd been the last to wield the mighty weapon before it disappeared again. Pride swelled in her. She would show herself to be his worthy descendant.

"Shall we begin, Highness?" Lord Sorma asked.

"Is Father not back, then?" She couldn't hide the note of disappointment.

"The king sends his deepest regrets, Highness. Mr. Drang spoke with him moments ago. He should be back by tonight, but his ship was delayed and he will need to miss this morning's events. He is very upset and wished me to convey to you his good wishes. He will watch over the quantum-net coverage."

Verena sighed. Her father often traveled incognito to get a good feel for the true situation of the kingdom, yet it sounded like he had been off planet. *How can Father miss the most important moment of my life?* Verena buried her pain. She had to concentrate on defeating the beast... well, on enduring as long as possible before dying, hopefully making a few dents in the creature's nearly impenetrable hide.

"Let's get started."

At her directive, the Lord Chamberlain turned to face the spectators. "Royal guests, ladies, and gentlemen." His deep, booming voice, augmented by the sound amplifiers, brought silence to the room. The audience readied themselves as the servbots hovered off, back to the castle's kitchens. "We gather today to bear witness to a momentous event. Our heir, Princess Verena Elidena Destavi of the House of Drav, shall battle the undefeatable foe, a venladon queen."

The polite applause ended abruptly. A roar shook the room into silence as the holopro switched on, revealing the ten-foot-tall form of a venladon queen. Verena froze at the simulation's realism. The creature threw back its massive head, its deep-throated call reverberating off the beige stone walls of the chamber.

The princess's mind ran through all she knew of the beast: The venladon drone workers walked on all fours, but queens could rise on their hind legs. This one stood with its long arms hanging loosely at its side. Thick, sharp claws emanated from each of three distinct finger-type appendages. The creature had thorn-like spikes covering its dark-brown scaly torso. This made attacks from the side difficult. Venladons could use their long muscular tails like a whip, doing severe damage and knocking their enemies off their feet. This venladon queen's elongated maw held three rows of jagged teeth. Its head featured a lethal crown of four short horns. Verena knew some could have upwards of ten or more. She wondered if they'd used the minimum number on record for a full-grown queen to make the battle easier. The princess hoped this was not so, for she was ready to face the challenge before her.

The creature stood, waiting.

With a single thought, Verena activated the virtual ginmra she had in her right hand. From the sword-like pommel came forth a simulated honrol double-edged blade glowing pink, her favorite color. The holographic monster came alive, roused by Verena's weapon readiness. Coming down on all fours, it lunged. The princess threw herself to the left and thrust the blade in between two spikes on the creature's lower abdomen as it went by, careful to avoid being impaled on her first move. The system registered the slight hit. It had little effect on the venladon.

"Well done, Highness!" Sir Eriq Seller's praise echoed in her ear. The com device allowed her to receive help from her weapons master, just as a warrior would receive orders on a real battlefield from their commander.

Almost too late, Verena noted the monster's mouth hurling down toward her. She slid to the right, twisting to land a glancing blow on the protruding snout. It cried out in pain and then thrust its head at her, aiming its horns at her chest. Verena dodged the spiked crown, but its maw slammed into her.

The sensors in her armor analyzed the impact and threw her back. Losing her balance, the princess skidded away and hit a padded column. The computer simulated the damage to her body, applying pressure to her rib cage. She gasped for air. Pain flashed through her. Another roar filled the chamber. The venladon rose onto its hind legs.

"Slash the softer abdominal hide!" Sir Eriq's voice in her ear instructed.

Pushing the pain aside, she ran toward the monster. The venladon drove its muzzle at her oncoming form once more, but Verena dropped onto the mat and rolled under it, jabbing her virtual blade deep into its stomach. Verena heard the crowd cheer. Without knowing what damage she had inflicted on the beast, she reveled in the gathering's response.

Distracted, she failed to see the venladon's tail as it swung into her shoulder. The sim-armor spun her body and sent her crashing into another column on the opposite side of the arena. Recording the damage to her left shoulder, the armor became heavier on that side.

"Foluc!" Verena cursed her failure.

The creature charged, jaw wide and ready to swallow her whole. With all her might, Verena used the column to push herself once more across the dojo and under the thick neck of the beast. She brought the ginmra up, but the move, slowed by her injury, did little damage. Turning, she saw the first gash across the belly and impaled her weapon again into the same spot.

A sharp-clawed arm grabbed her and flung her away as the venladon roared in pain. She landed hard on her hands and knees, her injured side giving way. Her head hit the floor. Pressure points across Verena's back simulated the fresh wounds the creature inflicted. Her armor became progressively heavier as the computer calculated the effects of the blood loss. She struggled to her feet.

Disoriented and laboring hard against the drag of her armor, Verena watched as her enemy turned toward her, breathing in short gasps of pain as the backplate pressed tighter from the simulated wounds. Every inch of her ached; every muscle screamed in protest. Only the adrenaline coursing through her system allowed her to persevere.

"Go for the cut on the stomach!" Amiel's whisper in the com device took her off guard. He was not authorized to access this private channel.

"How in the—"

"Just do it!"

"The prince's suggestion is good, Highness," Sir Eriq seconded.

"Right," Verena said between clenched teeth as she made a run at the venladon.

She evaded the talons rushing at her and slid under it for another pass at the abdomen. She managed to strike inches from the first cut.

"Foluc!" Verena cursed as she twisted to her feet, fighting the weight of the armor's pressure.

Jumping to the side as the tail came whipping at her, she thrust down, striking a hit. Her heart pounded as if it would come right out of her chest. She gasped for air. Strands of fiery hair had come loose and now fell across her face and over her shoulders.

The venladon squared off with her once more. Its scarlet reptile eyes narrowed as it zeroed in on her. Verena spotted the slash on its throat, a small drip of the creature's green blood oozing out as it rushed her again. She dropped and rolled as the open mouth passed over her head. She plunged the blade into the same simulated injury on its neck. The beast howled in pain, lifting onto its hind legs.

She lay beneath it, staring at a wrinkly knee. Her eyes found the gut wound. Scrambling onto her feet, she ran, half stumbling, across the animal's wide girth, pushing the blade in. The creature's pain-filled cry rang once more. As she dove to clear the venladon's body, its tail slammed into her stomach. The sensors in the armor threw her onto her back just as the monster's arms swung down. Long claws dug into her belly and chest. The DSI registered the death blow and switched off.

The venladon queen disappeared. The virtual ginmra vanished. The sim-armor released its pressure points. The room waited in silence as Verena sat up, panting. Each breath identified another painful spot on her body. Yet, none of that mattered as she anticipated the analysis. *How long did I last? Did I score anything against it?*

Three of her seven ladies in waiting brought a portable chair and helped her settle into it. Pain seared through her at every movement. Sir Eriq came toward her, leaving his place in the command box at the head of the arena.

"It will take a minute for the DSI to finalize its calculations," he said, handing her a towel so she could wipe the sweat off her face. "How do you feel?"

"Like a stampede of elhrin just hit me."

"It is a good thing your highness was not run over by a herd of pachyderms," he commented, a wide smile wreathing his rugged face. He stood beside her as they awaited the results.

Verena smiled at her ladies as all seven gathered behind her chair. They were all significantly older than her, except Lady Geld, who was also twenty-one.

Lady Geld handed her a bottle of nutrient-fortified water. "It's a good thing the ginmra effect doesn't happen with a virtual weapon, or you'd sleep through your entire birthday ball, Highness!"

Drinking deeply, Verena responded, "Yes." Her mind recalled how training with her ginmra could leave her comatose for up to a month or more. "It has always been that way for me. I don't know why."

"All knights who have the nodes to control a ginmra implanted need recuperation time," Sir Eriq said.

"None as long as her Highness. It is a bit of a concern, don't you think, Sir Eriq?" the Countess of Cartul asked.

It had been an embarrassing topic of conversation for Verena ever since the princess had been granted a ginmra. In spite of the assurances from Lord Horsef, the greatest of rajin masters, that it was nothing to worry about, Verena questioned the unusual response her body had to the weapon. She didn't like the weakness it revealed.

Lady Reflo's frowning face caught Verena's eyes. The representative of planet Drulin conversed with the other ambassadors and royals from the fifty-one planets of the Intergalactic Council seated in the right-hand spectator boxes of the second floor. Confident in her negotiating skills, Verena had carefully reviewed the reports of the growing discord among the allied planets over the allocation of access to critical natural resources on uninhabited worlds. As queen, she would soon be able to work with them on these and other intergalactic issues. The princess anticipated with eagerness having a chance to forge equitable distributions for everyone.

Her eyes drifted to the ground floor, where Dravidia's earls, dukes, counts, and barons sat next to those of the Principality of Aulden, the only other nation on her world. Amiel's clear blue eyes locked with hers. He smiled at her, and pride gleamed in his gaze.

A flush of warmth filled her, followed by a deep sense of loss. *Why did he change?* Flustered, she shifted her eyes to the opposite side of the room.

There, on the bottom floor, the representatives on her Council of Vassals, dressed in their finest formal business attire, sat alongside her military leadership. The princess smiled amiably at them, a sense of comfort in her well-established relationships returning her emotions to their normal calmness. Her gaze lifted to the second-floor boxes, where the Rajin Council of Masters and a few apprentices sat in their long scarlet robes embroidered with astronomical patterns in silver thread. A handful of elmalin, each attired in a cloak whose color and decoration represented the element of nature the bearer wielded, were beside them.

But her mind pulled her attention away from the powerful beings and back to her old friend. Amiel stood, tall and broad shouldered, beside the other royals. His wavy black hair framed his handsome face in its usual neat cut. Dressed in an elegant navy-blue silk suit, Amiel's good looks drew the attention of the ladies around him. Yet, his eyes didn't stray from Verena for long, which brought a smile to her face. Her fond childhood memories of their mischievous escapades warred against the growing fear of the cold violence she'd witnessed in the Prince of Aulden in recent years.

"No Calvernsin." Sir Eriq's comment brought the realization of their absence to the princess's attention.

She pushed her confused feelings for Amiel aside. "That is odd," Verena said, glancing up into her weapon master's face to read his interpretation of this. "What do you think that means? They were invited, as members of the council."

"They aren't very social, but..." the legendary knight's voice trailed off, a wariness entering his eyes.

Verena acknowledged it with a nod. The space-faring Calvernsin were by far the most difficult to work with among the alliance. She sighed wearily at the thought of the continuous skirmishes with these beautiful beings.

The Lord Chamberlain returned, his face wreathed in a wide smile. "The results are ready, Highness," Lord Sorma stated.

"You may make the announcement, Excellency," Verena instructed, butterflies flitting in her stomach. *Did I do well?* She lifted up a quick prayer to the Great I Am for a worthy showing. Top ten would be a dream come true.

Turning to the room, Lord Sorma used the voice enhancers to bring the guests' attention back to the arena. "Ladies and gentlemen, honored guests, the results are in." An expectant silence fell upon the chamber. Verena's belly roiled, and she willed her Lord Chamberlain to be done with the drama. "Five minutes and thirty-three seconds," Grahan Sorma finally announced. "Her Highness takes fourth place, surpassing her father, King Dekkyle's time, by a full two minutes."

An explosion of applause and cheers reverberated across the room. Verena's heart soared. Twenty generations of royal heirs had gone through the challenge, and she'd placed fourth. The urge to jump up and down with joy assailed her, but the strictures of royal composure that'd been drummed into her kept her from acting out her elation.

"And," the Lord Chamberlain broke in, silencing the crowd once more. "Her Highness made two cuts into the venladon's hide that would have bled. That adds a bonus twenty seconds per strike, for a final score total of six minutes and thirteen seconds."

It's done. Thank the Great I Am, it's over!

The Duchess of Fen, her mother's spinster sister, abandoned all decorum and rushed over to her. She hugged her tightly. "If she had lived to see this day, Irene would've been so proud. You remember the word the Great I Am gave her about you?"

"Of course, Auntie. Mama said I would be a woman who encompassed a man."

"And so you shall, child. The greatest female ruler ever."

Verena hugged her aunt tightly, feeling the ache of her mother's death. It had been many years, but the sense of loss remained.

The guests' hoorays resounded again in the dojo. Pride brought a triumphant grin to Verena's face. She allowed herself to be led away to the changing rooms. The most important guests lined her path, congratulating her.

Then he stood before her, Prince Amiel ra Aulden, ruler of the Principality of Aulden. His ice-blue eyes met hers, and a shiver ran through Verena. Her heart skipped a beat, and she berated herself for it.

"You were magnificent!" His words warmed her as he bowed over her hand.

"How did you access my com?" Verena asked, deflecting from the compliment he'd given her.

He winked at her, an arrogant self-assured smile splayed upon his handsome features. "I have my ways."

Verena shook her head and continued past him. Helen, one of the Garinquel servants, awaited her with her bathing toiletries at the ready.

The maid still bore the marks of Amiel's wrath on her back. A sadness filled Verena as she thought of his temper and how it could manifest in sudden violence.

Allowing her attendants to disrobe her in the dojo's locker room, Verena dispelled her mind of these musings. Tonight, she would dance and celebrate. Tomorrow, as custom dictated, her father would abdicate and she would take the throne. Now, while her guests attended the castle fair, enjoying food and shopping from the vendors she had personally selected, Verena would rest and recuperate for the evening's ball. *Will Father make it back in time for that? What could possibly be so important to keep him away on this day?*

CHAPTER 2

THE RAJIN

PRINCESS VERENA TOOK HER FATHER'S ARM. King Dekkyle had returned to the castle only an hour earlier, visiting her room still in his disguise. From the coneb desert attire, Verena guessed he'd likely come from Lataira, an arid planet very near to their own.

What were you doing there, Father? she'd wanted to ask, but after a quick kiss and cursory apology for missing her coming-of-age battle, his valet had rushed him away to change for the party.

His strong embrace, along with the look of pride and wonder as he congratulated her, had lifted Verena's spirits. Despite the great victory and the relaxing afternoon, the disappointment of his absence had weighed heavily on her.

Now, he stood beside her, attired in his full military uniform of royal purple with silver trim. King Dekkyle's fifty years on the throne had not yet turned his auburn hair, so like hers, fully gray. Verena smiled up at his emerald eyes. In the morning, she would ascend the throne, and his abdication would make her queen. The burden of state would shift to her shoulders. He would be there as an advisor, but he'd enjoy some peace in his latter days.

Not all royal houses held to this custom. For most, the heir waited in the wings until the death of the monarch. Verena had often felt pride that her kingdom moved away from such nonsense. At twenty-one, the heir who ascended to the throne was given the opportunity to reap the benefit of the abdicating monarch's expertise. Plus, Verena felt it engendered better relationships, as the heir wasn't waiting for their parent to die in order to rule.

Father and daughter descended from the second-floor mezzanine down the central staircase to the entry vestibule in a slow, stately manner. Her dark-purple gown with square-cut neckline and voluminous skirt shimmered with each step she took. Her fiery hair had been gracefully piled atop her head and held in place with a myriad of diamond rose-shaped pins. Below them, the guests had gathered for the commencement of the birthday dinner and ball. The beige stone walls were festooned with garlands of rose flowers in pink and purple hues, which accentuated the tapestries and paintings. The white marble floors gleamed, while the area rugs and runners had been brushed clean, their colors vibrant in the pink flow of light from the crystal chandeliers.

"I missed you this morning at the coming-of age-battle." Verena tried to keep the peevish tone from her voice.

"I'm sorry, my little kura," her father responded, using the nickname he and her mother had given her. It meant 'treasure' in the ancient tongue of planet Drulin and always filled Verena with joy. "I would have been here, but the investigation into the situation on Parthia took longer than planned. We will speak of all tomorrow."

"Situation?"

"Do not fret yourself about it now. This is your birthday. Enjoy your evening. We will have time to talk in the morning."

"The abdication ceremony will be—"

The king cut her off. "We will need to postpone it for a time."

Verena's foot slipped. She caught herself with the next step. Staring straight forward, she forced herself not to turn, not to demand an explanation. She was to be queen. *Why the change?* Her stomach lurched as her mind turned over this development.

"Why? I don't understand."

"Things will be clearer after tonight."

They reached the vestibule. The crowd parted. As they passed, men bowed and ladies curtsied, then fell in line behind them. They entered the great dining hall, but Verena's thoughts were still out on the stairway.

"But the arrangements—" Verena's voice quivered, the joy of her birthday overshadowed by her father's words.

"I've taken care of everything. Daline will make the announcement to the media."

As her father led her to the far end of the long honeywood rectangle table, Verena had an image of the plump and animated Daline Elviran, communications director for the royal family and head of the Media Relations Office, telling the news outlets of the kingdom and of the entire galactic wall that the king had opted not to abdicate, as tradition dictated. The vision of the reporters and their questions brought a heat to her face, and she willed herself to calm down. Her father pulled out the queen's chair for her. Ever since her mother's death, nine years earlier, Verena had sat in her stead.

I should be queen. The words echoed over and over in her stunned mind. *Why the delay?* No answer came back to her. Doubts assailed her as panic swelled in her chest. Her stomach tensed while she waited for her father to take his place at the opposite end of the table.

Amiel's whisper told her she'd lost the cool composure the occasion called for. "Are you all right?" He stood at her right hand waiting for the king to be seated in order to take his place.

A frown of consternation marred her face as she glanced his way. He returned a cheeky grin. The Prince of Aulden, as the only other head of state on their planet, should have been placed to the right of her father's seat. *Why is he near me? I didn't approve this seating arrangement.* Finally, her father took his place and the guests all followed suit.

"You look magnificent this evening," Prince Amiel commented.

"Thank you." Verena acknowledged his compliment.

The first course, a simmering vegetable soup, was placed before them by the dining hall hudroids. Dressed in the livery of House Drav, these robotic servants were fashioned to appear human. Only the charging port on the back of their necks gave away that they weren't real people. She liked them far more than the metal servbots.

Verena swallowed down the hurt and confusion of her brief conversation with her father. She turned to President Nichamir Vlanesport Linput of Sorusvia, one of the most powerful nations on planet Gelderant, who sat to her left. Since he was the person of highest social status seated closest to her, she conversed with him during the first course, expressing her condolences over the death of his wife.

"Did you get my gift?" Prince Amiel asked when the soup bowls were removed, and she turned to him.

"Yes," Verena answered, recalling the beautiful pink gown in the new Auldian style hanging in her closet. Amiel had never given her such a personal item before. It had struck Verena as odd. Still, Mrs. Denip, her nurse-maid hudroid, had not felt the gift inappropriate.

"I thought perhaps you would wear it tonight," he commented.

Letting her emerald eyes connect with his ice-blue ones, Verena explained, "I'd already had this gown commissioned for the occasion from Igog Tars. He is a great young designer I came upon in Dravidia City." She brushed away a wayward strand of auburn hair that had tumbled out of her coifed updo. "I did wear the brooch you gave me last year. It's most charming. Don't you think?"

"I'm very pleased you like it." His eyes looked at her with a strange intensity. "I'm told Elvar Grifold is all the rage right now among designers. He is the one who made the gown I gave you."

"There will surely be an occasion to wear it soon. This new look is interesting."

"Anything you wear, no matter how lovely, is eclipsed by your beauty."

The princess chose to take a bite from the succulent steak, cooked to a perfect medium rare, rather than respond. She couldn't deny Amiel was a very handsome man—really handsome, she admitted to herself, breathless from his gaze. His wavy black hair, classical features, and athletic physique made him extremely attractive. It was the arrogant, and, too often violent disregard for those he considered inferior that troubled and frightened her.

"May I have your attention, everyone," her father called out, lifting his wine glass. "Tonight, I wish to make a toast to my beautiful daughter. To Verena, mighty warrior and soon, Queen of Dravidia."

The guests responded in unison, "To the Princess."

Verena's puzzlement intensified. She held her composure as she smiled at her guests, but within, her mind whirled. *Is Father changing his mind? Will he abdicate tomorrow after all? Why would he need to postpone anyway?*

"I'm so proud of you," the king continued, his eyes meeting hers from across the gathering. "May the Great I Am bless you and keep you. May He make His face shine upon you and be gracious to you. May Our Lord look upon you with favor and give you peace."

"So may it be," resounded from the invitees.

Her father glanced about the room as he continued, "We may yet face times of turmoil, but I know the Great I Am is with us." He turned his gaze upon Verena. "And, House Drav will endure through your strength and courage, Verena." Looking back to the crowded dining table, he exclaimed, "Fourth place! To my daughter!" He lifted his glass once more to her.

Verena's heart soared. Her father's words gave her hope. Whatever the reason for the delay of her ascension to the throne, he believed in her as Dravidia's queen. Or, maybe he was changing his mind and would abdicate as tradition dictated. He'd mentioned turmoil, but the galactic wall was at peace. She shook her head and endeavored to focus on her guests.

The dinner continued. Verena caught a snippet of conversation between General Oldan, Dravidia's chief military officer, and the Earl of Sarnac. They seemed concerned about something happening on the continent of Parthia.

"We cannot know what they are planning." The earl's voice held a note of anxiety.

"It may be nothing, but we must..." General Oldan responded, but Verena couldn't catch the end of it.

President Nichamir spoke to her then. "Your Highness has shown exceptional skills in battle. Sir Eriq's training shows."

"He is a wonderful teacher." Verena strained to focus on the other conversation, but the gentlemen had already changed subjects.

Recalling her father's words, Verena wondered what the Gortive could be up to. They were such primitive natives that it seemed odd that someone as wise as the Earl of Sarnac would worry about them. A sense of normalcy settled back into her celebration. Perhaps the abdication ceremony would be delayed, but she was still the only heir to the throne. Maybe her father wanted to deal himself with whatever issue had arisen in Parthia first. Yet, sooner or later, she would be queen.

Two hours later, Verena found herself being led to the ballroom on her father's arm. Behind them, the guests spread out flanking the room around the honeywood dance floor. The king led her toward the far end, where the majestic thrones sat on a raised dais.

The backrest and seat of the royal chairs were upholstered in rich dark-purple satin and flanked in white gold. Verena had always loved the soft, supple fabric from the textile mills of the Vongar Valley. The seat's armrests, ending in the forged semblance of the Geldian eagle's fierce face, seemed to her the epitome of elegance. The mirror-shine of the metal surfaces reflected the light and color of the festivities, bringing a smile to the princess's face. Upon the purple velvet cloth of the canopy that draped behind the royal seats was the sigil of her royal house. Embroidered in silver thread, the image of the legendary sword, Marama, flanked with widespread dragon wings twinkled in the light of the crystal chandeliers.

The three master rajin leaders, heads of the order, waited to perform the Ritual of Endowment. Verena had always believed the name a misnomer. As she understood it, they would help draw out the fruits of the Sevenfold Spirit that were already within her, strengthening her for the task of ruling. The rajin existed in habitual presence with the Great I Am and drew from His power. Verena's confidence had soared from the morning's success against the venladon, and the meditation time of rest had brought her a deep serenity. But now she felt as ruffled as a bird caught in a tempest.

Whatever the situation with the Gortive on Parthia, surely as queen she would be able to handle it. Unbidden came the question: *Why would an heir not be ready to rule?* She had fulfilled all the requirements met by past heirs...

...By past male heirs.

Is that it, Father? Is that the reason? The tightness in her chest hurt more than any physical pain she'd experienced in mock battles, born from the understanding that her father did not have faith in her. *What will the Press Office announce tomorrow as the reason for the delay in my ascension?*

She breathed deeply, trying to calm herself and recall all that her tutor, Rajin Molent, had instructed her about the Endowment Ceremony these past weeks. She was supposed to clear her mind. She was supposed to be serene and open so that the energy of the Great I Am could flow. She was supposed to be receptive to any special vision or word that the Great I Am might bestow on her.

Verena was the opposite of all those things. Her mind was muddled with fear and doubt. Her emotions were muddled by confusion and hurt at her father's choice. Her soul was muddled by the marred vision of what she had assumed would be her secure destiny—to rule Dravidia as its queen. She caught sight of Rajin Molent among the guests. He smiled encouragingly, and Verena longed for his wise counsel.

Stopping before the triun head of the Rajin Order, the king said, "Masters, I present to you my heir."

Dropping her arm, he continued up the three steps and took his place on the throne. *Am I really, Father? If I am your heir, then why am I not ascending tomorrow? If you are really proud of me, then why don't you trust me to rule?* Verena felt abandoned and alone as she faced the masters.

Each of the master rajin wore a floor-length scarlet robe with various astronomical constellations embroidered upon it in silver thread. Beneath the ceremonial garment, Verena knew that each had on evening attire in the color that denoted their area of specialization.

Master Rajin Lord Horsef the Great was the eldest of the trio. Verena met his calm gaze as the tall and lanky lord approached. He wore his long gray hair pulled back and tied in a ponytail at his nape, with a matching beard reaching well below his waist. Verena smiled at the hints of purple, white, and gray that peaked out from beneath his robe, a sign of his work in the field of education sciences.

Beside him, on his right, came Master Rajin Lady Vivelda the Bountiful. Her blonde hair cascaded almost to her knees in glorious waves, and her clear blue eyes held warmth as they met Verena's. Hints of a golden gown could be seen, and the princess remembered that Vivelda was a master in the healing arts.

Verena turned to Master Rajin Lord Bral the Merciful to give him a polite smile. He always managed to appear and sound bored, yet his deep brown eyes held earnestness. His short brown hair was neatly trimmed, and the suit he wore beneath his robe was a bright orange, showing his interest in political sciences.

Once the masters had taken their places around Verena, an apprentice came forth, bearing a large silver bowl filled with water. The princess closed her eyes, taking in slow rhythmic breaths to still the turbulence within her. Master Horsef spoke first, his powerful voice filing the large ballroom.

"Almighty Lord, King of all Kings, may your Sevenfold Spirit's fruit flourish within this, your humble maidservant." She heard him dip his hand into the water and felt it sprinkle lightly with his finger over her head as he continued. "May she be filled with joy as the Great I Am grants her strength in the knowledge of His mighty protection. Heavenly Father, fill her with your kindness as you grant her compassion for all."

Verena's skin tingled, warmth covering her whole body. She opened her eyes and focused on Master Horsef's. A bright yellow energy field encased her. A hard, harsh voice spoke in her mind: *Your father will not abdicate the throne for you.* Sadness welled up in her. *Who will protect me from Father?* The question raced across her mind as her heart ached.

Slowly, the world turned orange as the energy around her changed. Verena let out a deep sigh. This was to make her a great queen, but she wouldn't be sovereign. *What will become of all this that the masters are performing?*

The rustle of skirts made her turn to Master Vivelda. The lady rajin spoke now, her sweet musical voice a contrast to the booming one of her fellow, yet retaining full authority within it. "May she be filled with peace as the Great I Am makes her whole in body, mind, and soul." She, too, anointed Verena lightly with water. "Heavenly Father, fill her with your generosity as you make her a person of excellence."

The princess watched the world turn a pink hue. *Peace. There is no peace.* She had been whole, confident in whom she believed herself to be. Now there was only doubt as to her future. The energy changed to green. Verena felt a strong longing to help others, to serve her subjects. *You will never rule over Dravidia,* the voice cruelly asserted. She had always desired to be the greatest monarch Dravidia had ever known. She could do it. *Why can't you see this, Father?*

"May she be filled with patience as the Great I Am grants her restraint and endurance in the face of all that is to come." Master Bral's tone held the underlying note of indifference that always colored his words. His fingers barely touched the water as he fulfilled the ritual. "Heavenly Father, fill her with self-control as you grant her mastery over her thoughts, her will, and her actions."

In spite of his lackluster method, Verena's body energy changed to a blue glow. She could hear gasps from the guests and wondered if they could see the colors changing around her. *Patience will be needed indeed. If I have to wait to ascend, can I find the strength to do so?* The hue became red, and Verena prayed silently for understanding, wisdom, and discernment to rule her people. She could submit to her father's wish to delay. The wait would surely not be too long. The voice spoke again: *You will fail.*

The world turned brown as Master Horsef spoke once more. "May she be filled with gentleness as the Great I Am grants her meekness." Verena bowed her head. *I cannot fail; I won't.* Her body shook as she wrestled with the need to be strong and the weakness she could feel in her.

The rajin masters created a circle with their entwined hands around her. Their voices rose in unison.

"May she be filled with love, as the Great I Am is love. May she be remade anew in His image." With a final dip into the water, the masters made the sign of a cross over her.

Raising her eyes to the mirrors on the ceiling, Verena watched as the energy surrounding her turned to purple. She closed her eyes, and tears spilled down her cheeks. The princess saw herself in a vast empty space embraced by a love so pure, so selfless, it was almost a physical pain in its intensity. A sparkling form stood before her, a crown in His beautiful hands. *I will not forsake you*, a voice, like the sound of rushing water, echoed in the vastness around her. Verena felt the heaviness of the symbol of sovereignty placed upon her head. The unwavering certainty that she had been born to rule filled her. Words of fire appeared before her shut eyes: *Love always wins.*

The cry of "So may it be!" sounded from the guests, and they burst into applause. The rajin stepped away, and Verena's heart ached to hold onto the vision that even now was dissipating. A slight glow remained behind, and Verena smiled opening her eyes and meeting the kind gaze of the masters.

She'd seen the rajin use their connection to the Great I Am before and had been allowed to witness an occasional ritual at their temple of Sanctal, but she had never felt it directly upon her. Now she shook slightly as her father reclaimed her hand. Tears streamed down his face, and he bent to place a kiss on her cheek.

"What the Great I Am has shown you is for you alone," he said, smiling at her. "It is a guide for your reign, and I trust in Him that you shall rule a long and prosperous time."

Verena couldn't speak. She throbbed with the wonder of the experience, and a warm glow lingered about her. She didn't know how much of it to believe. She was breathing hard, as if she'd been in combat. Rapidly blinking her eyes, she tried to regain her composure. This was her birthday party. What came tomorrow, she could handle tomorrow. *Just breathe and smile.*

Her father turned her toward the guests, then led her into the center of the room. Tradition dictated the heir open the dancing. Usually, it was a mother-son dance. For the first time in the history of her people, the king danced with his daughter. As they swayed across the room, they were accompanied by a holographic display featuring the beautiful scenery of their continent. Verena sensed a tension in her father and wondered again at the need to forgo the abdication.

"What's on your mind, Father?"

The king released a sigh. His eyes spoke of uneasiness and something else Verena couldn't quite define. She smiled encouragingly, hoping he'd share more of why he was taking such drastic actions.

"Amiel has developed a reputation as a great military strategist." King Dekkyle's eyes turned toward the crowds as he continued. "His battle against the Calvernsin on behalf of planet Fratern is a part of the new textbook at Stroleng Academy."

"Sir Eriq said I would have done well if I'd been allowed to volunteer." Verena's throat tightened. *Didn't I prove my combat skills this morning?*

"We can't risk you. You're all I have, my little kura." His gaze, on her once more, warmed her. His love shone in his eyes.

"You don't need to worry about me, Father." Verena squeezed his hand as the music came to an end, hoping he knew she'd do right for their kingdom.

As soon as the piece was done, the next partner on her holodance card claimed her.

CHAPTER 3

THREATS RISING

KING DEKKYLE ENTERED the private conference chamber connected to his office in the castle's central work complex. After handing Verena to her next dance partner, he'd signaled his key advisors to follow him. Amiel and his people were also settling into the comfortable chairs around the honrol table. As he took in the moment, Dekkyle's heart ached. He felt the momentousness of it and knew his relationship with Verena would never be the same after tonight. *Can she ever forgive me? Will she understand why it must be this way?*

Eldor, Earl of Sarnac, as Chief Peer of Dravidia, sat to Dekkyle's right. Beside him, Chief Military Officer General Oldan took his place. On the left of the king sat Rajin Horsef, whom Dekkyle trusted more than anyone else and, of course, Rajin Bral.

As a Consular Rajin, it was Bral who had the official right to be present. Yet, Dekkyle had never fully been at ease with the master of political sciences. Still, conventions had to be observed, and it would not do to insult one of the triad leadership of the Rajin Order.

On Amiel's right sat Figor, Duke of Aul, who was the prince's cousin. On the left sat Viscount Pembra. Dekkyle found this an odd choice. The House of Pembra had been formed only ten years earlier. There was not much clarity on why this man had been given a noble title or if the title would become hereditary. When Amiel had approached Dekkyle with the situation on Parthia, the king had ordered an investigation of all the main counselors of the Prince of Aulden as a precaution. Yet, his inquiries into the origins of the Viscount had not yielded much information.

Once they had all taken their places, Dekkyle began. "I will let Amiel recount our audience before the Intergalactic Alliance Council."

King Dekkyle sat down in his own chair at the head of the rectangular table. Amiel had taken the place at the opposite end, which was his due as the only other sovereign in the room. The king watched the young prince stand to address the members of their respective inner circle. There was no doubt he was a handsome, distinguished-looking man, and a brilliant strategist. But the temper and violence he exhibited upon occasion filled the king with unease at the outcome of these negotiations.

"King Dekkyle and I presented to the council the information concerning the sea-going vessels the Gortive are building. We requested permission to conduct a preemptive strike against the native forces." Amiel's face took on a look of disgust as he continued, "The council believes this development is nothing more than a natural progression. It is the council's ruling that we are to allow the natives to continue growing as a people."

"In a way, the council is right," Dekkyle stated, noting the responding nods from his people. "Native populations will, of course, progress technologically. What the council has not taken into account is the incredible leap this is for the Gortive."

Viscount Pembra cleared his throat before speaking. "With all due respect, are we not independent sovereign kingdoms? The politics of the alliance should not dictate our control over our respective nations."

Dekkyle frowned. He noted the arrogance in the odd amber-colored eyes of the man.

Rajin Lord Bral responded with his typical cold condescension. "You are new to politics, Viscount." He intoned in his nasal voice. "The alliance exists for our mutual protection. All planets have sworn fealty to the council. Each is represented there, and each has a chance to be heard. The ruling of the council was established in order to ensure the success of the alliance. What we have here is insufficient evidence."

"Indeed," Dekkyle chimed in. "The council needs definitive proof that the Gortive have created these ships for the purpose of attacking us and not simply to further their own society."

"We have been commanded to establish a trade treaty to help them build on this development," Amiel commented, having regained his seat once the discussion had begun. "Such a negotiation might help us get a better understanding of what is transpiring on Parthia."

"Sending emissaries to the Gortive to broach the topic could be very dangerous. They're well known for their violence." General Oldan looked about the room as he continued, "It is possible the person, or people, sent might end up dead."

"If they respond by killing the ambassadors, then we will have an aggression on their part that will open the door to a declaration of war," Amiel stated.

"But the people sent will be dead." General Oldan's words hung in the air.

King Dekkyle's brow furrowed into a worried frown at Amiel's willingness to sacrifice people in order to have a cause to arms. Still, approaching the Gortive had been ordered, and someone would have to go.

"May I suggest," Rajin Lord Bral commented, "that a rajin is the best person suited for such a mission. We are impartial, as we work for no government and are an independent order. We also have the power to protect ourselves without being military in nature."

"It is a good recommendation," Rajin Lord Horsef stated. "Sending a diplomat from one or both of your nations puts that person at risk. Sending a knight or general creates an instant impression of aggression. A Consular Rajin can assist in this."

"Lord Bral," King Dekkyle said, turning to the master, "would you honor us by being our emissary?"

"It will be my pleasure, King Dekkyle, to represent the united continent of Vidden."

"In regards to creating a united continent, I believe we are here to sign a betrothal." Amiel's voice held a note in it Dekkyle couldn't quite place. The boy would not sign a treaty without marriage included; that much had become clear in the past months.

"Amiel," Dekkyle spoke now in a last effort to avoid the union he was certain Verena did not desire. "A marriage alliance between our nations is not really necessary. The reality is that if and when the Gortive attack, we will need to fight together, just as we did when our two planets colonized Jorn and faced them the first time."

The light in Amiel's eyes changed. He became guarded. "King Dekkyle, our houses have worked together over these many years to create a planet that today is the fourth most important in the Intergalactic Alliance. Uniting as one in marriage will make planet Jorn's future even more secure."

The Earl of Sarnac cleared his throat. "Prince Amiel, it is not that we don't see the benefit of a marriage alliance, but rather that the timing is—"

"The timing is not of our making," Amiel interrupted. "Certainly, Verena should have been given years of reigning as Queen in her own right, but the Gortive will not hold off their attack for that." The prince locked eyes with Dekkyle, and the king felt the full force of the younger man's conviction. "It is not a coincidence that you have but one heir and she is a woman. It is not an accident that our Principality has a male heir unwed. This is the future of Jorn, united under a single banner."

"I thought the betrothal agreement had been settled," the Duke of Aul commented. "We've spent some time on it, and I believed we were in this room for the purpose of signing the final document, not renegotiating terms. Am I mistaken?"

King Dekkyle still held Prince Amiel's gaze. In his heart, Dekkyle knew this was the only and best choice. The agreement gave final say over all that was currently the independent nation of Dravidia to Verena, and of course, Amiel held control over his own lands. Yet, it created a new kingdom, Auldivia, which would be stronger. The thought of the name irked Dekkyle. They'd tried variations where Dravidia was more prominent, but none sounded right. In the end, it was this combination of their original nation's names that worked best, to the king's chagrin.

With a sigh, King Dekkyle signaled to the earl that he should bring out the leather-bound folder in which the final draft of the agreement lay waiting.

"You are correct, your Grace," the king stated. "We have the document ready. I have set the cancelation of the abdication ceremony in motion, and we will work to program the wedding as soon as possible."

Amiel's voice showed his surprise. "Why would you need to cancel the abdication?"

Dekkyle swallowed hard. In his heart, he knew Verena would not acquiesce to the marriage. Though they had been friends as children, something had brought a barrier between his daughter and Amiel a few years ago. Dekkyle had never pried into what it might be, but no one could mistake the coldness she showed Prince Amiel when he visited.

He wished he'd had time to talk to her ahead of tonight. It had been his plan to arrive several days ago. But Ternic, Dekkyle's longtime informant, claimed the developments of the Gortive were the work of a more powerful group. He had presented no reliable evidence. Dekkyle had instructed Ternic to find conclusive proof, for only then would the council allow them to act against the natives.

If it was as the king feared, they faced a much greater challenge, one that Dravidia could not bear alone, even with intergalactic help. The union of their nations would secure a stronger position in the coming war.

Now, Dekkyle locked eyes with Prince Amiel across the table so there could be no misunderstanding of the words he was about to speak. "As Queen, Verena can make her own ruling on the betrothal issue. She could set aside the agreement."

Dekkyle watched as the full meaning sank in on Amiel. A look of pain crossed the young man's eyes. No further words were spoken. None were necessary. They all understood the truth. The princess didn't want the marriage. It would be a forced alliance.

As they waited for the earl to return from collecting the folder with the document, King Dekkyle's mind wandered to the day some years ago when the Prophet Lord Orloff had come to him with a GenWord from the Great I Am.

"But that GenWord, Lord Orloff, was fulfilled many years ago." The king gestured to his personal secretary, who quickly handed him a hefty book.

Its silver title, *Book of the Prophets*, seemed to sparkle up from its thick, black hide. The leather-bound volume held the official pronouncements of the fifty-one Prophets of Ressord, the only acknowledged order of seers in the Intergalactic Alliance.

Dekkyle continued, "Was not that the divination spoken concerning the dark times when the Calvernsin first came to our part of the galaxy?"

The portly Prophet shifted his weight, leaning upon the honeywood walking stick he held. Seated as he was, the glowing gemstone at the top lent a kind of halo to Lord Orloff's graying jet-black hair.

"I too was surprised by this. When the words first came to me, I felt their familiarity and sought the prophecy in my own copy of the book. It is indeed the same oracular utterance by the Prophetess Dalactine from all those many years ago." A deep sigh escaped him, and the king could see the deep concern in the seer's gray-blue eyes. "Yet, as I prayed, the words would not leave me. I believe this is the GenWord for our generation."

King Dekkyle rested the tome on his lap and opened it to the table of contents. Scanning to find the page he sought, he flipped to the recording of Lady Dalactine's prophecies. His hand smoothed over the illuminated text. There the chronicler had noted the prophetic words and then the fulfillment of them.

> *Carnal passions outweigh the light; union hope beckons. Bound together forging a path, yet evil encircles. Arrogance of knowledge splinters the faith; dark power rises. Can love bar its way?*

As the king's eyes skimmed the words, he recapped needlessly, the dread of what this all could mean for them blinding him to the fact that Lord Orloff already knew the history.

"That prophecy foreshadowed the fights for independence among the colonized planets, the schism from the weak Pact of Commerce, and the arrival of the Calvernsin."

"Yes."

"It was Thyrein Dragonheart who took on the task of reorganizing the planets and defending them against the Calvernsin attacks. It was his marriage to the Calvernsin Princess Z'Agota'z that created the Intergalactic Alliance Council and the treaty of planetary use and commerce we go by today."

"All of that is correct," Lord Orloff stated. His gaze unwavering, he continued, "And the same GenWord that foretold of those turbulent times and gave rise of the peaceful intergalactic governance system we live in now has been given to us for this new generation."

"It has never been heard of before, Lord Orloff." The king glanced up from the page to look upon the seer. "A prophecy has never been the focus of two times, two eras. Once fulfilled, the divination is done."

The learned man shook his head and smiled wanly. "It was difficult for me also to accept. These words have lingered in my mind now for many months, while I prayed and asked of the Great I Am His confirmation. And two days ago, I received it. The Prophetess Rhy-Jun communicated to us that she has been given this GenWord as well. Others in the order also received the words." The Prophet rose and gave a bow to Dekkyle. "I will continue to inquire of the lord His will in this, but you must know that this GenWord is for now in this new generation and be vigilant."

"Indeed." The king gave the prophet a nod as Lord Orloff departed.

"Your pen, Majesty." Falhorn Drang, his faithful secretary, handed him the elegant writing utensil.

Taking the plumed instrument, King Dekkyle turned to the blank pages at the back. Starting a new entry, he wrote the prophetic utterance, labeling it a GenWord, and described its delivery by the Lord Armond Orloff and confirmation by the Lady Graceli Rhy-Jun. Closing the book, he handed it back to Falhorn, who would return it to its sacred spot in the castle's library.

Now, seated at the table, waiting to forge an alliance with the Principality of Aulden, King Dekkyle pondered if this indeed was the beginning of a new time of war. There had been and always would be minor skirmishes here and there, disagreements and political maneuverings. Such was life, but the tidings from Parthia hailed something different. From the moment Amiel had first sent the news the prince had uncovered, Dekkyle's mind had burned with the GenWord.

The emphasis on love in the prophecy worried the king. Verena and Amiel had been close until a few years back. It was evident to Dekkyle that Amiel loved his daughter. Yet, did she care for the prince? Could the close friendship they'd shared in the past build to a match of true affection? Dekkyle lifted up a prayer to the Great I Am that it would be so.

The earl returned with the betrothal documents and lay them before Amiel. The prince ran a hand over the leather cover. His eyes were fixed on the table so Dekkyle couldn't see his expression. The boy's movements let the king know he was hurt by the assumed rejection by Verena and yet determined to have her nonetheless.

Dekkyle watched as Prince Amiel, with deliberate slowness, opened the folder, thumbing through the pages, adding his initials. At the final page, he signed. The Duke of Aul handed him the lit black wax stick. Amiel took it and let it drip onto the page. With the ring on his right index finger, he embedded the crest of his nation into it with care.

Then the earl took the open folder gingerly and put it before Dekkyle. The king's eyes fell upon the yet malleable wax seal of the Principality of Aulden. His heart ached in his chest. Verena would see this as a betrayal. He had promised her she would pick her own husband after she ascended to the throne. He understood the depth of her desire to be queen, the first female ruler of their kingdom. And she would have made a great monarch in her own right.

But Dekkyle couldn't risk the future of their nation's existence. He needed Amiel's military mind to help guide Verena in the war that even now lay on their doorstep, waiting to spring. If this indeed indicated the beginning of the fulfillment of the GenWord, then it would be a time of long turmoil and much bloodshed. Amiel could keep Verena safe. He would ensure Jorn's survival through whatever might come.

The king added his initials and signature, affixing his insignia in the royal-purple wax provided by the earl. He sat back and breathed deeply. *It is done.*

"When will we make the announcement?" Amiel asked from across the table. His tone was guarded, but Dekkyle could feel the excitement emanating from him.

The prince did indeed desire Verena, and now Dekkyle had given her to him. The king lifted up a prayer to the Great I Am that the boy would prove a worthy husband.

"We shall announce it tonight."

"Tonight!" The surprise in the prince's voice was mirrored on the faces of all those present, except for the Earl of Sarnac, who'd known the king's plan.

"Yes." King Dekkyle rose, followed by all the others. "We cannot waste time. Eldor and I will be heading out as soon as the informant sets a time and place. We must be ready to mobilize. Therefore, it is best the matter be made public and all preparations set in motion tonight."

Amiel walked around the table to Dekkyle, who moved to meet him halfway. The two men squared off for a moment. Then Amiel stretched out a hand to him, and Dekkyle took it.

"I promise you, Sire, that I will take care of Verena. You've entrusted her to me, and I will not fail you."

"I'm counting on that... son."

CHAPTER 4
BETROTHAL

THE PARTY WAS IN FULL SWING by the time Verena took a break, settling into a sofa in a side alcove. She preferred sitting here, amidst the guests. It made her more accessible than if she sat on the throne dais. The princess smiled broadly as she scanned the gathering. The scent of the fresh flowers drifted like a subtle perfume throughout the space.

Noble ladies glittered in exquisite gowns and magnificent jewels as they floated around in the arms of their noble lords. Earls, dukes, and counts mingled with mighty generals, knights, and rajin.

Even the elderly Reverend Mother, Sister Perpa, of the Order of the Geldian Heights, had come to bestow her blessing on Verena. The holy lady, accompanied by the Mother Superior, Sister Galvi, sat in the place of honor to the right of the thrones. Sister Perpa's black habit, embroidered in silver thread, depicted a cross with a crown of thorns at its center.

Verena had, of course, studied the tenets of the faith, but found the idea of secluding yourself from the world for religious contemplation nonsensical. Inwardly, she rolled her eyes as people paid obeisance to the aged nun and her only slightly younger companion. A swirl of silver-blue in her periphery made Verena turn.

"Your Highness, may I join you?" Elmalin Nomri requested, bowing to her. The supple fabric of the elmalin's silver gown spread out as she curtsied.

"Of course, Misrim Nomri," Verena acquiesced, motioning for the second-most important member of the Elmalin Order's Abloir to take a seat. The title of misrim belonged only to the triad leadership that formed the elmalin's high council. "I have heard of your valiant work on planet Schol."

"Oh, thank you, Highness," Misrim Nomri said. "The elmalin wish me to extend to you their most heartfelt congratulations on your coming ascension to the throne. We offer you our allegiance and counsel and wish your reign the most prosperous success."

Verena looked admiringly at the learned lady's dress and its pattern of rolling waves. "Thank you, Misrim Nomri." Verena nodded her head slightly, ignoring the stab of pain that assailed her, knowing the abdication would not take place. *Who knows when I'll finally be Queen?* "I, too, look forward to being the first Queen of Dravidia."

"It is the Abloir's hope your reign will help demonstrate once more that a woman ruler is just as good, if not better, than a male." The elmalin smiled ruefully. "As you know, we continue to petition for a declaration from the Intergalactic Council making first-born status the only requirement for ascension."

"I know of your cause, and you have my full support." Verena returned the smile. "It is such an antiquated concept, setting the first male child as heir. I, for one, feel the law should allow the ruling monarch to select the best-suited person from among his or her descendants, irrespective of birth order or gender."

"I agree, Highness." Misrim Nomri gestured her frustration. "Ambassador Halden has coalesced a majority of the noble families to oppose us in just seeking first-born status as automatic heirship. I fear we have a long way to go before an edict such as you propose could have any hope of being implemented throughout Thyrein's Galactic Wall. Change is hard, especially when it comes to equity in gender relations."

"Is that not why your order separated from the rajin?"

"Yes, Highness. In all fairness, the rajin do acknowledge a woman's ability to wield the powers of the universe and to be anointed by the Great I Am for His service, but they still limit the number of women allowed to serve on the Rajin Conclave and often turn down female rajins' research proposals. They particularly feel the study of the elemental energies to be pointless, which, of course, our order believes to be crucial to a balanced existence."

"I'm not familiar with the other planets, but Jorn is represented on the Rajin Conclave by the Reverend Mother of the Geldian Heights and Master Vivelda the Bountiful is one of the Triun Heads of the entire order."

Misrim Nomri smiled politely. "We hold no ill will toward the rajin. They have shown us the way to the Great I Am through knowledge and research, rather than ancient superstitions, and for that we are grateful. The Elmalin Order seeks to work in tandem with them in service of all humankind and for the spiritual development of all sentient beings."

"Your order has not established a Cleyior on Jorn. I understand you have faced opposition to your temples on certain planets."

"Ambassador Halden has made us seem extremist since we broke from the rajin five years ago." The elmalin smoothed out a nonexistent wrinkle on her skirt before proceeding. "Your father prefers the rajin as his primary counselors, and Aulden, well, they follow only their own hearts' instructions."

Verena frowned but kept silent. Once she was Queen, she would reach out and welcome a Cleyior to Jorn. While she had often visited the Rajin Temple of Sanctal as well as the convent of the Geldian Heights, Verena did not care for the limitations on the research that the rajin imposed. There was much yet to be learned from the study of the natural elements, and she couldn't comprehend the reluctance to allowing the Elmalin Order an equal standing in the galactic wall.

"Well, I will rejoin my group, Highness," Misrim Nomri said, rising. With a parting curtsy, she excused herself. "A very happy birthday to you, Highness."

Backing away, Misrim Nomri strode toward the group of elmalin who had come with her to the celebration. Verena loved the way her gown flowed about her as she walked, as though it were as light as air. The princess smiled as she recalled Misrim Nomri was an elmess of air and water.

Verena summoned a hudroid and sent it to fetch her a glass of wine. The servant promptly returned with her drink. The princess turned her attention to the party and sighed with contentment. There were plenty of bachelors here, all eager to win her heart. Of course, she was not interested in selecting a husband, not yet anyway. Pride filled Verena, knowing she would be the first female successor to take the throne in the 300-year history of her house. Eventually, Verena would marry and have children. But first she wanted to rule. To show that she was capable of being Queen.

Ambassador Halden went by dancing with Lady Geld. His eyes locked with Verena's as he passed, an intensity in the gaze that made a shiver run down the princess's back. She had found herself dancing with him twice, back to back at the beginning of the ball. She had expressly forbidden that anyone be allowed to have more than one dance. Yet he'd managed to find a way. Verena made a mental note to discuss the matter with Mrs. Denip, her personal hudroid, on the morrow.

Lady Gar plopped down beside the princess and hollered out, disrupting Verena's thoughts. "Sir Eriq, doesn't our princess look ravishing tonight?"

The plump noblewoman took the last hors d'oeuvres from the tray of the waist-high servbot that drew near to the sitting area. The droid hovered off to the kitchen with a beep.

Sir Eriq, who'd been walking by, came to a stop. However, he couldn't respond as the garrulous lady continued without pause.

"Goodness, these are delicious. Just the very thing to celebrate your Highness's coming of age! I can't believe the excitement of it all. The king will abdicate, and you will ascend to the throne. Oh! For the first time, we shall have a Queen, not one by marriage, but a real blood ruler. And then, someday, a royal wedding. Oh, your Highness will make the very best Queen. The battle with the Venladon showed that!"

The matronly lady paused to chew the smoked nolrous fish, delivered fresh to the castle from the Bay of Drav that very morning.

"Your Highness does indeed look very beautiful tonight," Sir Eriq responded, taking advantage of the opening. He gave the princess a deep bow, exchanging a conspiratorial wink.

"Thank you, Lady Gar, Sir Eriq," Verena said, graciously accepting their compliments.

She smoothed the flowing skirts of her dark-purple gown, letting her lithe hands caress the silver embroidery depicting the star systems of Thyrein's Galactic Wall, of which planet Jorn was a part. A knot settled back in her stomach at the mention of the abdication that would not happen. Deflecting the feelings, she glanced at the chandeliers.

"I'm glad the king commanded Master Helvin to add pink tone to the light flow. It gives the party a very merry feel, and I do so love how the crystal sparkles."

Her weapons master and Lord High Marshal of Dravidia shook his gray-speckled head in lament. "If only we didn't have to worry about the situation on Parthia. Who would have thought it was poss—"

"Oh, yes, Highness," Lady Gar interrupted, having swallowed the savory fish. "I am surprised you didn't use purple, as it is the color of your house, but, of course, pink is such a feminine and beautiful color. The whole castle looks festive tonight. Why I was telling Baron Gar, as we arrived, how much I do love..."

Verena's attention wandered away as Lady Gar launched into a monologue describing all the accolades for the royal house she had expounded to her ever-patient husband. The princess wondered what her father discussed in his private study with Prince Amiel at that very moment.

They had disappeared shortly after the father-daughter opening dance along with all their primary advisors. Verena sighed as she thought, for the millionth time, how difficult her father made it on her when he didn't let her in on these meetings. *How am I to rule if I am left out of what is really happening? My coming of age should at least change that!*

The arrival of Count Tor ended Lady Gar's soliloquy of the splendor of House Drav. "I believe I have the honor of the next dance, Highness," he said, bowing. "I understand it will be a slower pace."

"It's my pleasure to dance with you, my Lord." Nodding goodbye to Sir Eriq and Lady Gar, Verena allowed the count to lead her to the floor. The new song started as they positioned themselves.

Verena smiled as the orchestra struck up a slow graceful dance. The old gentleman began extolling the virtues of his son, who would be knighted on the morrow. The princess responded politely, but she knew the foppish Viscount, though a good-natured young man, would not do for her.

Trumpets interrupted the dance. Lord Sorma's voice boomed into the room. "His Royal Majesty, King Dekkyle!"

Count Tor bowed to her and joined the crowd of guests. The gathering parted, making way down the center of the room for their sovereign.

"His Highness, Prince Amiel ra Aulden," the Lord Chamberlain stated, continuing his announcements. "Their Holinesses, Rajin Master Lord Horsef the Great and Rajin Master Lord Bral the Merciful. His Excellency, the Earl of Sarnac. His Grace, the Duke of Aul. The Viscount Pembra. Chief Military Officer General Oldan."

Princess Verena held the center of the room as her father, Prince Amiel, and their entourage of advisors came toward her.

"My kura!" King Dekkyle exclaimed as he approached. He extended both hands to her. Verena gave him a deep curtsy. "Are you having a wonderful birthday?"

"Yes, Father, though I have missed you since our dance."

"A pressing matter of state couldn't wait, but the results will be wonderful for our kingdom." He smiled fondly at her. "Prince Amiel and I have forged an alliance." He placed a firm hand on the younger man's broad shoulder.

"How nice," Princess Verena said in a wary tone. Her face maintained its polite expression as she acknowledged their royal guest. "Prince Amiel."

"Verena, I look forward to the strengthened bond between our adjoining nations and having the pleasure of your company."

Oh, Lord, Verena thought, though she kept her courteous smile. *That's all I need, this arrogant and mean-spirited royal visiting with increased frequency. How will I protect my staff from his viciousness and cruelty?*

"Come, my dear." Her father extended his arm, and she gracefully accepted it. "I wish we had more time, but this announcement must be made tonight."

Verena's stomach tightened at the thought of the words he would speak. *How would people react to the delayed abdication? What excuse would be given?* The pair of majestic silver thrones awaited them as they approached the far end of the ballroom.

Verena took a step up, intending to take her place on her mother's throne. Her father gently stopped her. He deftly positioned her on the second of the three steps leading to the royal seats, so that she stood next to Prince Amiel. Surprised, the princess stared at her father as he prepared to address the assembled company. The silver trumpets sounded once again, signaling the coming royal proclamation.

"My esteemed guests," the king began once everyone had settled around the dais. "Tonight, we gathered to celebrate the princess's birthday."

He waited, allowing for the applause and cries of "Happy birthday!" Princess Verena half turned to accept her guests' congratulations. Amiel turned as well, leaving them facing each other.

When the clamor died down, the king continued, "Now we will add to the joyous occasion. Our neighbor, Prince Amiel ra Aulden, has forged an alliance with the House of Dravidia. With great pleasure, I announce the betrothal of Princess Verena to Prince Amiel. We shall have a royal wedding!"

In the midst of the guests' hoorays and boisterous joy, Verena's stomach roiled and her hands clenched into fists. Her cheeks flushed, and her eyes threw darts at Amiel as he stood before her on the step. The look of shock in the prince's eyes told her the raw emotion consuming her was visible on her countenance. Dipping her head to hide her face, Verena slid, with great effort, the mask of politeness over her features once more. Her body trembled slightly from the rage within.

All her life, she had been told she would choose her own husband. Verena tasted bile at her father's betrayal. Amiel ra Aulden was the last person in the universe the princess would have chosen, having witnessed his brutality inflicted on her human servants firsthand.

The king took Verena's clenched fist and placed it in her betrothed's open hand. It took all her self-control not to rip her hand away. Leaving the Reverend Mother seated in her place of honor, Sister Galvi came hurriedly forward, her white baldachin habit softly swishing as she drew near.

Verena focused her eyes on the gold-embroidered depiction of the holy book with the seven blood drops around it on the Mother Superior's robe. Somehow it helped her keep calm as the holy lady, speaking the words of blessing, wrapped their joined hands with the silver rope of betrothal, which had been brought in from the vault by a liveried hudroid.

"Holy Trinity." The sweet voice of Sister Galvi filled the silent room. "We implore your favor and grace on our beloved princess and on her betrothed. May their union bring us all peace and prosperity, and may their rule be one of justice. Hear us, we implore, on this special day. In the sevenfold blood and spirit, may it be!"

The crowd cheered again with cries of "May it be!" The princess stared dumbfounded at her entwined hand. Verena had the surreal sense of being in a dream—a nightmare. Feelings of anger and hurt grew within her, but years of royal training helped her keep her tranquil demeanor.

Verena's mind whirled as her heart broke. *Was this always his plan? Did Father always intend to marry me off immediately? Was Amiel always the chosen king for Father's kingdom?*

Chapter 5

Amiel Ra Aulden

He held her clenched hand in his. The silver rope joined them. Sister Galvi's voice spoke the words of betrothal. All the while, Amiel's heart pounded within him, a wild mixture of emotions. She didn't want him. She would be his. The searing pain at the look on her beautiful face stirred again.

Amiel drew in deep breaths. He kept his face as impassive as he could. The orchestra began to play the first chords of the Felandine, the ancient betrothal dance of Dravidia. All these years, Amiel had insisted on practicing these musical pieces, the ones he hoped with all his being to perform some day with Verena Elidena Destavi in his embrace.

His tutors had shaken their heads at him. It was not certain that he would be her husband just because theirs were the only two nations on the continent, on the whole planet, really, because the Gortive and the other assorted riff-raff didn't count. He couldn't just assume a union with her would happen. Or so they'd tried to tell him.

But Amiel knew somehow, some way, he'd make her his wife. The Gortive stirrings on Parthia had given him the perfect excuse to push for a marriage alliance.

Verena seemed to have recovered from her initial shock. As he wove her arm into his and led her to the dance floor, her face held the cool politeness of civility. But she shook. Her body shivered beside him. Turning her into his arms, he felt the slight tremble as she fought to control her emotions. Verena's eyes stared at his medals, avoiding his gaze. The medals jingled as they danced.

Amiel smiled, recalling the day he departed to the Calvernsin skirmish that had earned him the awards.

A hudroid let Amiel know Dekkyle and Verena had arrived at Auld Palace to deliver the supplies and warriors they were contributing. After much discussion, including Verena's last-ditch effort to be given permission to enlist, Amiel found himself alone with her.

"I don't see why you get to go and I don't. I'm just as good a warrior as you are." The petulant tone did nothing to mar the beauty of her face.

He responded without thinking, "You're a girl."

"Women can fight, Amiel! Sir Eriq says I am gifted and would acquit myself well."

"What would your father do if you were killed?" Amiel looked into those emerald eyes, so full of self-righteousness.

"Your parents are dead and your principality needs you, but you're going." That beautifully shaped bow mouth beckoned him to kiss it. He stood so close to her.

"Figor could take over. Even my uncle Sabred would be better at being prince." He forced his eyes to meet hers, trying to forget those lips. "You are indispensable. Your people need you. You are a ray of light that brightens everywhere you go."

The startled look as she let his words in only made him want to hold her—taste her—more than before. They were isolated in the hangar. He could just take her in his arms and kiss her. He'd moved to do just that, when the doors swung open and her father came in, followed by the emissaries from Fratern.

Now, before all the guests from around Thyrein's Galactic Wall, Amiel held her firmly, swaying to the beautiful music. It had been made official. Verena would be his wife. A pang of pain filled him, knowing she rejected him, knowing she'd be his nonetheless.

Her emerald eyes met his, and his heart broke. She was hurting. He could see the confusion written across the perfect face of the woman he longed to make his own. There wasn't a time Amiel could recall when he had not loved Verena.

Amiel's mind sought words to comfort her. Perhaps this anger wasn't about him. More likely it was the fact she wouldn't get to be Queen by herself. Surely, she'd been planning on enjoying a few years of ruling. He smiled recalling the young princess sitting in a tree, talking about all the things she would do when Dravidia was hers. *Does she know about the threat our world faces?* Maybe she thought her father was making a mistake.

"Your father is a wise ruler," Amiel said, hoping to break the icy silence. "He realizes his kingdom will need a strong king to protect it. The Gortive are nothing to sneer at. The battles to come will not be easy ones."

"I will be Queen. You will be my consort, if anything," Verena retorted with blistering condescension.

"That's not the bargain we made," he informed her.

Tucked firmly in his arms, he led her through the steps across the honeywood floor. Her body pressed into his. The tantalizing curve of her hips and the pressure of her ample breasts ignited a fire in him. Every time they danced, their rhythm was perfect.

"I will be king with equal power to help you. You don't realize the dangers our continent faces." Extending his arm, he made her twirl out. Then guided her in a circle around him.

"Dangers!" She practically shouted the word. He watched her moderated her tone as the realization she could be overheard sunk in. "Vidden is secure. The Black Ocean and the Green Ocean keep us safe from the Gortives, the only possible threat. They would be fools to attack us. Surely as primitive as they may be, they realize we would crush them."

Amiel shook his head. She was so naïve. He'd wondered if King Dekkyle shared everything with Verena. Apparently not. No doubt she thought they lived in a perfect little fairytale.

"I can see why your father agreed to this alliance." He brought her back into his embrace, enjoying the warmth of her deliciousness against him again.

They swirled around the room in silence. Amiel leaned into her, his cheek up against the softness of hers. Her fragrance filled his senses, that intoxicating scent of lavender unique to her. His body reacted to her proximity. He'd need a cold shower for sure tonight.

Her whispered words sent a shiver through him as they caressed his ear. "I can assure you, Amiel. I don't know whose idea this betrothal was, but I have not consented to it. I will never be your wife." The words came forth firm yet measured.

Amiel clenched her tighter to him. She was his. Nothing she said or did could change that now. Anger stirred. King Dekkyle should have prepared her for this. The way her father had gone about this would make everything harder. But Verena, as he himself, had been raised to understand duty to country. She'd come around.

"You will be my wife, for the good of your kingdom," Amiel responded into her ear, the effect of her evident in the husky tone of his voice. He wouldn't be able to modulate that, and he didn't care. Maybe it would be good if she felt his desire for her. If she knew he cared and would be a good husband. "And if your intelligence matches your beauty, which is considerable, you will see we need to build a good relationship if we are to be successful." As the song came to an end, he turned her into an expert dip.

The strains of music stopped, and the guests applauded with gusto, swept up in their perfect performance of the love dance. Prince Amiel escorted Princess Verena back to the dais. He bowed over her hand as he watched her take her place on the Queen's throne. She belonged there, beautiful, serene, and full of kindness. But she needed him. She didn't have the ruthlessness it took to rule.

He made his way through the guests to where Figor stood.

"You've got what you always wanted, A," Figor said, a sly smile across his face as he handed Amiel a glass of champagne. "To A and V, the marriage of the century!"

Amiel smiled, lifted his flute and drank. "Dekkyle never told her."

Figor almost sprayed them. "What?"

"The announcement is the first Verena knew of the betrothal. I could see it in her face."

The duke ran a hand through his dark, wiry hair. His ebony skin took on a shade of red as he considered the situation.

Amiel had always envied his cousin the rich dark skin of his traditional Fraternese heritage. Amiel's side of the family had more Drulian and Gelderantic bloodlines.

"Do you think she will be okay with it?" Figor asked.

"Eventually." Amiel took another deep drink recalling the raw pain and hurt. "She wanted to be Queen, to get to rule and be on the throne for a while by herself."

"Understandable."

A pair of young noblewomen walked by, smiling coyly at them. Amiel noticed the gleam in Figor's eye. "Go on. You're still a free man."

"Technically, so are you, A," Figor said with a cocky grin. "You're not wed yet."

"There's only one woman I want." Amiel said, looking toward the throne. It was empty. He scanned the ballroom, but Verena seemed to have left. Maybe to speak with her father. "You go. Have fun."

The duke headed off in the direction of the ladies. The heady fragrances and body heat of the room stifled Amiel. He needed fresh air. Amiel headed to the courtyard gardens. Exiting into the warm summer evening, he thought how nice it would be once fall began and the air turned cooler, the foliage of their world preparing for winter's cold embrace. Now, the heat of the day failed to abate with the rise of Jorn's silver moon, Ryu. Amiel found a darkened alcove on the terrace overlooking the first of three interior courtyards in Castle Dravidia. He sat on the stone bench and considered the situation.

King Dekkyle had clearly bungled the whole thing. Verena should have been told ahead of time, given time to accept the news. Telling her on the eve of her ascension to the throne did not bode well.

Amiel unbuttoned his uniform's jacket and opened up his undershirt, trying to cool off a bit. Out of habit, his hand sought the amulet Godar had given him. Then he remembered he'd taken it off after the meeting with Dekkyle. The chain kept snagging in his thick chest hair. He'd have to do something about that, he thought, reaching into his jacket pocket and running his hand over the smooth, cold stone.

As he sat in the fragrant air from the myriad flowerbeds, Amiel closed his eyes and saw once more the anger, rejection, hurt he'd witnessed. Surely she knew he loved her. He had made no secret of it.

The image of the papier-mâché bird invaded his thoughts, and a frown marred his face. That had been the day everything changed between them. Before that, she had been his Rennie, his best friend. They had been inseparable.

Until that day.

He sat on the blanket cross-legged. Rennie lay on her belly, looking out over the lake. That was his name for her, Rennie. This had been their favorite boulder on the edge of Lake Oley deep in the Oldey Forest that surrounded Castle Dravidia.

"So, now you are an official knight," she said, turning her sparkling green eyes on him.

"That's right," he answered. "You'll need to show me more respect."

A burst of laughter came from her as she rolled on her back. "Please," she said when her mirth had subsided. "What valiant deed have you done?"

Amiel furrowed his brow. He turned away from her. The summer sun glistened on the mirror-like surface of the water. The heat of the day pressed down on him.

"I'll have my chance to prove my valor soon enough," he'd responded defensively. "Those Calvernsin are sure to do something stupid, and we'll have to beat them back again."

"I think they're beautiful."

Amiel had snapped his eyes to Rennie. "Beautiful! Are you kidding me? They're hideous!"

She turned to lay on her side, propped up on her left arm. "Have you ever seen one?"

"Many times," he responded. "My uncle Sabred has battled them on many occasions and showed me pictures."

"So, you've never seen one," Rennie asserted.

"Have you?" he challenged.

"As it happens, I have." Rennie had flashed him her cheekiest grin as she sat up to match his posture. Plopping a grape in her mouth from the fruit platter between them, she elaborated. "Mother went on a mission to Schol. The Calvernsin want to set up some business on that planet. She was asked to mediate. I went with her. Prince Z'Pau'z is very beautiful and very nice."

Amiel's frown deepened. "The Queen shouldn't have let you be anywhere near those heathens. You realize they don't believe in the Great I Am."

"That has nothing to do with how gorgeous they are. And Mother says what people believe is none of our business."

"They're ugly!" Amiel's stomach had roiled as he considered Queen Irene letting those disgusting creatures near his Rennie. Of course, Rennie would be thrilled. She loved everybody. "You don't seriously think you want to forge a friendship with a Calvernsin?"

"Well, I think that as rulers we should build good relationships with everyone. Really, Amiel, they just want resources to sustain their life on board their ship colonies."

Her face had taken on that grown-up seriousness he really liked. His heart had swelled with pride that, at sixteen, she was so intelligent and mature. Then his mind had recalled her words about the Calvernsin prince, and he'd scowled again.

"Trading with them is one thing, but liking them is another."

She shook her head vigorously, her wild auburn hair slapping about. He'd smiled. She'd always loved doing that.

"Prince Z'Pau'z is tall, taller than you, and his skin is so smooth and lavender. His face is beautiful, Amiel, and his eyes are the most gorgeous blue ever!"

Amiel had considered her, a deep disgust filling him. She obviously didn't understand. "Your father will make sure you don't mingle with them. He understands how things really are."

Her face, which had lit up as she spoke of the filthy creature, fell into a scowl. "My father—and mother—have invited the general and his son, Prince Z'Pau'z, to Mother's birthday celebration tonight. You'll see for yourself how nice they are."

Amiel's cheeks warmed, and the vein in his temple begin to throbbed. He lifted a hand to the amulet Godar had given him upon his knighting. The cool feel of the smooth red stone was pleasant and helped him think. Anger surged through him, roiling in his gut. How the hell would he be able to keep Rennie from mixing with it if her parents let it come here? The question filled his mind.

"Princess!" A squeaky voice broke from the trees surrounding the secluded spot.

"That's Helen." Rennie's face had radiated happiness. "She's from the Garinquel Islands and just arrived a couple days ago. Her skin is so beautiful."

"You're beautiful. Why do you always think inferior beings more lovely than yourself?" Amiel's disgust had intensified. The Garinquel were midgets, genetically flawed peoples who'd insisted on reproducing more of their deformed kind.

"I like myself just fine!" Rennie had said, rising and smiling. "I just happen to enjoy the beauty in others."

"Highness." The servant had broken through the tree line in an unseemly run. "The Queen... she commands... you return... to prepare."

"Of course, Helen," Rennie had said.

"Pack up our picnic things!" Amiel had commanded the midget with a glare. "I'll get our horses, Rennie."

"Okay," Rennie had said. "Oh, Helen, be careful with that."

Amiel had turned then. His perfectly formed papier-mâché bird, the gift he had worked on for so many hours, imagining the glorious smile it would elicit from Rennie, was now squished under a heavy bowl. Ire, hot and blinding, had seized him. Before he knew what was happening, he'd given the deformed little beast a thorough whipping with his riding crop.

Rennie had screamed, pushed him, and almost gotten hurt. She'd hurled words at him and ridden off with the bleeding thing to get it medical attention. In the end, he'd had to collect their things. As he'd entered the ballroom that evening, Amiel recalled thinking she'd probably gotten over it. But she hadn't. She'd refused to talk to him. She sat next to that Calvernsin prince and smiled and laughed with him.

Now, in the warmth of her castle's courtyard, Amiel shivered. It hadn't been long before the Calvernsin overstepped themselves. He'd found himself pitted against Z'Pau'z in the battle. They'd fought each other. Amiel had disarmed the pathetic prince's space fighter and killed him. Things had never really gone back to the way they had been with Rennie, before Z'Pau'z came into her life. Since that day in the forest, she'd been cooler around him. They'd never hung out again just as friends, just them two.

She was his betrothed. As of tonight, he would be the only man in her life, as it should always have been. Her father should have better prepared her for this. Maybe he was with her now. Dropping the stone, Amiel drew out his com device to send a message to King Dekkyle.

<I'm worried about Verena. She was not prepared for the announcement. Is she with you? Perhaps we can speak with her together.>

Amiel clicked send and waited.

<Don't worry. I will speak with her and she will be fine. She knows her duty. I sent her back to the ballroom.>

King Dekkyle's response flashed on Amiel's com. *Duty. Is that what I want to be for Verena? A duty?*

Amiel sighed and put away his com. There were marriages that had worse beginnings. They had been friends for a long time—all her life and most of his. He would be able to win her over. He was sure of it.

Chapter 6

Ruling

VERENA RAN DOWN THE HALLWAY. Her bare feet padded on the marble floors. Clad in her night clothes, she gave no heed to the stares and gasps of her scandalized staff. The matching robe, which she had failed to secure in her haste, now flapped behind her like a flowing cape. Arriving, panting, at the north tower's hangar, the princess noticed the hustle and bustle of the hudroids and servants as they prepared her father's ship.

He can't leave again without talking to me!

"Father!" Verena cried out, chest heaving.

All activity ceased as the room's occupants turned shocked faces to where she stood. Ignoring everyone, Verena scanned the space until her eyes found the king. He stood at the top of his ship's loading ramp. His brow furrowed, no doubt at her state of undress, but she didn't care. *This is too important.* She stomped forward, determination burning in her.

"Verena, for Pegot's sake, you should not be here dressed..." He stopped, shaking his head in consternation.

Verena worked her way up to him, tightening the robe about her scantily clad form.

Before she could speak, he continued with a sigh, "I know you have many questions, but I must go now." Turning to the immobilized spectators, he commanded, "Load up!" The flurry resumed as men and droids sprang into action around her.

"Please, I must talk to you... You must know how I feel..." her gasping words spilled out. Her emotions threatening to overcome her, Verena placed a hand on his arm, fighting back tears.

Her father's palm on top of hers felt comforting as he gave her a quick squeeze. The golden-brown, lightweight coneb desert gear he wore told

Verena he would be heading back to planet Lataira. He had barely returned from there an hour prior to the arrival of their guests for the dinner the day before. He'd been away for two months. Why did he need to leave the planet at all? Verena wondered at his prolonged absence from the castle only to return for one night and go back out again. For what purpose? Why didn't he just tell her?

"My kura," he said to her, "I will be back soon, and we will talk then. An important development requires I go right away. For now, just know that I am doing what I feel is best for us all. Trust me." The king leaned forward, planting a kiss on Verena's forehead as he had done ever since she could remember.

There was so much she longed to say, but all she managed to speak was "I can't marry him." It sounded pitiful.

His voice held a slight note of regret, yet firmness, as he responded, "Yes, you can. It may be hard at first, but political marriages are a necessity sometimes. There are situations that require of you this sacrifice. When I return, we will talk further."

Verena stared into her father's emerald eyes, which mirrored her own, willing him to understand. Placing an arm about her shoulders, he led her off the ship.

"Rest. Enjoy shopping for the wedding." He held her at arm's length when they'd reached a safe distance. "All will be well. Amiel may not be ideal, but we need this union. Trust me, kura." His eyes held a sadness mingled with some other emotion Verena couldn't place.

She stood there, watching the king, the Earl of Sarnac, and a small retinue of knights climb aboard the petite E-Class transport. The simple commercial freighter had no markings and would go unremarked at any port. The dark matter engines roared to life, filling the hangar with a brown glow. The tower's roof opened like a flower bud spreading its petals. The hot air of the final month of summer filled the hangar, overcoming the interior's cooling system. As her father's ship took off, she sighed, wishing she could leave too.

Verena turned and trudged back toward her chambers. Entering, she found Mrs. Denip sorting the mail and watching the news cast. Daline Elviran, communications director for the Royal Family and head of the Media Relations Office, stood in an elegant black pin-striped suit at the podium. The coat of arms of Dravidia emblazoned on the dark ebony wood stood out.

"Ladies and gentlemen of the press," Daline's commanding voice began. "As you know, this morning the abdication ceremony was to take place. However, the king has opted to postpone transferring the throne until his daughter's wedding to Prince Amiel in order to preserve the security and prosperity of the realm."

A barrage of questions followed the pronouncement. Verena fell into the nearest seat and doubled over. Mrs. Denip rushed to her and patted her back, saying something. But Verena couldn't understand the words. It was as if she'd been punched in the gut, and she struggled to breathe. The communication director's statement began to sink in: "postpone transferring the throne until his daughter's wedding... preserve the security and prosperity of the realm."

There was a tap at the door. Mrs. Denip scurried to open it. She returned with a folded piece of paper.

"What is that?" Verena asked, straightening into the back rest of her chair. A cloud of confusion and hurt filled her mind.

"It is a note for you, Highness," Mrs. Denip handed it to her and went to the cart that held a water jug. She poured out some of the refreshing liquid and brought it to Verena.

All the princess could do was sit and stare at the monitor displaying the media conference. Nothing registered anymore. Looking down at the missive in her hand, Verena opened it.

"Highness?" Mrs. Denip enquired.

"Tell the elmalin I will see her. Then help me get dressed." Verena glanced up at her longtime nurse and confidant.

The faithful old hudroid was so lifelike. Fashioned to seem like an old granny, the droid's kind eyes acknowledged the command.

Moments later, Verena found herself seated in her private office with Elmalin Misrim Nomri. The room had once been her mother's, but Verena had redecorated it in pink and white when she took over the space.

"You wanted to meet with me, Misrim Nomri," Verena stated, her voice even and calm despite the inner turmoil.

She'd dressed in her simple black slacks and a matching silk shirt. The princess hadn't realized the choice of color until she'd walked past the gilded mirror in the hallway.

"You must appeal to the Intergalactic Council, Highness." The elmalin launched straight into the matter with no preamble.

"I am—" Verena's shock must have been evident as the elmalin continued.

"Word has spread that King Dekkyle made the agreement without consulting or receiving your consent. I'm certain that if you make an appeal to them, the Intergalactic Council will forbid the union if you do not willingly accept it."

Verena took in a deep breath.

"Misrim Nomri, I appreciate your concern. However, whatever rumors may be going about, I assure you, they are wrong." The princess fixed her gaze on the elmalin. "While my father's announcement did come as a bit of a surprise, I will honor his wishes, as it is a good course of action for my nation."

The elmalin studied her. Storm-gray eyes tried to peer into her soul. Disbelief shone in Misrim Nomri's gaze. Verena sensed the elmalin might press the matter.

"I see that your petition for a hearing before the Intergalactic Council on the motion for a change in heirship law has been granted," Verena deflected.

"Yes, Highness."

"The hearing will be held in a few days." Verena glanced down at her desk calendar. "I will make it a point to be present. I would like to help in this matter as much as I can."

Resignation settled on Misrim Nomri. She bowed her head respectfully to Verena, thanked her, and excused herself. Long after her departure, Verena sat there, contemplating the option the elmalin had proposed, but her emotions were so raw, no coherent thought materialized.

The heat of summer gave way to the chill of autumn. The Duchess of Fen had remained with Verena and filled their days with wedding dress boutique visits, florist appointments, and cake tastings. The princess was grateful for her aunt's assistance, though with each new decision about the wedding, the very real prospect of a matrimony to Amiel haunted her. Now, Verena felt solace as she prepared to preside over the Council of Peers.

Sitting in the king's tall-backed black leather chair, she watched as the council members took their seats. Her father's custom of going undercover from time to time had made him a beloved ruler. Verena often read comments of praise on the holonet from the people about their sovereign's willingness to find out for himself their condition so that he could make the best choices for the kingdom. People, it seemed, enjoyed the hide and seek that resulted when the king was away from the castle, each hoping to catch their monarch incognito.

The princess pulled the rolling desk table toward her, settling in. After her mother's assassination, when she'd been too young to sit in for him, the Earl of Sarnac would preside over the kingdom when her father absented himself in this way. Upon Verena's eighteenth birthday, the king announced that she would rule in his absence. The earl then accompanied his sovereign on the adventures, which the princess noted made her father happy, as Eldor was the king's closest friend.

As she looked around the oval room, watching the members take their places at the honrol table in the center, Verena wondered why her father felt it necessary to have Amiel as king. She had been ruling in his stead for years with no problems.

"Highness," Count Tor, who took the place of the earl as Chief Peer, initiated the meeting. "We have several proposals of a minor nature from the Council of Vassals. Most are regarding treasury disbursements for various public works. We also have the ambassador from planet Drulin here, seeking an audience."

"Let's begin by hearing the ambassador so as not to keep her waiting. We can review the proposals after. Send her Excellency in," Verena commanded.

Ambassador Relfo entered, dressed in her official long blue robe, as protocol required. She approached the podium from which formal requests to the Council of Peers and the Monarch were made.

Once situated, she began. "Royal Highness, Mighty Peers of the Realm, I am here on behalf of several mining corporations to request access to the liog reserves identified in the Parsqual section of the Torsgeld Wildlife Preserve."

"By law, a wildlife preserve must remain inviolate," Verena interjected. "Did we not grant mining rights to your corporations on the Vayard Plains of Parthia?"

A look of arrogance marred the ambassador's beautiful face. "Your most generous father did grant us access to that section of the Parthian continent," she responded. "However, the Vankihi have made it impossible to sustain a profitable mining base. In the last few years, the Gortive tribes have become increasingly disruptive. There are daily reports of attacks on the workers' compound, as well as raids at the mining sites themselves. The Torsgeld is here, on the continent of Vidden. A much safer and more profitable grant for us."

Verena graced Lady Relfo with her most supercilious stare, irritated by the tone the ambassador had chosen to adopt with her. "When we signed the grants to you, we were clear on the likelihood of Gortive offensives against your sites. You accepted, knowing the risks. It behooves you to ensure the safety of your personnel."

Silence engulfed the room. Verena kept her eyes on the ambassador, peripherally aware that various council members were nodding at her statements.

"Highness, it is true that we did accept the responsibility for the wellbeing of our workers in a hostile environment, and we have taken many steps to do so. But the situation on Parthia is fast becoming volatile—"

"The Gortive are well known, since the war of colonization, as savage warriors," Lady Soane commented, interrupting the ambassador. Her blue-gray hair, piled haphazardly upon her head, looked like it might come cascading down at any moment when she turned to speak to Verena. "Highness, we might assist by providing a maniple of soldiers—"

"One hundred and twenty men will do us little good. The reserves of liog in the Torsgeld—"

"The ambassador is right," Verena said, speaking to Lady Soane and interrupting Relfo. "A single maniple is too small. Can we spare to send a full cohort?" She directed the question to the Earl of Geld, who was Secretary of the Royal Defense.

Ambassador Relfo's pale complexion had turned ruddy. Her eyes threw darts as she commenced again to explain her position. "We are not ask—"

"I believe sending a cohort can be arranged, and would suffice to secure the Drulian investments," the earl spoke, facing Verena. "However, the expense is considerable. Will the crown be paying for it or... Drulin?"

"Considering that Drulin could send its own soldiers, I don't see why we should pay." Lady Soane, keeper of the banks of Jorn and Royal Treasurer of the Realm, commented. "The corporations who will benefit from the security forces would be well able to pay for them in full."

"Highness, Drulin is not interested—"

"Ambassador Relfo." Verena adopted the tone of authority she had so often heard her father use when he wished to end a discussion. "The Wildlife Preserve is off limits. However, we would like to assist our home planet in safeguarding the lives of your people while they work the mines. We will dispatch a cohort to assist your companies' security. We will cover half the cost. I suggest you discuss the other half with your corporations."

There was a small harrumph of disapproval on her last statement from Lady Soane. Verena understood her concern but felt the concession would be more meaningful this way.

A disgruntled but resigned look came over Ambassador Relfo's countenance. "Thank you, Highness. I am sure it will make some difference. Do you know when your father will return?"

"When he does, he will uphold the preservation of the Torsgeld." Verena's voice dripped ice.

"I didn't mean to—"

"That is all." Verena lifted her hand in dismissal.

Once the Drulian Ambassador had left the room, Lady Soane reassured her. "Your father will uphold the Torsgeld. We all know what happens to a civilization that doesn't employ proper stewardship of their planet."

A round of concurrence from the other council members resounded in the chamber. Verena smiled, glad her people stood with her decision.

"So, now let's look over those proposals." Verena took out the first one, as Count Tor activated the holonode to project critical information in the center of the table. "I see the Vassals have approved funds for the renovation of Fort Iark to the north. Let us begin there."

Verena sat ensconced in her favorite nook of the castle's library. She was alone, thankfully, as her ladies had locked themselves in the Blue Salon to plan the series of wedding showers that would begin the following week. Tearing her gaze from the window overlooking the back gardens that led to the cliff promontory and the Green Ocean beyond, Verena placed the pair of silver nodes, each no bigger than the pad of her index finger, onto her temples. The holonet display arose before her eyes.

The red dot next to the king's handle indicated he was not logged on. All the messages she had sent him remained unopened. Frustration gnawed at her. Turning to a news source, Verena noted the headlines continued to indicate Amiel was amassing an army. There had been much discussion on the political channels about the purpose behind the appropriations he had authorized. His choice to construct fortifications along the coastline of the Strait of Dralden were also a topic of hot contention.

What is he doing? Verena had been filled with consternation when she discovered her father and Amiel had requested a private hearing before Thyrein's Galactic council shortly before her birthday. *What did they ask of the Intergalactic Alliance's main governing body? Why don't they just tell me what is going on?*

General Oldan's words about something happening on Parthia lingered. *Does Father think I won't be able to manage the native disputes? Does he believe I am unable to rule successfully if there is conflict with the Gortive? Have these years of helping him rule meant nothing to him?*

Verena's body tensed as her mind turned over the dawning understanding that her father did not trust her leadership. Whatever the issue with the Gortive, the king felt her unequipped to handle it alone. A flash of realization struck her. They expected a war with the natives. The fortification of Iark and of her own coastlines had been approved by the Vassals and by herself only a few months ago.

The pain that seared her heart made her double over in her window seat. The Gortive were primitive, albeit barbaric, warriors. *Does Father think so little of me? Yes, he must. No doubt he thought Amiel best suited to be King of Dravidia.* The stab in her heart and the growing anxiety built up tension in her limbs. Wishing to rid herself of the stress, Verena rose and made her way to the castle's dojo to work out. The exercise would do her good and keep her mind from dwelling on these things.

CHAPTER 7

WEDDING PREPARATIONS

THE WINTER SEASON DAWNED, blanketing Dravidia in lavender-hued snows. Yet, her father remained absent. The kingdom was in full royal wedding fever.

The big ceremony would take place in seven days. The feasting and the celebrating would last for fourteen. Guests from the fifty-one planets of Thyrein's Galactic Alliance had already started to arrive.

These days prior to the wedding were scheduled as a whirlwind of parties and balls. Specially selected vendors would showcase their wares in the castle's inner courtyard as part of the fair, and knights from around the galaxy would demonstrate their prowess during the jousting tournaments and mock battles.

Princess Verena went through the motions, each day feeling more and more adrift, isolated in a sea of gaiety. She'd been barred from communicating with the king.

"Can't I even send him a letter? I could write him, and someone can sneak in and give it to him," she had suggested to Rajin Molent after months of digital messages to her father went unread. Perhaps he was in a place where accessing the quantum net couldn't be done. Though, the signal was supposed to reach across the vastness of space at the quantum level.

Her lanky tutor had turned a placid smile on her as he responded, "I am afraid that is also out of the question, Highness. We've been told that your father is in a place and situation that doesn't allow any communications with him." Misinterpreting her frustration, he continued, "But don't worry. He has the best knights with him, and the king will return safely very soon."

Now, seven days before a wedding she did not intend to go through with, he had yet to arrive. At first, she had considered doing her duty, like she'd mentioned to the elmalin. But the more she pondered the situation, the more her conviction to run away grew.

The ladies of her own court, along with the guests from around the Intergalactic Alliance, assaulted her with their cheerful banter as she sat in the castle's Blue Salon, suffering through yet another bridal shower. Staring out at the snow-covered gardens, Verena's morose thoughts of a life with Amiel swirled in her mind as the wind whirled the falling lavender flakes past the glass panel doors.

The Duchess of Fen settled into the sofa next to her. "Are you all right, my dear?" She asked in a low whisper.

"I'm okay, Auntie," Verena lied, summoning a wan smile.

"Tsk, tsk." The beautiful duchess shook her golden head, eyes gazing into Verena's. "I can see that you are not. It is always hard marrying for political reasons. Your mother was terrified of wedding your father, you know."

"What?"

"Oh, yes. He had a dreadful temper and was well known for his love affairs."

"Father?"

"Yes. I know you wouldn't think so now, but when Irene first got married, it took a lot of courage. Then they forged a friendship, which, I am glad to say, became true affection in the end."

Verena leaned in to her spinster aunt's shoulder. "I suppose it will all be okay for me as well."

"It will." The duchess placed her arm around Verena and gave her a loving squeeze. "Just give it time. Think about how you can build on the friendship you already have with him."

"I just wish I had been given the chance to rule a few years before..." her voice trailed off. She took a deep breath. Looking into her aunt's gentle brown eyes, Verena confessed the deep wound in her heart. "Papa doesn't trust me to rule."

"Your father thinks the world of you. There are, no doubt, some things that make it expedient for you to wed and unite Vidden. I'm sure he will explain all when he returns. Be patient, Verena."

"I'll try. Do you know why he needs this marriage?"

"I only know that it has to do with Parthia and the indigenous people there. What are they called here again?"

"Gortive."

"Yes, something to do with them, it seems." Her aunt gave her leg a pat. "Come on. Enjoy the moments and focus on building a sound marriage for your kingdom's sake."

"I'll try."

Verena and the duchess joined in on the tittering and giggling of the other noble ladies. They were planning her prenuptial celebration. The princess wanted to have a positive attitude, but her mind didn't allow her much peace.

True, as her auntie had said, the king had a short fuse. However, Verena had never seen her father physically harm anyone in anger as she had seen Amiel do. Despite the duchess's assurances, Verena felt her situation was significantly worse than a simple arranged marriage.

"I heard that Prince Amiel is quite gifted in the bedchamber." The Countess of Cartul's saucy statement snapped Verena's attention to the gathering.

"Countess!" The Duchess of Fen feigned shock, but the smile across her face belied it.

"Well, I'm just saying that our Princess will have nothing to worry about in that department," the countess explained herself. "Unlike poor Margy here."

"It's true. Hert is terrible in bed. Two seconds and he's done. And me, oh well. I get to finish my own pleasure."

Verena felt her cheeks bloom at Lady Margy's words. Giggles and guffaws filled the room, as the other ladies all spoke at once, expressing their condolences to Lady Margy.

"I don't think a prenuptial celebration is needed." The princess's statement effectively ended the ladies' mirth.

"Oh, but you must have one, Princess," Lady Geld insisted.

As per court tradition, Verena had, upon turning eighteen, selected seven ladies to attend her and assist in what she might need. Lady Geld, the youngest among them, had been a controversial choice, as her mother had run off with a Calvernsin. But Verena felt she was the one who more truly had the princess's best interests at heart.

"Look, let's face it. I don't want to marry Amiel."

A solemn hush fell on the party.

"I don't think any of us blame you for your... misgivings, dear," her aunt said. "But bringing the two nations together is for the best. It will create a stronger continent of Vidden. Perhaps even someday, the whole planet will be under a single house rule... your house."

"I heard he beat a pleasure lady to a bloody pulp." Lady Margy's words sent a chill down Verena's spine. The older lady turned a stern gaze on her. "Yet, in other instances, he's touted as a gifted lover. We have all heard the tales of the punishments he dishes out to his servants. And then there are the moments when he has shown great mercy and compassion. He is a man of complex character. You must be cautious as you deal with him, Princess."

"He is a bit scary, but he's also very handsome. I think he truly loves you, Princess," Lady Geld spoke.

"His desire for you is clear," the Countess of Cartul concurred. "In that, you have an advantage. You will be able to manage him better given the intensity of his interest in you."

All the ladies looked at her then, and Verena felt herself blush again under their scrutiny. "He is handsome, but with my own eyes I have seen him beat servants. And I don't know that I want to marry a man who visits the pleasure ladies."

"Well, then you'd be a spinster like your aunt, my dear." Lady Margy's guffaw set the ladies to tittering.

The Countess of Cartul chimed in. "Most of our noblemen have their... indiscretions. The bordellos they visit are carefully regulated to ensure compliance with the health codes. We can't be blind about our positions, ladies. We marry for convenience and political power. The trick is to develop a relationship that allows you to pursue your own life's goals while ensuring their benefit."

All her ladies' comments sunk into Verena. This was very much a marriage foisted on her for some political gain that her father hadn't bothered to explain.

The Duchess of Fen tsked. "This isn't helping. Verena, dear, you will find a way to be happy together. He may have a temper, but your father also has one. Your mother and father were able to forge a good life for themselves. You must work on building respect and understanding between you." She rose, walked over to the table piled high with wedding gifts, and returned with a rectangular one wrapped in silver paper and fashionable purple ribbon. "Now, let's open some of these wedding presents."

Verena watched as her aunt turned the mood of the gathering. They all went back to twittering about the wedding.

Returning to her sitting room after the tedious event, Verena plopped down on the cushioned window seat. Her mind reeled with the newly learned information about Amiel. She wasn't naïve. Obviously he'd been with some women; he'd had girlfriends. Paid-for sex was something entirely different. *Why would a man need to visit the pleasure houses?* Verena couldn't fathom it. And that bit about beating a woman was exactly what scared her the most. He'd never harmed her. *But what, if someday he does?*

The princess thought about intimacy. Warmth pooled in her abdomen when she recalled the feel of Amiel's desire against her as they danced. Her face burned as her mind entertained the image of the prince touching her, kissing her, having him inside her.

The day she'd stood so close to him in the hangar came to her. The look in his eyes, the way he'd stared at her mouth, had made her heart pound. For a moment, it had seemed he would kiss her goodbye, and her stomach had filled with butterflies.

She'd never been with a man. Most courtiers were too respectful to make any such advances on her. Those who'd been a bit bolder, Verena had rebuffed. She believed that level of relationship was too personal to be engaged in casually. Sharing her body with a man was something Verena considered special, reserved for the one man with whom she'd also share her life.

The idea of Amiel making love to her brought a tingle through her body. She did care for him as a friend, once. He was handsome and she'd always felt... something... pleasant somethings, when he held her or touched her hand.

Verena reflected on the noblewomen. They had settled into a life of comfort and social position. Accepted husbands and did their duty for the privilege of power and wealth. Only a handful, like her spinster aunt, held positions and land in their own right. The rest married to secure their house's political wellbeing and were satisfied with "true affection." *Is that enough?*

An avid reader, Verena had indulged in romantic stories. The idea of falling deeply in love appealed to her. *But is that unrealistic given my position in life?* Regular women served as heads of large companies, owned their personal businesses, or even served in the Council of Vassals and other government positions.

The princess had believed her father's words when he said she would select her own husband. Now he was imposing a life of conformity and lovelessness upon her, possibly even physical pain; at the least, an existence filled with fear.

With the elmalin's support, the council might back her, if she went before them and said she was being forced to wed against her will a man known to physically harm people. But will they act?

The matter hadn't worked out for Lorifa when she had tried to have the council intercede and prevent her wedding to King Derin of Ontenue. They'd backed her father on the choice. Oh, there had been news stories and protests for women's rights.

In the end, the power and wealth of the nobles had won. The ceremony had been small and private, and now Lorifa was trapped in Ontenue Palace, never allowed out. *No. I'll get no help from the Intergalactic Council. Their power should be for all people, but it is never applied fairly.*

Entering through the servant's door, Mrs. Denip carried a tray with a silver tea service upon it. "I thought this might help settle your nerves, Highness," the faithful hudroid said. She placed it on the coffee table and poured Verena a cup.

Verena smiled at the B-10 model, welcoming the beverage. Mrs. Denip had been the personal maid to her mother, her grandmother, and all the way back to her great-grandmother. Though some felt the droid should be replaced entirely, Verena wouldn't allow it. The hudroid was a connection to her family, and the grandmotherly appearance of the unit gave the princess comfort. And it could yet be upgraded, so there was no need to replace her as far as Verena could see.

"How can I get Father to call this off if he isn't here? What if he arrives the day of, like he did for my birthday? I'm not going to marry Amiel, Deni. I can't." Verena's isolation in this left her confused as to why her once-loving parent wanted to turn her over to a monster. *If he isn't willing to listen to me, then he leaves me no choice; I'll have to flee.* "I'll run away!"

"That's madness, Highness, madness!" Mrs. Denip exclaimed in horror.

"I can't marry him, Deni; I just can't. Papa will not listen. Maybe he thinks I'm not capable of ruling. Maybe he thinks with Amiel as king things will be better. But I know that won't happen. Amiel won't make things better. He'll make my life hell!"

"Hush now, child. Your father wouldn't have spent a fortune on the best tutors to provide you with the skills for governing if he thought you wouldn't be a good ruler." The hudroid gave a furtive look around before continuing. "There is talk, Rennie, on the net. Some say the warring Gortive tribes on Parthia are uniting. A leader has arisen among them. Rumor has it the tribes may seek to cross the Black Ocean to Vidden. Reclaim these lands."

"For Pegot's sake, Deni! The Gortive don't even have small fishing boats. Rajin Molent said they are primitives. They live in mud huts and such." The princess shook her head, wisps of auburn hair whipping her face in that way she had always enjoyed. Verena could feel the resentment as she said in aggrieved tones, "No, Deni, Papa doesn't trust a woman to rule, to keep his kingdom safe. And I will not be the wife of Amiel ra Aulden."

"Come, come, sweet," Mrs. Denip said. "I remember when you and Master Amiel were mere children playing in the forest. Why, you two were inseparable friends."

"That was before," the princess said resolutely.

"Before what, child?"

"Before he beat little Helen!"

Verena remembered the incident well. Amiel's face contorted in anger, the riding crop crashing down on little Helen, the ripping sound of the servant's shirt, the stickiness of the blood splattering on Verena, all remained embedded, seared into her mind's eye.

After that, the princess had sought to spend as little time with Amiel as possible. Her mother had been horrified as she oversaw the tending of Helen's wounds that evening. Her father had spoken to Amiel's parents, but as the years went by, Verena continued to notice his cruelty and arrogance. The princess was continually shocked by his indifference to the pain of those whom he considered "sub-human." Especially after the assassination of his parents.

"No," she spoke now with a vehemence born of resolute purpose. "I would rather die than become that man's wife."

Verena sat on her bedroom floor, tubs full of old journals surrounding her. She had spent her whole life writing her thoughts as well as assorted stories and poems into these, and now she would need to leave most of them behind. She could only realistically take one or two with her. *Which to take?* Cross-legged in her pink cotton pjs, the princess skimmed the precious volumes.

Reaching in to the nearest container, she drew out a white leather notebook with sparkling red crystals in the shape of rose on its cover. Verena's throat constricted.

Reverently, she opened it and began to flip through the pages. Her hands stopped at the picture of Prince Z'Pau'z and his father, General Z'Tro'z. The Calvernsin had visited for the occasion of her mother's birthday, the last they would ever celebrate, when Verena was sixteen.

Looking at the smiling royals, the princess recalled the conversation her parents had the self-same evening. Her father's reaction at her praise of the beauty of the prince's skin had shocked her.

"You can never trust a Calvernsin, kura," he said, caressing her cheek as she gazed up at him. "We must work with them, but we can never align ourselves too closely with their kind."

"But, papa, Thyrein married Z'Agota'z. Aren't we part Calvernsin?"

"You are Dravidian, and your blood is Drulian."

"Darling," her mother had chimed in, "Verena is right. To a certain—"

"Verena will wed one of her own kind when the time comes." His voice held a sharp tone that surprised Verena. "And a prince she shall have. One who is her equal. One she already has a good relationship with."

"We must not choose for her," Queen Irene said. "Surely she will be able to select for herself. And you saw what he did to little Helen."

"One temper outburst is not reason to discard the clear path... but yes," he held up his hands before her mother could speak again, "Verena will choose who she will."

Now Verena saw it. All these years, her father had already chosen a husband for her—Amiel ra Aulden. Perhaps that was why he had not set aside his marriage to her mother when the Queen could not bear him a son. He had chosen his heir, and it was never her.

The realization pierced Verena. Her mother had wanted her to have a choice. *If Mama had lived, would things be different?* It was a pointless line of thinking. Verena continued to turn the pages. In here, she would come upon her mother's assassination. Tears welled in her eyes at the loss that now seemed so much worse, if that was even possible.

A picture of a Sehy stopped her. The blue amphibian humanoids had attacked Amiel's parents, killing them in a horrible manner. The news story she'd pasted here was of the prince's response.

Amiel had all but annihilated the Sehy people. Her father had gone to the council and interceded for him. Genocide was a major violation, yet the alliance had been swayed by the grief and horror of his parents' deaths. They had sanctioned Amiel and ordered him to restore the Sehys' home.

Of course, he had proceeded to enslave them and use them to mine the honrol Aulden had been after from the start. It had been Amiel's father who'd invaded the atoll where the Sehy lived and tried to take the land so he could mine it. Verena's mind spun as she read the words she had written all those years ago.

How can Father be on Amiel's side? This is evil. Mother says he sees Amiel as a son, but I would be ashamed to call him my brother.

Verena closed the journal, tucking it and two others into the bag she planned to take with her. The princess was about to add the newest one, a gold-filigree bound notebook, when she recalled it had been a gift from Amiel. He was always sending presents. Hesitating, she tossed it instead into the nearby tub and tucked her bag under the bed, where it would remain until she made her escape.

After putting everything away, she curled up in bed with her mother's antique Drulian music box beside her. Verena lifted the top and watched the figurine dancing in the red and blue traditional dress.

Her father had made his choice. Amiel was the son he'd actually wanted. *Father didn't worry about a male heir, because he'd decided from the start to marry me to Amiel.* The painful truth dawned on her.

She'd never been meant to rule. She had been groomed to be a consort, with more power than most, maybe, but never a Queen. Everything she'd thought she was had been a lie. The destiny she'd believed in had never been intended for her.

Verena thought of her people. If she stayed, Amiel would be their king. If she left, her father would surely sit Amiel on the throne somehow. No matter what she did, Amiel would rule. *But he won't hurt me if I'm gone. I can save myself at least.*

Opening her new journal, she picked up her pen. Writing had always been a balm to her. She spilled her emotions into a poem.

> Life keeps going, flowing,
> You think you're knowing, growing,
> Secure in who you are, destiny awaits.
> Innocent and trusting, the world seems yours.
>
> The evidence all around, surrounds,
> Blinded by love, oh silly dove,
> Then it slaps you, what you've known.
> Wrapped in bitter truth, you drown.
>
> Your firm foundation cracks, fracks,
> Painful questions loom, bloom,
> Who you are is shattered, life in shreds.
> Destiny snatched away, supporting role to play.
>
> With woman's flesh adorned, thus born,
> Meant to rule, you mindless fool,
> Men decide your fate, the lies revealed.
> It was never meant to be, it's not your place.
>
> By gender bound, unworthy found,
> Men alone sit the throne, your heart torn,
> You paid your dues, followed the rules.
> Crowned you'll never be, for you're a woman.
>
> Open up the gate, a new fate,
> Forge your own way, into the fray,
> In the myriad stars of space, there you'll find,
> A fresh beginning, oh crownless queen.

A tear splattered onto her page. She dabbed at it with her bedsheet. Closing the book and the precious memento from her mother, she bent and tucked them both into her bag.

CHAPTER 8

IN THE WILDS

KING DEKKYLE CROUCHED NEAR THE FLAME, gloved hands outstretched to ward off frostbite. His insulated honrol armor distributed the warmth of its thermal heating unit evenly over his body. In spite of this and the red-gold minox fur coat draped upon his shoulders, planet Fridgia's inauspicious climate pierced through. He could feel the bite of the evening wind's bitter cold down to his very bones.

The king stood, stretching his sore limbs from the time riding on the fremels. The squat horse-like creatures, native to the snow planet, had cloven hooves that allowed them a strong foothold on rocky ground. The white fuzz helped them blend into their environment and avoid the large predators of the continent. They were the only conveyance that could make it in the winter season.

Eldor had found this shallow cave of ice-rock tucked into the side of the mountain pass, and they'd made camp in its protective walls. Dekkyle walked over to the opening and looked out across the narrow path that spiraled up the side of the snow-covered peak. The king had to admit the glistening landscape in the green light of the planet's two moons was a magnificent sight.

Eldor, Earl of Sarnac, handed him a bottle before sitting on the frozen ground by the fire pit and digging through his backpack. "Here, I think this should help a bit. The fremels are settled," the earl reported.

"I wish they were hardy enough to allow us to ride through the night," Dekkyle commented, going back to the warmth of the fire.

"The planet's too cold in the chill of darkness even for their thick fur. The hovercraft's dark-energy engines freeze in daytime out here."

"I know. I'm just frustrated. So far we've been led a merry chase and have nothing to show for it." The king took a hearty swig of the distilled liquid. The liquor burned its way down his throat in a welcome blaze of heat. "Where did you manage to get us savok?"

"Stole it from the pilot's mechanic aboard the Latairian freighter."

"Glad to know he was good for something! I can't believe he dropped us here this way."

"Even our own ships would be unable to bear the planet's cold, Sire. We should have hired a Fridgian vessel. Then we wouldn't be out here having to ride to the rendezvous point."

"The fifth attempt at a meeting! I'm beginning to wonder if Ternic has anything at all to tell us."

"We will get the information we seek. I have no doubt of it. Ternic wants to be cautious, that's all."

Dekkyle knew the earl was right. The pressure of so many months hunting down leads only to end up with nothing had become unbearable as Verena's wedding day drew closer. He wouldn't even be out here if it weren't for Ternic.

When the king had been a young man and he and Eldor had gone on missions on behalf of Dekkyle's father, he'd met Ternic. The man was a chameleon, blending in anywhere. The informant could get anyone to tell him anything. When Dekkyle had saved his life, Ternic had become the king's number one spy. Now Dekkyle was counting on him to bring him the information needed to prove his suspicions.

"Time is running out. I need to return and speak with Verena. But I can't abandon this thread of clues just when it could yield us the proof we need. Having to go by fremel is too slow."

"Perhaps we might have Coronel Folgero carry on for us. His Royal Elite Investigation Services team is already working this from a different angle. If we contact—"

"No." Dekkyle refused to give up. He was too close. "If the truth is as I fear, I wish to confirm it myself. Anyway, you know full well Ternic will never meet with someone else. He insists on giving me the information directly. It protects him, and he has been priceless to us through the years. I must honor his wishes."

"It is costing you dearly, with Verena, I mean. I'm still unsure what you are thinking Ternic will be able to give us, Sire."

Eldor's voice held a slight tone of resentment at Dekkyle's refusal to share the theory that had brought them to the wilds of Fridgia in the middle of the ice planet's winter season. Perhaps it was wrong to keep his suspicions from the earl. Ever had the House of Sarnac served as advisors to the crown. And Eldor had been his best friend since his knight's training at Sarvon Hall, the earl's ancestral home. Still...

"We'll know soon enough. Let's hope we reach Drapo peak before our contact. I want to make sure we set up at our advantage." As Eldor had insisted on scouting ahead, the king inquired, "Did you spot any Picog encampments?"

"No sign of them, but the port master mentioned when we docked that there is a tribe who likes to hunt on the ridge. We'll need to go around to avoid their territory."

"The clock is ticking, Eldor. I think the risk is worth it to get there faster." Seeing the earl about to protest, the king continued, "Come, let's set up the thermpro, and we can get some rest. We'll discuss the plan of action tomorrow."

Dekkyle drew out the black box with the thermpro logo emblazoned on it. He placed it on the cold stone floor and pushed down on the shape of a flame. The unit beeped and green light emanated from it, scanning the space. Once the measurement was taken, the unit emitted a bell toll and the energy field ignited lining the cave space. The air grew warm at last, and Dekkyle took off his thick, cumbersome winter gear.

Once in lighter attire and having cooked a simple meal of beans and rice over their camp fire, the king asked, "Do you think we will be able to find definitive evidence that the Gortive are uniting with help from some exterior source in an attempt to retake Jorn?"

"I believe Ternic is able to get us actual evidence." The earl's face showed concern. "If only the Intergalactic Council had given us the green light for a preemptive strike, this expedition would be unnecessary."

"Verena would not need to wed Amiel if that were the case." Dekkyle recalled the look on his daughter's face as she pleaded with him to call off the wedding. Even now, there were hundreds of messages from her that he'd refused to open. He knew their content, but the conversation required face-to-face interaction, not digital. *I've already made a mess of it; I'll sit down with her and explain.*

"I know there are concerns about his temper, but I must say Rajin Horsef's assertion that Amiel loves our princess is correct." The earl paused briefly to stoke the fire, adding another flame chip. "By wedding the Prince of Aulden, Verena will become Queen of the entire planet."

"She doesn't wish to marry the boy," Dekkyle reminded his best friend.

"Why did the council refuse to grant the strike? The unification evidence and satellite feed of the Gortive shipyard off the Bay of Parthos that Amiel collected seemed to me strong proof of their intent."

Dekkyle shook his head. "The council felt the fact that the natives are building sailing ships only showed they were progressing to more civilized creatures. They said, and they are correct, that we had no proof they intended us harm." The king ran a hand through his gray-kissed auburn hair. "Chief Councilor Laurenga believes the native development should be encouraged. I don't know what luck Rajin Lord Bral is having, but I can't fathom the natives will be interested in trade treaties."

"Laurenga may be as senile as rumors from her home planet of Drulin have stated." Eldor's tone showed his disgust with the Premier's benign view of their enemy.

"That is why it is crucial we follow the current lead and gain the evidence that will show with certainty there is malicious intent." Dekkyle shivered as he considered the implications. "The Gortive tribes uniting, making sailing ships, cannot be anything but a plot instigated by powers beyond our planet. Someone very specific in their intent is pulling the natives' strings." The king's eyes locked with the earl's as he continued, "Such a sudden leap forward in their development can only mean they have outside help. They don't even fish for their fear of water, yet suddenly they are building ships?"

Eldor nodded his ascent. "We need to know who is supporting them and why. If they are being provided knowledge of ocean-going craft, why not spaceships as well?"

Dekkyle contemplated the question. It was the very one that plagued him. The outsiders using their natives had a plan, but it wasn't to help the Gortive. They were just pawns in all this. The bigger threat, at least to the king, seemed plain. The Calvernsin had to be behind this. He reached into his pack and took out the velvet pouch with the odd jewel the trader in Lataira had given him. The man claimed it was a gift for the rincess in honor of the coming nuptials.

Eldor had spread out his sleeping bag and was now cozily rolled up in it. "Are you going to give it to the princess?"

"No." Something inside of Dekkyle told him the fascinating piece was not what it seemed. "I'm going to give it to Master Rajin Horsef. He'll be able to discover why it makes me feel so apathetic when I touch it."

"Apathetic?"

"When I held it, I was overcome with this sense of... I don't know... just not caring about anything." The king spilled the beautiful pink stone onto the floor. The silver chain cascaded around it. Gazing at it, Dekkyle could see a light within the iridescent jewel. "There is something wrong with it, but I can't figure it out."

"The Rajin will know. Their power and connection to the Great I Am will reveal the truth of it to them."

Silence fell, each lost in his own thoughts. The king scooped up the gift and placed it back in its scarlet pouch. The moment his fingers touched it, he felt a sudden lethargy. *Why am I even bothering with all this?* I should head home and be happy. When the necklace was once more tucked in his pack and his mind cleared, Dekkyle returned to the multitude of unopened messages from Verena. She had used the private back channel he had taught her. He'd installed the master code that accessed everything and the private network so as to safeguard the castle and its communication system. Beside him, only Verena and Eldor knew of the code.

Verena's beautiful face filled the king's mind. The look of anger, pain, hurt on her birthday, and of complete desperation the morning after, made his heart ache. Verena's rejection of the betrothal was understandable, Dekkyle thought, wrapping himself up in his sleeping bag and staring up at the ice cave's ceiling. With Dravidia at peace for so long, it had seemed as if Verena would have a choice in who she married. Moreover, she would be able to rule for a time as Queen, something Dekkyle knew she longed for and wished he could give her.

But political marriages were essential. His own had been arranged by his father as a way to cement the trade routes with Planet Drulin's Dukedom of Fen. Before the betrothal, he had barely given a thought to the scrawny little Lady Irene. Happily, for him, she had blossomed into a curvaceous beauty. Slowly, they had forged a friendship that had sparked into a love match.

His stomach turned recalling the assassination of his beloved Queen. The natives of planet Schol, whom she'd been trying to help, had turned on her. Dekkyle wished he could have done as Amiel had when the Sehy killed his parents. But he was too old to claim youthful zeal and too levelheaded to risk his nation on revenge.

Shaking away the memory of Irene in his arms dying, Dekkyle lifted up a prayer to the Great I Am. Perhaps Verena could find the same bliss with Amiel someday, with God's blessing. Now, Verena would have to come to terms with the need for this union. She was a sensible girl. She would do her duty.

Hours passed. The wind outside the cave howled as a sudden storm ran past. The king fidgeted, while his friend snored peacefully. Sitting up, bundled in his blankets, his gaze fell upon the curtain of snow swirling at the entrance, shielding them from prying eyes.

Noticing his sleeping friend, Dekkyle smiled, recalling the days of their knight's training at Sarvon. They had been an unruly pair in their youth. The flames of the fire cast eerie shadows on the ice-rock walls. The king longed for the comfort of his home and berated himself for not having made time to talk to Verena. He had left her in the dark about the reasons for his choice. Refusing to abdicate had been the right course of action. Once installed as Queen, it would have been harder to make the alliance happen.

Pulling out a pair of holonodes, he placed the silver discs no bigger than the pad of his index finger on each temple. He accessed his private journal on the back server with the master code. The king added to the pages, noting what had thus far been discovered about the situation on Parthia.

He reread the series of questions that he'd started out with about this circumstance all those many months before. Sadly, he'd gained answers to only a very few, despite days, months really, tracking down leads. The king looked at the virtual display of his notes and felt heaviness blanket him.

The messages from his kura beckoned. *He should write to her. What he had to say was better done in person.* His hand hovered over the virtual display. *He was too tired to write anything to her right now, he decided.*

He logged off and put away the nodes. Settling back down, he smiled. She would have made a magnificent Queen. He had provided Verena with the best training money could buy. After the murder of Irene, he'd insisted the princess be well trained in the art of war by Sir Eriq himself.

The legendary hero had reported with pride Verena's skill, especially with the ginmra weapon. His daughter was smart, and though a little naïve, she had a strong sense of justice and fairness, coupled with a tender heart. She would have ruled well on her own. The king let out a heart-weary sigh.

He would meet with Ternic on the morrow. If all went well, he would have the answer to who really was backing the Gortive in less than seven days. *No*, the king thought. *I will head home in five days. I owe Verena an explanation, and I'll deliver.*

Two days later, King Dekkyle stood atop the flattened mountain peak of Drapo. The awe-inspiring view of the vast Dray mountain range towering over the valley lands of the south left him breathless. The snows blanketed the entire world in a glistening green that mimicked grass. The Poy River, which cut across in zig-zagging turns and bends, served as a mirror, its frozen waters a silver thread in the landscape.

The beauty of it all failed to alleviate Dekkyle's growing irritation. Ternic was a no-show. Again. *Had the man been captured? Found out? Killed?*

Releasing a growl of frustration, the king turned back to Eldor, who sat on a short boulder, a book in his hands. "We must go. It will take us a day to get to the ship and at least two days to return to Jorn. If we wait longer, I'll miss her wedding. Good thing Fridgia is in the same system."

"We don't seem to have much luck," Eldor said, closing his book and rising into a stretch. "I'll send a message to Captain Groeg to meet us at the port in Albantu. It will be an easier climb down if we go west instead of returning the way we came."

"Excellent idea."

They gathered up their packs, mounted their fremels, and began the climb down. Dekkyle concentrated on managing his animal's footing. As he scanned the area ahead, the king spotted something shiny in the pathway.

"I see something. Stop." Bringing his animal to a halt, he dismounted and strode to the object half embedded in the snows. Cleaning it off, he picked it up. It was a data chip, still in its protective case.

"A data chip!" Eldor spoke over the king's shoulder.

"Yes." Dekkyle scanned the area closer. A trail of crimson led toward the mountain side and into a possible cave. "Look, blood."

"Ternic?"

"Maybe." Rising, Dekkyle strode purposefully, following the splatter drops. Fear gripped the king's heart.

The cave was shallower than its counterpart on the eastern slope, where Eldor had found them shelter. Against the far wall, a man lay face down, his skin almost blue.

"Ternic!" Rushing forward, the king bent over the body and turned him. Checking the victim's vital signs, the king swore under his breath as he confirmed, "He's dead."

The earl came over and began to search the knapsack nearby. He pulled out a set of clothing, a thermopro, and some coins. "Jornian desert currency."

The king stood. The use of physical money had long been extinguished. The banks of the various planets kept tight control digitally. Only the desert people on a handful of planets used coins due to the heavy metals in the sands that made the digipayers malfunction.

"If he was on Jorn, why have us meet him here?" Dekkyle asked.

"Who knows when he was last there? The clothes in here seem to be from Eesh."

"Isn't Arwace from Eesh?"

With a cough, Eldor responded, "Yes, she is. I doubt—"

"Perhaps this man was in her employ. He may have been coming from Eesh with whatever is on this data card."

"How did he die?"

The king turned the man's body, looking for signs of the cause of death. "Well, it wasn't an energy weapon. He bled and was able to drag himself to this cave from out there. See the hand marks in blood."

"Let's bring him with us. We can have Dr. Koll examine him."

"It will slow us down... but yes... let's do it."

CHAPTER 9

A FATEFUL DECISION

VERENA RECALLED HER ASTRONOMY LESSONS. She knew that the wormhole pathways, which allowed intergalactic travel, were veins, running through and between the galaxies of the universe. As an ocean's undercurrents allow its aquatic inhabitants to travel quickly across a planet, so the wormhole portals opened gateways to far flung regions of the galactic wall. Using these intergalactic highways, the princess planned to travel to a planet far from Jorn, where she could start a new life.

"Where shall I go, Deni?" the princess asked as she pored over the maps and charts in the castle's well-stocked library four days before the dreaded event.

Her nurse gave her a stern look, no doubt disgusted by her blithe tone. *Too bad! It's my life she wants to sacrifice, not her own.* With doggedness, Verena returned her attention to the chart in front of her.

The library had been her favorite place since childhood. It encompassed the eastern tower of her home and rose ten stories high. Its roof ended in a stained-glass depiction of the final battle for the independence of Jorn, which was visible from the ground floor. Verena moved to the railing and glanced up at it. Over 300 years ago, her family and Amiel's had led their respective people in establishing independence from the imperialist planets of Drulin and Fratern. Many planets had become independent during those years.

Before that time, Thyrein, then regent of the colonies of Drulin on Jorn, had basically formed the Intergalactic Alliance. The legendary sword Marama had chosen him to wield it. Only a warrior with the purest of hearts could even lift the weapon forged, according to the stories, by the hand of the Great I Am Himself from the heart of a dragon who'd made the willing sacrifice. Her family had a great history with strong leaders, yet her father refused to let her rule. *Because I'm a woman? Is he so ridiculous as to believe only a man can defend our people?*

Verena sighed and turned to look down. Each level of the library formed a circle with a railing overlooking the rotunda of the first floor. The circular inlay of black marble with white streaks from the quarries in the Tarsidian Mountains had, at its center, the statue of the first King of Dravidia, Larenos I.

Surrounding the marble likeness of her grim-faced ancestor were the data readers and node boxes that contained all the wealth of books in virtual holo-digital form. The princess, however, had always had a fondness for the actual paper books and charts. One of the functions of the Royal Library included the preservation of the written word in all its formats. If she had not been born a princess, Verena had often thought she would have loved a life as a librarian, a keeper of ideas and history.

"I still don't see a need for you to go anywhere," her nurse finally replied from the comfortable sofa near the window that she had chosen to occupy. "You should do your duty as a Royal Princess and marry. It is your father's prerogative to select a suitable husband. As a good daughter, you should submit to his wishes and wisdom, child."

They were on the ninth floor, and the musky smell of the fragrant blackwood of the shelves was relaxing in spite of Denip's nagging. With renewed zeal, Verena returned to the charts of the systems that made up the known universe.

"There are fifty-one planets in Thyrein's Galactic Wall that match our advancement in technology," inhaling deeply, the princess muttered to Helen, who stood on a stepstool beside her assisting in her hunt for a new home. Being a native of the Garinquel Islands, Helen had the beautiful bronze skin and short stature, only four feet two inches tall, of her people.

They studied the plans of each solar system and skimmed through books on the different planets. King Dekkyle would have an easy time finding her, should she settle on any of these. The connectivity between the worlds through interstellar commerce thanks to the Intergalactic Council would make the effort futile. Even with forged documents, the DNA analysis required to get a job would make hiding Verena's identity impossible.

"This is hopeless! Papa will find me and drag me back for sure."

"What about the more primitive planets?" Helen suggested in her sweet, childlike voice. "Perhaps on one of the colonized worlds the technology is not yet in use."

"What do you think, Deni?" Verena stole a glance at her sulky hudroid. The servant opted for a disapproving silence.

The princess threw the recalcitrant droid an irritated glance. *Why did they have to give personality algorithms to these things?* Still, many times her nurse's love coding had comforted Verena.

With a shake of her head and a conspiratorial smile at Helen, the princess turned to the next map and scanned its contents. There were three interesting planets in the Golan Galaxy. Enthused, she sent Helen to fetch the volumes from the stacks on the fourth floor. After several hours of research, the pair shoved the collection of books irritably aside, nearly spilling the ever-growing pile of tomes onto the floor.

"I can't believe it, Deni, Helen! Not one of these planets will work! The natives are seriously hostile, and the colonists continually have to be rescued from attacks. It would be suicide!"

"There now. You see, best to marry Prince Amiel and live here with your people in peace, Princess."

Peace—ha—no way that will happen. Verena shivered at the thought of a marriage to Amiel. Given his violent proclivities, he might even go so far as to beat her someday. Lady Margy's words yet lingered in her mind. It was a horrible rumor. There had been no way to corroborate it, and Lady Margy had a history of telling tall tales. Still, Verena couldn't risk it. *No, there will be no peace for me here.*

"There must be somewhere, Highness," Helen chimed in.

Verena turned to the next set of charts, smoothing out the maps with her hand. The first depicted the galaxy for the sacred planet. Verena's mind recalled what she'd been taught about the planet that mattered the most to the Great I Am.

Intergalactic Statute 136 Section C Subchapter 3.4 declared the sacred planet a prohibited zone. Captain Galev had stressed this when he was teaching her to fly her personal space craft.

"It is forbidden to go near that solar system," he stated firmly.

"Why?"

"The sacred planet is to be unaware of our existence."

"Yes, but why?"

"It's the law. Now, look at the hedligan controls, Highness..."

Unable to get a straight answer from the Captain, Verena had inquired of her tutor the reason for the prohibition upon their return to the hangar that same day.

"Well, that question leads us nicely into a history lesson," Rajin Molent, dressed in his purple and gray tunic and pants, responded. Sighing heavily, the princess sat down to the monotone lecture.

He began by explaining that the special planet had first been discovered by Drulian imperialists.

"When they first came upon Earth, as they named the sacred planet, they realized its people were yet in the very beginnings of developing civilization. Do you remember the Intergalactic Alliance criteria for colonization?"

With an inward grumble, Verena responded, "The natives have to be sentient beings, with civilized governments, nearing technological advancement that would allow interstellar flight, and be able to record information through the written word."

"Excellent, Highness." The rajin smiled warmly at her. "In the times when Earth first came to our attention, these requirements were not in place as these were established much later." He paused to wipe his glasses. Placing them back on his slightly crooked nose, he continued, "So, the Drulians interacted with the humans of that world, even taught them some building techniques appropriate to their developmental stage, of course."

"But Master Molent, what makes this planet so special? I mean, it's very behind us in advancement."

"In the year 2020 TGW..." He paused and looked at Verena. "And what does TGW stand for, Highness?"

"Thyrein's Galactic Wall."

"Excellent!" Rising, Rajin Molent walked behind his desk. Opening a drawer, he pulled out a metal-bound book. The gold-plated cover with a filigree-engraved title gleamed in the light of the classroom's windows. Returning to the table, he set the volume down between them.

"In the year 2020 TGW, the fifty-one prophets of the sacred Order of Ressord came together for their annual gathering. Each brought a book they had written, inspired by the Sevenfold Spirit. And do you know what book it was?"

"The Book of Illumination. The Holy Word of the Great I Am as given to the prophets."

"Very good. Indeed, each prophet, without ever speaking to each other, had written the exact same book. Every word identical across the fifty-one copies."

"How can that be?"

"The Great I Am was sending us, not only His Holy Word to live by, but a sign. Earth was identified as the planet upon which the events of the book either had taken place already or would do so in the future. Those that had happened could be traced to that planet, but much of the text was yet prophecy back in those days. So, the council, presented with this evidence, declared Earth sacred and prohibited all contact with it."

Now, glancing at the table in the library, Verena ran a hand over the small, blue dot that represented the holy planet on the chart before her.

"I think I found the perfect hideout," she muttered at Helen. "It is far more primitive than us, but that's to our advantage. Happily, there are no other species on it that would threaten our life. Nope, just good old-fashioned *Homo Sapiens!*"

"I think it is a wise choice, Highness," Helen concurred.

"Deni, Papa will not be able to marry me off. I will make my own destiny."

"As you please, child," her nurse responded. Mrs. Denip continued to sit, staunchly opposed to lending any assistance.

"Tomorrow, I depart," the princess said, going to stand before her. "I know you don't think it's necessary, but I cannot sacrifice my happiness."

"Selfishness is not a trait becoming of a future ruler!"

"Ah, but I won't be a future ruler," Verena countered. "I will be a librarian. This is my chance to be me. To find out what I can do. Not subjugated to a husband, but my own person."

Going to where Helen had started collecting the books to help reshelf them, Verena gave her instructions for the next day's escape. The diminutive servant agreed she would be ready.

"Come on, Deni, let's get lunch." Verena turned and Mrs. Denip rose, following her charge.

As they approached the lift, Verena gave the hudroid a hug. Then she moved behind the servant and accessed the interface portal. The panel sprung open. Verena swiftly wiped the memory banks clear for the past week just to be safe. She hoped the information would remain deleted forever, though she knew data could always be found again by a skilled droid keeper. Confident that by the time someone retrieved these conversations, she'd be well hidden on Earth, the princess closed the hudroid's panel.

Verena clutched her ginmra firmly. Clad in tight-fitting black pants and shirt, her hair bound and tucked into a black cap, the princess moved through the darkened castle corridors with the stealth of a jungle cat.

Security had been tightened with so many royals and government leaders from around the Galactic Wall attending the wedding. Getting to the launch pad meant navigating through the various groups of guards. A couple times, she had been forced to wait in nooks along the wall for the right moment to slip past unseen. It had been nerve racking, but Verena finally made it to the north hanger, where her personal ship was housed.

Now, she lingered in the shadowed alcove outside the hanger's massive blackwood doors. Her foot tapped the white marble floor, and she wondered if Helen had backed out at the last moment. *At least, it seems she has not alerted anyone to my plan. But will she tell them where I went when questioned?*

Amiel had arrived that very morning. Several times, she noticed how he tried to get her alone, but Verena had evaded him thanks to the ever-present guests and her seven noble ladies. Dinner had been excruciating. She had fulfilled her last duty as a royal. She would forge a new future, one in which she was free. *If Father thinks Amiel is a better King for Dravidia, then so be it.*

The sound of approaching footsteps echoed from the hallway leading to the east wing of the castle, bringing her back to the moment at hand. The princess pressed herself deeper into the darkness and held her breath.

"Highness?" the tentative whisper broke the silence.

"Helen." Verena stepped forward, a note of relief in her voice. "Everything's ready. Come on."

The Garinquel servant, dressed all in black and carrying a small bundle containing all she owned, turned to follow Verena. Earlier, the princess had requested her vessel be made ready. It was an order she issued with regularity, as she occasionally enjoyed morning forays. The silver ship gleamed in the lights of the chamber, perched, like a falcon, awaiting her mistress. Together, Verena and Helen made their way toward the open ramp. The boxes of wedding supplies, which had arrived that very afternoon, made for good cover as they approached.

"Almost there," Verena whispered, as they crouched next to the last set of boxes before the open space leading to the craft. "Okay, quickly now."

The pair set off. The hangar was dark, save for an occasional lantern sconce. The deep shadows made the trek feel ominous. A shiver ran down Verena's spine as the reality of what she was doing set in.

"You there. Halt!" Three guards rushed toward them. These were human beings, not the usual hudroids that patrolled the hangars. Verena felt a cold sweat drip down her arm pit and at her spine.

"Get on board and start her up," Verena commanded.

With a single thought, the princess activated the ginmra, its special honrol alloy flowed out, fashioning itself into a foot-long hammer. It glowed with a soft pink light. Wielding it from its sword-like pommel, Verena ran toward the oncoming guards.

With lightning speed, she thrust herself into the air. In a single fluid movement, she kicked one guard down with her right leg, knocked out the second on the head with her ginmra, and brought the weapon around, delivering a blow on the third guard's forearm.

Rising from the crouch of her landing, Verena rushed to the guard recuperating from the kick, hitting him on the head just in time to twirl round and manage a hit on the leg of the third guard. As the wounded man fell to his knees, Verena brought her hammer-shaped ginmra down on his head as well.

All three lay unconscious at her feet. Bending, she checked their pulses; they were alive. *Good!* She was loath to kill innocents to make her escape to freedom.

Verena turned toward the ramp. A powerful hand yanked her back. She struck a pile of wood boxes and crumpled to the floor, landing face down. Gripping her ginmra, Verena twisted up and onto her feet while simultaneously thrusting forward.

His ginmra was in the shape of a double-edged sword, lit up in a fiery red. She swung, trying to knock it out of the guard's hand. He ducked. Recuperating quickly, he attacked.

Squatting to avoid being cut in half, Verena rolled away. He brought the ginmra back around toward her. Verena willed her weapon to transform into a matching sword. The pink radiance changed to a deep purple as the princess realized this fight might be to the death. Sparks of light exploded as the blades clashed.

Using his upper-body strength, the guard gave a mighty shove, attempting to push her onto her back. A gasp of surprise escaped him as Verena, unaffected, returned the move, sending him crashing into a pile of boxes. She smiled at the sight of him covered with silver ribbons. The under-wing lights of the ship illuminated her face as the engines burst to life.

"Highness?" Righting himself to his feet, the Dravidian guard stood, uncertain how to proceed, confusion at the realization of who he had been trying to kill written on his face. He gave her a deep bow to show his respect.

Transforming her weapon once more into a hammer, Verena took the advantage. She lunged, knocking him unconscious. His body swayed. Verena took a step back, slamming her hand into the corner of the boxes.

"Foluc!" The curse word slipped out as the pain caused her hand to open, releasing her ginmra, which switched off instantly.

The guard's body fell heavily onto her as they toppled to the floor. Without the weapon for extra strength, Verena struggled to rise from under the unconscious guard's full weight. Harsh voices echoed in the hangar. The princess realized she had no time to search for her ginmra. With a final shove and a wiggle, she freed herself from the cumbersome body. She boarded the ship, closed the ramp, and made her way to the cockpit.

"I've started the mechanism for opening the roof hatch," Helen informed her as she entered.

The fellow fugitive stood on the co-pilot's seat, stretching to reach the final controls that would guide the ship into space.

"Here we go!" Verena couldn't keep the note of excitement from her voice. The princess took over, piloting them out and away as more guards rushed into the hangar.

It was not easy; the blackness of the ginmra's after effects assailed her.

They were out of the atmosphere now. She fought to hold onto consciousness long enough to make the jump into the quantum stream and set them on the correct pathway coordinates. Approaching the access point, the wings of her ship swung up, forming a circle. The quantum drive activated, filling the space between the wings with an energy stream. The responding energy portal opened, and they entered the pathway.

Once they were safe, Verena set the autopilot and made her way to the sleeping quarters. Helen helped support her as the princess swayed, struggling to stay awake for just a little longer.

"It's a little worrisome how the ginmra affects you, Highness," Helen commented. "The royal guards are weakened, and they need to eat and drink. Some even faint for a couple hours, but you, Highness—"

"It has always been this way. Rajin Horsef assured my father it was not a problem, so don't worry, Helen. Though it looks like I'm gonna sleep all the way to Earth. We will reach the planet in two weeks, but I may be out longer than that. I never can tell. So just hover the ship in interstellar space until I awake. I'll help you put her down. She isn't easy, and I don't want you crash landing us!" Verena settled into her bed, its warmth enveloping her.

"You can rest, Highness. I'll get us there in one piece, even if this bird is a bit too big for my size."

"Wait for me to..." the princess couldn't finish the sentence. The darkness claimed her.

CHAPTER 10

GODAR

GODAR'S AMBER EYES GLEAMED as he stared into the murky water of the red-granite bowl before him. He'd refused to attend the wedding, though he could have donned his Viscount Pembra shape.

Godar's veiny hand clenched violently, recalling the ridiculous betrothal agreement that had almost laid waste his careful stratagems. *The besotted fool of a prince, for the chance to fuck that insipid princess, had accepted an empty title, leaving the final say in all matters to his queen.* It had been hard to keep his rage in check when he found out the terms Amiel had accepted. *All my hard work to bring it about, and Amiel threw it away for the chance to warm that woman's bed!*

Godar's grip relaxed. His almost-translucent thin pale skin showed his thick blue veins. A cruel smile curled his slim lips, snaking them up across his wrinkled face. The news from his informant pleased him tremendously.

With a bang of the massive blackwood door, Amiel barged into the nijar's chambers in the catacombs of Auld Palace.

"She ran away!" he growled through clenched teeth. "How could she have done that? Doesn't she..."

The prince stood there shaking, the veins in his neck throbbing, eyes ablaze with anger. The talisman Godar had gifted him years ago glowed red beneath his shirt.

"I'm sorry, Highness," Godar feigned ignorance, looking up at the angry noble. Inwardly reveling in the opportunity, he inquired innocently, "I'm afraid I've been here researching... What are you speaking of, my Lord?"

"Verena!" the words, curt and sharp as broken glass, came forth from the irate prince. "She ran away. Disappeared! Two days before the wedding!" Amiel began to pace, punching the far walls of the stone chamber when he reached them. "The whole galactic wall... She's made a laughing stock of me!"

"What did King Dekkyle have to say?" Godar strolled calmly toward his comfortable chair. A pair of black reclining seats beckoned by the blazing fire of the round bronze brazier that took up the middle of the large room. "Please, sit, my Lord. Let us take council calmly." He stood, waiting for the prince to sit.

Amiel dropped into the chair opposite the nijar's. "I... Why would she do that?" The anger was dissipating, replaced now by the deep hurt of spurned love. The look of pain in the prince's blue eyes spoke of the years of longing for this one woman.

Godar knew he had to keep Amiel focused on the political—and very public—slight. Deliberately arranging his midnight-blue robes as he took his seat, the nijar asked again, "What of King Dekkyle?"

"Oh, he says he had no idea she would do that. He says he never had a chance to really explain to her the need for the union—"

"He did try to forge a treaty without the marriage, if I recall, even at the last..." Godar's hopes were not disappointed. Understanding of the implication of his statement burst to life, rekindling Amiel's anger.

"Treacherous bastard!" The prince sprang to his feet, storming the chamber once more. "He hid her. He plans to force an alliance from us without the marriage. Well, if he thinks he can make a fool of me like that, he is sadly mistaken."

"Do you really think war is the best course of action?" Godar queried coolly. "After all, if the Gortive attack... well, we'll need the Dravidians. And there is the rajin. Long have they protected the House of Drav." He reclined back into the black satin cushions. Folding his hands and interlacing his fingers, he rested his chin upon them in a contemplative pose.

"You can deal with the rajin, or are they stronger than your nijars?" The prince came to a stop before Godar. The look on Amiel's face made the nijar laugh inwardly. The fool thought he was so smart, pricking Godar's ego to bend him to his will. Of course, it was Amiel who was playing so nicely into Godar's plans.

"The rajin will pose no problem. Can you guarantee a victory against Dravidia? The Principality's forces are not particularly large, even with the preparations you've made for when the Gortive offensive comes."

"We won't fight alone." Amiel's smirk pleased Godar. "I spoke with King Delvag before leaving Castle Dravidia. He was disgusted by the situation and has pledged planet Fratern's forces if we should need them."

"Still... Dravidia will no doubt be reinforced by Drulin."

"You're a nijar. Do you mean to tell me you can't find a way to have Drulin refuse to aid them?"

"Well... perhaps we can let the Drulians know that if we succeed against Dravidia, we would be willing to let them mine for liog in the Torsgeld Wildlife Preserve. They have wanted to have access to this natural resource that is so essential to their special kelling machines. I understand Princess Verena thwarted their latest attempt to gain access."

"Perfect." Amiel rushed out as quickly as he'd arrived.

Godar leaned back. This was better than what they'd originally planned. He'd have to send word of this new development to the Grand Nij.

Godar's ship began its decent from space, having been cleared to land at the south hangar of Auld Palace. Out the porthole window, the nijar took note of the muddy grounds surrounding the building.

He'd been working behind the scenes to secure Drulin's promise to refuse aid to Dravidia. In the backrooms of the Intergalactic Alliance Council's Chambers on Eskopock, in his Viscount Pembra guise, Godar had met with the Drulian Ambassador. It had proved pathetically easy to break the centuries old alliance with Dravidia. *Childish and petty idiots! But useful... for now.*

As he disembarked, the excitement of the coming war filled him. He made his way to Prince Amiel's study, having returned from the moon that served as the seat of power for the Intergalactic Alliance.

"We now have two-thirds of the council on our side," Godar announced by way of greeting.

"This is fantastic news!" Figor, Duke of Aul, stated. "We stand a much better chance of actually winning now, A."

"Yes. You've done very well, Viscount Pembra." Amiel gave Godar a short nod of the head.

The prince's use of his title made Godar aware he was still in disguise. He froze, about to speak the words to return him to his natural form, when he realized Lord Sabred, Earl of Udeep, uncle to Prince Amiel, was also present. Godar recoiled to the farthest corner of the room as surreptitiously as possible. The man always made Godar feel as though he were burning.

"This is not a good idea, Amiel." Lord Sabred's reedy voice and emaciated look had fooled many into believing him a weakling.

Godar knew, of course, the lord had been trained in the rajin arts. As such, he wielded a considerable power. Nothing that could threaten Godar's own abilities. *Still... best to keep my distance from him, the nijar thought.*

"Uncle, it's clear King Dekkyle is hiding Verena. He hopes to force us into an alliance without the marriage."

"I don't believe that for a second, but... suppose it is so." Sabred stood before Amiel, placing his hands on the prince's shoulders. "If she doesn't love you, why force the issue? She ran. It hurt your pride. Move on. The Gortive are the real enemy."

"The jilting came before the eyes of the entire Galactic Wall," Amiel's pain resonated in his tone. "Dekkyle will pay for it."

"I had hoped after these many months, you would have let that go, A," Lord Sabred's voice softened, using Amiel's nickname.

Shaking free of Sabred's hands, Amiel turned to where Godar watched the exchange.

"We have been building up our forces during wauger. As far as Dravidia is concerned, Dekkyle believes this armament to be preparations for when the Gortive attack us."

"Excellent, my Prince," Godar concurred. "The past three months of wauger's rains and flooding have proven useful. Now that spring approaches and the land is drying, we can launch our attack."

"Where shall we strike first?" Amiel turned to the table, a map of the continent of Vidden lay spread out on it.

"Sanctal must be destroyed." A thrill of bliss went through Godar as he made the pronouncement. At long last, the Rajin Order would fall.

"What? Are you mad?" Lord Sabred's disbelief at the suggestion hung in the air.

Reiterating his words, Godar explained, "The temple must be brought down, the rajin removed, so that they cannot help Dravidia. They have always sided with the House of Drav since before their regency on Jorn."

"I'm sorry, Uncle Sabred. I know you are fond of them." Amiel stood by Godar's plan. *Good. The little princeling was falling in line nicely thanks to that stupid princess.*

"There is no power in the universe that can stand against the Great I Am. That will be the beginning, and end, of your war," Lord Sabred said. His eyes filled with concern.

The fool truly believes this is the God of the universe. He will see... they will all see... when Ahrinox reigns at last.

"We have... weapons... that will do the job." Amiel glanced sideways at Godar.

The nijar understood. The time had not yet come to make known that the only real power in the universe backed the house of Aulden. He held his tongue while Lord Sabred tried, uselessly, to dissuade Amiel.

After much discussion, Amiel brought the matter to a close. "We shall attack Sanctal. You will not warn them, Uncle."

"I am your kin. I will always be with you, A."

"Thank you."

This wauger season had felt like an eternity to the nijar. Godar had been forced to remain on Eskopock while the rain poured down in sheets and the rapid thaw of the snows and ice inundated Jorn. Wauger was not a fit time for battle as the planet became a virtual water world. Yet, Godar longed for the moment when the nijar leadership could arrive and defeat the rajin of Jorn.

At last, the meeting adjourned and Godar waited for Lord Sabred to leave.

Once he was alone with Amiel, he stressed, "You will not allow them to return, ever. Once defeated, the rajin must be exiled from the planet."

"Godar," Amiel's tone held a note of irritation, "I have already pledged this. The Nijar Order will have its first official and fully recognized home here on Jorn once I am king."

The temperate spring breezes brushed past Godar as the night's darkness shielded the army of his prince encamped around the Rajin Temple of Sanctal. The fragrant wildflowers of the open fields lay crumpled beneath their booted feet.

Finally, the moment had come. Reinforced with Fratern's armies and secure in the secret agreement with Drulin, Aulden would begin the war on Dravidia by annihilating the rajin.

"Our men are in position, Godar," Amiel stated, coming to stand beside the nijar.

Godar's heart rejoiced. The heads of his order had arrived on Jorn that morning. The High Priests stood around the temple. Thirteen men spaced out evenly around the seven thousand square foot monastery and its grounds. Their blue cloaks flapped softly in the wind. A red glow around their bodies indicated they'd performed the ritual, opening the door to channel Ahrinox's greatness.

For a moment, Godar longed for his time on planet Magdezb. But there was work to be done here if they were to usher in Ahrinox's rule.

"You won't need to fight this battle." Godar turned bright-red eyes to the young ruler he'd mentored. "It will be between us and the rajin. Watch and see the power of the true lord of the universe. Ahrinox will bring down your enemies, my Prince."

"We shall see. First we must get past those walls. The ships are ready to fire from space."

Amiel's lack of faith irked the nijar. He turned away from the pathetic princeling. *Will he ever learn? All this time and he still doesn't understand the true source of power!*

"Do as you wish," Godar said. "Your technology will not avail you here."

He heard Amiel scoff as the prince walked away toward the Fraternese command liaison. The prince's voice carried to the nijar as he gave the order to attack. Fratern's warcrafts in orbit unleashed their firepower upon the temple. Their blue blasts illuminated the force shield protecting Sanctal. A golden glow emanated from the now visible bubble.

A cackle escaped Godar's lips as the energy field withstood the attack with ease. *Fools! This move only served to alert the enemy.* Alarm sirens filled the night air as rajin stirred, mobilized to defend their home. *Good, come out and fight. See the power of Ahrinox!*

The yellow limestone walls of the monastery gleamed in the rising moon. The soft chant of the nijar began. The words, spoken in the ancient long-forgotten tongue of true power, rose on the breeze. A shimmer of red mist formed from the incantation. It glinted, swirling in serpentine motions as if it were a living thing.

The startled rajin lined the outer wall's parapet. Energy crackled upon their outstretched palms. The night glowed with a myriad of colors. Godar scanned the group. He searched for the masters. Those would be the strongest, the ones to defeat first. His eyes found only filear.

Apprentices! Godar's face burned as his ire rose. *Our first appearance and we're fighting weaklings! Where are the masters?*

Whoosh!

The scarlet mist burst into fire.

Raising their hands up toward the walls, the nijar launched it forward. The flames struck the walls of Sanctal. A brilliant glow of color burst from the temple, blinding Godar for a moment.

Energy sizzled as fire slashed at the force field. Through the gaps in the fire, Godar watched the filear rajin's hands rise, sparkling light flowing forth from them as they sought to reinforce the shielding. The nijar priests' song rose in the air as their flames intensified. Like iron welded together, the enchantment gripped hold of Sanctal's protection. As their magic engulfed their nemesis, Godar could no longer see what their enemy did behind the shield. Minutes passed. The nijar took in a deep breath, his thin lips exhaled the chant, as he joined his power to that of his brethren.

Boom!

The fire burst through in a blinding blaze. Then the stone melted, the temple's spiraling towers dripped down like candle wax from the heat. The ijar priests erupted into dance. Their voices, strong and deep, continued the chant, unleashing a red glow of power upon their enemy. Swirls of crimson mist rose about each cleric, then rushed forth filling the halls and chambers of the rajin sanctuary.

Screams of agony pierced through the crackling roar of fire. The scent of burning flesh mingled with the fragrance of the flowering buds of spring. Godar breathed in the sweetly acrid perfume, letting it roil within him. His body shook with ecstasy.

What a sight!

His fellow nijar, stood around the scorched edifice, their nemesis trapped inside. The chant reverberating in the air as the rajin scum's supremacy waned. The followers of the Great I Am had no inkling of the true power rising. So arrogant in their own understanding. Little wonder they lost the elementals, too.

The sounds of agony subsided. The High Priests called as one, "Ahrinox!"

The fire twirled, gathering into a single column. With a final whoosh, it was gone.

Turning to Amiel, Godar took in the shock on the boy's face. *Good! See what real power is, little princeling!*

"Now, my Prince, you can finish off any yet living."

Godar strode away to his camp tent, where the High Priests were gathering to celebrate. They had just the prize awaiting them. A lovely young girl and her would-be lover had been captured as they snuck about for a tryst. The nijar felt his body's readiness to enjoy the delicious orgasm the pair would bring.

Nine months later, Godar stood in the midst of Dravidia's Great Plains. It's waist-high purple grasses lay buried beneath the thick blanket of winter's snows. The second month of the season brought with it ice-cold blasts of winds that ran unimpeded across the open prairie lands and exhilarated his senses. Godar's midnight-blue robe and hood sheltered him, covering his lanky form. His lack of stature, being only five foot six, did nothing to hinder the imposing sight of his nijar attire. His burned amber gaze took in the gleeful sight of Eporue City burning; its walls of thick granite melting. Each city, town, village had faced the cleansing fire of Ahrinox.

The High Priests had returned to Magdezb. There they would continue the preparations for the real offensive. For now, Godar continued to forge the path to victory for his puppet princeling.

Another gust of winter wind ran wild with nothing to hinder it, filling his senses with the sweet scent of burning flesh. His hood slipped back. Godar's thin brown hair whipped his face, but it didn't matter. The nijar rejoiced.

After this battle, they would take Castle Dravidia. Then Amiel would be king by right of conquest. The Intergalactic Council's predictability in refusing to intervene along with Drulin's refusal to aid their former colonists had yielded the Dravidian downfall.

They fought alone, and with reduced numbers as the stupid king sent out search parties for his worthless daughter. *Did the pathetic monarch believe they would end the war if they found her?* A scowl splayed across Godar's face as he realized Amiel would do just that. *He'd give up all his power for the chance to bang that bitch!*

"Retreat!" King Dekkyle's cry to his men rang across the open field before the decimated walls of Eporue, drawing the nijar's attention to the battle field.

Godar scanned the countryside looking for the Dravidian leader. His eyes needed no assistance to focus on the scene so many miles away and see every detail.

The nijar watched as a blood-splattered figure prepared to flee into the safety of the Oldey Forest. The AJ10 jorse he rode had the royal crest of Dravidia upon its saddle. *Ridiculous how these nobles insist on riding astride on the AI machines built to look like horses. They would do better to ride within the seat and protected. Still maneuverability was an asset.*

Godar scanned the Auldian forces. About a thousand yards back from the king, a lone Auldian archer drew his honrol bow. The electrified molecules formed into the shape of an arrow, glowing brown. *The fool is too far. He'll surely miss.* The friction with the air would disperse the energy.

Godar murmured in the ancient tongue of his order. The runes upon his cloak began to glow scarlet.

The archer let go, and the crow was airborne.

Godar intensified his incantation. The winds of the prairie swirled around his feet, rising with a howl. As they reached his lips, they snatched the nijar's words and flew to the projectile, which had started to wane and lose its momentum. It was descending a good 200 yards from its target.

Then the missile rose, reforming, as it was propelled on the back of the spellwinds. It flew swift and sure. The king turned to look behind just as the crow would have struck him, causing it to hit his jorse's neck instead. The artificial intelligence vehicle sputtered as the energy blast short circuited its systems.

"Foluc!" Godar cursed.

The nijar watched the king reflexively tense on the reins of his AI as it tumbled to the ground. Godar's face shone with glee. The fool was trapped beneath the heavy metal beast.

Godar took off. In a rush of inhuman speed, he ran to the spot where King Dekkyle lay. Though it should have taken hours to reach the fallen sovereign, with the runes aglow and the special incantations flowing from his mouth, Godar arrived within seconds. Pushing the king back to the ground as the monarch tried to rise, the nijar straddled the startled man.

Around them, men fought, some retreating as the king had commanded, others yet trying to press forward. Isolated by the nijar's shielding spell, Godar held the King of Dravidia pinned with his left hand. Reaching into his glowing robe, he drew forth his right hand, bearing a long black claw on his index finger.

The tip dripped a white liquid. The poison would consume the monarch's body in a fast dehydration no amount of medical intervention could prevent. The thought of the strong king shriveling away sent a ripple of gratification through the nijar.

With a quick movement, Godar embedded the claw into a wound on the king's shoulder.

The king cried out in pain. Then, perplexed, he asked, "What are you doing? Who are you?"

"You will die and your kingdom will belong to my prince," Godar stood, twirled around, and with the same unnatural speed, ran toward the burning city. The wind caught his wild cackle and carried it across the prairie.

Seated in the dark corner of Prince Amiel's royal tent, Godar let the knowledge of the imminent death of their enemy roll through him in an orgasmic burst of pleasure. Amiel would be happy to know of the great service his faithful nijar had done him today.

His gaze fell upon the broad table in the center of the room. It held the map of Vidden spread upon it. The flag of Aulden marked the places ablaze from their conquest. Soon, Amiel would assign portions of the continent to his knights and lords. They would divide the spoils. Their thoughts focused on humiliating their old rivals, the Dravidians. The nijar's smile held no mirth as he contemplated the future.

Jorn would be the first. Here, on the world that had given birth to Thyrein Dragonheart, the Nijar Order would rise. True power would rule the intergalactic system. The rajin and their ridiculous limitations kept them subservient to the ordinary men who called themselves kings. But the nijar would not be under these weaklings for long. Their time had come at last. A sound at the tent's doorway drew Godar's attention away from these happy musings.

Entering, Amiel took his helmet off as he discussed the next phase of the war with the Duke of Aul, "...the Oldey Forest. That will be hard to get through. They have some well-planned defenses around Castle Dravidia."

Imbeciles! Godar felt the bile of disgust and scorn rise in his throat as he beheld the absurd lordlings. They trusted their weapons, when it was the power of the universe that had brought them the real victory.

"My Prince." The nijar rose from his shrouded corner. Bowing, Godar greeted his liege.

"Godar!" The Duke of Aul jumped at his sudden appearance. "We didn't see you there."

"So it would appear."

"It was a great success!" Amiel approached and placed his hand on Godar's shoulder. The nijar recoiled. "I forgot you don't like being touched." Amiel withdrew his hand. Turning to the table, the prince continued, "They have turned to the refuge of Castle Dravidia and the Oldey Forest. This will be our greatest challenge."

"We must plan the offensive with care," the duke commented, his gaze on the map.

"Indeed," Amiel concurred. "But first, we must deal with you, good sir."

Godar followed discretely behind the prince as he turned toward the lords that had followed him in to join the meeting. Behind them, dressed in an ill-fitting soldier's uniform, stood a young man.

Godar studied the newcomer. Something stirred within the nijar's mind. This man would be important somehow. The aura of destiny glowed about him.

"You have saved our Lord Uld," Amiel was saying to the soldier. "And what an amazing move. Such bravery must be rewarded. Tell me, what is your name?"

"Andross Draneg." The man's ebony cheeks turned a slight red hue. His emerald eyes looked upon his liege lord with obvious admiration.

Godar noted the blond hair, and knew he was a mix-breed. Black skin with light hair was a sign of blending of Auldian and Fragmian blood. The Fragma Tribe in the Jornian desert, as indeed the other six tribes, were allied to Dravidia. This man's heritage spanned the two nations, a not necessarily good sign as far as Godar was concerned. The nijar moved closer to Andross. He needed to touch him, to understand if this man was enemy or friend.

"Kneel, Andross Draneg," Amiel commanded. Taking out his ginmra and shaping it into a double-edged blade, the prince tapped the man on each of his broad shoulders. "I hereby dub you Sir Andross Draneg.

Rise, Sir Knight. Lord Uld, you will give this man a reward purse of ten thousand auls for his great deed."

"As you command." The boy was known to be a miser.

Godar noted the tone of irritation in the rash lordling's voice.

"Thank you, Prince Amiel," the newly knighted Andross spoke with such reverent tones as if he were addressing a deity.

Pathetic, Godar thought. *Doesn't have a clue what real power looks like.*

"I will do my best to be worthy of the title you have bestowed on me," the new knight gushed.

"I am sure you will." Prince Amiel looked over to the war map and began discussing stratagems for taking the castle.

Lord Uld chimed in, "We should attack from above. The fleet can rain down fire on the castle and forest alike."

"As before, attacks from space are futile," Lord Sabred the dragon slayer, Earl of Udeep, explained.

The older knight exuded a light that hurt Godar's eyes. The nijar often felt afire in his flesh when the legendary warrior was present. Lord Sabred came toward the table and leaned in as he continued, "The force shields will deflect any attack from above. Ground forces, however, can penetrate the energy barriers with the enop canon."

Other lords and generals concurred. Pointing and hypothesizing, they explored the likelihood of success of various proposed plans of action. Godar reached Andross, who happily had moved away from the center of the room and from the Earl of Udeep. Touching the newly minted knight lightly on the arm, the nijar waited.

Nothing.

A strange coldness rippled down Godar's spine. Releasing the man, the nijar stepped up to the table where the discussion had become heated.

"Might be best to wait for the death of the king."

"What?" Lord Uld turned at Godar's words. "Was King Dekkyle wounded?"

"Indeed." The nijar couldn't resist the smirk on his face. "A deadly poison runs through his veins. He won't last more than a few days."

"Excellent!" Lord Uld's glee rang in the near silence that followed the nijar's announcement.

Amiel spoke in a soft, but firm, tone that brooked no argument. "King Dekkyle is a good man. His death was unnecessary. It would have been better to force a surrender, or a treaty with him."

The silence thickened. Godar bent his head, making his hood drop in tighter to hide his countenance. The nijar's eyes, the color of burned amber, glowed. The wrinkles of his forehead settled into a furrow over them bringing his bushy graying eyebrows together. His stomach roiled and his fists, tucked into the folds of his robe's long sleeves, clenched tight. *Ingrate!*

"What is done is done," Amiel continued. "I appreciate that you intended the best. Still... It would have been good to work with King Dekkyle. We will need to gain control quickly and treat with the Dravidians. We need to be one land by the time the Gortive strike comes against us. They are still the main foe."

Godar slid quietly back to his chair in the dark corner. A calm settled over the nijar. The Gortive would not be an issue when they outlasted their usefulness, but let them fret about it. Now, his thoughts were on this Sir Andross.

It was rare for Godar not to have a vision when he touched someone. It could not bode well that the knight's future was veiled from his sight. Unless perhaps it was Lord Sabred's proximity that made the connection difficult. He would try again later, when the earl had left.

CHAPTER 11

INEVITABILITY

"THE CASTLE'S TOWER HAS GIVEN US permission to land," Jolyon, Viscount Tor, informed her.

"Okay," Princess Verena rose from the space ship's comfortable tan leather seat and prepared to step out once more upon Jornian soil after a year of self-imposed exile on Earth.

During all that time, her nation had been at war. The shock of this, and the fact Amiel was winning, had motivated her return. The possibility that Amiel would fight her father had never crossed her mind.

In her heart, she'd believed the king would find a way to sit Amiel on the throne without her. That her departure had thrown their lands into a bitter conflict had never entered her thoughts. Nor the possibility that her father would be defeated and fall ill.

As she gathered her things, she glanced over to where the Viscount stood. It had been Jolyon who'd discovered the princess's whereabouts.

Verena had been flourishing in her new role on the sacred planet, alone. She had awoken with a jolt from her ginmra sleep to find the ship alarms blaring. Something had gone wrong. Helen had tried to make an emergency landing, but lost control and sent the craft hurtling toward Earth. The crash landing killed her beloved companion instantly, leaving Verena to make her way out of the hot New Mexico desert by herself.

Having no time to mourn, the princess had salvaged what she could from the decimated vessel. With the superior technology tools from Jorn and her new false identity, Verena had succeeded in integrating herself into a comfortable life as a teacher in the nearby small town of Dexter, New Mexico. She had even risen to some acclaim locally with her article on using multiple novels in the language-arts classroom.

It had been that very text that had given the Viscount the first clue as to where on Earth he might find her. He had stumbled upon a copy of the small magazine in a bookstore and recognized her picture. But it was her birthmark that had confirmed her true identity.

Birthmarking had become a common practice on planet Drulin, which spread to its colonies. Great houses, to ensure purity of blood-lines, had fetuses marked with the charge of the father's crest on their shoulder. The procedure was painless to the developing babe and required the father's written permission after DNA testing confirmed parentage. Verena's shoulder bore the mark of her house—the sword with the dragon wings outstretched. It seemed an unnecessary risk to take with a fetus, yet many did it anyway.

"We'll be landing at the north tower," Jolyon informed her.

"I am looking forward to seeing Father again and finding out from the doctors what is going on with him."

She had not been eager to return. However, Jolyon would not take no for an answer. He stalked her for three months, accosting her to plead his case at every opportunity. *Earth really was backward,* the princess had thought resentfully when confronted with the lack of anti-stalking laws on Earth. Of course, she knew the Viscount would not do her any physical harm; *he is a knight, after all. Still, he can be the most annoying pest!*

"Your father is dying," he had stated bluntly one Saturday afternoon, inviting himself into her booth at the local soda shop. He had been wearing a white linen suit. On his head, he bore an ivory felt fedora with a black ribbon adorned with a single ostrich feather. His feet were clad in black and white saddle shoes.

"What are you talking about?" Verena had asked irritated as she rearranged her pink poodle skirt on the red and white vinyl seat of the eatery.

"The Battle of Eporue went terribly bad for our side. Prince Amiel has won another victory and the king has been gravely wounded. The report states his Majesty's situation has been complicated further by a strange illness. The doctors don't seem to know what it is."

"Nonsense. Father has never been ill a day in his life!" she had protested, convinced the Viscount was lying. "Besides, Dr. Koll has the most up-to-date equipment in the galaxy. There is no way she would fail to make an accurate diagnosis."

"Check for yourself, Highness."

That evening, Verena accessed her account using the quantum-net. The truth of Jolyon's story was soon confirmed by the report on **IGNA**, the Intergalactic News Association.

Using the special code her father had shared with her long ago, Verena read the king's classified medical reports. The blood work showed the cells were weakening and eventually bursting. The deterioration was speeding up. The toxicology report had come back negative of all known poisons.

This meant the substance was new and must have been injected into the king. Verena wondered if this connected back to the Battle of Sanctal. The video she had found showed a group of strange people, clad in flowing midnight-blue robes, their faces covered by hoods, and strange runes on their cloaks glowing scarlet during the onslaught.

Now, as the ship entered the hangar, Verena prepared to descend and see her father again. She was not plagued by any sense of worry at her reception. Being an only child, the princess had grown up secure in her parents' affection.

Of course, her main focus was this poisoning. She'd sent word to the rajin moon, Ghoukas, to Lady Vivelda at the Temple of Artaxyoun. While at war and given the strange attack on Sanctal, Jolyon had informed her the rajin had been barred by the Intergalactic Council from returning to Jorn. They would be needed if the poison destroying her father was to be stopped.

Verena sighed as she considered that once her father's health was restored, she'd have to face the consequences of her escape to freedom. Still, she had to fight for her father's life.

An idea formed.

In this moment, she could rally the troops and lead a campaign to push Amiel back. She had read up on his tactics and a plan began to fashion itself in her mind. If she could show herself strong, militarily, it might make her father see her differently.

As the spaceship's doors opened, she heard the sound of harsh voices and Prince Amiel's sneering face came into view.

"Well, well, what an interesting development," he drawled out as he entered the vehicle and insolently surveyed her person. "If you come to nurse your father back to health, Verena, I'm afraid you are too late."

"He's dead," her voice broke on the final word. *Of course he was. Why else would Amiel be in the castle?*

"Your father passed away two days ago," the prince spat out unsympathetically. "I took the castle yesterday. Aulden is now in complete control of Dravidia."

"I seriously doubt that," Verena mustered the strength to match the haughtiness and self-confidence in his tone. "Holding one castle does not give you control over the entire nation. I am Queen of Dravidia now."

Amiel's tone held mockery as he bowed, "Your kingdom, Majesty, is under my control, whether you choose to believe it or not. Do you have a plan on how you will reclaim it? Being as how you are yourself my prisoner, I must say I would be very interested in seeing you try."

At his words, the guards who had boarded the ship with him drew their ginmras. Viscount Tor and the small crew prepared to fight, but Verena stopped them with a wave of her hand. She didn't want innocent blood spilled in a battle they clearly couldn't win.

"When my people learn of my return, their efforts to save Dravidia will be renewed. Yet, if the reports Viscount Tor showed me about the Gortive threat are true, would not a truce be better than a divided land when the attack comes from the natives? Are you aware of what is transpiring on Parthia?"

Amiel's crystal blue eyes regarded her with contempt. He closed the space that separated them so that she had to look up at him.

"I am very well aware of what is happening on Parthia. As I recall, I attempted to inform you of the issue we faced during our betrothal dance," his voice was low and steady, his eyes glacial. "However, a truce is not as strong as a marriage. Your father was a wise man to realize it. United we can stand against the Gortive."

"We can face this threat as two kingdoms, strong and unified against a common enemy. A marriage is unnecessary."

Everything in her hoped he could understand. *Why did he want this wedding? Surely after leaving him the way I did, I should be the last woman in the universe he would wish for a wife. What am I missing here?* Something flickered in his eyes, but it was too fleeting for her to identify.

"I fought and won. Your lands are mine. You are my captive." He paused and Verena felt a chill go through her at the look in his gaze.

"I'm offering you a chance to help your people instead of living out the rest of your days in a dungeon cell."

The cold fingers of dread wrapped themselves around Verena's heart. *Would he do that to her?* The implacable iciness of his eyes told her he would.

"Under my father's terms?" She had meant for it to be a statement though it snuck out as a question instead.

"When I conquered your nation? I think not!"

"If we want to end the war and unite the land we must be on equal footing. Otherwise the Dravidians will continue to rebel." She held his gaze.

Silence stretched between them for what seemed an eternity. Verena couldn't read him. He'd always been good at hiding his true feelings.

"King Dekkyle's betrothal agreement will stand." He chuckled a mirthless laugh. "I do believe your wedding gown is still in your room where you left it. I'll have my guards take it and you to your new chambers."

Turning, he strode off the ship. His royal guards herded her to what had been her mother's rooms. They were being hastily aired out and prepared for her as she entered. Nothing had been changed since her mother's death all those many years ago. A melancholy settled on her as she stood in the threshold of the elegantly appointed suite.

"You've made a pact with the devil," Viscount Tor said as he followed her into the private living room.

"No, Jolyon," Verena responded. "The pact was made by another." *I just get to be the human sacrifice*, the princess thought bitterly. "Did you reach the Earl of Sarnac? Any of the others?"

"The message went out and it showed received." Jolyon stood shifting from foot to foot, clearly uncertain what to do. "They abandoned the castle when Amiel's forces overran the forest defenses and stormed the walls. That was the last notice I had. It's unclear whether the king was alive or dead at that moment."

Verena placed a calming hand on his arm. "He must have been dead. They would never have abandoned him if it were otherwise. Find out where they are. We must get word to them about the truce."

"Right away... Majesty."

Auldian guards escorted Verena to the throne room the next evening. Their black and silver uniforms had the principality's crest emblazoned on it—the auger seashell through the coronet. She had been locked in her rooms the whole day. Verena's grief her only companion as the realization she would never be able to set things right with her father nor see his smiling face again filled her being.

Finally, Mrs. Denip had been sent up to attend the princess and make her ready for the gathering. Verena had been instructed via holonote from Amiel that the leadership of both nations would meet in the throne room.

Verena was glad to have her faithful nurse back at her side. She would need all the help she could get and from what little she'd been able to see, Amiel was quickly removing the human staff faithful to Dravidia. No doubt the hudroids would be reprogrammed soon as well.

"Highness." Mrs. Denip's tone was formal as she curtsied before Verena.

"You were right. I shouldn't have run. So much death and destruction for nothing. And my father..."

"It is good to have you home." Mrs. Denip stated hugging Verena as the tears began to pour down the princess's cheeks once more. "Everything will be all right; you'll see."

Mrs. Denip helped her dress in the comfortable black pants and blouse, of the finest Earthian silk, for the event about to unfold.

"I didn't know they had polisk on Earth!"

"Yes, though I have to say I think theirs is softer than ours." Verena extended the edge of her top for Deni to feel.

"Hmmm, yes. What jewels shall you wear?"

"None," Verena said, feeling the pain of her father's death still raw in her heart.

Amiel had sent out the announcement of the king's death, her return, and the truce they had reached. Dravidian and Auldian nobles, generals, and knights had been summoned to the castle to bear witness to the war's end. Tonight, peace would be proclaimed.

"Interesting choice," Amiel commented as she joined him in the hall outside the throne room.

"I'm in mourning."

"Pants? For a formal occasion?"

"They're comfortable," Verena extended her hand and he took it, intertwining their arms. A familiar shiver went through her at his touch. As children, they'd scaled trees together. As adults they would have to figure out how to overcome the ravages of war and re-forge their relationship. Yet, her fear of him persisted. The concerns remained, but she was out of options. Verena squared her shoulders and drew in a steadying breath.

The ten-foot tall blackwood doors were opened by the liveried hudroid footmen, which Verena noted wore Auldian uniforms now. A voice she did not recognize announced them. She wondered what had happened to Lord Grahan Sorma, their Lord Chamberlain. *What of the other staff members of the palace? Are they dead or just removed from office?*

As Amiel led her through the long rectangular room, she took in the harsh faces of the men gathered. Mirror-paneled walls reflected the warriors from both nations, magnifying their number. The black marble floors with their silvery white streaks echoed as they made their way to the dais with the great thrones.

The awning and backdrop of dark violet was framed in silver thread. The great seal of Dravidia embroidered directly behind the thrones had been altered. The sword's blade now ran through the Principality of Aulden's coronet diadem symbol. The magnificent crystal chandeliers illuminated the space with a slightly lavender light flow that glimmered throughout the chamber. The effect was augmented by the matching mirrors on the ceiling.

"Gentlemen and ladies," Amiel began once they had been seated on the thrones. "Today is a bittersweet day. King Dekkyle is dead, and, after nearly a year of war, the Houses of Dravidia and Aulden will be united as he had originally intended."

Verena kept her eyes straight ahead, refusing to look at the accusing faces of the war-weary Dravidian nobles and generals. She had spied Jolyon and the Earl of Sarnac, but Verena could not meet their eyes. *Coward!* she chided herself.

"As the Duke of Aul has been explaining to you, the tidings from Parthia are not good," Amiel continued. "The king knew of the rising Gortive leader, Lorgan. His fears of a union of the four Gortive tribes has proven true. A new nation, the Pavah-Onglonac, has been born."

Fearful murmurs of concern rippled through the war-hardened audience. While the Gortive were not as technologically advanced as the humans, they were brutal and skillful warriors, whose savagery was well documented in the annals of the colonization of Jorn.

The settlers from Drulin and Fratern had fought together to gain control of the planet. Verena remembered Rajin Molent's history lessons. The interstellar laws against genocide were strictly enforced, even in those days. Thus, the conquered natives had been relocated to the less desirable lands of the Parthian continent, while the human population enjoyed the rich fertile soil of Vidden.

The Rajin Lord had not shared with her the extent of the violence, but the princess had sought out the information on the conflict in the library's archives. A cold shiver of dread ran down her spine as she recalled what she had discovered of their barbarism.

"King Dekkyle, foreseeing this development, intended to strengthen our land," Amiel continued, turning to look at her with a glacial stare. "His plans were thwarted and now we are weaker than ever before."

Verena blushed from the embarrassment of this public humiliation. Her father had kept the truth from her, but that was no defense. She was a royal princess and she should have done her duty. Her selfishness had brought them to this. She wiped her moist hands on her slacks, keeping her eyes averted from the hostile faces of the men and women gathered before her.

"Princess Verena and I have chosen to honor King Dekkyle's betrothal agreement and bring an end to the division. We will work to prepare, and strengthen, our united house against the native attack," Amiel's proclamation brought dead silence as both sides considered the implications.

The silence broke.

Murmurs spread like wildfire across the prairie. Both sides reacted to the announcement with consternation and dissension.

"Princess Verena doesn't speak for Dravidia," General Oldan, leader of the army, stated in a booming voice. Verena noticed a fresh raw cut across the general's face and felt a pang of guilt. "She left, effectively abdicating her royal rights. If an end to the combat is to be had, then the true leaders of Dravidia will meet with you to create a legitimate treaty."

Verena's heart plummeted. She couldn't blame them for not wanting her, but it still hurt.

"Why should we accept these terms?" a young lord on the Auldian side called out, forestalling Amiel's response to the general's comment. "We beat them! Always they have acted as though we were nothing. Yet, here we stand in possession of their lands and castles. To honor the betrothal would mean those who have fought for you, my Prince, would return to our estates without spoils, without the riches we deserve by conquest!"

The Auldian nobles took up a clamor of "Victory! Victory!" They stomped rhythmically as they chanted.

Great! My people reject me and his people want the riches of revenge. We'll never have peace! Despair invaded her mind and heart.

"We have not surrendered!" General Oldan's commanding voice put an end to the Auldian's chant. "You have won some battles, but so have we. We can yet oust you from our lands and squash you like the impudent dogs you are."

The Dravidians began their own chant of "War! War!" The sound of more stomping and the banging of armored breastplates reverberated through the chamber.

Verena had to do something. She sensed Amiel's tension as he sat on her father's throne. If she could find a way to bring them together, it would strengthen her position with Amiel. *Maybe? She must try.*

"Stop!" Verena's voice was firm and clear. All eyes shifted to her as she stood up and addressed the crowd. "It is true I ran away and brought about war. My only defense is that I wasn't told the true purpose for the union. My father didn't entrust me with the knowledge of the Gortive threat."

Grumblings went through her listeners, particularly the Auldians. No doubt they took it as a slight to their leader. She'd left him at the altar after all.

Verena pressed on. "Nevertheless, I am guilty of forfeiting my royal rights, and I do not deserve the honor of speaking for you. Running away was a selfish and cowardly act that threw both our nations into chaos. Both sides have suffered losses and won victories. The men of Jorn are mighty men of valor, our history proves this is so."

The room was silent again. All eyes focused on the princess as she stood with her arms open, palms facing them as if to embrace both sides.

"But I beg of you, my fellow citizens of Vidden." Verena knelt on both knees upon the hard platform. "Do not let the bloodshed continue. Let us unite these lands as my father and Prince Amiel had planned. Let there be peace, and above all, let us regain our strength and defend our species from the Gortive that would seek to destroy us. Do not let the animosity that my shortcomings have stirred between our nations keep us from fighting the true enemy. Forgive me, as Prince Amiel has done, I beg of you." She bowed her head and waited, hoping that her act of humility might be enough to heal the rift her departure had caused.

She heard the distinctive sound of the Earl of Sarnac's voice. The crowd of Dravidians parted to allow the revered nobleman to come forward. The earl commanded more respect than any other person, save the king himself, for the Dravidians. The sound of his footsteps thundered in her ears in the near silence of the room. Verena's stomach churned and clenched with apprehension.

What will this great man say? She raised her face and looked him in the eyes, battling the tears that threatened to spill out. She could feel her cheeks flushing red, their heat burning her as her mind willed him to be kind, to forgive.

He looked at her briefly, on her knees there before him, then he turned to face the crowd. The roiling in her stomach intensified at the disrespect the action implied; no one would dare to stand with their back to their sovereign.

"Our princess has asked our forgiveness," the earl's voice was strong and commanding. Turning to her, the great man knelt. He beat his chest with his right hand formed into a fist three times in the Dravidian sign of respect to their monarch. "May our Queen live forever!"

Slowly each Dravidian there joined the earl in paying homage to their new Queen. Verena looked at the faces of her people, her own wet with the tears that could no longer be contained. Her people forgave her. She, too, thumped her chest with her closed fist three times, unable to speak.

Then Amiel was there, standing beside her. He extended his hand to her and helped Verena rise. She struggled to suppress her emotions and regain her composure.

Of course her people forgave her. The alternative was to have Amiel as King of Dravidia by conquest.

She had no right to hope that the forgiveness meant anything else. Yet, a small spark lit within her. She could regain their love. She could rule beside Amiel and bring peace, prosperity, and justice. She could be a worthy Queen.

Intertwining his fingers with hers, Amiel gazed at his Auldian nobles. "Lord Uld has spoken well. We have conquered and we could set about to plunder and destroy. Meanwhile, as we grow weaker, a horrible enemy would be revolting against us. Together, we are stronger."

"What of the lands you have already given us?" the noble Amiel had called Lord Uld pressed. The group of young, brash lords around him murmured their ascent. "Are we to forfeit them? Return them to the enemy?"

"The prince is right!" The Duke of Aul's voice rang out. The House of Aul had served the Principality of Aulden with great honor for centuries and was kin to the royal house. "We have a common enemy. While we have been at war, the Gortive have come together. We must join. We are not enemies anymore. We will be one house, one kingdom."

"There is much to work out," Prince Amiel placated, seeing Lord Uld was about to speak again. "We shall merge our Council of Peers and create a leadership of joint Auldian and Dravidian representation. Then we can begin the process of healing and rebuilding, and address the issues of becoming one kingdom. Most important of all, we must prepare to defend our home against the real foe, the Gortive."

CHAPTER 12

A NEW BEGINNING

VERENA BOARDED THE HOVERLIMO that would take her to the capital. The king's embalmed body had been placed on display in the Great Cathedral at the heart of Dravidia City for the past three days. The people had been given this time to parade past the marble sarcophagus and say their final goodbyes to the sovereign they had loved so dearly. Many had traveled to the capital for this in spite of the ravages left behind by the war.

Verena marveled that Amiel was allowing her to attend her father's funeral. Over the course of the past week, she had been escorted from her mother's chambers to the Council of Peers room each afternoon to discuss and coordinate first the funeral for King Dekkyle, and then the joint wedding coronation ceremony.

Besides herself and Amiel, the Earl of Sarnac and Sir Eriq Seller from Dravidia with the Earl of Udeep and the Duke of Aul from Aulden attended these discussions. The new Council of Peers would be finalized and convene after the wedding. It had not surprised her that Sir Eriq remained Lord High Marshal. He and Lord Sabred had formed a strong friendship over the years. The two legendary heroes often fought together on missions for the Intergalactic Alliance.

All her meals were served in her rooms and she was allowed no visitors. Today, however, she had been permitted to breakfast with the group of select nobles gathered for the funeral. Now, they sped through the Oldey Forest in the elegant royal-purple vehicle, the crest of her family emblazoned on its doors.

Amiel, the Duke of Aul, the Earl of Udeep, and the Earl of Sarnac were the other occupants of her limo. Sir Eriq, as Lord High Marshal, rode by jorse with the other elite guards making up their procession.

No one spoke. The sorrow of the occasion lay like a thick wool blanket over the day.

Normally, Verena would be enjoying the forest scenery and the beauty of the city's diverse architecture. Instead her eyes stayed on her mother's ancient copy of the Book of Illumination. The black leather-bound volume held the sacred texts given by the Great I Am to the prophets. Her heart ached within her. Verena's eyes stung with unshed tears. She opened the tome to a random page and read the words.

It spoke of a good shepherd who lays his life down for his sheep. A strangled sob ripped from her as her eyes followed the passage. The hired hand flees, leaving the sheep to be destroyed by the wolf. She ran and left her people to face the wolf alone. Her father had stood his ground. Now he lay dead, as a good shepherd. Tears streamed down her cheeks, plopping onto the pages.

She glanced up for a second then averted her face. The men in the vehicle sat silent, staring at her, unsure what to do. Her body shook as sobs erupted no matter how she struggled to regain control.

She'd failed.

Her father had asked her to lay down her life for her people's good and she ran instead. Her eyes shut, her body shaking with the pain of the loss and the condemnation of her guilt, wrapping her arms around herself, Verena swayed.

Amiel knelt before her, his scent invading her senses. His strong arms took her and slid her off the seat and into his comforting embrace. Verena burrowed her face into the black uniform jacket replete with jangling medals of his victories in the fight with the Calvernsin. His voice spoke words of consolation that her mind refused to interpret. She could only cry, grief mingling with guilt.

Everyone fails and comes short of the glory of God, that is why I lay my life down. Rise up now, daughter of kings, become who you were meant to be.

The words floated in her mind. They repeated three times. A sense of wonder filled Verena, her being covered in a warmth she recognized from the ceremony with the rajin. The Great I Am didn't hate her for her stupidity. He forgave her and asked her now to take her rightful place.

"We're arriving," Amiel's voice in her ear brought her back. "Do you want me to have the chauffeur do a lap around the city?"

"No." Verena lifted her head and looked into his blue gaze. Something odd flickered there. "I am ready."

Struggling out of his arms and back onto her seat, she used the handkerchief the Earl of Sarnac offered her to wipe her eyes and dry her face. She smiled at him as she handed it back. He gave her hand a comforting squeeze.

Lord Sabred, Earl of Udeep, leaned toward her. "This day is a new beginning as much as an end. You and Amiel will make things right."

"Yes."

The vehicle came to a stop at the foot of the white marble stairs that lead to the cathedral's massive double doors. Verena squared her shoulders. *I can do this.*

Verena stood at the bottom of the family crypt, a twenty story hexagonal column buried under the far right back tower of the castle. The spiraling staircase from the ground floor led down a wall of casket-sized spaces that served as the final resting place for the House of Drav. Filled from the bottom up, the top spaces awaited her and someday her children and her children's children. Awe had filled her as she'd followed the High Priest who led the procession down.

The few nobles who'd been honored with attending the interment sat on the white wood pews surrounding the gray marble coffin, with the king's youthful likeness sculpted on its lid. When all had paid their respects, the crane, which had deposited it here after the service in the cathedral, would lift it again, depositing it in his assigned slot.

Glancing up from her place, Verena took in the strange sight. The silver plaques for the names of those entombed twinkled in an almost joyful manner as the light from the single crystal chandelier suspended from the ceiling fell upon them.

At the High Priests command, she stood to lay her single pink rose bloom on the sculpture of her father's hands. Her own lingered over the cold stone beneath which his body lay. If he had but spoken to her, if she had been a better daughter, he would still be with her. Guilt numbed her mind and heart. Recalling the words from the limo ride, she straightened. The time for her to become the Queen her people needed was now.

She turned to head back to her seat. Amiel stood up as she approached. His eyes still held that strange look from when she'd cried in his arms. Somehow, Verena had to find a way to mend things.

The wedding would take place on the morrow. Verena sat in her chamber, locked in, as she had been since her arrival.

Restless, Verena meandered about the room aimlessly. Noticing near the door the still packed bag of personal belongings she had not let Deni put away, she decided to use her pent-up energy on something productive. Anyway, she was marrying Amiel for real this time, so she might as well settle in.

The princess started putting away her things. She pulled out the Dior ensemble she had used to wrap the more precious items for the trip home. The beautiful white waist-cinching jacket with the black full calf-length skirt she had purchased on Earth held various items that could have been damaged. Verena reached into the folds of the skirt and drew out her mother's music box.

The image of her mother on a long ago and deeply cherished summer day came strongly into her mind. In this very room, the Drulian-made box nestled on her mother's lap had shone with blood red grooves in its rich black wood. It had mesmerized the young princess who sat at the Queen's feet. The open window let the warm breeze in, carrying the scent of the salty ocean beyond. She remembered her mother's words on that occasion.

"If ever you find yourself in a desperate and unsolvable situation, remember this box," her mother had counseled her. "It will help you when you need it most."

"How, Mama?"

A sigh had escaped Queen Irene. Putting the box back on her desk, the Queen had pulled Verena into her arms.

"I will show you when the time comes." With a kiss to her forehead, her mother had set her down once more. Queen Irene had opened the music box. "Let's do the dance together."

For years, Verena had treasured this memento that contained the few inconsequential pieces of jewelry from her mother's childhood. Now, the princess sat at the elegant desk near the window and began a closer inspection of the precious item. She noticed the funny old Drulian runes etched on the sides. If they held a secret meaning, Verena couldn't figure it out, though she could read them well enough thanks to Rajin Molent's lessons.

The verses upon the box where an old Drulian proverb:

Life and time are what you make of them; wish neither away. Truth revealed will set you free; let love's heart light the way.

It was a nice saying, but try as she might, Verena couldn't see how it might help her solve this particular situation. It seemed overgeneralized.

The antique box itself had been handed down from mother to daughter for generations, since before her family had left their home planet of Drulin to forge a new life on Jorn. After a moment's hesitation, she opened its top. The old Drulian folksong she had heard it play so many times before started while the pretty little figurine in a traditional dress danced around on a small platform inside.

The song finished; then started again. As always, nothing magical happened.

What had her mother meant that day? If only she had not died and could have helped her now. Of course, if her mother had lived, Verena might not have made such a mess of things.

Giving up on the cryptic comment from so long ago, the princess glanced around the room, seeking a special place to display the sentimental piece. A small nook built into the wall beside the hearth caught her eye. Verena decided it would make a good spot. Rising, she placed the music box in its new home.

She had turned to continue her unpacking, when she heard a series of clicks followed by a loud clack. Looking back, she gave a startled cry. The nook had been covered up and was no longer visible. Indeed, it was hard to tell where the space had been.

The princess placed her fingertips tentatively to the spot. The secret panel lit up with dots around the pads of her fingers. A sliver of pain shot through her arm, followed by a long beep. The mechanism had taken a DNA sample.

The cover rose again, revealing the nook and its contents. Only now, the front of the music box had flipped open and a small silver bottle twinkled from within a secret compartment. Reaching in, she drew the now exposed item forth. The princess examined it. There were intricately etched star systems and galaxies decorating it and a silver cap closed by a clasp held its contents secure. More curious than ever,

Verena opened it with trepidation. It was filled with a gleaming golden liquid. Cautiously, the princess poured out a few drops onto her mother's desk. The moment the drops touched the surface, they solidified into a mirror-like flat disc.

Verena touched it with the tip of her finger, drawing away quickly in case it was dangerous. But it didn't burn, or sting, or seem to cause harm. The hardened liquid was cool to the touch. Sliding it slowly unto her hand, the disc liquefied as soon as it was tilted, then re-hardened on her palm. Her mother had said it would help find a solution to the most unsolvable problems. *But how is it used? What will it do?*

Verena sat in one of the comfortable sofas near the hearth for a long while, perplexed by the enigma of the strange substance. She could find no further clues or guidance in the box or on the bottle. Tilting her hand, the movement caused the firm disc to liquefy once more. Nothing else happened. She replaced the material in the bottle, careful that none should drip. She needed to tell someone and ask questions, but who could she trust?

She rang for her nurse.

"You sent for me, Highness," Mrs. Denip inquired, arriving in Verena's private chambers moments later via the servant's entrance.

"Deni, do you know what this might be?" Verena extended the silver bottle for her inspection.

The princess had no qualms about Mrs. Denip's loyalty. The hudroid had served her family for generations and Verena hoped somewhere in the depths of her digital drive there would be something about this bottle.

Mrs. Denip scanned the item with her eyes, then closed them to access the memory files locked in her main frame. "I'm afraid I can't help you with this," the faithful lady replied after a long moment. "Where did you find it?"

"It was my mother's," Verena explained. "She said it could help find solutions to problems, but she never explained how it worked. Mother said I was too young, but then she died before I grew up." Verena's voice held steady, but the lump in her throat tightened as she realized that now she was a complete orphan; she had no one.

"Perhaps you could look up information on this using the nodes?" Mrs. Denip suggested.

Verena moved to her mother's desk and took out the silver discs. Placing them on each temple, she activated the virtual screen. Entering the holonet, Verena used a variety of descriptors in hopes of locating the source of the liquid. No matter what key terms she used, nothing even remotely similar surfaced. Removing the nodes, she inspected the bottle once more.

There was no name, no markings that might help narrow the search. Returning to her net search, she put in the Drulian proverb. Its origin came up on the holosite, but there was no reference to any golden liquids connected to it.

She looked up the data archives containing the information on her family's history on Drulin. After several long hours on the net, she had found nothing; no clues to go by and, with no real name for the liquid, the search seemed futile.

The history of the box itself began with Duchess Nuri of Drav. It was a gift from Rajin LaRoo the year before Duke Lorenos, her husband, was made regent of the colonies on Jorn. It seemed to be part of a thank you gift for saving the King of Drulin's life. There had been a coup and the duke and duchess had been an integral part in stopping it. As always, Verena's heart filled with pride at her family history. There were many tales of valiant deeds. But there was nothing about any special liquids among these.

Frustrated, Verena closed the net connection, placing the nodes back in their box. Securing the bottle in its secret compartment and leaving the music box hidden in the wall nook, Verena decided to wait and see if maybe she could work her own miracles, for the mysterious container and its shiny contents seemed to offer her no help at all.

CHAPTER 13
WEDDING DAY

AMIEL STOOD IN THE KING'S DRESSING ROOM. He'd had the bulk of his clothing and personal belongings brought over from Auld Palace. They filled only a small portion of the wood paneled closet. King Dekkyle's things had been packed up and taken to one of the empty rooms. Verena would need to go through them and decide what should be done with each. Glancing down at his right hand, Amiel admired the signet ring on his index finger. It fit perfectly. Dekkyle had thought of everything. He'd fashioned a pair of rings, one for Verena and one for Amiel, with the united crest he'd concocted. Amiel liked the look. The legendary sword with dragon wings outstretched from the hilt and the Principality's coronet surrounding the mighty blade.

He took it off and placed it back into the cushioned box his valet held. The two rings would be part of the coronation ceremony. Today, he would make Verena his wife and become her king. *But at what cost?*

"I have to urge you to call this off, A." Figor, Duke of Aul, sat in a chair near the threshold into the bedchamber. "I know you love her, and marrying her is not off the table, but you can't honor the betrothal agreement. Not after the conquest. There is growing discontent among your lords."

His valet drew close with the amulet. Amiel reached for it, then drew back his hand. He really didn't need it. They were all safe now.

Waving the jewel away, Amiel commented, "After the wedding, we will come together as a new nation with a United Council of Peers." Amiel bent to allow his valet to place his uniform's coat on him. The medals on it tinkled. "We can move then for an amendment of the terms to better reflect the new circumstances."

"You need to have the final say in all matters, not her," Figor pressed.

"You won."

"The power should be shared equally." Lord Sabred the dragon slayer, Earl of Udeep, entered the room. Dressed in his finest navy-blue suit, the medals on his emaciated-looking chest jingled. He strode forward, coming to stand before Amiel.

Uncle Sabred's legendary exploits made him Amiel's personal hero. Tall, thin, seemingly weak, his uncle had cut open a massive space dragon from the inside after being swallowed by the beast. Amiel knew that Sabred had trained with Amiel's great uncle, Rajin Zegan, in spite of the Rajin Order's prohibition of this kind of thing. It was believed to be dangerous, allowing those not fully in the order to have a portion of the knowledge.

Amiel had never given credence to the tales of the rajin and their power. They had seemed to him just another arm of bureaucratic control over the Galactic Alliance. Yet, having witnessed the nijar's abilities, Amiel wondered if beings with such power should even be allowed to exist.

"Equal?" Figor's tone showed his disgust at the idea. "We won."

"Amiel, the only path to peace is for you and Verena to share power equally. Otherwise, you will always have one side dissatisfied and likely to revolt." The Duke of Aul made a noise as if to interrupt, but Sabred continued in his reedy voice, "During a Gortive attack, the last thing you need to be worried about is having to fight your own people or looking out for a moment when hers might use the distraction to move against you and re-establish themselves."

Amiel placed a hand on his uncle's shoulder. "I am not sure my people will go for that at this time. We did conquer, but I think the first meeting of the new council can hash this out. Right now, accepting the betrothal agreement," he looked to Figor as he continued, "has brought her to the marriage and that is what we need more. We can't rule Dravidia as conquerors and face the Gortive. If she remained defiant of us, there would surely have been an interior revolt at a critical moment. But with her by my side, we can find a way to move forward."

Sabred smiled and nodded his ascent. "That is wise, Amiel. I am glad to be back in time for your wedding."

"Me, too, Uncle." Amiel returned the smile.

Figor chimed in, "Where were you, by the way, Uncle? I didn't know you'd been sent on any—"

"Sabred was gathering information for me," Amiel said.

"Ah." Figor rose from his seat. "Well, I think it is time for us to head out to the cathedral."

The hoverlimo passed through the Oldey Forest at a leisurely pace. There were signs of the battle as they went. Charred trees and pink-stained snow tainted the beauty of the winter woodland scenery. The black craft with the Auldian crest on its doors, a silver seashell with the Principality's coronet circling it, zoomed along creating soft flurries in its wake.

His cousin, Figor, and his uncle, Sabred, accompanied him. They rode in silence. Amiel let his mind wander to the woman he'd left in the castle, dressing for her wedding day.

He'd refused to look at the dress when he'd taken control of her home. Hurt at her departure pierced him at the thought of beholding the gown Verena would have worn. Somewhere deep inside, the vain hope that she'd wear it one day remained, a soothing balm to the pain of her jilting. Now, she would be arriving in it as he waited for her at the steps before the altar.

She'd agreed to marry him because she had no other choice. Her arrival had been a turn of good fortune for him. The Gortive would attack, no one could say how soon, and he needed the support and backing of Dravidia's forces to combat them. Ruling as a conqueror would leave him open to a mutiny when he could least afford it. Verena as his wife secured their allegiance.

But she still didn't want him. Just as a year ago, this was a forced marriage for her. Amiel stared at the walls of Dravidia City as they approached and wondered if she wished she'd stayed hidden; if she regretted having returned. A deep ache settled in his heart. They would stand before the Great I Am and vow to love and cherish and support each other. *Will she mean the words? Will she turn on me if she has a chance?*

The war-torn capital made for a melancholy backdrop, having been hastily festooned for the Royal Wedding and Coronation. Ruined buildings, potholed streets, and missing sections of hover lanes, made the royal procession a dismal sight. Signs of the bloody battle fought only a few weeks earlier served as a vivid reminder that he had taken a country that didn't want him, just as he would take the woman who'd been born to rule it.

Tonight, they would consummate their union. Amiel had fantasized about the moment when he would make love to Verena for the first time for longer than he could even remember. He'd loved and desired her all his life. Every man who drew near to her was his enemy. Any one she gifted a smile to, a dance, anything that indicated she might favor another cut him deeply. But now she was his and would be his forever. He longed to touch her, pull her naked body to his, fill her and feel himself buried within her.

Amiel adjusted in the seat to relieve the pressure in his well-tailored uniform pants. *How will it be? Will she resist? Can I force myself on her?*

No. He could never do such a thing. This was his challenge: to forge a united nation by building a strong marriage and keeping the damn Gortive creatures off their continent.

The people of the capital were out and lining the streets. Others from around the continent had journeyed to see the king's funeral and the new monarch's coronation and wedding. They waved and cheered as his hoverlimo passed on its way to the Great Cathedral in downtown Dravidia City. Amiel was amazed and humbled by the turn out. There were thousands of citizens bundled up along the royal procession route. Auldian and Dravidian flags waved in their hands. It was good to see them mingling.

This was Verena's doing. It was her acceptance of him, publicly, that had brought the nations together. *Hers longed for peace and his expected... a better future, to grow stronger.* The crowd's hopeful gaiety in the face of the destruction filled Amiel with a sense of faith. If they could come together to cheer this union, he would find a way to make the alliance work.

"This moment is critical for Jorn." Sabred echoed his thoughts. "I know you have it in you to be a great leader, Amiel. Verena, too. It won't be easy, but you can do it."

Amiel let the impact of his words sink in, sighing deeply. Figor sat across from him with Uncle Sabred. Both men looked at him with a mix of concern and encouragement.

"We'll find a way," Amiel reassured them.

The limo came to a stop. The white marble building loomed beside him. The stone had come from a special quarry at the foot of the Ydar Mountains. It struck Amiel that the Ydar formed the border between Dravidia and Aulden on the north side. The marble it yielded was pure white with no streaks of any kind. It was so rare, the church had claimed it for their cathedrals not just for Jorn, but for around the Intergalactic Alliance.

He stepped out unto the royal-purple carpet. He made his way up the forty steps to the silver-gilded front doors. When he reached the top step, he and his entourage turned and posed for the media pictures. Amiel waved at the cheering people. The square before the cathedral was lined with the parliamentary building that held the Council of Vassals on the left, the main postal office of the realm cattycorner to the temple, the offices of the primary agencies and departments opposite the church, and the Jornian Offices for the Intergalactic Council to the right.

In the center of the square rose the spinning ten-foot by twenty-foot sculpture of the Thyrein's Galactic Wall's planetary alignments. It was a smaller replica of the one that had once stood before the monastery of Sanctal. Like that one, it spun in perfect precision, mimicking the movement of the cosmos.

A chill swept through Amiel as the memory of the battle at the rajin temple filled him. There would be retribution. He'd promised Godar to keep all other orders off Jorn, but Amiel knew that would be near impossible. They were well established in the alliance and would return seeking to rebuild.

Amiel turned and entered the church. The main vestibule before the sanctuary's doors was lined with wide hand-woven tapestries portraying key moments from the Book of Illumination. The workmanship of these masterpieces struck Amiel, but only for the marvel of the artistry. He felt nothing spiritual and never had, even as a child.

He did feel something with Godar.

Perhaps the nijar had the truth and the rajin and Official Church of the Galactic Alliance had hidden it from everyone else in order to establish their power. The sound of the Principality of Aulden's national anthem came through the thick honeywood doors. They parted on silent hinges and Amiel made his walk down the aisle. His uncle and cousin behind him followed by other members of Aulden's royal family and government.

The gleaming white stone was decorated with garlands of fragrant blooms in ivory and purple. The well-brushed carpet beneath his feet muffled his steps. Guests had poured in for the fast-tracked wedding and coronation as well as for the funeral. The Intergalactic Council had issued a statement of praise for the move and an appeal for it to bring peace. Amiel arrived before the three steps leading to the altar. He turned and waited, his uncle and cousin coming to stand beside him. The others filing into the reserved seats near the front.

Loud cheering erupted from outside. It startled him at the strength of the sound given the closed doors to the sanctuary and to the square. The cry of "Queen Verena" resounded within the solemn walls of the temple. Verena had arrived. Amiel's heartbeat quickened. He was grateful for the white gloves that kept his sweaty palms at bay.

The crowd's chanting became louder as the outer doors opened. Amiel visualized the vestibule. Verena in a beautiful gown, the Earl of Sarnac along with the Duchess of Fen and the four other ladies in waiting that had survived the war would be standing there now. Perhaps they were fixing her dress, or adjusting her veil, preparing her for the walk down the long aisle.

Dravidia's royal military march started. The doors to the sanctuary swung open. The four ladies in flowing lavender dresses made their way up to the front with the Duchess of Fen bringing up the rear. Minutes passed as they slowly managed to get into position. Amiel made an attempt to see if he could catch a glimpse of her, but she was too far back from the doorway.

"Patience," Uncle Sabred's whisper, brought him back to his feet from the tiptoe he'd been balancing on.

The music stopped. The Dravidian national anthem started.

And there she was.

Clad in a voluminous silver gown embroidered with the symbol of her house in beautiful purple thread. The corseted top accentuated her ample bosom and the tight curve of her waist. Her gorgeous fiery hair was piled into a well coifed updo sprinkled with diamond pins. She wore no veil. A beautiful diamond necklace rested around her graceful neck and matching earrings swung from her earlobes. Amiel forgot how to breathe. Everything in the room disappeared. Each step brought her closer to being his. Nothing could stop that now.

Then her eyes locked with his. Emerald gems that held a look of...

he couldn't name it. She averted her gaze, fixing it on the High Priest in his white robe who stood behind the altar. The Earl of Sarnac came to stand beside him between them, having escorted her up the aisle.

Amiel extended his hand and the earl placed Verena's soft and trembling one in it. As the earl took a step back, Amiel twined her arm into the crook of his. He led her up the three steps to stand before the altar.

High Priest Glovel's nasally voice rang through the now silent chamber. "We are gathered here today in the sight of the Holy Trinity and of man to bear witness to the commitment of union between the Princess Verena Elidena Destavi of House Drav and Prince Amiel Harlan Orlic ra Aulden of House Auld. Who presents this bride?"

"I do." The Earl of Sarnac climbed the stairs, holding in his hand two white fliare blooms that the Countess of Cartul, his daughter, had given him. Handing them to the High Priest, who had come around the altar, the earl made his way back to his seat.

"May the union be blessed with the great fire of unending love and understanding that flows from the Great I Am, through his son, and flowers in the Sevenfold Spirit."

Amiel had to release her in order to take from Glovel the proffered flower. He watched as she went to the left side, circling around the silver water bowl that stood before the altar. He circled around it on the right. He timed the release of his bloom with hers, placing it into the water. The carefully crafted mechanism swirled the fliare into a circle that led them toward each other. They crashed, as designed, in the center of the bowl. Upon contact with each other, the flowers caught fire, a unique feature of the fliare, and merged into a single blue-white flame.

Returning to their place before the High Priest, Verena tugged at her skirts to position them again. Amiel made a move to help, but then pulled back, uncertain how to do so. He smiled as her eyes alighted on him briefly before withdrawing back to Glovel. The holy man launched into his sermon.

"The union between a man and a woman is a most sacred trust as two become one in a lifetime journey of discovery. Together..."

Amiel stopped listening. He could feel Verena beside him. A small tremor went through her periodically and he longed to comfort her. To take her in his arms and tell her everything would be okay. His eyes drifted to the burning flowers in the bowl behind the priest.

Two become one. Would that prove true for them?

The fragrant lilies nestled in verdant garlands around the hollowed hall filled the solemn room with their sweet scent. Despite their strength, Amiel could distinguish the light lavender of Verena's personal perfume. The color from the arched stain glass windows danced on the white marble floors and on the silver of her gown. It all felt like a hazy dream.

A year ago, he had been on the cusp of this moment. She had left him at the proverbial altar, a laughingstock of the Galactic Alliance. The sting of the slight filled him and he clenched his fists. He felt his cheeks burn, recalling the pain and anger of her departure. Now, she stood beside him, listening to the words admonishing them to build a strong bond for their future and that of their united realm.

Amiel's attention returned to the moment when he realized Aunt Nataya, Uncle Sabred's wife, had moved to stand beside him. The Countess of Udeep draped the white linen prayer shawl, with its long blue and white dangling tassels, over Amiel's head. High Priest Glovel instructed him to turn toward Verena. She was covered now in her matching prayer shawl, placed over her by her aunt, the Duchess of Fen. Amiel took Verena's right wrist with his left hand and she did the same with him.

Their aunts took the strands of their respective shawls and used them to bind the bride and groom's hands together. Thus entwined within the prayer closet, Amiel listened as the woman he loved pronounced the marriage vows. A sudden peace filled him. The sound of Verena's voice engulfed him in a sweet embrace.

"I, Verena Elidena Destavi, do solemnly swear before the Great I Am that I do, of my own free will, join myself in the holy union of life partnership to Amiel Harlan Orlic. From this day forward, until the day the end of my time shall be fulfilled, I shall be his mate. At his side will I face the good times and the bad and through all that life may bring shall remain faithful to him and him alone in all things."

Amiel's heart swelled. In a clear and strong voice, he proclaimed, "I, Amiel Harlan Orlic, do solemnly swear before the Great I Am that I do, of my own free will, join myself in the holy union of life partnership to Verena Elidena Destavi. From this day forward, until the day the end of my time shall be fulfilled, I shall be her mate. At her side will I face the good times and the bad and, through all that life may bring, shall remain faithful to her and her alone in all things."

Waving his hands in the sign of a cross, High Priest Glovel pronounced them man and wife. The noble ladies withdrew the shawls from them. Together they stood arms yet entwined, as the Dravidian High Council of Lords and the Auldian nobles chosen to serve on the United Council of Peers stepped forward and formed a circle around the newly wedded couple. Together, their voices completely in sync with one another, Amiel and Verena repeated the words that ascended them to the throne of Dravidia.

"I do solemnly swear to uphold and protect the kingdom from all enemies, both foreign and domestic. That I shall seek the Great I Am's wisdom in all matters and rule with justice and fairness to all my subjects. As sovereign of this land, I shall persevere in all things to ensure its continuous wellbeing for all its people and the nation as a whole. This responsibility I do hereby take upon my shoulders on this day until such time as my heirs are ready to relieve me and reign in my stead."

With holy oil, High Priest Glovel anointed them each in turn, forming the sign of the cross upon their foreheads, on their lips, on their breast, and on their hands.

"By the power bestowed upon me by the Great I Am and His most Holy Church, I hereby anoint you rulers of Dravidia. May His wisdom through His Holy Word reign in your mind, on your lips, in your heart, and may He cause all that you touch to prosper. In His Holy Name, so let it be."

The Earl of Sarnac stepped forward on Verena's side and the Duke of Aul on his. They carried the new crowns. The High Priest pronounced a blessing and placed one upon their respective heads. The Mother Superior, who had blessed their betrothal, now put the royal robes upon each of their shoulders, saying a blessing and asking the Holy Trinity to give them wisdom to rule justly.

Fashioned from white gold, the crown consisted of a pair of dragon wings spread open wide whose tips met at the back. In the center of the forehead, the wings attached to the hilt of a sword the blade of which rose as a peak. The grip was made of an amethyst with the principality's black opal on the pommel. The jewels were held in place with talon-like clasps. Both crowns were of equal size so that neither was distinguishable from the other.

"They're beautiful," Verena's whisper reached Amiel's ear.

"One was supposed to be smaller, more petite, for you, in Dekkyle's original drawing, but I made sure they were made this way instead."

"My father designed it?"

"Yes. I found the drawing."

Her eyes met his and for the first time Amiel felt warmth from them. "Thank you for making that change. I appreciate it... as will my people."

He gave her a quick nod. Amiel removed his gloves and tucked them into his coat's pocket. Then he took her right hand in his, the softness of her skin eliciting a sliver of pleasure. The Duke of Aul drew near with the ring box, and Amiel took the one for Verena out. His voice filled the temple as he proclaimed.

"May these new rings, with our united crests, along with our new crowns, equal in size, demonstrate for all time our commitment to forging a united and strong kingdom." He slid the signet ring onto her index finger.

Verena's hand trembled as she grasped his left hand. Amiel's brow furrowed, but he said nothing. She took the larger signet ring from the box and tried to force it onto his left index finger. His left hand had always been slightly bigger and she had some difficulty sliding it on him.

"May this ring, with our united crests, along with our new crowns, equal in size." She glanced up into his eyes as she spoke the words. "Demonstrate our commitment to a united and strong kingdom."

The ring, designed to fit on his right hand, failed to go in all the way. Amiel noticed the consternation on her beautiful face. She was nervous and hadn't noticed she'd grabbed the wrong hand. He covered hers, still struggling with his ring, and smiled. Giving it a squeeze, he released her, placing his hands together behind his back and stealthily sliding the ring onto the correct finger.

The High Priest turned them toward the gathering. With the heavy new crown on his head, covered in the black velvet robes lined with silver fox fur, and the signet ring on his hand, Amiel looked out at the guests and felt a sudden bliss. This was, and had always been, his destiny.

"My Lords and Ladies, gentlemen, and esteemed guests," High Priest Glovel intoned with all the gusto he could muster, "It is my honor and privilege to introduce you to their Royal Majesties, King Amiel and Queen Verena of the united kingdom of Auldivia."

The applause within the edifice was overtaken by the shouts from the crowds outside. The ceremony had been streamed live over all the news networks of their world and across the intergalactic system. Strategically positioned along the streets, high-resolution holopros had let the gathered citizenry of the capital watch the event as they kept their spots along the procession route back to the castle. It sounded like the whole planet had exploded in joy at the union. Perhaps he was being fanciful.

Amiel held Verena's arm, entwined with his, and lead his new wife and queen down the aisle. The doors opened to the vestibule, but Amiel didn't pause. He continued out the front steps. There, atop the forty stairs to the cathedral's entrance, he stood, letting their people get a good look at their new king and queen. The media could take as many pictures as they wanted. Around them, their noble entourage filled out the panoramic of the new realm. Next to Verena, Amiel noted the Earl of Sarnac, Viscount Tor, and other great men and women of her kingdom, while beside him the Earl of Udeep, the Duke of Aul, and other Auldian nobility came to stand. But it was no longer her or his, but their people, their kingdom.

"Do you see that glimmer?" Verena's whisper to the Earl of Sarnac reached him.

"Yes," the earl responded.

Amiel glanced to where the earl was gazing. Atop the far building, something glinted in the winter sun. A cold sweat dripped down Amiel's arm pit as understanding of what was about to happen dawned. Gripping Verena, he threw himself down onto the hard, cold stone. She fell with him in a tumble of skirts and robes. The Earl of Sarnac had shoved her toward him and the impact of Verena's body on his knocked the wind out of him. Amiel struggled to breathe and emerge from the cloth that seemed to drown him. He managed to roll over and cover her with his body, gasping for air.

Popping noises reverberated through the crowded square, the sound bouncing off the walls of the buildings that flanked it. People screamed and ran in panic; others hit the pavement covering their heads as best they could. Amiel's peripheral awareness of it all helped clear his mind. He lay on top of his newly crowned Queen, the horror on her face etched into his soul.

"There's blood on your face," Verena's voice held a shrill panic in it. She lifted a shaking hand and swiped his cheek.

"Someone's shooting at us." He tried to sound steady and calm, though his insides felt like releasing a messy bowel movement into his perfectly pressed pants. "It's all right." She shook now in the violent throw of hysteria. "We'll be all right." He reassured her.

"Come, Majesty!" The Earl of Sarnac pulled Amiel up and off Verena. Amiel struggled for an instant, but met the nobleman's eyes. Understanding the intent, he allowed the earl to rush him down the steps and into the hoverlimo. Guards had formed a living shield, clearing a path for their monarchs.

Entering the vehicle as fast as he could, Amiel turned to receive Verena into his arms. Figor had grabbed her up. Now, his cousin and the earl jumped in and ordered the driver to head full speed to the safety of Castle Dravidia.

Amiel straightened a frightened Verena onto the seat of the conveyance, assisting in adjusting her skirts and their respective robes. "Where is Sabred?"

"He and Nataya headed off to try and capture the shooter, no doubt," Figor stated.

"Good." Amiel held Verena's shaking body.

There was blood smeared on her skirt now. He realized it was from her hand. Blood she'd cleansed off him. *But whose was it? Not mine.* He looked at the Earl of Sarnac, who held his shoulder. He'd been the one to take the hit. *Good man.* As the vehicle sped through the forest, Amiel's mind reeled. *What the hell just happened?*

CHAPTER 14

WEDDING NIGHT

THE FOUR OF THEM SPED TO THE CASTLE, leaving Dravidia City and flying through the Oldey Forest. The journey, which had taken Verena an hour at a leisurely pace earlier, took them less than half that time traveling at the hoverlimo's top speed. Descending from the vehicle, they were ushered into the nearest drawing room by the royal guards.

Amiel was shouting orders, but Verena's mind couldn't register any of it. Her gaze was fixed on her hand, still smeared with blood. The shaking was back. She tried to control it. *Get a hold of yourself!* But her body wouldn't comply.

"You've been wounded!" The Queen's voice was a harsh croak as she looked up and noticed the Earl of Sarnac's bleeding shoulder. Focusing her mind on someone else helped calm her down a little.

"No need to worry, Majesty," the brave man replied. "A mere flesh wound."

"I sent for Dr. Kolls." Amiel took her hand and wiped it off with a moist napkin he had picked up at the bar tucked into one corner of the room. "Drink this," he instructed as he pressed a glass of brandy into her hands. He adjusted her royal robe more tightly about her.

"What just happened?" She verbalized the question that had been ricocheting around her mind.

Verena took a long sip of the amber liquid. It burned its way down her throat filling her with warmth. She hadn't realized how cold she felt until just then.

"An assassination attempt, Majesty," the Duke of Aul answered her. She noticed he was helping the earl by holding a handkerchief to the wound.

"On whom?"

Her question hung in the air. Amiel had gone over to the large stone hearth and was leaning both hands on the mantle, staring at the charred remains of a fire. The earl and duke both avoided looking at her. Questions raced inside her head: *were they going to kill her or Amiel? Who had ordered the hit? The Gortive were not so bold or well equipped, were they?*

"Let's not worry about that," Amiel said. "We'll investigate later. Let's enjoy the banquet. We have the wedding dance in front of us. Let's just try to get through that for now."

"Yes," Verena seconded, her voice still shaky. "We must not let them know it shook us up."

"Begging your Majesties pardons," Sir Eriq Seller, the Lord High Marshal, spoke up.

Verena had not noticed him standing by the doorway. Now, he stepped forward and addressed them with a respectful bow.

"I don't believe it would be wise to continue with the celebration. For all we know, the assassin could be among the guests. There may be a second attempt." His gravelly voice conveyed the authority of his office as he pronounced. "I have secured the castle, and it would be best to remain on lockdown."

"Unacceptable!" Amiel's tone was imperious. "You will immediately allow guests to enter and guide them to the throne room. The wedding will continue as planned."

"But, your Majesty, your life could be in—"

"Our lives will always be in danger." Amiel put an end to the Lord Marshal's objection. "We are sovereigns. Our people must see that we are unharmed and unimpressed with this feeble attempt at destroying the peace for which much has been compromised. You will supervise the investigation of the crime scene personally, of course, and report back to us your findings."

The Lord Marshal's eyebrows rose in surprise at the directive, but he bowed deeply. Turning, he headed to the door to do his king's bidding.

"Wait, Excellency," Verena commanded before he left. "Double the guards in the castle and see to it they are placed strategically, but discreetly, in the rooms we will be using. Then you can join Lord Sabred at the scene. I believe he will already be onsite."

"Yes, Majesty." Sir Eriq stated. "It will be a pleasure to work with Lord Sabred once again."

Amiel's eyes locked with hers questioningly.

"Sir Eriq and Lord Sabred have engaged in various missions for the Intergalactic Council from what I understand," Verena informed him. *Surely, he knew that. Lord Sabred was his uncle. Perhaps it was her giving commands he questioned?*

He smiled. It was pleasant, but it didn't reach his eyes. *He'll have to get used to me issuing orders. We are to rule together now.* She lowered her gaze to the swirling liquid in her glass. She was still shivering a bit, but not as intensely. Noticing the blood splatter on her gown, the Queen excused herself and headed to her chambers followed closely by the guards that had been her constant escort since her arrival. Mrs. Denip helped her change into one of her other gowns, a deep emerald green embroidered with marigolds in yellow thread. The beautiful four petal flowers of the Vale of Tor helped lift Verena's spirits.

The Queen began to ponder the various combinations for the assassination attempt and their implications. Dravidians out to kill Amiel was by far the worst scenario. The whole wedding and truce would be for nothing and her people would suffer more war. Auldians trying to kill Amiel seemed the least likely, after all he had led them to victory over Dravidia, which had never been done before in the whole history of their nations. Auldians trying to kill her was a possibility, but what would be Amiel's response to that? Dravidians trying to kill her could be the least harmful option, but again, what would Amiel's reaction be to an attack on her?

"Deni," she said with a sigh. "Get me a couple aspirin. My head feels like it's going to explode."

"Right away, Majesty."

"Are you ready?" Amiel inquired as they stood before the blackwood doors of the throne room. They were flanked by six guards each.

"As ready as I'm going to be," Verena responded with a slight smile.

With a nod, he took her arm and they entered the great hall. The tension in the chamber was palpable. Hudroids had distributed champagne and hors d'oeuvres were being passed around by the servbots. Guests mingled in clumps, murmuring with concern about the assassination attempt and its implications. In place of the excited twitters and joyous laughter of other parties, there were subdued voices and worried glances. As they walked, Verena noted there were significantly less people than they had anticipated and invited. No doubt some had chosen not to attend or thought the remainder of the ceremony would be canceled. She was proud of Amiel for going forward with it. They would show themselves unafraid.

Dravidians and Auldians segregated into groups, keeping to their own side of the dance floor, which had been put in for this one dance. Its golden toned honeywood installed over the black marble stone of the chamber had been positioned between the chandeliers so that its reflection was unobstructed in the ceiling's mirrors.

The Senud, composed 500 years ago, had originally been danced at the weddings of the clicks of the desert tribes. Its fiery, yet sensuous tempo recalled the hot and cold contrasts of the Jornian desert and the tempestuous nature of its climate. It was not until King Larenos III that a set of formalized steps had been choreographed.

As she passed the post hooked to the dance floor's north edge, Verena had no doubt this rendition would be a fiasco. At least when they tumbled over each other and became entangled in the cords, it would provide some much-needed comic relief. She had been learning the intricate steps since she was ten years old. Amiel had only practiced them a few times that she knew of during their engagement.

The worst part was not the quick tempo or footwork requiring heel tapping at specific moments, it was the silver cords Verena dreaded. These would be hooked to their respective waists. Each would start in one corner, their cord attached to one of the four corner posts. They would begin diagonally opposite of each other. As the music progressed, they would cross and meet at intervals, setting and locking round silver discs to represent each of the fifty-one planets. Coming together at the end in the center, they would unhook the cords at their waist locking them in place with a single gold disc to symbolize Jorn. When done perfectly, the resulting reflection on the mirrors would be the lines of wormhole portals that connected the planets of Thyrein's Galactic Wall. The quantum streams mimicked the form of a giant eagle in flight.

They reached the dais and turned toward their guests. Verena was relieved to see guards standing in the periphery of the room. In their alcove, local and intergalactic media outlets were set up to report on the celebrations. Live feed would allow the whole nation and people across Thyrein's Galactic Wall to join the festivities. Glancing at the dauntlessly empty dance floor, she recalled that only twice before had the royal dance been performed entirely without error. Not even her parents had managed that, and they'd practiced together for an entire year. Amiel had never practiced with her.

"What?" Amiel whispered.

"At least we have practice tumbling all over each other," she struggled to keep her composure and suppress the nervous giggling that threatened to overcome her. The pent-up energy of shock, which at first had manifested itself in shivering, now sought release through silly laughter.

"We will be perfect," Amiel spoke each word with confidence holding her gaze. "Ours will be the most accurate picture of our cluster ever."

Taking her hand in his, he led Verena to her starting position. Bowing, Amiel lifted her gloved hand to his lips as she curtsied to him. She had to admire his confidence in light of the spectacle they were about to make of themselves. The new king strode to his post with the air of a man fully able to perform the intricate dance.

The music started and Verena concentrated completely on her steps. Releasing the silver thread as she went, she twirled, unwinding it from her waist, and met up in his embrace setting the first disc. Taking the lead, Amiel stepped and tapped faultlessly. Turning away for a few steps then joining again at the north left post, they clasped the next disc. Whirling away and coming together again, they set the next disc, and then the next, and the next. He held her eyes with his and she felt the rhythm of the music pulsing through her veins. Amiel directed her flawlessly through the dance. As the song came to a crescendo, the final steps led them into a tight embrace right in the center. Clasping the gold disc in place, which released them from their cords, Amiel grasped her around her waist. Holding her tucked in his arms, he kissed her passionately, the music's fire burning through both of them. She returned his kiss with the same intensity, caught up in the moment.

Thunderous applause filled her ears. Their guests, forgetting the anxiety of the earlier events, cheered heartily at the sight of their newly wedded sovereigns in a heated embrace.

Separating from his arms, Verena blushed bright red with embarrassment. The perfect outline of the eagle, its golden eye twinkling back in the light of the chandeliers, reflected down at her from the ceiling mirrors.

"Wow!" She smiled at Amiel, whose eyes never left her.

"Told you." He gave her a bow.

Smug bastard! Still, she couldn't stop smiling. Many times, she had watched the video of her mother and father tripping over each other, entangled in the cords, in their attempt at their wedding.

"Wow," she whispered to herself in awe of what they had just accomplished.

Shaking her head in disbelief, Verena remembered that the last time the pattern had been put together this ideally had been over 150 years ago.

Verena stood in the shower letting the warm water soothe her. After the dance, they had led the way to the dining hall for the banquet. Then it was on to the ballroom for the continuation of the celebration. The party had settled into a happy, semi-relaxed event, recovering somewhat from the horror of the assassination attempt.

As the scented water massaged her shoulders, Verena recalled there had been no rajin present. Their absence had been marked, especially as they would have presided over the blessing of the crown. That entire section of the coronation ceremony had been cut. She had sent word to them at the main temple upon arriving, but had received no response. Verena could only assume that the attack on Sanctal by Amiel's forces had made him persona non-grata for the Rajin Order. This, too, would be something she needed to heal.

Rinsing off her soap, the fact that the Dova Elmalin Jafra and her two subordinates, Misrim Nomri and Misrim Andiera, had attended the wedding struck Verena. She noticed the coldness in the way the Dravidian nobles addressed them, often turning their backs to these knowledge wielders. It had been Jolyon who'd mentioned the widespread belief about the strange figures in blue robes at the destruction of the rajin temple being the elmalin, though the leadership of their order publicly refuted the rumor. Verena couldn't believe they would do such a thing, but then so much that had always seemed impossible had now happened.

As the lavender scented water continued to pour over her, Verena's tension eased. The pressure and stress of the days since her return and the events of the day had knotted up her shoulders. The strong pulse of the massage shower head helped with her overwrought nerves. Yet the most frightening part of the whole thing yet loomed before her.

"Highness?" Mrs. Denip's gentle prod to leave her sanctuary forced her to turn off the water.

Stepping into her sandals, Verena allowed Mrs. Denip to engulf her in a warm towel. The new queen moved toward the vanity area, drying herself off. As she pulled out her chair, Mrs. Denip handed her the lush bathrobe and took the now moistened towel away. Verena sat before her mirror and felt her stomach knot up at the thought of facing Amiel in the intimacy of her bedchamber. Her reflection stared back at her.

"Queen of Auldivia," Verena tried on her new name with a whisper.

The past few weeks flashed through her mind as she allowed Deni to dry her hair. *What will marriage hold for me?* Verena pondered as she perfumed her body on autopilot with her lotions and talc. The very thing she had sought to avoid had come about. It had seemed as if the wedding would solve the crisis her leaving had caused. But the assassination attempt was a wrench thrown in whose ill-effects were yet to be fully felt. The tension returned as she considered once again the possibilities. Above all else, she lifted up a prayer that it would not have been the Dravidians at fault.

For a moment, Verena wondered at the possibility of Amiel having been killed. A pain stabbed at her heart. He'd been in her life since always. Once a good friend and playmate, the thought of a world without him in it felt strange, empty. And, such a fate would be horrible for Dravidia. Surely any person with intelligence could see that. The Auldian army held much ground. If Amiel had died, how could they overcome the enraged Auldians who held key portions within their nation? Dravidian forces would need to make a hasty retreat to the north. *Yes. That would be the best place to strike out from.* Anco City with its fortified walls and war machines would be a great place from which to launch a counter attack. Or perhaps Fort Iark in the north east. It had recently been refurbished. *Amiel couldn't die. At least not yet.* Not until the situation was more settled and an offensive could be launched simultaneously.

Verena froze. She stared at her face in the mirror. *Was she really considering killing the man she'd just married?* A cold shiver ran through her. He'd be in her room shortly. They would consummate their wedding vows. Her cheeks burned at the thought of what that entailed.

No more death. They would find a way to make a life together and lead their nation to a victory against the Gortive. *Time now to heal, not continue battling each other.* She rose from her vanity determined to make the marriage work. She untied her bathrobe, letting it slip to the ground. Verena raised her arms and allowed her pink nightgown to cascade over her body. Suddenly, she became aware of just how transparent the garment was. Of course, as she had never intended to wear any of these clothes, it had not mattered what her aunt had selected for her a year ago.

Why didn't I check what we bought when I returned? True, there had been the conquered nation to salvage, her father's funeral to organize, and then the combined wedding and coronation to prepare. Now, though, standing there practically naked, Verena regretted her failure to give this more attention. She put on the matching robe, which offered no additional coverage, as it was just as transparent as the frock itself. Mrs. Denip slipped out the servants' exit quietly, leaving her in the brightly lit bathroom. Taking a deep breath, she opened the door to her bedroom, finding it in complete darkness. *She hadn't turned the lights off when she had come through it to undress, had she?*

A sharp intake of breath from the reading nook at the far end alerted her to his presence. She could hardly make out Amiel's silhouette in the darkness. Verena realized, framed in the light of the bathroom, the translucent fabric of her gown was all but nonexistent.

A deep embarrassment took her and she reached over to turn off the bathroom light. Darkness would be a welcome ally in this next part. His firm and sudden grip on her wrist stayed the action. She hadn't heard him move, but he stood in front of her now, having crossed the room quickly. Heat rushed to her cheeks and she was glad her face was turned from him and covered by her long flowing hair. Loosed and rolling down to her waist, the auburn tresses provided subtle coverage.

He let go of her wrist and she let her arm fall to her side. His hand reached her face turning it toward him, cupping her cheek. She closed her eyes. *This was really going to happen!* Her frantic breathing gave away her agitation. *Get a grip on yourself!*

He kissed her. His mouth was hungry, devouring, deep and urgent. He ran the hand on her cheek down to the back of her neck, where he twined his fingers into her hair. She felt his other arm go around her waist and hold her tight to him. She trembled slightly, but shyly returned the kiss.

Separating, his voice a husky whisper, he said, "You always did love pink." He grasped with both hands the garment she wore and pulled both robe and nightgown over her head in one fluid movement.

A gasp of surprise escaped her when the cool air of the room hit her exposed skin. The shock made her open her eyes. Verena turned her head and fumbled again for the light, but his hand stopped her once more. She stared, entranced at his strong hand on her wrist. His arm was bare. She realized Amiel must have taken off his shirt. His chest was covered in thick curly hair. She wondered, ridiculously, if he liked being so hairy. The urge to burrow her fingers there struck her, but instead she dropped her hand to her side.

Slipping both his arms around her, he cupped her butt and pulled her to him. Her arms came up defensively to his chest. Looking at her fisted hands, Verena chided herself; *he was her husband now and this was supposed to happen.* Relaxing her palms, she splayed them flat, her fingers nestling and weaving themselves of their own accord. Verena kept her head low, eyes averted. She could feel the hardness of his manhood pressing against her through the fabric of his pants. Amiel lowered his head to her shoulder. His lips began at her birthmark and he kissed his way up her neck. The hunger in his touch sent an involuntary shiver through her.

"Am I so repulsive to you?" His voice was deep, almost unrecognizable.

She shook her head.

"I don't understand then, why..." He stopped and looked at her, pulling her face up. "Look at me."

Her eyes opened and the tears of trepidation that Verena had been holding back spilled out.

"Have you never been with a man?"

She shook her head. Her cheeks burned with embarrassment. *What would he think? Would he be annoyed that he had to teach her? Would he like it that he would be the only one?* She tried to turn her head, but he had her chin firmly in his grip.

"You're so beautiful, I assumed..." his voice trailed off. His eyes softened.

"I'm not a whore. I'm a Royal Princess of the House of Drav." The pride in her name and her family helped Verena restrain the tears and gather her courage.

He took her face between his hands, combing her hair back so that he could look at her. His mouth was on hers, but this kiss was different.

It was slow, gentle, almost tender. He wrapped his hands around her waist; his grip soft but firm.

Lifting her into the air, he deposited Verena on her bed. He lay down beside her, touching, caressing, making her skin come alive. At first, she lay there stiff, feeling awkwardly exposed and uncertain. He kissed her neck, her breasts.

A gasp of pleasure escaped her as his mouth sucked in one of her nipples. After a moment, he moved to her other breast, his tongue playing with its hardened peak while he used his free hand to continue teasing the other one. She arched her back, expanding his access, lost in the thrill of it.

She placed her hand in his thick black hair and felt him moan against her chest. *He liked her touch.* The realization warmed her. Verena twirled her fingers in the thick tufts at the nape of his neck and felt a shiver of delight as her caresses elicited another deeply masculine groan from him.

"Rennie," her nickname spoken against her neck sent a shiver of pleasure through her.

She felt Amiel's hand reach between her legs, its touch magical. He lifted his face to hers and kissed her deeply, as his fingers probed and massaged. Relaxing in his arms, Verena returned his kisses. *He had been a great friend once, perhaps...* waves of pleasure unlike anything she had ever felt were crashing through her just then and thinking became impossible. She clutched the sheets as she felt an eruption of sensation roll across her body.

"Mmmm." She tried to control the sounds seeking escape. After all, she was a lady, and ladies did not yell. But she felt like yelling. She felt like releasing everything and letting herself go completely.

"I never thought a woman could come so quietly," Amiel chuckled, looking into her eyes in the aftermath of the explosions he had caused.

Is he displeased? Embarrassment returned with a vengeance. He had taken her to heights of delight she had never dreamed possible. *Was he about to slap her with how poorly she compared to his former lovers? He no doubt had many,* the depressing thought brought tears to her eyes and she slammed her lids shut, refusing to give in to them.

Amiel stroked her cheek gently. "Your response was beautiful." He kissed her eyelids, her mouth, lingering against her lips. "Ready for more?" The words brushed over her swollen lips.

Had he been inside? Verena opened her eyes as the question popped suddenly into her head. *No, she was sure he had been beside her the whole time.* Verena had studied anatomy and reproductive health; she knew how things were supposed to work. She could say almost definitively he had not been inside her, well his fingers had. The sound of his zipper interrupted her thoughts. *He had his pants on the whole time!*

Firm hands spread her legs as Amiel positioned himself atop her, resting his weight on his arms. The woodsy smell of his body filled her senses like a walk in the forest. His fingers stroked strands of her fiery red hair. His mouth found hers. He trailed kisses down her neck, and to her breasts. Cupping them in his strong hands, he teased her nipples with his tongue, sucking them into his mouth. Verena arched her body up, giving herself up to the pleasure that rippled through her at his touch.

Returning to her neck and mouth, his right hand trailed a delightful path down the rounded curve of her hip. The lovely waves of pleasure were back and she let them roll over her again, gripping his arm as she felt the crescendo rising. Then he eased himself into her. At first, there was a discomfort, a strangeness to the moment, but then it felt so right, like when she was in his arms dancing.

His hips moved with a rhythm she instinctively understood and matched. Every fiber of her being clung to him, seeking the wondrous friction of his skin on hers. As the waves of her orgasm exploded through her again, she heard him call her name. A warmth spread inside her and she tightened her legs around him. She didn't know when she had so completely wrapped herself about him. He nuzzled her neck for a moment, his body relaxed and heavy on hers, spent. The feel of him fully in her arms, still within her, was a pleasant crush. *This is very nice. I could go for doing this regularly. She smiled at herself.*

Rolling off her, he gathered her into his arms, nestling his face into the soft curls of her hair.

"Are you okay?" he asked.

"Yes... this was... very nice."

He pulled her face up to look at her. As usual, she couldn't tell what he was thinking, but the heat of his gaze made her feel oddly satisfied.

"Just nice?" He gave her nose a quick kiss. "Guess I'll have to work on it then."

"I didn't mean... no I..." A chuckle rumbled through his chest and she frowned. Then, rising on her elbow and looking down at him, she found herself saying, "I think we need to work on this a lot actually." Elaborating, she continued, "In fact, I think we need daily sessions."

A full laugh erupted from him. His eyes held a heat that sent a thrill through her.

Amiel desired her. *Is it purely physical? Or, is there deeper feelings behind it?* Their friendship had been shattered by his brutality. *Can we rebuild it?* That look he was giving her filled her heart with hope. *Perhaps, I'll have a good marriage after all.*

Rolling away, he stood and headed for the bathroom. Verena heard him moving around, turning on a faucet, but she couldn't glimpse what he was doing. She sat up, moving to the head of the bed just as he returned with a moistened towel. Verena was amazed at how comfortable he seemed to be with his own nudity as she used the cloth to clean herself. Uncertain what to do with it, he took it from her hands. Picking up his shirt from the floor, Amiel offered it to her on his way back to the bathroom. She put it on. The scent of him filled her senses, heightened from their lovemaking, and brought a thrill to her.

A glimmer of red on the white carpet caught her eye.

"What is that?" she asked as he returned.

He reached down and picked up the necklace. A red stone, the size of his thumb, on a gold chain sparkled in the light from the bathroom. "It was a gift from a friend," he said, reaching the bed and sitting on the edge beside her, the bright jewel in his hand.

"May I see it?"

"Certainly."

The moment she touched it, bile rose in her throat. As she gazed down at the strange charm, its fire leaped to life, coiling around in serpentine motion. *Something is terribly wrong with this necklace.* But she couldn't quite determine what about it seemed off, made her uneasy. Shaking her head, Verena let the jewel slip from her hands onto the bed beside her.

Her eyes rested on it. *What is it? Why did I react to it that way? Does it affect him or is it just me?* She wanted to ask him about the red stone, share how it affected her, yet she couldn't find the words. Her mouth refused to speak aloud her questions.

Instead she heard herself saying, "It's beautiful. May I have it?"

Amiel looked into her eyes. Verena could feel he was about to give it to her. The afterglow of what they had shared was still on him. Her heart gladdened that he would make a present of it for her.

"It would make a great wedding present, and it's my favorite color," she lied. Why had she done that?

He knew it. They had been friends since childhood. How often had she said red and gold was a gaudy combination? He was well aware her favorite color had always been pink. The warmth in his eyes dissipated, replaced by suspicion. She had lost. It was written on his face and the momentary connection between them slipped away.

"I can't give it to you. It was a special gift presented to me upon my knighting." He picked it up and pulled it over his neck, the stone resting near his heart. Standing again, he pulled on his pants.

He reached for her, pulling his shirt from her body. She covered herself with her hands, shy again suddenly in spite of the shared intimacy. Pushing her hands away from her body, he stared at her naked before him. The look in his eyes juxtaposed to the tenderness they had exuded only moments ago. Verena's heart plummeted at the change in him. Straightening, Amiel walked out of her bedchamber without another word.

The lie had been unnecessary, Verena berated herself. A shiver went down her spine recalling the final look on his face as he left her. She scampered off the bed and put on her clothes, despite the poor protection they offered. Climbing back up, she slipped under the covers and cried herself to sleep.

CHAPTER 15

MISDIRECTION

AMIEL STORMED THROUGH TO HIS BEDROOM via the connecting door. His hand caressed the talisman Godar had given him. A restless energy surged through him. Making his way across his bedchamber, he tore his clothes off on his way to the bathroom.

He stepped into the shower, letting the hot water run over his body. The image of Verena in the doorway of her own bathroom filled his mind. Everything he had ever imagined about being with her paled to the reality. A smile curved his lips as he thought about her suggestion they should make love every night. The recollection of her lips, her breasts, the feeling as he filled her body, the deliciousness of the release roiled over him as he showered.

Toweling off, he put on comfortable clothes. Stopping to collect the talisman where he'd tossed it, he let it hang from his fingers. She'd wanted it. *Why? Bad enough to lie. But, why?* He knew her well enough to realize she didn't really like it. Shaking his head at the incongruency, he wondered if she'd just wanted something of his. His heart warmed at the thought, the vision of her in the middle of her first orgasm making him smile.

Amiel pulled the jewel on and headed out the door. Anger coursed through him as he thought about the attack. Walking purposefully down the hall to the lift, he accessed his com device and sent messages to Lord Sabred, Sir Eriq, Figor, and Godar. He instructed them to meet him in the king's private conference room.

Arriving there, Amiel turned on the holopro and pulled up the images from various news networks. The varying camera angles of them exiting the cathedral pulled up, floating over the table. He ran through each in slow motion. His stomach roiled and he pounded the table with a clenched fist after the third. *They'd intended to kill me. Who would dare do such a thing?*

A respectful knock on the door pulled his attention away. "Enter."

"Good evening, Majesty," Sir Eriq said. The man had obviously dressed in haste. "I brought all the material we uncovered so far about the assassination attempt as requested."

The Lord High Marshal bowed as he extended a holonote chip.

"Thank you, Sir Eriq," Amiel said. "Please take a seat while we wait for the others to join us."

"Of course, Sire."

Amiel stole a glance at the time piece over the side table at the far end of the room. It was nearing three in the morning. He'd obviously pulled this fine man from his sleep. The others were no doubt delayed by having to dress in order to attend his call. They should have realized a matter of this importance would not be left until sunrise.

"Cousin, for Pegot's sake, its three in the foluc morning!" A disheveled Figor came in throwing himself into the nearest chair.

"You realize you're addressing your king?" Amiel threw the Duke of Aul a cold glare.

"My apologies... Majesty," the duke said, sitting up straighter.

"Majesty," the Earl of Udeep greeted from the open doorway that Figor had failed to close. "You know this could have waited for morning."

"Technically, it is morning, uncle." Amiel felt the restlessness growing. *Someone tried to kill me and these people wanted to sleep!*

"Your Majesty summoned?" Godar's raspy voice filled the space.

Amiel felt a chill as the nijar entered. There was always a coldness that surrounded the knowledge wielder. Godar's real appearance had been shifted to the semblance he'd adopted for Viscount Pembra. This persona allowed Godar to attend Amiel without revealing his true nature as a nijar. Amiel had seen to it he was granted lands to go with the title, but as far as the king could tell, Godar had never bothered to so much as inspect his holdings. With a shrug, Amiel turned his attention to the matter at hand.

"Everyone take a seat and let's begin." Amiel straightened and placed the chip Sir Eriq had provided him into the holopro.

They went through the evidence. As they did, Amiel watched Sir Eriq's discomfort. He was the only Dravidian present. Amiel trusted the man given his legendary status and friendship with Lord Sabred. His uncle had always spoken in the highest terms of his friend and of their exploits together on occasion.

"Doesn't seem we have learned much." Amiel commented. "What next steps will be taken in the investigation?"

Clearing his throat, Sir Eriq answered, "We must question Count Tor and his son, have them account for their signet rings. If one is missing, that might indicate a possible framing of the Tor. We would—"

"Framing Dravidians for the attempt on King Amiel would imply Auldian involvement." Figor played with his nails as he spoke. "I doubt any Auldian would raise a hand against the man who has led us to such victorious status."

"I would not doubt a possible Auldian involvement." The Earl of Udeep's eyes met Amiel's. "We know that there is a faction of nobles who are upset at the betrothal agreement in light of the war, and I wouldn't put it past that group to do something rash, like trying to kill you."

"Auldians cannot have done this, uncle," Figor insisted. "Certainly, there are some who are upset, but to try and kill our national hero..." his voice trailed off and he shook his head in disbelief.

"Sire," Godar spoke for the first time. His amber eyes glowing in that unnatural manner they had, which made Amiel feel so uneasy.

"Godar, what do you think of all this?" Amiel asked, deferring to the nijar.

"While the evidence, on face value, suggests Dravidians at fault, it is entirely possible Auldians could have planned it. There are murmurings. When denied the right to loot the conquered people, the group we all are thinking of might not reflect far beyond to the deeper consequences of such an action as murdering their ruler."

Amiel sat back in the black leather executive chair. His mind filled with a very real certainty. This had not been Dravidians. They had their queen back, and they had a favorable status as far as they knew. He could see the faces of Lord Uld and several other younger noblemen who followed him. They wouldn't hesitate to execute such a plot. Their small minds wouldn't understand the full implications of these actions' consequences. Fear gripped him. He would have to tread carefully. Play the part and then, in the right time, bring them to justice for the traitors they were.

Another thought niggled its way in. With this evidence, he might be able to push for the removal of the betrothal agreement. *But can I do equal status for Verena as Uncle Sabred suggested?*

She is a weak ruler. When faced with hard choices her instinct was to flee. She had intelligence and good training, thanks to King Dekklye, but he really couldn't trust her to provide strong leadership. This moment could be the one to bring him the full power he should have.

He became aware of the silence of the room. All eyes were on him.

Straightening, he said, "Sir Eriq, we will proceed as you suggest. Bring the Tors in for questioning. Find out about the rings. Uncle, you will work with Sir Eriq and discover if the plot might have come from Auldians. In the meantime, Figor draft a statement to be put to the Council of Peers for the setting aside of the betrothal agreement in light of the plot to assassinate me being Dravidian."

"Amiel," Lord Sabred said. "Do not act on this evidence. Present the council with the motion because a more equal distribution of power is a—"

"Do you honestly believe Verena can rule?" Amiel felt a twinge at his belittling the woman he loved. Then again, he spoke only the truth. "She doesn't have what it takes. With this, we can move to take full control and establish a strong kingdom. We must be ready for when the Gortive attack us."

"I believe it wise for you to have full control, Sire," Godar chimed in.

Turning to Sir Eriq, Amiel impaled the man with a hard stare. "Sir Eriq, you serve me now."

The statement filled the chamber. All eyes switched to the Lord High Marshal. Amiel watched the warrior struggle with the decision he was being asked to make. Then the man's face told Amiel all he needed to know before he ever spoke.

"Sire, I had the honor of training Queen Verena in war and she is a fine warrior. I know that she had the very best tutors for the preparation of becoming a great ruler. When the king would be away and she sat in his stead, she showed great skill in ruling," his voice was firm and strong as he defended his sovereign. "However, when the moment to make a difficult decision came, when she was called upon to sacrifice for her people in a way that is not uncommon to women of her social status, she failed us. I will not interfere in the matter and will serve the kingdom."

Amiel smiled at the room. "Excellent. Let's proceed with the plan." With a long yawn, he rose and dismissed them, making his way back to his room. She wouldn't like it, but it was what was best. Gazing at the closed door that connected to her, he slid into bed.

Amiel waited in the family room on the north side of the castle. It was a smaller, more intimate chamber decorated in forest green and white. The double doors that led out to the rose garden and promontory beyond were closed, their stained-glass depiction of the beautiful blooms cast vibrant color into the room.

He'd summoned Verena and ordered the Earl of Sarnac to take his breakfast in his rooms. The Duchess of Fen had tried to defy the same order that he'd given her, but he'd had the guards refuse her entrance and escort her back to her rooms.

"Good morning, Majesty," the duke rose in greeting when Verena entered.

Turning to her, he commanded, "Come sit by me." He pulled the chair out as he spoke so she had to sit near him. She had been heading to the other side of the table.

As she took her place, the delicious scent of her filled him. Everything in him wanted to tell Figor to get the foluc out and make her his right there on the table. A sigh at the unpleasantness he was about to bring between them escaped him as he retook his own place.

"Where is the earl? And my aunt?" She glanced about the chamber as she inquired.

"The earl is taking breakfast in his room, Majesty," the duke replied. "We thought it best to have him rest after the wound from yesterday. The duchess, I was told, is yet asleep."

Amiel watched disbelief flash across her beautiful face. She knew the earl's wound had been take care of by Dr. Koll and required no bedrest. And they all knew the duchess to be an early riser. Amiel waited for her to push them on this, but she remained silent. He gestured to the hudroids to begin service.

They ate the delicious breakfast with only the occasional pleasantry exchanged. When the table had been cleared of all but the coffee, Amiel reached over to her and placed a pictode in her palm. His hand brushing against the softness of her skin brought a sliver of pleasure to him. He could change his mind. Give her a chance to rule beside him. Then he remembered the derisive looks from those who hated him when she'd spurned him. *She deserves what's coming.*

"This is the evidence recovered so far from the rooftop. Take a look." He sat back in his chair, gazing at her impassively.

The holoimages appeared before Verena. He watched the emotions roll over her. Shock, disbelief, fear, settled into determination. She didn't believe it and she would push hard now against it.

"Do we know who their target was?" her voice was cautious.

Amiel watched her zoom in the holoshot revealing the seal of the House of Tor open before her. It was clearly visible in the packed ice-snow on the ledge of the roof, where, presumably, the culprit rested his hand to hold the weapon steady.

"From the video, using the various news media's positions, we have been able to ascertain that the target of the assassination was King Amiel, Majesty," the duke answered in a matter-of-fact tone.

"This is a setup. You do realize that, don't you?" Verena pulled her gaze from the image to look at him.

Did she even care if he'd died? Maintaining as calm an exterior as possible, he responded, "The evidence is clear cut." He kept his voice quiet, emotionless. "The real question is who are the conspirators. I hope you had no part in ordering this."

Silence filled the room. His accusation hung in the air. The duke busied himself stirring his coffee cup, while the newlyweds engaged in a staring contest.

"Jolyon is not a fool. He would never engage in something like this. He was with us in the church! Again, this is a setup. Someone wants a divided Vidden," Verena argued ignoring his suggestion of her treason. "Your people stand to lose more with our union. Mine have nothing to gain with this move."

"Actually, Majesty, with the king dead," the duke countered, "you would have full control. It would resolve things neatly in Dravidia's favor."

The tension doubled. For a moment he saw her panic, then she regained her composure. A surge of pride filled him. *She needs more practice at this, but you're doing fairly well, my Rennie.*

"Please," she retorted. "There is no way the Auldians would have simply accepted me as their queen if Amiel had been killed. There would be war again for certain. Plus, the Earl of Sarnac saved our lives. He pushed us down and took the hit himself," she pressed. "He is the most important nobleman. If such a plot had been hatched by Dravidians, they would have sought his support and he wouldn't have saved us if he was in on it. And if he wasn't in on it, he would have told us. His honor is beyond question."

"Now I think on it, you were definitely not involved, though at first I thought you might have been," Amiel stated, leaning toward her. "You did wear a gown with the emblem of the House of Tor on it, replacing the blood-splattered one. But, you saw the glimmer, probably of the weapon's telescopic sight. You mentioned it to the earl. At that point, he had to act to throw suspicion away from him. He could be in on it."

"No, he didn't have to act," Verena countered leaning toward him as well and holding his gaze. He felt a shiver of excitement roll down his back. They were toe-to-toe, and it excited him to make her work at convincing him. Of course, his heart already knew who it really was, but he wouldn't lose such a great piece of leverage for power.

Her creamy skin was flushed a rosy pink. His mind recalled other parts of her that turned the same color after he'd enjoyed them. A frown furrowed his brow. He had to be careful. He didn't want to lose access to the deliciousness of her body.

She was speaking now, defending the earl. "He could have let you be killed. He would have no reason to believe your death would grieve me. I did after all runaway from marrying you before. And Viscount Tor couldn't be in two places at one time. Someone is framing him and my people. Most likely your people."

"The king led our armies to a historic victory over Dravidia," the duke exclaimed as if the very idea of a mutiny among the Auldians was ludicrous. "Why would his people want him dead? He is a hero to us."

Figor really is a great actor.

"So, beloved a hero that your people will just docilely give up their spoils of war?" She countered, keeping her eyes on Amiel, watching him for a reaction.

He denied it to her. He'd had much more practice at this. He slipped a mask of indifference over his face.

"That young lord was most adamant that they didn't want to give up the lands you already gave them. In the preparations for the wedding, you have been delaying the issue of reconciling the betrothal agreement with your conquest. Maybe they feel you will deny them the wealth they deserve. Men will kill anyone over money." Her eyes pleaded with him to come around and accept her argument.

"Any evidence it could be as the queen has said?" Amiel directed the question to the duke, but his eyes stayed on hers, as impassive and cold as he could will them.

A glimmer of hope crossed her face. She was so gloriously beautiful. And she was his. Now, he would take full control of her kingdom. If she hadn't run, they could have been co-rulers. But, she didn't deserve it. She'd be his wife, a queen consort, never a queen. His hand reached to his chest, feeling the talisman. He hoped the power Godar had laced it with would indeed keep him safe.

"No evidence to support that theory at this time, Sire," the duke affirmed.

"Have Sir Eriq continue investigating." Amiel pushed his chair back and stood. "In the meantime, you will forgive me but we must take action in light of the evidence we do have." He stretched his hand to help her rise.

Verena rose without his assistance. "What action?"

"Don't worry yourself about it." Amiel led the way to the door. A liveried hudroid footman quickly held it open. Amiel stood there expectantly. "You best prepare for the Allegiance Ceremony."

Minutes ticked by while the latently hostile silence blanketed the room. The Duke of Aul, who had stood up when the queen rose, now shifted awkwardly from one foot to the other. Amiel noted his discomfort but held her determined gaze. He extended his arm toward the door in a gesture indicating she should leave the room.

"I will have an answer, sir, make no mistake about that!"

"The appropriate action will be taken," Amiel's voice was cuttingly precise. He motioned to the guards standing outside.

They came in and flanked Verena. They didn't touch her, but the message was clear. The queen could leave of her own accord or be taken out of the chamber.

Her hands clenched at her sides and a fury sprang in her eyes. He watched her struggle with the decision. Stay and continue demanding he tell her what he was going to do and risk him ordering the guards to drag her back to her rooms, or leave with dignity. Would he do it? Could he inflict that on her? She'd inflicted worse on him with her public shunning. A little humiliation would do her good.

Her expression changed. She'd made a choice. She turned and left, followed by the ever-present escorts. For a moment he felt disappointed that she hadn't held her ground. *But then, that is her way.*

Chapter 16

Unlikely Allies

THE EARL OF SARNAC STOOD before the windows of his chamber over-looking the side yards of the west wing of Castle Dravidia. A deep sigh escaped his thick lips as his gray eyes gazed out beyond the carefully sculpted verges toward the Bay of Drav and its softly rolling waves. Eldor Falmer Sar of the House of Sarnac, earl of the bountiful lands of the Vongar River Valley, which lay between the Sarnac and the West Vongo Rivers, had served for most of his life as the main advisor to the royal house of Dravidia. He was more at home in the castle than at his own estate, Sarvon Hall. He, like his father before him, and his father before that, functioned as the most important personage in the land, second only to the king. *I would give anything to be able to do as Verena did and simply run away from this whole bloody mess!*

Thanks to the Great I Am, she has returned. With the king dead and Amiel's forces firmly in control of the southern portions of the kingdom, Eldor had led the remaining Dravidians north to Anco City. His plan had been to hold the banking centers and use them as leverage to treat with Amiel. Verena's return and her ability to get the boy to accept once more the original betrothal agreement had been a godsend.

Getting Dravidia's troops to support her proved a hard sell but in the end the idea of a planet under Amiel's rule was enough to bring them to the table. No one wanted Amiel as king over them. Eldor had made it clear to his followers that with Verena wed to Amiel, their kingdom would be safer.

For a blessed moment, everything seemed to return to balance, back on the right track. *Then those shots rang down on it all!* Eldor had no doubt they were meant to strike down Amiel. As the preparations for the king's funeral and the royal wedding had taken shape, Eldor had noted with growing concern the disgruntled mumblings of Lord Uld and his band of scornful young lordlings. There was no doubt in the earl's mind that the assassination attempt had emanated from this group of Auldian "nobles" who were eager to loot and pillage.

A knock at his door broke into his reverie.

"Enter," he commanded.

"I am sorry to disturb you," the Duke of Aul entered, dressed in his usual austere yet elegant manner. The earl had to admire the young man, who served as Amiel's trusted advisor. Many in the court favored the more colorful and foppish vestments put in style by the great actor Nor Drolby.

"What can I do for you, your Grace," Eldor extended his arm, gesturing the duke to take a seat on a sofa in the chamber's sitting rooms. Eldor settled into the plush chair opposite him.

"I thought you might want to know what the preliminary investigation has found." The duke extended a pictode to him.

The earl's eyebrows rose in surprise at the duke's willingness to share information. Wondering if he could trust this young Auldian, Eldor proceeded to access the report and accompanying pictures. His stomach clenched and his cursory breakfast threatened to make its way back up.

"What does Pr—King Amiel have to say?"

"He will need to follow the matter up, of course. But... I don't believe it was as the evidence would seem."

"I see." Eldor locked eyes with his counterpart in the Auldian court.

The young man's ebony skin took on a slight red hue at the intensity of Eldor's inspection. Lanky thin, with green-speckled brown eyes, the duke didn't seem as self-assured now as he had been during the preparation days.

Good, the earl thought. "What can I do for you, your Grace?"

"If we can get to the truth of this matter quickly, find the true culprit, I think we can keep the kingdom on track." The duke leaned forward slightly as he followed up his statement, "I fear the queen may get in the way."

"Has she been shown this evidence?"

A weary sigh escaped the duke and he settled back into the sofa's cushions. "Yes. She and the king had some tense words about it over breakfast." The young man made an apologetic gesture with his hands before proceeding. "By the way, I'm sorry that you were kept from being there. That was not my advice."

"I understand. How did the king approach the subject?"

A wry smile crossed the duke's face. "Not well. He blatantly suggested she might have had a hand in the attempt on his life."

"It seems we may have our hands full if we are to be ready for the Gortive offensive."

"Yes."

"I think we need to move quickly on this investigation." Eldor rose and headed for his com. "I have a contact whose special skills may be of service. May I call her?"

"Please, do. I have contacted some of my people. I will follow up with them." The duke rose to take his leave. As he drew near the door, the duke turned back, concern knitting his brow. "They are very volatile together. It will be tough keeping them both calm and steady. I'm glad to have your help... with the queen."

"That's what we do... you and I... make sure the realm survives by helping keep the hands at the helm balanced."

The duke nodded solemnly and departed.

"Eldor! I was expecting your call," the sultry voice at the other end of the com always sent a thrill through him.

"Arwace, I need your services."

"Hmm... never the ones I would like to bestow on you, Eldy."

The earl could see her in his mind's eye. The most beautiful and deadly woman in the universe was as voluptuously curvy as she was petite. No doubt that perfectly shaped mouth now pouted beguilingly. From the moment they met, the chemistry between them had been undeniable. Remaining faithful to his wife proved a constant struggle around the intrepid lady. As wife to the leader of one of the desert's most powerful tribes, Clicktess Arwace dur Falahar was accustomed to having her way and his refusal to give in to her served only as a continuous challenge.

Shaking his head to clear his thoughts, Eldor got down to business. "There is preliminary evidence I'm sending you now from the assassination attempt. I need—"

"Please, of course I know what you need. I am already working on it, darling. The evidence implicating the House of Tor is too blatant."

"Yes, it's nothing but boogwak."

"Tsk, tsk. Such language from a nobleman of your stature!" Her throaty laugh echoed down his skin, and Eldor found himself wishing he could burrow his face into the smooth bronze skin of her graceful neck. "I am traveling to Eagle's Nest as we speak. I will contact you when I have something for you... other than just me, of course."

"Thank you, Arwace, I knew I could count on you," Eldor couldn't hide the note of sincere appreciation for this master spy and patriot.

"Always."

"Any news on Lord Horsef?"

"He is definitely not dead."

The statement shook Eldor. While he'd hoped the rajin master had survived, the utter decimation at Sanctal didn't bode well. "How can you be sure?"

"The rajin master contacted one of my informants. He's gone under-cover. Something connected to the attack and a pink stone? I believe Lord Bral may be with him. No one has seen that master since King Dekkyle asked him to lead a mission to Parthia. It is unclear what transpired there, but I have people working on it."

"Interesting. Arwace, I've been pondering this for some time but haven't had a chance to find out anything. Why would the rajin not attack Amiel after he orchestrated the destruction of their temple? I thought Lady Vivelda would've had an army of rajin here. If she had, things might have been very different for us!"

"Drulin, Eldy."

"Drulin?"

"At first, when the Drulians didn't support Dravidia against Amiel, I thought it was pettiness over Queen Verena's refusal to grant them access to the wildlife preserve. I thought they would eventually come around. But there is more to it, I fear." He could hear disgust in her tone as she elaborated.

"Why would Drulin block the rajin from defending their order?"

"Because they didn't want Dravidia to win."

Eldor plopped down on a nearby chair. *Drulin sought to ruin Dravidia. Why?*

"Vivelda went before the counsel and requested permission to fight," Arwace continued. "You know there are strict rules for rajin involvement in any disagreements, much less wars, given their powers."

"Yes. They need council approval. How is it they didn't get it?"

"Two-thirds of the council voted to deny the rajin request to fight on behalf of Dravidia and in defense of Sanctal. Drulin and those planets allied to them as well as Fratern and their allies blocked them. My father's Councilman told me, he'd never seen such a power move."

"Does your father know his Councilman is an informant for you?" Eldor couldn't hide the surprise in his voice. Aumend was a powerful king with strong misogynistic leanings.

"Of course not, Eldy, don't be foolish." She tried to make it sound flippant, but the earl could hear the pain. "He thinks I'm a dutifully compliant wife of the desert click he married me off to." After a short pause, she changed the subject. "Keirmish told me they even blocked the elmalin."

"Those witches wanted to come to Jorn?" The earl scoffed. "For what?"

"When King Dekkyle was ill. Their top leadership Dova went before the council seeking to be allowed to find a cure. They were forbidden, as was Vivelda."

"Something bigger is going on. We must find out what."

"Vivelda was spotted leaving the rajin moon Ghoukas. She spent all this time there at their main training temple of Artaxyoun. From what I gather, Verena sent word of her arrival at Jorn and asked the rajin to assist her in forging a peace with Aulden. Seems the queen didn't expect to find herself Amiel's captive."

"No, I dare say she didn't expect any of this. Doesn't she need the council's approval?"

"Yes. And now she has it. After Amiel married Verena the council informed the rajin they could return to Jorn and re-establish Sanctal, but they must not seek vengeance or retribution for the attack. War is war."

"Vivelda's arrival will prove interesting. I doubt the rajin will let it go that easily. Stay in touch."

The line clicked off. Eldor stood staring once more at the castle's magnificent gardens. Arwace would find the answer; he felt certain of it. The Allegiance Ceremony would start in a couple hours. He watched as a pair of blue seagulls flew by his window on their way to fish in the sea beyond the promontory. Their piercing cry set him in motion. Turning, he gathered up his portfolio and his holopad. It was his turn to call on his esteemed colleague.

The Duke of Aul's suite of rooms were similar to his own, the earl thought as he entered. The younger man had selected the blue rooms, whose elegance was matched by its utility. The earl had never used these, preferring the wood paneling of the rooms that overlooked the back gardens and sea.

Eldor enjoyed the surprise in the duke's face at his arrival. "I've made contact and we should have more information soon," Eldor stated, crossing the room purposefully and settling at the round breakfast table near the windows. He gestured for his host to join him. "Come, join me here. There is much we must discuss."

"Make yourself at home." The duke's wry smile took the edge off the comment as the nobleman settled in one of the chairs. "May I ask what this is about?"

"Indeed." Eldor drew out his holopad and turned it on. A holographic map of Vidden appeared before them. Six of Dravidia's cities were pinned on the virtual relief of the continent. "The real threat to the king's life comes from his own lords." The earl watched the duke tense, a protest forming in the loyal nobleman's mouth. "Now, let's dispense with insincerity. We both know the assassination attempt was about money."

The duke settled back into his chair, intertwining his fingers and resting his chin on them. "The king is a hero to his people, defeating Dravidia as he did. Why would his lords seek his life?"

"I know the House of Tor didn't do this. And I know Dravidia is... well... glad to cease the war and have Verena home." The earl set his device on the table and extended his hands in a gesture that spoke volumes. "The only angry and discontent group is the Auldians who fear they will be deprived of their spoils."

The duke's eyes were veiled, but the way he fidgeted as he sat made it clear that the very same idea had already crossed his mind. The earl watched as the duke schooled his features and measured out his thoughts. "Assuming you are correct... and I by no means believe that can be the truth... the land distribution issue becomes paramount to securing the kingdom."

"Yes. Hence the map."

"Where do you want to start?"

"How many lordlings have you noted making comments or seeming disgruntled? I counted five main ones in Lord Uld's entourage."

The duke's grimace made the earl chuckle. It was good to note that his counterpart held the ridiculous thug with a title in the same low regard. "There are six actually that follow his lead. They are the primary ones stirring dissension."

"Then I suggest we proceed as follows. Peour, Eporue, Srat, Garp, Redelfa, and Namonuv are all cities with surrounding land that were lost during the battle, burned practically to the ground. But they are very well situated and have many natural resources and businesses that yet thrive there." The earl pointed these out on the map as the duke leaned in. "The families that held these cities were killed and have no direct descendants for their titles. We can bestow these upon the Auldian lords of the king's choosing with little to no ill will from Dravidian nobles."

"They are good choices, but we can't just give those six lords lands and leave the rest of the nobles, the ones that would actually deserve them, with nothing."

"I am not suggesting we give these lands to those fools! None of that!" The earl looked the duke straight in the eye. "We grant these titles to worthy Auldian lords. The king sends a message, you can't make me give you what you don't deserve. Not even a threat to my life will make me do what is not right. He shows himself fair and just, as a king should be, and fearless."

The duke sat back. He appeared to ponder the plan. After a prolonged silence, he rose and headed to his desk, picking up his com.

Dialing, he spoke to the person on the other line, "Sire, the Earl of Sarnac and I would like a moment of your time. We have a plan we feel is viable." The duke stood listening to whatever Amiel was responding. "Thank you, Sire." The duke clicked off the com and turned toward the earl. "Let's go see if the king will approve your plan."

Eldor wondered if this might be his opportunity to share with someone what he had gleaned from King Dekkyle's dying moments. *Can I trust this new would-be ally?*

"These lands have no direct descendants. They are good grants for your lords, Sire." Eldor pointed out on the map, going through the various business and natural resources of each region with King Amiel.

The Duke of Aul chimed in suggesting the names of the lords that had shown exceptional bravery and loyalty during the war.

"It is a good plan, Excellency." Amiel complimented. "It is doable, and I like the appropriateness of it. However, I will need to give Lord Uld some lands. He was instrumental in the Battle of Peour and almost lost his life. If it hadn't been for that young soldier that saved him. Do you remember his name, Figor?"

"I believe it was Sir Andross Draneg, Majesty. You knighted him for his bravery," the duke responded.

"Yes, that's right. Sir Andross. I have heard he has been doing very well as a knight."

"So, it would seem, Majesty."

"If you feel Lord Uld must have lands, may I suggest giving him Redelfa." Eldor wondered at the interest in this Sir Andross, but didn't wish to allow the focus to shift from the main issues. "It's a good size keep with fine orchards that lies very near to Aulden."

"But that leaves Count Pembra with nothing. He is a very important member of the Auldian court. I wouldn't wish to leave him out."

After a short silence, Eldor suggested, "I would be willing, Sire, to grant the city of Cartul and the surrounding river valley lands to Count Pembra. They are currently part of my holdings, but can easily be redistributed. My eldest daughter has the title of Countess at present. Perhaps if Count Pembra has an heir or is willing to marry her..."

The duke chimed in then. "The young Viscount is unwed. He is forty-two. How old is your daughter?"

"That will be excellent," the earl exclaimed. "Darlina is just turned thirty-five."

King Amiel held his eyes for a long time, a calculating gaze. Eldor grew a little uncomfortable under the scrutiny but refused to avert his eyes. He was unaccustomed to such treatment; after all, he had served as primary advisor for Dravidia since coming of age. Not to mention, he was sacrificing some of his best lands and his own daughter to appease the situation.

"That will do then," Amiel stated at last. "We will need to take Count Tor into custody today. The evidence we presently hold regarding the attempt links his house and we must take action."

"This attempt on your life, Sire, surely you—"

"The investigation will continue," Amiel cut him off. "I don't believe the House of Tor was necessarily involved. But we cannot simply ignore the information we have. My uncle, the Earl of Udeep, has been assigned, together with Sir Eriq, the task of finding out the truth. I'm confident they will get to the bottom of it."

"Of course."

"It would be wise if you would let them know ahead of time and perhaps the other nobles from Dravidia that will be attending the ceremony," the king suggested. "To avoid unpleasantness."

"I will take care of it, Sire."

Returning to his rooms, Eldor began to dress for the Allegiance Ceremony. He was pleased with the outcome of the conversation with Amiel. The new king clearly had good sense.

As he stood in his dressing room, the Earl of Sarnac had to admire the king's approach. It was clear from his interactions with both his liege and the duke they were aware the attempt had likely come from Auldians. Now it was just a matter of making it clear that the king would act with fairness, unafraid of his own nobles.

The sound of the servant's door opening made the earl turn. "Majesty!" Queen Verena, entering from such an unexpected place, took him aback. *Why is she going through the serv... of course, it's her way to get rid of the guards King Amiel posted on her.*

"Excellency, Amiel is planning something, but I don't know what. I need your counsel. Something horrible is going to happen. I just feel it. We must warn the others. Oh my Lord, I just don't know what to do! You were my father's most trusted advisor will you help me now?" Queen Verena paced his chamber, an anguished look on her beautiful face.

"Of course, Majesty. It has been an honor for me to serve the House of Dravidia. Please, sit down." The earl ushered her to a chair. He hastily buttoned up his formal shirt, heat invading his cheeks at being caught in such a state of undress by his queen.

"Don't worry about that, Excellency." Verena waved off his discomfort. "You must listen to what has happened. We must think what we are to do!"

"Of course, Majesty." Continuing to straighten his clothing, he took a seat opposite her.

"This morning, at breakfast, Amiel showed me some pictures taken on the rooftop where the shooter lay—"

"If I may, Majesty, I am aware of the situation."

"Wha... how?"

"Well, first I had a visit from the Duke of Aul, who shared the evidence with me. Later, we, the king, duke, and I, discussed the likelihood that the attack on King Amiel came from his own disgruntled lords—"

"Uld for sure!" The queen's emerald eyes filled with disgust. "I'm certain he had a hand in it all."

"I concur, and I think King Amiel would agree. However, there is no evidence implicating him at this time—"

"We must investigate for ourselves, Excellency. We cannot allow Amiel to railroad our Dravidian nobles when clearly they are innocent."

"I believe the king intends to continue investigating." The earl lifted both hands palm up noticing that Verena was about to interrupt him again. "Of course, I will put our best people on the job. Never fear, Majesty, we will get to the bottom of it."

"Good." The queen's eyes clouded over with concern. "We must warn the Tors and inform the other nobles. I don't know what Amiel meant by "appropriate action," but I know he will do something very soon. I would hate to have open warfare again."

"I have already taken the liberty of informing the Tors and high nobles. King Amiel let me know that he intends to have Count Tor taken in for questioning during the Allegiance Ceremony today."

A strange look came over the queen. Eldor realized that she might be taking offense at his discussions with the king behind her back. She was the ruler of Dravidia and he should have cleared his plans with her first. The earl berated himself for not having considered this slight to his sovereign earlier.

"Majesty, I want to apologize for not having come to you first on this—"

"I'm sure Amiel took you by surprise. I just wonder why he wouldn't just simply share with me his thoughts. Why leave me with this "appropriate action" line, yet go to you with the actual plan?"

"The king is used to making decisions on his own, without consulting anyone. He simply informed me because I am the person who could let the others know about it. I don't think he realizes that the betrothal agreement calls for the final decision on all matters to be in your hands, Majesty."

"Yes... well, I'm glad you've taken care of things." She rose to leave.

Rising with her, Eldor considered it wise to inform her about the land grants. His loyalty was to her and he would need to remember that she was now queen. It felt strange. She had abandoned them, caused a war. Yet, she was his sovereign and he had accepted her back. Her father would not have been pleased at the way she was being treated. Eldor would need to watch himself and ensure he was faithful to his true monarch. Though he didn't feel loyalty toward her. But supporting her would help keep Amiel in check.

"Majesty, if I may have one more moment of your time."

"Of course." She turned back to him. The look in her eyes remained sad and confused.

"I have developed, with the Duke of Aul, a plan to provide eight cities with accompanying lands for the Auldian lords of King Amiel's choosing to help bring peace with regard to the war situation."

"What of the families that presently hold these lands, Excellency?"

"The lands selected are currently without a direct descendant. The families that held them were without heirs and inheritance would pass to members far removed. I thought these would be the best to use for this. One of the cities is Cartul, which is within my holdings and I have ceded it to make this possible. It will be necessary for my daughter to marry Viscount Pembra, but I'm sure she will make the sacrifice."

She stared at him then, the same scrutinizing look King Amiel had given him. The earl focused on her eyes, hoping she would sense that she had his allegiance. Eldor chided himself again for the fault. She would be a good queen, he hoped.

"All is in hand then." She turned and left through the servant exit.

"I messed up, Rud!" The earl commented to his trusty valet hudroid, as the faithful servant helped him with his suit's coat.

CHAPTER 17
APPROPRIATE ACTION

VERENA MADE HER WAY through the dusty servants' passages. As a child, she would often sneak around the castle this way, especially when her mother or father would forbid her to go outside. Amiel had not thought to put guards in these halls. It gave Verena the opportunity to move about her home freely. On her way back from the earl's quarters, Verena made a quick stop in her former chambers. The furniture had been covered up and the bed divested of its linens. The queen went quickly to her former bathroom and dressing rooms. She stood before her vault. Drawing out the key she always carried with her, tears spilled down her cheeks.

"I think this necklace will look beautiful on you, my little kura," her mother's voice was clear and sweet in Verena's memory.

"Can I have a special closet, too, papa?" the young princess had begged her father as she'd sat cradled in his lap. She had looked from him to her mother who'd stood holding the beautiful pink rose necklace.

Verena had been seven and was to attend her first queen's Picnic Luncheon, where powerful ladies from around the kingdom were hosted in the rose gardens once a year. The queen would address those gathered concerning issues of specific interest to women. The ladies had the opportunity to share with their monarch their perspectives and suggest solutions. The royal family had met up in the queen's dressing room to select the jewels Verena was to wear from her mother's vault.

"Why, my sweet," her father had exclaimed giving her a squeeze. "You do not need one."

"I do, Papa." Verena looked up at him with her emerald eyes aglow at the thought of having her own vault. "I need it to hold all my treasures, like Mommy's."

Her father's laughter echoed in her thoughts and she could almost feel his strong arms around her again. Naturally, her vault had been installed the very next day. The first treasure to be housed there had been the rose necklace.

Now, Verena opened the vault. The beautiful piece, depicting six of the delicate pink blooms spaced out evenly on a silver chain, sat on its cushion. Each rose was exquisitely lacquered in glazed enamel extending from the orange-gold centers to the curved tips of the pink petals.

Next to it sat the papier-mâché bird Amiel had given her when she turned sixteen; mended as best as it could be after being crushed in the picnic basket. Verena's heart sank thinking of the loss of Helen during their crash landing on Earth. So much loss... her father, her mother, Helen... and of course, her people's confidence in her.

Even the Earl of Sarnac now seemed to feel Amiel had more right to rule than she. He'd gone straight to Amiel with his plans not bothering to include her. She had proved an uncaring shepherd and Amiel had shown himself strong. Could she win her people back? Could she earn the respect of the Earl of Sarnac, who'd been her father's strongest ally and advisor?

Shaking her head to clear away these depressing thoughts, Verena ran her fingers over the delicate gift and wondered why Amiel had changed so much. What had happened at the Duke of Aul's during his training to make him be as he was now? Did the strange necklace he wore have something to do with it? Or, was it his parents' assassination that had brought this angrier more violent Amiel out?

As her fingers caressed the gift, Verena recalled how Prince Oraum and Princess Hara had been ambushed en route to visit the Earl of Udeep by members of a militant Sehy group protesting the Principality's motion before the Intergalactic Council. Prince Oraum was claiming ownership of the Seinhy Atol off the coast of Aulden. The Sehy, a race of amphibious humanoids, claimed to be an independent nation. The fact that a sizeable deposit of honrol had been discovered there and that the Sehy refused mining activity gave the corporations across Thyrein's Galactic Wall reason to support the Principality's claim over the Sehy people. Princess Hara's gruesome disembowelment created outrage against the natives of Seinhy. Amiel, as the new Prince of Aulden, had been only fourteen. Verena remembered the stories she'd heard about how Amiel had all but exterminated the Sehy people, taken control of the Seinhy Atol, and established Aulden's control over the honrol mining there as a response to his parents' assassination.

The council had given him a reprimand, believing the violence he'd inflicted a result of grief and misguided youthful zeal. Could it be that this incident had tainted him so much as to change his character entirely? He had been such a great friend and so kind before. Or perhaps, he had always been this way and she had just been too young and naïve to notice.

With a heart-heavy sigh, the queen moved the jewelry trays aside, and reached for the weapons drawer. A squeak of joy echoed in the small chamber as she drew out her ginmra. Its silver-plated grip was etched with the star systems of Thyrein's Galactic Wall and crowned with an amethyst on its pommel. Thank goodness it had been found and placed back in here after her escape. Had it been her own father who had returned it? Only he had the duplicate key. She felt a tightening in her chest as she held the weapon.

After her mother's death, King Dekkyle had insisted she learn to defend herself. Eventually, Verena had graduated in skill to earn the use of her own personal ginmra. It was used only by the most elite forces in the intergalactic system; the cost and skill required being extremely prohibitive to an ordinary soldier.

The ginmra's pommel, like that of a sword, contained liquid honrol. Grasping it with her right hand firmly, she activated it with a single thought sent from the implanted node located at the junction of the frontal, parietal, and temporal lobes of her cerebrum. The metal alloy came forth solidifying into the shape of large garden shears. It gleamed a soft pink hue. Mentally shutting it off, the honrol disappeared back into the silver hilt.

Making her way to her room again, the queen thought about what she would wear for the Allegiance Ceremony. It had to be formal, yet flexible, and loose fitting enough that she could bear the weapon concealed on her person. Verena finally decided on a Coco Channel suit she had brought with her from Earth, light blue with comfortably tailored pants and a matching jacket. A white satin blouse with a collar tied into a bow completed the outfit.

"Deni, get food and lots of water for me. I need to energize in case I need to use my ginmra."

"Lord preserve us, Majesty!" Mrs. Denip bustled away to the kitchens to do Verena's bidding.

The throne room was full to capacity with the highest-ranking noble families. Each would step forward when called by the Lord Chamberlain to swear allegiance to the new king and queen. The lesser nobility and knights of the realm would swear as one afterwards. Presently, they watched the proceedings from one of the large drawing rooms via the holosets. The media companies from other planets had left, choosing to televise only the wedding and coronation. However, local Jornian media outlets would televise the Allegiance Ceremony to the whole planet.

Verena glanced around the room. Her stomach clenched as she took note of the Auldian guards positioned inconspicuously on the periphery of the space. Verena wondered at how yesterday their presence had given her a sense of relief, but now they filled her with foreboding.

The earl had informed her people about what was most likely to occur so the shock would be minimized and the reaction controlled. Dravidia would need to be cleared of the assassination attempt and she hoped the earl could help keep her people calm during the process.

Amiel guided her through the curtsying throng to the raised dais at the far end of the room. The banners of the aristocratic families of both nations hung from the ceiling. The pattern of their placement, as if they were on a map designating the seat of each noble house, created the shape of their continent. The spacing had been adjusted as now they ruled over a united Vidden. They took their seats on the silver thrones, the new symbol of their united kingdom stood out behind them on the purple backdrop and awning.

"Before we commence with the ceremony," Amiel's voice resonated across the cavernous room with authority thanks to the voice enhancer. "As you know there was an attack on the royal family yesterday. Thanks to the queen's perceptiveness and the quick actions of the Earl of Sarnac and of the Duke of Aul, no life was lost, though the earl suffered for his loyalty a slight wound. The investigation into this matter has only now begun. However, the preliminary evidence points to the House of Tor."

Forewarned the Dravidian nobility, for the most part, remained silent and calm. The Auldian nobles, Verena noticed, murmured among themselves, all but the small clique around Lord Uld. Verena's eyes locked with the young man's. His smirk and the insolence in his eyes struck her like a slap on the face. The queen smoothed her palms on her lap to keep herself serene.

"At this time, I am instructing the Lord Marshal to take Count Tor into custody for questioning," Amiel said the words in a matter-of-fact tone.

Verena was aware peripherally that he had turned to look at her. She looked to where the Earl of Sarnac stood by the Count of Tor. That nobleman's wrinkled face registering shock that he was truly to be arrested.

Sir Eriq Seller looked up at her, awaiting her confirmation of the action. Next to her, Verena noticed Amiel tense. Without glancing at her husband, Verena gave Sir Eriq a short bow of her head, indicating her consent with this course of action. The Lord High Marshal then strode to where the members of the House of Tor stood, the crowd parting for him. He was followed by two guards ready to assist him, if necessary. Verena's heart felt heavy as she looked at Count Tor's eyes. It was preposterous to detain an old gentleman. Her fists clenched in her lap.

Then she felt Amiel's palm. Verena looked down and saw his hand unfurling one of her fists and lacing their fingers together. Surprised, she looked at him. His crystal blue eyes wore a softened expression.

"My father has done nothing wrong." Jolyon's voice made Verena turn back to the unfolding scene. The Viscount had moved to stand in front of his father. The yellow marigold floral pin on his emerald green hat glittered in the light of the chandeliers. Coupled with the rest of his dandyish outfit, his stance appeared somewhat comical. "He is an old man. Please, arrest me if you must arrest someone. House Tor will stand trial. We have nothing to hide."

"Calm yourself, my son." The count placed his hand on his son's caped shoulder. Moving the young man out of the way so that he no longer blocked the Lord Marshal's access to his person, the count reassured him as best he could. "I may be old, but I am not frail. I will answer what questions they may have of me. Our name will be cleared soon enough and the true culprit brought to justice."

Verena sat straighter as she watched with pride how the count stepped forward with dignity. The Lord Marshal prepared to place the manacles around his wrists. Her whole body clenched at the indignity.

"That is unnecessary." Amiel's voice stayed the action. "He is being held for questioning. He is not being charged at this time."

The Count of Tor was escorted out of the throne room unshackled. The crowd of nobles whispered among themselves at the handling of the situation. Verena barely noticed them. She had turned to look at Amiel, surprise on her face at his words. The look in his eyes gave her pause. Something flickered there she could not identify. She wished she could read him, but he was truly an enigma.

The ceremony seemed to last a lifetime. Verena's back stiffened after hours of sitting in the same attitude on the throne. At long last, the final allegiance was sworn in unison, broadcasted from the drawing room through the holocom system.

As they exited into the hall and boarded the lift to the floor of their private chambers, Verena realized that through the entire event Amiel had held her hand. He held it still, their fingers laced together. It felt odd, the sudden realization of it. His touch reminded Verena of the gentleness with which he had made love to her, heat rising to her cheeks.

"So, now that I am queen and we are married, I expect to be able to move about my home freely," she stated as they entered the lift. "I was still locked in my rooms this morning. I fail to see the point of this now." She slid her hand from his as she spoke.

"Of course, I will see to it that the order is given. However, you will have guards protecting you while we find the true culprit." Before she could formulate her protest, Amiel continued. "The duke believes the attack was meant for me, but what if they decide to switch tactics and kill you? We don't really understand the full motivations behind the attempt. Please, allow me to be cautious and assure your safety. Even if you feel it an intrusion, it is only meant in your best interest."

How could she argue with that? He was right about not really knowing the motivations of the attackers.

"Very well," she conceded. "But I will go where I please. This is my home."

He nodded his head in ascent as they walked toward their bed-chamber doors.

"I will see you at dinner this evening," he said as they stood outside her room. "I need time to rest. That was the longest, most dreary, royal event I have ever had to endure." His lips twitched into a conspiratorial smile.

"I agree." Verena smiled back at him. "I thought it would never end."

"I noticed you fidgeted and slouched. I had never seen you do so before."

"I guess my time on Earth made me relax a little too much. I will be mindful of it. Thank you for bringing it to my attention."

"Yes, well, none of that can diminish how beautiful you look." He gave her a bow.

Once alone, she changed into some comfortable leggings and a loose fitting oversized shirt. Tucking her ginmra into her waistband holster behind her back, where she had housed it all day, Verena stepped back out into the corridor. Without a word to the guards, she headed back to the lift. They followed.

Castle Dravidia stood atop a foundation of honrol walls buried into the hard soil. The metal had been poured in a solid block. This special alloy, discovered on planet Gildenheld, had many unique attributes, among them its unbreakablility once hardened. Within this foundation, burrowed twenty stories deep below the ground, the one and only prison of the realm was housed. Growing up, Verena found the thought of prisoners living under the castle singularly disturbing. She had not visited often.

Each cell was no larger than six feet wide and eight feet long, furnished only with a small bed, toilet, shower-area and sink, all open and visible through the bars. When she first saw the tiny rooms, the young princess had been overcome by a sudden shortness of breath. Panic had gripped her. It had taken all of Verena's willpower not to flee, but the shame of such an action gave her the strength to continue the tour with her father.

No one had ever escaped the dungeon's walls and life within was as unpleasant as humanely possible. Verena felt downhearted as she thought of the count in such a dreary and demeaning place. She recalled the dance they had shared at her last birthday celebration. If she had but done her duty back then...

Arriving at the main control station on the first level through the only access point, the queen was surprised to see that the sentinels here were a mix of Dravidian and Auldian knights. Elsewhere, the castle was now manned by Auldians almost exclusively. It made sense, however, having the original guards with new Auldian members in this sector to ease the tensions between the two now joined nations. She hoped inwardly that this trend might spread and a peace be reached at last.

"I wish to see Count Tor." They hesitated a moment, looking at each other. "Did you not hear my command? Are you deaf?"

Mobilizing, two of the guards led her down to the fourth level oubliette where the count was being held. Entering the cramped prison cell, the queen fought off tears as she looked at the proud elderly gentleman living in such conditions. The feeling of guilt that now seemed her constant companion overwhelmed her. Her selfish act had brought this all about. How could she ever begin to make amends to her people?

At her entrance, the count rose from the bed and bowed to her.

"You may go," Verena commanded.

The guards looked at each other with nervous uncertainty.

"Close the door and leave!" The imperious tone moved them to action. Once she was alone with the count, Verena got right down to the heart of the matter. "I must know, how many signet rings do you have, sir? And are they all accounted for?"

"Signet rings, Majesty?"

"Yes, my Lord, signet rings. Quickly now, think, how many do you have and who has them?"

"My son and heir, the Viscount, has the one I presented to him on his knighting day, the one I used to wear when I was a Viscount." The nobleman's eyes clouded over. "I, of course, have mine, passed down to me by my father upon his death. And, there is the one that belonged to my late wife. It is smaller, more delicate. It should be housed in the vault of the countess's suite of rooms at Eagle's Nest, our manor house."

"And where is yours, my Lord?" Verena asked, noticing from her position sitting on the chilly and hard bed that his hands bore no rings at all. He had chosen to remain standing.

"May I?"

"Of course."

The count sat beside the queen, rubbing his hands together, massaging the joints of his fingers.

"I'm afraid old age is upon me, Majesty," the count said with a self-deprecating smile. "I suffer from jarith and my joints ache, often becoming quite swollen. I have not worn my ring for the past year. It should be in my personal vault."

Verena turned as she heard voices coming down the corridor. "Do not despair," she comforted the count, rising quickly. "We will clear your good name, sir. You have my word on that."

The door swung open. The Duke of Aul stood in the threshold. For a moment his mouth hung open, taken aback at the queen's presence.

"Majesty?" he said bowing to her respectfully. "I am surprised to find you here, ma'am."

Thinking quickly, Verena decided the old adage was right: the best defense is a good offense.

"What is your purpose here?"

"I... am... here to question the count, Majesty."

"I do not see his lawyer here," the queen commented, peering round him into the corridor and finding only guards, Auldians, with him. "You do, of course, invoke your right to have counsel present during any inquiry, do you not my Lord Count?"

"Absolutely." The nobleman followed his queen's lead.

"Your questions will need to wait until his attorney arrives," Verena spoke with firmness and looked straight into the duke's eyes, gracing him with her most condescending stare.

"He... is not under arrest... a lawyer is not necessary," the duke fumbled.

"Under Dravidian law, anyone brought in for questioning has a right to have council present. Has that changed? I am not aware of any legislative changes having been made."

"The king is waiting to speak to the count," the duke pressed. "I have been asked to bring him into the king's presence."

"Then let's not keep the king waiting."

The duke's pencil-thin eyebrows rose in surprise as Verena moved purposefully past him through the door, followed by the count.

Returning in uncomfortable silence to the first level, they passed the main station and turned right into the long corridor of interrogation rooms. Verena paused. With an imperious gesture of her hand, she allowed the duke to step past her to guide them to the room where the king awaited. The duke held the door at the far end of the corridor open for her.

"Rennie?" Amiel rose from the chair at the head of the rectangular, nondescript interrogation table. "What are you doing here? And what in the name of all that is holy are you wearing?" He approached her, his face a mix of surprise at her presence and irritation at her casual clothing.

"I am told you wish to question the count without giving him the benefit of counsel." Verena extended her hand for him to kiss, which he did automatically.

"He is not under arrest, Madam." The king's tone was back under control. He led her to the chair beside his. "We wish only to ask a few questions."

"I am not fully versed in the laws of Aulden, but in Dravidia anyone brought in for questioning, whether under arrest or simply for information, has the right to invoke the presence of counsel, which, by the way, the count has done. His lawyer must be present before any interrogation can be held."

She gazed purposefully into Amiel's eyes, a confident smile brightening her face.

"I see." Turning to the duke, who had remained standing in the threshold next to the count, the king commanded, "Have the count contact his lawyer and set up a time for the interview, then return him to his cell." Turning to her with a certain condescension in his tone, Amiel explained, "Of course, this means his lordship may end up spending more time in the prison than necessary. We could ask him our questions now, which would perhaps have him home sooner?"

"I think it best for us to follow the law," Verena responded firmly, but within she felt a twinge of uncertainty. What if he was right and she was causing the count unnecessary discomfort?

"If I may," the count's voice interrupted her thoughts.

"Of course," Amiel said magnanimously.

"I would feel more comfortable if I did have representation. Though I am innocent of all wrong doing in this matter, it is always best to rely on professionals to aid one in such moments."

"Yes," Amiel's tone held a slightly peevish note. To the Duke of Aul, he reiterated, "Your Grace, kindly handle the matter as dictated by law."

With a nod of acquiescence, the duke left to do as he was bid. The others followed, closing the door behind them. Alone with Amiel, Verena's confidence waned and she began to shift nervously in her seat. She turned her sights on the door.

"Well, I suppose I should head back to my room." Verena attempted to rise and make a hasty get away, but Amiel's hand on her wrist held her there. She looked at him again.

"I believe it will be prudent for you not to interfere in these matters in future."

"Under the betrothal agreement, I am queen and you have equal rights beside me as king, but I am queen. You need to realize that. You are my consort when it comes to Dravidia. If you had consulted me, I would have informed you about the need for a lawyer. I am Dravidia's ruler. You are my help mate."

The coldness in his eyes sent a shiver down her spine. He was angry. She felt the controlled ire vibrating between them, heating up the air molecules that separated them. For a moment, Verena tensed, fearing he might lash out and strike her. His hand lifted to his chest, his fingers rubbing the jewel Verena knew he wore. In her mind's eye, she could see its serpentine glow.

"If the Dravidians plotted to assassinate me, then the betrothal agreement is void, is it not?"

"It was not Dravidians and you know well it was not. You admitted as much after the ceremony."

"Did I?" His expression became derisive. "I agree the House of Tor might be framed, but that does not mean it couldn't be other Dravidians." He rose and gave her a mocking bow. "See you at dinner."

Rising, she walked to the door with as much aplomb as she could while his eyes bored holes in her back.

"Tell me, Amiel, who has control of Eagle's Nest, the Count of Tor's seat?" Verena threw the question over her shoulder as she exited.

CHAPTER 18

BETRAYAL

AMIEL SAT IN THE COUNCIL CHAMBER the next afternoon for the first session of the United Council of Peers. All of the nobles selected were present. Beside him, Verena sat rigidly, looking out into the chamber.

They'd barely spoken at dinner the night before. He'd stood in front of the door connecting his bedroom to hers, wanting to enter, to have her in his arms again. In the end, he'd turned and taken a cold shower. The final blow would be delivered now, and then, once it was done, he'd find a way to make the marriage work.

The king glanced around the circular room with its white marble floors and walls. The dais with the twin royal chairs sat at the far end of the room opposite the main entrance. Unlike the white-gold thrones, these were executive-styled seats in supple white leather.

The floor-to-ceiling stained-glass windows on the east side, depicting the great battles of Dravidia's origin, cast multi-colored shadows over the stainless honrol table in the middle. Amiel gazed at the bloody scenes of the war for independence, mirrored eerily on the reflective surfaces. His mind recalled the battles leading to this moment. He deserved to rule; she deserved to lose her power. After all, she'd abdicated her throne when she left. He was doing the right thing.

"Let us begin our meeting," the king announced, silencing the noblemen who'd been mingling around the chamber. They each took their newly assigned position at the table.

The Earl of Sarnac had worked with the Duke of Aul to decide on the members of the council. They had presented their list of names to Amiel who had approved them. A smile crossed his face as he recalled. Her own people came to him and worked with him now. They never once consulted her on who should be on the council. He glanced at her beside him. His hand rubbed the amulet tucked under his shirt.

Amiel leaned in and whispered in her ear. "You're fidgeting."

Verena's eyes met his. He could see the worry in them. *She's weak.*

"We would like to propose starting with a discussion of the land grant issues, Majesties," the Earl of Sarnac, who had remained Chief Peer, proposed.

Amiel had always admired the man. Figor hadn't liked the idea of not becoming Chief Peer. But the earl brought more to the title than Figor could ever hope to.

"I second the motion," Figor, Duke of Aul, affirmed.

"A more pressing matter first, ladies and gentlemen," Amiel countered. Verena turned to look at him, surprise and suspicion on her face. "Given the assassination attempt, should the betrothal agreement be honored?"

There was a collective gasp around the room. Amiel took in the guards he had ordered placed in the periphery of the chamber. If things unfolded poorly, he was ready to assert his power by force.

"Dravidia is not responsible for this attack," the Earl of Sarnac stated firmly, rising to address the king, queen, and other nobles. "While the evidence presently would point to the House of Tor, it is shaky at best. There is cause to doubt its validity, but that is a matter for a court of law. What is important is that the investigation has only begun. Choosing to void the betrothal agreement, to which we all accepted to be bound, would be precipitous and unwarranted."

"It is duly noted that the investigation is still on-going," the Duke of Aul countered. "However, the king may be in danger from Dravidian co-conspirators that remain anonymous. We should take measures to ensure his safety." Murmurs of ascent rose from the Auldian lords.

"Without accepting that the House of Tor is responsible for the attack, which I firmly believe they are not, there is no evidence to link anyone else to the aggression," Lady Soane stated. "Setting aside the betrothal agreement would be, at least in my mind, an act of war."

The great lady's statement was greeted by outcries on both sides of the table. Amiel's stomach tightened. Heat rose in him. The arrogance of the statement brought bile to his throat.

"War," Amiel paused, staring steadily at the lady. His voice silenced the room. "Rash words, Lady Soane. If the House of Tor committed treason, and there is evidence to that effect, how likely is it that they acted alone? Dravidia would have broken the oath to be bound by the agreement. Aulden would be in their rights to consider it forfeit."

"Majesty," the Earl of Sarnac spoke calmly. "It is understandable that you are upset by what has happened, especially as it would seem you were the intended victim. However, a decision as important as this should not be made on partial evidence. We should wait for the full results of the investigation."

"And in the meantime, our king's life could be at risk," Count Ydarb of Aulden exclaimed. "Traitors would wander about the castle free to attempt a second assassination, perhaps meeting with success."

The situation was becoming increasingly heated. Everyone was talking at once, with wild gesticulations. Amiel sat back, watching Verena through hooded eyes. He could see the emotions roiling in her. The move had taken her by surprise, but he'd basically told her what he planned after her interference with Tor. Had she not picked up on the hint? How could a woman of her intelligence be so naïve? Did she really think he would grant her power, after what she'd pulled? Her eyes found his. Those emerald gems flashed condescension at him.

"Yes, let's go back to war!" Verena's voice filled the chamber, sarcasm drenching every word.

Silence ensued. All eyes turned to the queen.

"Let's fight each other some more. Let's go back to the killing and the destroying. And, when the Gortive attack, what then?"

Soft murmurs spread as the lords and ladies considered her reminder of the reason the betrothal agreement had been accepted. *Nice move!* Finally, she was showing some fight in her. Too bad he had to crush her.

"The Gortive threat is beside the point," Amiel countered.

"It is very much—" Verena began.

"No, it's not. The point here is who will rule and under which conditions." Amiel leaned toward her, a smirk on his face. "In the betrothal agreement, King Dekkyle assured that the bulk of the decision-making authority would reside with you. This made sense at the time given the disparity in power of our respective nations. But the war changed that. Aulden won. We conquered Dravidia, which should have given me full command over both countries."

"Begging your Majesty's pardon, Dravidia never surrendered," the Earl of Sarnac put forth. "We accepted an end to the war when Queen Verena came because of your pledge to honor King Dekkyle's agreement."

"The earl is right. When I returned, we agreed to the original terms. Setting that aside is not warranted," Verena's voice quavered.

Weak. Amiel let his eyes show his thoughts. Who would follow a ruler like her? *No one.*

Amiel pressed his point. "On the contrary, Dravidia plotted to kill me. I am within my rights to set aside the betrothal terms and assert control as conqueror of these lands."

"Doing this, Majesty, will leave Dravidia with no peace treaty and send us back to open warfare," Lady Soane asserted, her blue-gray head shaking in sad consternation.

"At war, and at risk of annihilation by the Gortive when—" Verena tried once more to redirect them to the true enemy. *She had brains, too bad she lacked backbone.*

"Annihilation!" Amiel chuckled in derision. "Really, Rennie, you give the savages too much importance. We must be ready, certainly, for their attack, but they will be no match for us when the time comes."

"Amiel, this is not the way—"

"Enough," the single word reverberated through the chamber. "I am setting aside the betrothal agreement. I will rule as king and sole sovereign."

"This is unacceptable," the Earl of Sarnac strode confidently toward the royal couple. "Dravidia's queen is Verena and if need be, we will fight."

"There will be no more fighting, Excellency," Amiel countered. He flicked his wrist and an Auldian guard approached with handcuffs. "Verena, as my wife and queen, will have an important voice in the council. But I will be king with full powers and final say in all matters. You can accept this or be jailed for treason."

As the guard drew near, the earl retreated and pulled his ginmra from an underarm holster. Other nobles rose, readying for combat, on both sides of the table.

"Guards, take the queen to her rooms and keep her safe," Amiel ordered her escort.

He stood and drew his own weapon. Activating it with a single thought, he brought forth a mighty double-edged blade, a deep blue glow around it. He watched his guards drag a stunned Verena out of the chamber.

"Put down your weapons and accept my rule or be arrested for treason." Amiel heard himself speak the words with a finality that echoed in the chamber. *This was it. This was the moment it had all lead up to. He would have her and her kingdom.* "Lock the doors," he commanded the guards noticing Lady Soane had stood and headed toward the exit. "We settle this now."

The king's eyes locked with the Earl of Sarnac's, willing the man to understand the truth. He fought for a ruler who did not deserve his loyalty.

"Dravidians to war!" the earl's shout mobilized the combatants on both sides. Weapons clashed, sparks flashing as the Auldian guards and counselors fought the rebelling Dravidians.

For a moment, sadness filled Amiel. *How could this great man prefer her? Didn't he see this would be better?*

Then, Godar stood beside him. He'd changed to his nijar visage from the Viscount Pembra look he'd born moments ago. His dark blue robes covered him as he mumbled the incantations that had so often brought Amiel victory. The runes on his cloak glowed scarlet. The Dravidians began to falter. Guards cut down Lady Soane and Amiel watched her body slump across the table.

Several Dravidians tried to engage him, but the guards cut them off before they could reach the dais. Restlessness ran through Amiel's body. He needed to fight. He glanced around and found the Earl of Sarnac and several Dravidians cornered. A click and the sigh of the doors opening brought his attention to the other side of the chamber.

She stood there. Ginmra activated, a purple glow emanating from her weapon. *Verena!* The gloriousness of her, a warrior queen, stunned him.

"This way!" she yelled into the chamber.

The Dravidians held their ground. Two others beside Lady Sloane lay dead near the table. Ginmra weapons slashed the air; their various forms reflective of their wielders. Sparks of energy sprayed as weapons connected in the fray.

For a moment, time stood still. Beside him, Godar's cloak ceased to glow, startled by Verena's entry.

"Come," the earl's command rang out. "Our queen has shown the way."

Verena mobilized. Her weapon met with Figor's, who was closest to her. Amiel's heart pounded. He moved toward where the Duke of Aul fought his wife. Her attacks were ferocious. He was drawing back away from her, barely able to parry her onslaught. Pride swelled in him. Maybe she might prove worthy after all. Amiel's eyes met Figor's and motioned him to draw Verena in to the far end, where the king could take her. With an imperceptible nod, the duke began to move toward the back side corner. Amiel made his way there, ready to meet his wife in battle. A thrill ran through him.

"The gates, Majesty!" the earl called to Verena.

Amiel watched Verena shove Figor, sending the duke skidding across the floor. Then she turned and ran to where her people were now exiting. The fleeing Dravidians were fighting their way out to the inner bailey. But she turned in the hall. *Of course, the castle control tower would keep the gates shut unless she could reach it and let them flee.*

Amiel took the back door behind the dais and ran through the antechamber. He could circle around and intercept her at the tower walkway. He picked up his pace. His heart pounded. As he came near the turn, Amiel heard her breathing, a smile spread across his face. *He had her!*

She turned the corner and slammed into Amiel's wide chest. Verena stumbled back and almost fell. Reaching out and wrapping his arm around her, Amiel crushed her against him, keeping her on her feet. His hand grasped her ginmra wielding arm and twisted it behind her pinning her.

"Bastard!"

"Incorrect. My mother and father were lawfully wed when I was conceived!" He knew he was smirking, satisfaction filled him as he gazed down at the ire in those beautiful green eyes. She tried to wiggle away against him. He held her tight with some difficulty. Amiel had always marveled at the extra strength her ginmra gave her. Yet, she was no match for him. He felt her breasts on his chest and enjoyed the friction of her efforts. Lifting her off her feet into the air for a moment, he thrust his legs between hers, forcing her to return to the ground with feet outspread, just in case. *Wouldn't want her to resort to damaging my manhood.*

"You heartless monster!" Verena brought her free hand up to deliver a stinging slap to his face. He flinched. But she never connected. Verena stopped her hand inches from making contact and let it drop. *His mind wondered why, but he shrugged it off.*

"We could have ruled together with unity and peace," her voice quavered. "This was so... so..."

"Necessary."

"Ruthless. A cruel waste of human life..."

"Couldn't be helped," Amiel drew his face close to hers. "If you had not run away, if I had not conquered your kingdom, yes we could have had peace and a co-rule. But that is not the case now. If I want to stay alive, I must give my people the spoils they deserve. There's no reason not to, really."

Verena straightened as much as she could, being that she was still held captive in his strong and unyielding arms.

"Let me save them," Verena pleaded, unwanted tears flooding her eyes. "Let me open the gates. Maybe there might still be hope for us. If they all die," his queen announced between shuddering sobs that now ran through her body, her voice breaking. "I will leave. Somehow, some way! I shall not be bound to a murderous tyrant."

Heat filled Amiel. The hand around her waist clenched into a fist. His stomach roiled as the bile rose in his throat. *Run. That was all she knew how to do. There would be no leaving. She belonged to him and would be his for the rest of her life.*

He twisted her away from him, pressing his finger into her wrist, taking the ginmra. It shut off instantly. Verena cried out in pain, stumbling, trying to keep her balance. Her knees hit the floor, but he yanked on her arm to bring her to her feet again. With a vice-like grip, he lugged her after him to the control room.

"Out!" Amiel ordered the operators and guards.

They rushed past, tossing their monarchs speculative glances as they emptied from the room. The screen showed the inner bailey. That open-air space held the last of the Dravidian nobles, fighting against his Auldian guards. The portcullis gate remained closed behind them. They were pinned. Amiel noticed Sir Eriq and his Dravidian knights were not on site. Storing the information away, Amiel turned to Verena.

"Now then," he released his hold of her and walked to the controls. She shook, her back pressed against the wall. "If you want them to live, you will make a statement to the nation agreeing to take me as ruler of Dravidia. You will apologize, on behalf of your people, for the plot against me, order them to surrender and accept me as their sovereign."

At the control panel, Amiel readied the system to receive the video footage. He plugged in his personal com device and aimed the camera lens at her. "And, Verena, if you leave me, rest assured I will not hesitate to hunt down and kill every last man, woman, and child of Dravidian noble ancestry."

The carnage on the screens gave his threat credence. Verena swayed, her eyes glued to the monitors showing her trapped people. He watched the struggle on her face as she made her decision.

"Fine." Her voice was a whisper.

A thrill of pleasure ran through him at her surrender. Taking his handkerchief from his pocket, Amiel wiped her face clean of the blood splatter and tears. She stood there. He could see the ginmra effects on her. He would need to ask Godar about this. It couldn't be healthy for her to undergo such extreme side effects when using the weapon.

"It is what has to be." He let his eyes take in her face. She had slid a mask of indifference now, but he could see her pain beneath it. "You cannot have believed I would let you rule after all that has happened?"

Turning back to the com, he clicked the button. Her face filled the screens, the signal breaking into the major networks automatically.

"Beloved subjects of my kingdom." Verena began her speech. "The king has set aside the betrothal agreement. The assassination attempt is believed to have been orchestrated by Dravidians. As such, the agreement is null and void."

The bailey was still now, as everyone listened to the broadcast. Amiel noted the consternation on their faces. He spied Uncle Sabred in the entry way to the castle, standing next to Sir Eriq. Neither had participated except to bar the entrance. For a moment, Amiel wondered what Sabred would say to all this. His uncle was one of the few people he trusted and admired completely. He'd been proud of him for the marriage. *Would he still be proud of him?*

"I hereby formally accept Amiel ra Aulden as sole ruler of Dravidia," Verena said, pausing to steady her voice, which had begun to quaver. "While the terms may not be those of my father, together, the king and I, will secure our borders against the Gortive and rule our united lands. I urge all of you to accept this change and move forward together as one kingdom. Let us not fall back into war, but unite and rebuild. I may not have always done the right thing, but I promise, I am doing it now."

Amiel switched off the transmission. It was done. The kingdom was his.

"Open the portcullis for them," Verena said. "I have done what you asked."

He punched in the code. Returning his gaze to her, he noticed she desperately fought the ginmra effects. She was losing that battle as well.

"You need to lie down."

He tried to grab her, but she forced herself harder against the wall. Her eyes glued to the monitors.

"I... will hate you... to the day... I die."

Her body swayed. Amiel moved quickly to catch her before she could hit the floor. With Verena passed out in his arms, he watched as the defeated Dravidians left the bailey.

His gaze fell upon her sleeping features. He'd won. He would be sole ruler. Her face as she told him she would welcome making love nightly filled his mind. His heart beat quickened.

Then the last words she spoke to him rang in his head:

I will hate you 'til the day I die.

Maybe... Amiel's mind swirled with pain... *I actually lost.*

CHAPTER 19
PICKING UP THE PIECES

VERENA RAN. Her bare feet stumbled through the brush. Tree branches snatched at her thin pink nightgown, ripping it to shreds about her body. The bite of broken twigs brought jolts of pain as her feet propelled her onward over the rough terrain. *Where am I going? Why am I running? Where are my shoes and why don't I have on proper clothes?* The questions raced across her mind. Stopping, she gazed up at the towering mountains of the Vidia range. They were the sentinels protecting the castle on its northern flank.

Protecting? She thought derisively. Amiel had taken it and her whole kingdom. *No protection here!*

The cold stone against her nearly nude body made the climb ever more uncomfortable. The slope slanted gently but the ragged edges of the rock face cut even deeper gashes into her already bloodied feet. Her smooth palms bled as well. The strips of nightgown constantly caused her footholds to slip. Reaching up to lift herself along the mountain's side, Verena wondered why it was so difficult. The ascent to the Grotto of the Prophets had never been this steep before. *In fact, where is the nice trail that leads there? Why didn't I just follow that?*

Scuttling over the edge, Verena stood on the flat top. The precipice loomed before her, the roar of the waterfall gushing from the grotto's mouth filled her ears. The waters pummeled the boulders as they crashed down into the crimson flow of the Evongo River. It would be so easy to just let herself fall over the edge. She had handed him her kingdom, what good was she as a ruler? Running away was all she seemed good at. Wasn't that what she was doing now? The weight of her immense failure crushed down upon her chest.

A majestic five-foot-tall Geldian eagle landed on the craggy point of the rock face opposite her, its head level with hers. Golden eyes looked at her quizzically over its hooked beak. As the great bird took her in, its look turned stern, damning her for the weakling she was. A throaty cry pierced the still air, as the bird of prey flapped its golden wings. Sharp talons cut into the hard rock face of its perch. It flapped and cried out and gashed at the rock while its eyes locked with hers. A fierceness gleamed there.

"Fight! Fight! Fight!"

Wait, is it talking to me? The realization that she was dreaming dawned. *Of course, it was a dream; it had to be. The terrain was all wrong.* The grotto's waterfall was not this steep, and it fed the purple waters of the Tarsus, not the red flow of the Evongo. And the Geldian eagles would not travel this far north.

The sound of the beating wings snapped her attention to the mighty bird of prey. It thrust itself upward, for a second heading straight toward her, then veering off and disappearing. Her eyes focused on the long slashes and clefts its colossal talons had left behind, marring the once smooth stone.

The ginmra sleep was upon her. The events in the council chamber, her speech, her people leaving the outer bailey in defeat, returned to her. *How long have I slept?* A ginmra made most people weak and the faint that followed lasted a short while, but not her. From the first, her use led to days, even months, of coma-like slumber. It had scared her father and the royal physician, but the Master Rajin Lord Horsef had not been alarmed. He kept her father from having the node removed from her brain.

I can't be out for that long; not this time. No! No! I must wake up! Amiel would have complete control of the kingdom. He would assert his power while she just lay there, immobilized. A black fog whirled around her. Darkness filled her vision.

Wake up! She screamed the words in her mind. *Wake up!* How much time had passed since the events in the Council of Peers?

No! Her heart was pounding now, the rapid beat rushing blood through her system.

Wake up! She willed herself to open her eyes. The lids refused to budge.

What can I do? How can I awaken myself? How long has he been in control now? Oh God! No!

Tears spilled down her cheeks. The impotence of her situation pressed into her consciousness.

Okay. Breathe. Just... just breathe. Concentrate. Verena focused her mind. If she could get her arms to reach out and grab hold of the night stand, she could pull herself over the bed's edge and might wake up.

Her breathing steadied; her mind cleared. She thought she could hear Amiel's voice. *Is that Deni responding? No, it could be the pull of another dream. Concentrate.* She commanded her arms to move, lift up, *r-e-a-c-h.*

They were lead weights at her side. *Come on! R-e-a-c-h!* The pull of peaceful rest beckoned at the periphery of her awareness.

What's the use? He was probably already creating new laws. Reorganizing her lands to his personal liking. How many of her people would be dispossessed of their inheritance? How many would die for their loyalty to her pathetic rule?

R-e-a-c-h! L-i-f-t! She commanded her defiant body.

A burst of intense pain shot through her, then another. *What's happening?* Slowly she felt her body responding. Verena focused on her arms. She could feel the softness of the satin sheets on her skin, the hardness of the night stand's edge. *Yes! Yes! Come on!*

Another burst of pain. Verena's eyes flashed open. She focused them on the ornately carved edge of her night table. One of her hands was gripping it so fiercely, her knuckles were white. Relaxing her hold, she pulled herself up into a sitting position against the cushioned headboard of her bed.

"You're awake!" Amiel's voice assaulted her ears.

"Water."

"Of course." She watched him rise from the reading nook chair and cross over to her. He wore the same clothes she had last seen him in. The dark blue suit pants and baby blue satin shirt. The coat was gone, as was his elegantly tied cravat. The shirt was open and his bare chest bore the gem. Its blood color glinted in the dimness of the bedchamber as it swung from his neck when he poured the water.

"Thank you." Verena gulped down the refreshing liquid. "More."

He refilled her glass, settling himself on the edge of her bed this time as he handed it to her. She drank with smaller sips. Deni approached from the bathroom. She held a wet towel in her hands.

"You... you're awake!" her mouth hung open in awe. "Why I never...

the shortest you've ever been out has been four days, Majesty."

"I was motivated." She smiled at her own response, truth though it was.

"We've summoned Dr. Koll," Amiel informed her.

Verena shifted her gaze back to him. Her body was beginning to relax, cuddled by the warm pillows. Drowsiness blurred her vision, threatening to take her back into the sweet darkness. She had to move. Walking would make her wake more fully.

She grabbed a fist full of the purple damask bedspread and sheets. Thrusting them off her body, she slung her legs over the side of the bed. The movement kicked Amiel on the side and he slid away from her, giving her more room. Too bad she didn't have the strength to cause him any real pain.

Sitting upright, Verena swayed with the onslaught of a dizzy spell. Holding the edge of the bed to steady herself, she focused her mind again, willing herself to remain alert. Another blast of pain shot through her body and she cried out. Amiel's hand reached out to help her. She felt his palm on her back.

"Don't touch me!" Verena thrust herself onto her feet. She wobbled until she reached the wall and used its strength to steady herself. Planting her bare feet firmly into the plush carpet, she twirled to face him, her back supported by the wall.

"You're still very weak. Come lie down again, before you hurt yourself, Rennie." His tone, as if he were speaking to a child, grated on her nerves.

"I'm fine," she said, raising her chin defiantly. Smoothing her white cotton nightgown that reached only to her knees, Verena glanced around.

She decided the best place to sit would be one of the straight back chairs near the window and doors that led to the balcony. They were there mostly for decoration. *Definitely uncomfortable and hard, they will keep me awake. No risk of falling back into sleep there.* Verena straightened. Clearing her mind, she focused on walking. One foot in front of the other, carefully, with increased steadiness, she managed to make it to the chair and settle into it. Amiel followed her. *Damn him! Why didn't he just go away?*

"I'd like to be alone."

"I'm not leaving you."

"Why? So, you can gloat at how well your Machiavellian schemes have worked?" Verena enjoyed the flinch her cutting tone elicited on his impassive face.

"Makia what?"

"Machiavelli." She enlightened him with as much condescension as she could muster in her present state. "The Earthian writer of The Prince? That great piece of literature has clearly become your personal handbook."

"By your tone, I'm guessing this 'prince' is not a very nice fellow." Amiel's face lit up with a smile.

God how I wish I could slap it off you!

"As it happens, Rennie, I just want to make sure you're all right." The smile disappeared. "Contrary to what you might think, I actually do care about your wellbeing."

A heavy silence filled the room. She stared into his eyes, shocked at his uncharacteristic confession. Was he looking at her with actual caring? What game was he playing now?

"Majesties, Dr. Koll is here," the Duke of Aul's voice broke their staring contest. The duke ushered the doctor in and left the room, closing the door behind him.

"Majesties." Dr. Koll curtsied as she entered, then headed straight to Verena. "This is astounding! You are awake!"

"Yes, a real miracle." Verena regretted the snide remark the moment it was out. Dr. Koll had been her physician from the moment of her birth. She was a very caring and excellent doctor. "I'm sorry... I... have a horrid headache."

"No need, Majesty." Dr. Koll set her bag down.

Retrieving a camriner ring from it, she hooked it up to the holopad in her hand. The screen lit up and the doctor inputted her password. When the home screen came on, she opened up the camriner's software. Expanding it, she placed the ring around Verena's head like a crown and turned the sensitive instrument on.

Verena heard the hum as it scanned her brain, sending the images to the doctor's holopad. Amiel sat across from her on the arm of the nearest chair. He actually did look concerned, though she wasn't buying his "I care about you" act. If he cared, would he senselessly kill people? No, this was just another ploy. Cold–Hot–Cold, that little game of his designed to throw her off balance.

The Geldian eagle's cry from her dream echoed now in her mind: *Fight! Fight! Fight!*

"What..." Verena shifted her attention once more to Dr. Koll, who was shaking her gray-speckled head in consternation.

"What is it?" *Oh, no, do I have some horrid tumor in there?*

"Oh... ah..." The doctor glanced at Amiel furtively. Verena saw something cross Dr. Koll's eyes, a sudden guarded expression. "Everything is in order. I would like to run some further tests. Perhaps your Majesty might come to the clinic so I can just make sure everything is as it should be? Tomorrow morning... fasting so we can get blood work as well."

"Did you note something wrong? Should she go now?" Amiel looked at the doctor with what seemed like genuine worry.

"No. All is well. But in the morning would be best so that we can get fasting blood samples." Dr. Koll gave Amiel a stern look.

"Why would you exclaim that way if everything—" Amiel's irritation augmented when the doctor cut him off.

"Well, I expected damage. The queen awoke too soon, not in her usual long sleep, so I was surprised." The doctor smiled placidly at Amiel.

"Then all is well?"

"Yes, but her Majesty needs to be at the clinic early so we may conduct the tests. See to it she is there promptly."

Verena watched as Amiel digested the doctor's command. He didn't like being told what to do, but objecting would go counter to the game he was currently engaged in to convince people he cared about her. The clink of porcelain disturbed the tension. The tray of delicious smelling food shook slightly in Mrs. Denip's hands. The faithful nurse had scurried away when Verena awoke and was now bringing much-needed sustenance.

"For Pegot's sake, Deni, put that tray down before you spill its contents," Verena snapped, unnerved by the tension and the tinkling sound of the porcelain plates.

"Yes, Majesty," Mrs. Denip placed the tray on the nearby desk.

Silence returned. Verena's stomach grumbled, reminding her of the need for some food.

"I'm hungry."

"Here, Majesty." Mrs. Denip hastened to pull the small lap table over and place the tray of steaming victuals before her.

"Thank you, Dr. Koll," Amiel dismissed the physician. Settling himself back on the chair in front of Verena, he commanded, "Show the doctor out please, Denip."

"I would like to further examine the queen, Majesty," Dr. Koll spoke with as much authority as her position of court physician afforded her. "And I may need to prescribe medication to help her Majesty—"

"How do you feel?" Amiel was looking at Verena. "Do you want the doctor to prescribe something?"

"Perhaps to let you sleep, Majesty," Dr. Koll chimed in. "Your body needs to repair from the ginmra use."

"No!" Verena's vehemence took all of them aback, shock registering on their faces. "I do not need to sleep. I'm fine now, thank you, doctor. You may go."

"But..." Seeing the determined look on the queen's face, Dr. Koll retrieved her instruments, collected her bag, and bowed out of the room.

"Thank you, Denip." The dismissal was clear as Amiel turned to the nurse, who remained by Verena's side.

"The queen may need help—"

"She has me."

"Yes, of course," Mrs. Denip's tone reflected her lack of trust in his ability to keep her charge safe.

Verena couldn't help the smile that stole across her lips at Deni's disapproving air as she left them. Verena ate ravenously the savory steak, cooked to a perfect medium rare, and the steamed vegetables fresh from the castle's gardens. She was keenly aware of Amiel's presence and of the smothering silence of the room.

"I suppose I should have known you'd fight, my little Rennie," he commented. "I remember your battle with—"

"Where are the rajin?"

"You don't know?"

"No," Recalling the strange man with the glowing runes on his cloak, she asked, "Was it a rajin in the council chamber yesterday... today... how long have I been out?"

"Four hours, and, no, he isn't a rajin."

"Where are the rajin?" Verena asked once more, wondering what the cloaked figure was if not one of the masters.

"I don't think this is the best time to discuss the battles of the war."

"Why?" Verena let each word drip with sarcasm. "Too ashamed of your deeds, are you?"

"No. I'm not ashamed of anything I've done." Amiel gazed calmly into her eyes. "Ruling requires ruthlessness. You have a soft heart, Rennie, but you're gonna have to toughen up a bit."

"Ruling requires justice and honor," she spat at him. "Not the killing of innocents to allow the greedy to plunder at will. And I'll thank you to stop using that nickname."

"I'm sorry these necessary actions hurt you." Amiel's eyes remained cool, as if her concerns over the rightness of his choices were completely unfounded. "More pain will be inevitable, but everything will be all right in the end. Why may I not call you Rennie? If memory serves, I gave you the nickname a long time ago."

"That was when we were friends and had real feelings for each other."

"I have real feelings for you still."

She stared at her now empty plate. "What's your game?" Her bluntness surprised them both. "You don't really expect me to believe that you're in love with me? Do you? Not after all that has transpired?"

"Eventually, I believe you will realize that what I have done I have had to do," Amiel's voice held itself in check, but his irritation was evident. Crossing his arms, he continued, "Why would I marry you when you returned? There was no need for this marriage, Rennie."

"You had to marry me to bring the nations together."

"You are so naïve." His derisive chuckle echoed in her ears. "I had your nation crushed and conquered. From Castle Dravidia, I could have turned and launched a final battle against your father's remaining forces before they even knew of his passing. I had no need for marrying you, angering my nobles with the betrothal agreement, risking my life—"

"So, you admit the assassination attempt was an Auldian plot against you, not Dravidian!"

"You're missing the point."

"You may have fought many battles and maybe you fought very well, but deep inside Amiel ra Aulden you are a coward!"

Lowering his arms, he placed clenched fists on his thighs. Had his eyes been implanted with lasers, they would have cut her down.

"Coward?" His voice was soft, controlled, the rage held in check.

"You married me to ensure my people would follow you and you betrayed us out of fear for your life. Do you really think that your nobles are gonna respect you, now? They know you fear them. They have seen you give in to them. They will rebel before you know it."

The words spewed out heedlessly. She could see his ire rising. His face reddened and the blood vessel at his temple throbbed. He lunged at her. Grasping the small table, he sent it flying across the room. The porcelain smashed into pieces as the dishes hit the wall. Verena retreated as far into the chair as she could, which was unfortunately not at all. The back was too straight and she found herself face-to-face with him. Her breathing was coming fast and her heart was beating as if it was about to jump out of her chest.

"Are you going to beat me now?" She forced herself to smile at him. Her anger replacing her fear, she continued, "That's how you show you love someone, of course."

His nostrils flared and his lips tightened. In her periphery, she could see the muscles of his arms constrict as his grip on her hapless chair intensified. The red gem swung from his neck, glowing. The fire in its depths swirling. Taking the jewel in her hands she yanked it off his neck and threw it against the wall. It landed, unharmed, amidst the debris of what had been her tableware. Verena wasn't sure why she had done it. But a strange feeling of satisfaction filled her.

"What the hest!" Amiel straightened, rubbing his injured neck with one hand.

"Oh, I'm sorry, are you the only one allowed to throw things around?"

Amiel stilled. He looked toward the mess he had made and burst out laughing.

"I don't find this amusing," Verena's voice came out in a pout.

He laughed on, doubling over now and slapping his thigh with the hand not soothing his neck. *The bastard is laughing at me.* The tension left her body, the weakness of the ginmra effect returned, making her limbs feel heavy. An overwhelming misery covered her. The righteous indignation that had made her strong only moments ago was gone. The urge to cry consumed her and she found herself sobbing inconsolably. Sliding off the chair, she rocked herself on her knees and cried.

"Rennie." The name was spoken in her ear as his arms surrounded her and he lifted her onto his lap, holding her close. "Don't cry, please don't cry."

"I don't understand..." The words gushed out between shudders. "I just don't understand..." Hot tears soaked into his shirt where she burrowed her face. "I hate you... I wish I could go home... I want to go home..." The whine in her voice stung her as she struggled desperately to stop herself from this unseemly demise of all dignity.

"You are home." His words hit her like a slap in the face.

Verena pulled away from him, crawling on the carpet they both sat upon. The realization that she was stuck here... forever... with him iced her veins. They sat there looking at each other. Time stretched.

"We are together in this," he echoed her thoughts. "You are my wife. I am your husband. We have to find a way to move forward from here, together."

"How?"

"Good question." He smiled at her then. "I'm not entirely sure." He shrugged his shoulders. "You should rest. It has been a difficult day."

"Yes."

He rose to his feet and extended his hands to help her. She pushed herself up off the carpet without his assistance. But her knees buckled and she ended up with his arm around her waist, leading her back to her bed.

All the fight left her, and the drained feeling was back with a vengeance. He tucked her in and she curled up, away from him. He padded around the room. The sound of broken crockery and the clank of the jewel being picked up told her he was not leaving it behind. *Too bad, the opportunity to have it go missing would have been nice.* The door to his room opened and shut quietly. At last, she was alone.

The tension in her muscles relaxed. Warmth surrounded her. Sleep called her back. She needed rest, but what if she didn't stir again for a long time. The languid feeling of her body told her she was on the verge of returning to her slumber. She had to do something.

The dojo. She'd not practiced her *katas* in a long while. The exercise and precise concentration of the routines would spur her body to resist whatever residual effects the ginmra might yet be having on her. Rising, she dressed for the workout and headed to the castle's indoor training arena.

CHAPTER 20

HOPE RENEWED

THE WEEK FOLLOWING AMIEL'S COUP D'ÉTAT went by like torture. The earl and a large number of nobles declared war. Amiel mobilized a contingent of soldiers to fight them. They knew their lands well. Engaging in guerrilla attacks, the Dravidians kept Amiel's men on the defensive and unsuccessful. She'd stayed in her rooms, trying to reach out to them, hoping to put an end to this new conflict. But her entireties went without reply.

Now, rising from her vanity, Verena picked up her riding crop. Garbed in the traditional Dravidian winter riding gear, she headed out. She needed fresh air. A ride in the forest would help her think, she hoped.

At the door of her chamber she met her new armed escort. She had slaughtered the others to get back into the Council of Peers chamber. She decided not to even acknowledge their presence. This was her home, and she would go where she pleased.

Verena made her way to the inner bailey, with them in tow. She glanced about the open space before the gates that lead from the castle. To the left were the stables. Many young men were busy there, but none of the grooms were familiar. They all bore Auldian livery. Catching one of the younger ones staring at her, she waved him over.

"M... m... Majesty," he stuttered, gazing at her with open admiration.

"What's your name?" she asked him kindly.

"I... my name... wel... I am Venik, ma'am."

"Venik, you will be my personal groom from now on." Verena struggled to keep her face from breaking into a smile at the bemused and excited look on the boy's face. "Fetch my horse. The animal, none of the AI vehicles. Her name is Gusmas. Tack her up for me. Oh, and be quick about it," she added when he remained there gaping at her.

"Yes, Majesty." He dashed off to the stables.

Verena meandered about the space. Evidence of the battle that had transpired here had been diligently washed away. An ache in her chest pressed upon her the great tragedy of that day. One that had begun with hope for a new future, had ended in division and strife.

Verena noticed the open stares of the bailey's occupants. Mustering her composure, she smiled warmly at each as she passed them, which made them quickly rise and show their respect. They bowed and curtsied and their eyes followed her as she continued her trek through the yard.

"And what exactly do you think you are doing?" Amiel whispered in her ear.

Startled, she spun around, having been completely unaware of his approach.

"Amiel," she recovered quickly. She'd assiduously avoided him, locking the connecting door of their chambers and taking all her meals alone in hers. "Why I'm going for a ride, of course."

"It is too dangerous."

"Nonsense, I have my guards to protect me."

"No," Amiel's voice was steel.

"The surveillance around the castle extends to the edge of the forest, and I won't go too far from the walls."

"There might be... danger... you could be kidnapped."

"You can come with me if you like? If you're afraid I'll run away, you should remember I gave my word I would remain." She challenged, standing her ground.

"It is better for you to remain indoors."

"I need the fresh air and the exercise. I will be fine. Would they attack if you were with me?"

"Fine. I will go with you if you absolutely must go."

Turning he led the way back to where Venik had brought out her saddled mare. Before long Amiel's slick black destrier stood alongside her gold-toned palfrey. They made their way through the inner courtyard and then the outer bailey's portcullis to the Oldey Forest, accompanied by their respective retinue of heavily armed guards.

Verena took in deep breaths of the crisp winter air. The leafless trees with their snow-covered limbs hardly moved in the late afternoon breeze. The crunch of her horse's hooves in the crystalline snow that blanketed the forest soothed Verena. It had been a long time since she had indulged in her most favorite activity.

"How about a little race?" Amiel's suggestion brought her back from her reverie.

"A race! If I recall correctly, I beat you the last time." Verena looked at him askance. "Are you sure you want to risk another loss?"

It felt odd talking as if not a thing had happened. Yet... what else could she do but try to get a handle on this situation.

"For your information, I let you win." He grinned smugly at her.

"Foluc!"

"I cannot believe a proper young woman like you would use such language," he pronounced with feigned disbelief.

"Please, you taught me most of the curse words I know."

"I would never do such a thing, Madam."

"Right." She shook her head, the sun glinting fire sparks off her auburn hair. "Where shall we race to?"

"We are about four miles from Lake Oey." He calculated stilling his horse. "We could go from that boulder there to the shore of the lake."

"You're on." Verena turned her mare in the direction he spoke of.

"Whoa, before we start, we should decide on a prize for the winner."

"Prize?"

"Of course, the winner has to have a prize."

They were silent a moment. The wisps of steam from their beast's breaths and the nervous pawing of their hooves on the ground surrounded them.

"A story," Amiel asserted.

"A story?"

"Yes." He explained, "the winner can demand the loser tell them something about their lives."

"A true story?"

"Yes."

"Okay."

Verena began the count. "One, two—" spurring her horse into a gallop, she shouted behind her, "Go!"

"Cheater!" He exclaimed.

The chilling wind of the day's end approaching slashed her face as her trusty mare rushed them toward victory. Her senses heightened, as branches reached out to sling her from her seat, Verena ducked just in the nick of time. A fallen log lay in her path. She lifted herself from her saddle. Balanced on her stirrups, she felt Gusmas lift her front hooves.

Shifting her weight expertly, she stayed astride her horse as the palfrey jumped the obstacle cleanly.

Verena became aware of Amiel's horse just at her rear. The pounding of hooves and the rush of air was exhilarating. As she hurled over yet another log, Verena lost herself in the moment. A squeal of delight bubbled out of her mouth.

The sound of their guards mounts seemed distant. They would need to stay close yet not interfere with the race. Verena didn't envy them the careful balance they had to keep. Near enough to protect, but giving them enough space for privacy.

A gasp of shock escaped Verena, when Amiel's horse came up neck and neck to hers. He rode hard. She rode harder. Loosening the reigns, Verena gave Gusmas her head. The quick-footed mare took flight, leaving Amiel's heavier war destrier behind. Then he was catching her up again. *Oh, no he isn't gonna win this!*

Veering slightly to the right, Verena went off the trail and over the boulders. She caught a glimpse of surprise on his face before he was lost from her view by the thick mounds of rock. The smooth surface of the stone and the gaps between them made this path treacherous. She had to slow, loathe to risk injury to her faithful palfrey. Then she hit the ground once more and spurred Gusmas back into a gallop. Verena had gambled on the slightly shorter path.

And she won! Arriving just seconds to the shore before his horse lurched out from the trail.

"Ha! You lose Amiel ra Aulden!"

"So, it would seem, cheater!"

"Cheater?"

"That's what I call it when you take off before the other rider and then choose a short cut."

"Sore loser," Verena accused him, laughing.

"Foluc."

"Oh, oh, who's using foul language now?"

Amiel dismounted. Coming toward her, he lifted his arms to help her do the same. Allowing him, she was aware of the strength of his grip on her waist and the purely masculine scent of him. Placing her hands on his shoulders, she noticed he had not buttoned up his shirt. It fell open, his dark chest hair visible.

His arms held her for a longer time than absolutely necessary. His blue gaze locked with her emerald eyes. Then, he released her turning to her horse. She liked this Amiel, the one not killing anyone, but whose eyes lit up with mirth. The one she used to consider a friend. While he took care of Gusmas, Verena walked over to her favorite boulder. It jutted out over the lake and was perfect for dipping your feet in the cool waters.

Tugging off her boots and rolling up the tight riding pants, Verena allowed her legs to dangle. A shiver at the coldness of the water ran through her, but she splashed them idly until her skin acclimated to the temperature. Amiel sat beside her. He too had taken off his boots and was enjoying the lake.

"So, I won." She gave him a shove when he groaned in protest. "And you have to tell me a true story."

"What do you want me to tell you?"

Verena considered the possibility of asking him the story behind the jewel he wore, though it wasn't on him now, she noticed. Then a better idea struck her. Maybe she could make him remember when he was different. When he was a nicer, better person. Then again, what if she discovered he had never been who she thought? It was worth the risk. Like it or not, she was stuck married to him. She had to find a way to make this situation work, for her and for her people. She'd already failed them too many times. She wouldn't do so again.

"Tell me the story of your favorite birthday."

"My favorite birthday." He looked at her quizzically. "They were never like yours."

"Obviously." She rolled her eyes exaggeratedly. "You mean you never got to wear beautiful gowns and dance all night?" She tipped her head and flashed him a cheeky smile.

"My favorite birthday moment was when you got stuck in that tree behind the palace."

"What?"

"You remember, you were what, eight, at the time." He grinned at her sheepishly. "I was sitting in the tree, at the highest branch possible, when you arrived. You wanted me to come down, but I challenged you to join me. Then up you went and we sat there for a while, eating the biscuits I had stolen from the kitchens."

"You ogre!" She gave him a shove on the shoulder, and he busted out laughing.

"It's not my fault you could never resist a challenge." He turned with his hands palm up as if he were so innocent. "I told you if you did it, you'd get stuck, and then..."

"How can you laugh about getting an innocent little girl stuck on a tree branch?"

His laughter echoed in the clearing.

"You looked so... it was hilarious."

"I didn't find it one bit funny."

"Well, you wouldn't, would you?" His mirth subsided.

"What happened to you?" Verena asked, staring into his eyes, so open and warm, the Amiel she remembered from her youth.

"I grew up." He stood. Briskly putting on his boots, he admonished her, "so should you. You act like this is a fairy tale, but it's real life. A war was fought. Men need to feel there was a purpose. You talk about justice and honor like you think we're living in some fantasy world."

"Justice and honor have a place in the real world, Amiel. You could have given your nobles land and wealth and cities to govern without destroying the peace we had forged. The earl's plan was perfect. You didn't betray your word because you're grown up, you did it because you were afraid—"

"Silence!" Amiel clenched his fists at his side. "What do you know? Your solution to tough realities is to run away!" He turned, as if to fetch the horses.

"Yes, I ran. But that's the past. We have—"

"Why?" He turned back toward her. His eyes were hooded, unreadable. "Why did you run?"

"I was scared."

"Of what?"

"Of you."

Shock registered on his face. He shook his head with disbelief. "Why? We have known each other since forever. How am I scary?"

Verena looked down at her hands in her lap. "You beat people when you're angry."

She found herself suddenly on her feet, his arms tight around her.

His eyes stared into hers as he said, "I will never hurt you. Never! Don't you know that?"

"No, Amiel, I don't. I was told... about that pro..." She couldn't finish. Feeling suddenly foolish talking to him about castle gossip, Verena averted her eyes. "And I saw you beat Helen, and your groom, and others." She tried to push herself out of his arms, but he tightened his grip on her. "And even a few days ago, you almost hit me as I sat there."

"You are not a servant. You are not a whore." Her eyes snapped back to his, surprised at the admission that what the ladies of the court had said could actually be true. "Yes, I know what is being said about me. You are a royal princess, and I didn't even come close to hitting you. I smashed dishes instead."

"And what happens when smashing dishes isn't enough?" She dared to stare into his eyes. All the warmth left them. They were as glacial as the winter mountain air that had already begun to descend upon them. A chill went through her.

Releasing her, he turned to where the horses awaited. She put her boots back on and made her way back to her mare.

"I will never hurt you. No matter how angry I may be, you are my wife, my help mate, and my friend."

The ding of his com device sounded. Drawing it from his pocket, Amiel glanced at the incoming message. Verena waited by her mare.

"I have to go back," he said, his tone matter-of-fact. Lifting her unto her horse, he instructed the guards, "Stay with the queen. See to it she is safely returned to the castle."

Turning, Amiel mounted quickly and gave his destrier his head, plowing headlong back into the forest. Verena followed at a slower pace. Her mind reeling from the conversation. He had all but admitted that the story she'd heard the ladies tell was true. Her stomach clenched at the thought of all that it implied. That he had been with others was one thing, but whores! Would he still visit bordellos now that she and he... this line of thinking was grossing her out and served no purpose, she chided herself.

Her mind focused on the last thing he had said instead. He had called her his friend. Somehow, they had to find a way to heal the nation. Amiel said she had to grow up. He was right, she did have to start thinking as a queen. What did she have to do now to—

She was snapped out of her reverie when a loud crack rent the stillness of the forest. A rotted branch from an old judas tree splintered and came crashing down, missing Verena by only inches. Gusmas startled and reared up on her hind legs. As the queen struggled to control her horse, the frightened animal took off in a wild gallop.

Verena held on tight. She could hear the guards galloping to catch up and rescue her. As the mare jumped over another fallen log that lay in its path, Verena tightened her grip and closed her eyes. *Not the wisest move*, she berated herself.

Seconds later, she felt a hand pull on her horses' reins. The frightened animal slowed. She opened her eyes expecting to see one of the guards. Instead she found herself looking up into a pair of emerald eyes and a ruggedly handsome face framed by thick curly blond hair. His ebony skin was smooth, with a slight hint of a stubble on his square jaw. For a moment she was breathless. *He is beautiful.*

"Thank you for saving my life. I thought for sure Gusmas would throw me." Verena's voice quivered from the fright of the wild ride. Recovering herself and taking the reins back from him, she said, "May I ask your name, sir?"

"Of course, my Queen," the handsome stranger responded with a deep sexy voice. "I am Sir Andross Draneg, your Majesty's most humble servant."

"How did you know I was the queen, Sir Andross?"

"The royal purple of your saddle pad with the royal seal of Dravidia on it, Majesty," he responded with a flirty smile.

"Well, that makes sense." She giggled like the silly school girl she had never actually been. *Keep your composure!* She scolded herself. Verena brought her mare to a halt.

As he drew on the reins to bring his brown rouncey to a stop, she noticed that his attire, though of good quality cloth and mail, showed considerable wear. It didn't seem to fit him all that well either. Perhaps he had bought it used?

"Stay away from the queen!" One of the guards shouted as he drew up to where they'd stopped their horses. Verena noticed he'd drawn his solun, aiming the silver barrel at her rescuer.

"Put away your weapon! No need to shoot this brave man," Verena commanded. "This knight has saved my life."

The Auldian guards took position around them tightly. Verena turned her attention to Sir Andross once more.

"So, where do you come from, Sir Andross?" Verena asked.

"Originally, I am from the small town of Dran on the banks of Lake Uld," he explained. "Since the war, I have been roaming your beautiful kingdom in search of work."

"How is that?" she asked confused. "You are a knight. Do you not have your own lands? Are you not attached to a noble house? How came you to be a roaming mercenary?"

"I was not born of a noble house, Majesty," Sir Andross explained. "I was knighted after the Battle of Eporue. Before that I was a farmer's son. When war broke, I enlisted as a foot soldier for Lord Uld. He was killed at Eporue. I saved his son's life, so your Lord husband dubbed me and gave me a reward purse. The new Lord Uld would not allow me to enter his service, so I look for work now where I can."

"And what work do you find these days, Sir Knight?"

"Well, not a lot, I must confess, but I do what I can to help. Some of the more remote farms and towns have been victimized by soldiers. War is not a pleasant business. I have found myself defending some of these."

"Can't imagine they pay very well?" Verena smiled at the earnestness in his eyes. He clearly liked the idea of being these small towns' savior.

"Well, no, but they feed me and shelter me so I consider it all an even trade." He flashed her a captivating smile.

Verena smiled back. "Well, Sir Knight," Verena said, getting Gusmas going once more. "You must join us this evening in the castle. Perhaps, we might be able to offer you better, or at least, more consistent work there."

"I would be deeply honored to serve you, Majesty, and the king." He had turned and kept his horse in a steady pace with hers.

"Excellent."

CHAPTER 21

SIR ANDROSS DRANEB

THE SCENT OF CHLORINE BLEACH AND VINEGAR filled the inner bailey of the castle. The pungent scent assaulted Sir Andross's nostrils as he rode in behind the queen. The king stood at the top landing as Sir Andross dismounted. The queen beckoned and Sir Andross approached. She led the way up the stairs to where the king stood.

"I was about to send a search party. I shouldn't have left you out there." The king addressed Queen Verena, concern in his eyes.

"As it happens, Gusmas was spooked and this knight saved me. That is why we are late returning." The queen turned toward Sir Andross.

"I believe I know you, sir?" the king commented as Sir Andross bowed to him.

"Yes, Sire," the knight responded, amazed that the king remembered him. "You knighted me at the Battle of Eporue."

"That's right!" the king exclaimed. "I recall your valor on that occasion, sir. How is it you no longer serve the House of Uld?"

"The new Lord Uld let me go," Sir Andross responded with what he hoped was a tone of indifference, though the slight had injured his pride. "He gave no reason."

"You are welcome to remain and serve here, Sir Andross," the king offered. "Indeed, you have already done me the greatest of services. The life of my beloved wife is priceless and no amount of reward could begin to recompense you."

"Thank you, Sire." Sir Andross was overcome with gladness. He had never wanted a mercenary's life, and service to the castle was the greatest honor he could ever aspire to.

The king drew forth his com. "I am sending a message now to the

Lord Marshal. You will find him in the east wing's guard offices. He shall take care of you and get you situated."

"Thank you, Sire."

"So what was so urgent you had to return right away?" Sir Andross heard the queen ask as he made his way into the castle in search of the guard office.

Having never been at Dravidia Castle before, Sir Andross had some difficulty in finding it. He was distracted by the object d'art he saw as he passed through the great marble halls that opened up to the elegantly appointed suites and salons. His university studies had been in husbandry and agriculture, in preparation for taking on his father's modest farm, but he knew a thing or two about the great masters. Dravidia's royal family had been known as collectors of the finest art.

Not wanting to be late meeting with the Lord Marshal, Andross found a lovely maid who, after a brief flirtation, was kind enough to guide him there personally. At last, he finally stood in the presence of the legendary Sir Eriq Seller, Lord High Marshal of Dravidia.

Andross was taken aback that the legendary hero had been allowed to stay as head of the Royal Guards. Of course, when peace was forged, the Lord Marshal had no doubt sworn fealty to the new king and queen. Andross had read about this exemplary knights' exploits during the Tribal Uprising. He had aided the Earl of Sarnac and King Dekkyle in bringing the desert tribes back into line.

"Well, now, let's have a look at you," Sir Eriq said, turning from the desk strewn with papers.

"Sir Eriq, I'm—"

"I know who you are, son. You sure took your time getting here. Did you get lost?"

Embarrassment spread upon Sir Andross's cheeks. He could feel the heat of it on his face. "I—"

"No, no worries." Sir Eriq waved a dismissing hand. "It's easy to get lost in this vast place. I've been asked to assign you to the queen's guard. You will begin tomorrow. For now, you will go with Tel here who will get you properly outfitted." Sir Eriq approached Sir Andross, who had remained standing in the middle of the office. "I will keep a close watch on you. If my queen comes to any harm by your hand, you will answer to me, boy. Do I make myself clear?"

Swallowing down the lump in his throat, Sir Andross managed to speak firmly, though his knees quaked a bit. "I would have wanted to serve in a different position, Sir. Perhaps—"

"The order came from the king."

"He does me a great honor. I won't fai—"

"See to it that you don't. We are all one united realm now, or trying to be. So, make sure my queen is safe."

"Yes, sir."

"Tel," Sir Eriq turned to the young Dravidian who clearly served as his orderly. "Get him dressed and housed."

Without further word, the Lord Marshal went back to the papers he had been looking over. It was then that Sir Andross realized there was another man in the room. Tall and lanky, he bore functional, though clearly expensive, honrol armor with a crest emblazoned on it.

It was the Earl of Udeep's crest. Sir Andross had been enthralled as a youth by the tales of the legendary knight and dragon slayer. Now, he recalled that often Sir Eriq worked with Lord Sabred. Was this why the Lord High Marshal had retained his position? His friendship to the Earl of Udeep was well known.

As Sir Andross filed out of the room in Tel's wake, he caught the words, spoken in a reedy voice, of the warrior's conversation with Sir Eriq.

Lord Sabred commented, "That kind of ammunition is not easy to get. The report shows the markings..."

The door closed and Sir Andross had to follow Tel. He wished he could have overheard more. *Why am I being saddled with guarding the queen?* Sir Eriq's insinuation that the queen would be in danger under his protection irked him. It stood to reason the Dravidian would object to Auldian guards for the queen. But Sir Andross would show this valiant warrior that he was worthy of his trust. Though guarding a royal was not his idea of a proper knight's job. He felt honored the king had chosen him.

The next morning, he presented himself before the queen. She sat in what he had learned was the garden room. He found her ensconced on the bench that looked out over the rose flower beds.

"Well, Sir Andross, seems you are to be our guardian from now on." Her emerald eyes sparkled with mirth. *By the Great I Am, she is a beauty!* Sir Andross had long held a crush on Verena. Her picture and all her goings on were often on magazine covers and media shows.

"It will be my pleasure," he said to her now, bowing respectfully in his new castle armor.

She was surrounded by Auldian ladies. He wasn't sure of their names, but he recognized a few like the Countess of Udeep and Lady Ydarb. He wondered what had become of the ladies who'd waited on her previously, but really one set of hens was just as good as another.

Hours ticked by. He stood around, watching the queen, listening to the empty conversations of the ladies that accompanied her. They sat twittering about the new fashion styles. Sir Andross thought he might as well just throw himself off the nearest rampart.

"Well, ladies," Verena rose from her seat, "as you know, I do love to have some quiet reading time. I will see you all again at dinner."

The gathering of ladies got to their feet and curtsied as the queen made her way to the door. Taking his cue from the other three guards, he followed Verena along the hall to the library tower. Upon entering, she went straight to the node boxes. Settling in on the couch near a window, she was soon lost in the digital display only her eyes could see. Her delicate hands danced in the air as she surfed the quantum net. Her brow furrowed slightly as her eyes darted across the information visible only to her.

Sir Andross stood by a column, mimicking the other guards. His thoughts wandered to the queen's exquisitely shaped mouth, so rosy pink; the sweet fragrance of her perfume, which flitted through the air at him. He wished more than anything in the world that he could be Amiel ra Aulden just for one night.

Winter's end drew near and the snows were beginning their melt. The ground was mushy and moist as their horse's clopped along. The other three guards kept their normal, respectful distance, while he and the queen rode side-by-side. She had insisted he chat with her as she took her daily morning ride.

At first, he had been flattered and glad. But after a while, his fellow guards where showing their resentment of his preferential treatment. Still, he couldn't exactly refuse, could he? She was the Queen, after all. And he was a knight, a station above that of royal elite guard.

"So, Sir Andross," the queen asked, as they rode through the forest. "What do you enjoy doing on your free time?"

"That can't be of interest to you, Majesty," Sir Andross said, amazed she would even care.

"Why wouldn't it be?"

"Well... You're a queen. What a lowly knight does on his spare time can't be that interesting."

"Well, it is. So, tell me." He liked that tone of her voice. The playful note, sweet and yet bossy at the same time.

"If you truly want to know, I am writing a book."

"Really!"

"Yes. I don't know that it will ever be published mind you, but I enjoy doing it." He shrugged his shoulders.

"What is it about?"

"Back in Dran, there lives an elderly lady, we always called her Old Glessa, and she used to tell us about legends and folktales, usually designed to scare little kids into good behavior." He smiled reminiscing of those days.

"No doubt. And now, you are retelling them then?"

"Yes. Some. Others I came across as I traveled your country."

"Is that so?" The queen turned a curious glance at him. "Tell me one of those."

"Hmm." Sir Andross dug around in his mind for a good one to tell the beautiful queen. "There's the one that involves your family... well, your ancestor."

"Oh!"

"Long ago, Princess Nuri, of the House of Drav, was given in marriage to Cliek Elvig of the Fragma desert tribe. Larenos the Great, her father and King of Dravidia at the time, felt the union would help cement the loyalties of the desert people. The Fragma are one of the most powerful of the tribes."

"Ah, yes," the queen said, drawing up Gusmas as they came to the shore of Lake Oey. Dismounting, she commented, "Indeed, Nuri is remembered as one of the most heroic female warriors of her time."

"That is so." Sir Andross tended to the horses. Joining his queen as she sat on a boulder near the water's edge, he continued, "The situation she faced, when she first wed, however, was not at all positive. The Fragma people resented her, and the cliek was not exactly a very loving husband."

Sir Andross paused, realizing that the situation her ancestor faced might be hitting a little too close to home for the queen. She had averted her face, but the tension in her shoulders and body indicated the similarity was not lost on her.

"Perhaps the tale of the building of the rajin monastery of Sanctal would be better."

"Another day." She turned and looked at him. Her emerald eyes held something Sir Andross found difficult to define. "I want to hear Nuri's tale. Finish her story, Sir Andross."

"So, there she was. Lonely and facing a hard time winning over her new people. Then, she remembered that her mother had given her the Shrang LaRoo."

"Shrang LaRoo? What is that?"

"Oh, Majesty, why that is a special golden liquid, created by the Master Rajin Lord Shrang LaRoo. The power in them, well, it's of mythical proportions."

The look on the queen's face made him stop once more.

"Tell me, Sir Knight, what does this legend say those mythical liquids do?"

"Well, Princess Nuri, guided by the Master Rajin Lord Horsef the Great himself, accessed their power and was able to change, it is said, a single moment in time, the moment when she first met Elvig. For, not realizing that she would be his bride, she had insulted the click upon first meeting him, and so earned herself his animosity."

"That's it."

"Yes, well, I plan to embellish the tale a bit, of course, but—"

"Sir Andross, if the liquids can turn back time, then how is it that anyone would know what the original situation had been, if she went back and changed it?"

Sir Andross looked out across the lake. The waterline was already rising. The marker that denoted the level showed the slight increase. As the rainy season drew neigh, the flooding would begin. He focused his mind on this, rather than on the feeling of embarrassment at the queen's obvious contempt for his ridiculous enthusiasm over an absurd tale.

"You are correct, of course, Majesty." He struggled to keep a light tone. "The hour grows late. Perhaps we should return."

"Yes, we should. The Council of Peers meeting is coming up."

They remounted and headed back in an awkward silence. He knew he shouldn't be hurt that she had called him on the obvious problem with his story. After all, it was rather evident. But it smarted anyway.

"Sir Andross." The queen's voice snapped him back. "You said that the princess had to get the help of the rajin to use the liquid. Why couldn't she just access it herself?"

"There are many flaws in these stories aren't there, Majesty."

"No. I don't think that's a flaw. I mean it might make perfect sense. The rajin have incredible powers. Perhaps only one of them can use the liquid."

"The tale doesn't indicate that," Sir Andross said, taken aback by the keen interest in who could work the mythological liquid. "What the legend says, at least how I heard it tell, is that the liquid responds only to the female bloodline of the House of Drav, but a rajin is needed to help create the... I don't know... link?"

"Ah." The queen smiled at him then, such a beautiful smile that Sir Andross had a sudden difficulty breathing. "Well, that makes sense. I wonder what such liquids would really do?"

"Time travel seems to be out," he managed with a smile.

"I think so, but it is an intriguing thought, isn't it?"

"There are several times in my life I wouldn't mind going back and changing." He gave a wistful sigh.

"I know what I would change in mine." It was said with such a tone of pain, he didn't know how to respond.

Hoping to turn her thoughts to something happier, he said, "I came up with a poem for the tale."

"Really!" She smiled again. "I want to hear it."

"I'm not sure it's particularly good..." he trailed off, self-conscious.

"Don't make me command you to read it, Sir Knight." Those emerald eyes gazed at him.

"If you insist." He dug in his saddle bag's pocket for his miniholopad. Accessing the file in question, he cleared his throat.

> "Golden flow
> Shimmers,
> Within silver constellations
> Encased.
> Liquid elixir

Turning,
Solid disc
Firming.
Red flow
Seeps,
Life's essence
Drips.
Within Eternity's dimension
Awestruck standing
Before mighty presence.
Power, Love, Justice,
Wisdom pours out
New beginnings
Golden flow."

Sir Andross concluded his poem.

"Sir Andross," Verena said with a smile, "I do believe you will make a very good writer."

"Did you know, Majesty," Lady Ydarb said in a feigned whisper, though he could hear her well enough from way across the sitting room. "Sir Andross once saved the life of a young woman who was about to be violated by some ruffians."

"I don't doubt it for a second." The queen's response thrilled him. "He is a valiant and honorable gentleman."

"Indeed, he is, though why we are discussing a guard is beyond me," Lady Den said.

Sir Andross couldn't stand the old biddy. Her false piety disgusted him. He knew for a fact that she kept a young lover, yet went to temple daily for prayer and meditation. As if spending a couple hours in a church each day could wipe away her filth.

"Well, I am glad to hear of his exploits," his queen said. "Sir Andross."

"Yes, Majesty," he responded approaching the group of ladies.

"It would seem there are a lot of stories about you and the good deeds you have been doing since you were knighted."

"I have tried to be worthy of the title bestowed on me by my king."

"And so you have, Sir Andross," the Countess of Udeep spoke up. She was always the more serious of them. Perhaps because her husband was Lord Sabred, the mighty dragon slayer. She should help the queen more, he thought. "I know the king and queen are proud to have you here protecting them."

"Thank you, your Excellency." He bowed deeply, returning to his post.

"So, Majesty." The countess turned the conversation. "What preparations shall we make for the Wauger Festival?"

"Hmm, I hadn't given it much thought," the queen responded.

With the ladies' attention on the frivolities surrounding the celebration of the start of the rainy season, Sir Andross was blessedly off the hook. Surely, the king could have found him something more exciting to do than stand around listening to women's talk. Sir Andross knew just the rampart he could jump from.

CHAPTER 22

TRUCE

VERENA SAT ENSCONCED in her favorite alcove of the library. She searched the databases of Aulden's royal history, glad to get away from the new ladies that had been foisted upon her. Amiel had apparently ordered the codes to the holonet and to the castle changed shortly after the betrayal, for that is how Verena thought of the battle in the Council of Peers chamber.

A smile wreathed Verena's face as she logged in with her master password and initiated her search. He wouldn't be able to keep her out; her father had made sure no one could by creating the master code.

Curled up on the cushioned purple satin sofa, Verena tucked her feet within the folds of the long and voluminous canary yellow skirt. The matching chenille sweater hugged her form displaying her bosom without being overly low-cut. This was one outfit Amiel had approved of when he had nearly collided with her as she turned the corner toward the library wing.

"You look stunning."

"Thank you." She had tried to maneuver past him, but he had stepped purposely into her path. "Yes?" she had queried, gazing up at him.

"I suppose I will see you again in the Council of Peers chamber." There was a slight note of irritation in his comment.

"Of course, I will be there." She had pushed past him and swept down the hall as quickly as she could. He had tried to keep her from the meetings by changing their schedule, but Verena kept close tabs on this and showed up every time. She was queen and she would have her say, even if they didn't like hearing the truth.

Now, as she uncurled herself from her seat, Verena dreaded the possible confrontation. Stretching, she massaged her aching limbs. After having spent a good three hours searching for a reference to the gem that Amiel wore, she was no closer to learning its provenance or anything about it. The persistent feeling that something just was not right about the jewel, made her determined to investigate. Every piece of jewelry, whether owned by the crown or personal property of the individual queen or king of Dravidia, was registered in their royal archives. The Principality of Aulden, however, did not keep as careful records.

Realizing she was running late, Verena rushed through the hall toward the lift, followed by her guards. Sir Andross had been among them for the past four weeks. She liked this Auldian knight. He was so naïve and earnest. It was refreshing. She smiled at him as they all got in and headed to the Council of Peers chamber floor. Entering the room, Verena's heart sank as she laid eyes on Lord Uld's sneering face.

Taking her seat, Verena noticed that Amiel had dark circles about his eyes. He had clearly not slept well these weeks. Actually, neither had she. At first, she had fought sleep, fearing the ginmra effects might yet take over. When she was sure the likelihood of a deep slumber had passed, she found herself plagued with the thought that Amiel might come to her bedchamber.

After the violent events of his betrayal, and in spite of the pleasant, often flirty attitude he took with her, Verena felt it was unlikely he would pursue intimacy. But she lay tormenting herself as to how she should respond, what she should say, if he did come. Night after night, he hadn't come. The fact she had felt disappointed brought on a whole other realm of introspection. Of course, he might have tried only to find the door locked.

She'd made sure it stayed that way, though a few times, when she'd checked it, the bolt was open. *Had he ordered it or had it simply been a servant passing through leaving it unlocked?* That she cared brought such mixed feelings, Verena shrugged the thoughts away.

"We have word from our reconnaissance senords. The holoimages they sent back show the group of Dravidian rebels have set up a base using the caves of the Perthiark Mountains," the Duke of Aul informed the council. He was now Chief Peer in the earl's place.

Verena's heart ached thinking of the Earl of Sarnac and the others who still fought on for her. She'd sent word to the houses of her realm to accept, for now, the situation. Most crucial had been Soane as they controlled the banking city of Anco. Many had chosen to follow the Earl of Sarnac instead and fight a guerilla war against the invaders. She couldn't blame them for not trusting her judgment, but it hurt to think of them in these circumstances.

"If you give me a contingent of soldiers, Sire, I will go in there and slaughter them for you," Lord Uld declared. Verena's distaste for him was hard for her to hide. He looked at her now with impudence and animosity.

"The caves of the Perthiark are a sinuous and complex system," Verena spoke with secure confidence. All the council members turned to look at her surprised. "Any attempt to attack them while they are in those caverns would be disastrous."

"What does a woman know of war," Lord Uld spat out insolently.

His comment amused the younger members who'd been added. They seemed to be the cohort of nobles that accompanied Lord Uld everywhere. Verena was pleased to note that the older nobles gave the younger ones disapproving looks.

"I am Dravidian," Verena's voice was firm and clear. "I know my lands." Turning to look Amiel in the eyes, she asserted, "If you want your soldiers to be massacred by all means follow Lord Uld's plan. However, if you truly desire a resolution, why don't you send messengers and meet with their leadership to work out mutually beneficial terms?"

All eyes shifted to the king. Verena kept her gaze on him. Something flickered in his eyes; then his look became glacial. She saw his hand reach for the gem he bore beneath his white linen shirt. This was something he did often, she'd noted, and it never boded well.

"We will not have our soldiers rummaging around in caves, Lord Uld," he spoke, a slow audacious smile spreading across his lips. "We shall seal the caves up. Blow the entrances and let them rot there."

Unable to stop herself, Verena flinched as though he had delivered a physical blow. *Was he truly so inhumane, so cruel?* She knew by the gleam in his eyes that he was enjoying her distaste for his proposal and she berated herself for her weakness in letting her emotions show. She had to learn to rule her countenance better.

"Wasteful," she retorted, controlling her tone with difficulty.

She clicked on the control panel of her chair's arm. An image appeared in the holosite over the center of the council table. Holographic video started rolling.

"This was taken by satellite 2-14 over the continent of Parthia's Thospar Valley. As you can see the Gortive tribes, all four, are present here," Verena took joy in zooming in closer so there could be no mistake about what they were witnessing. Next, she focused in on a Gortive male bearing the black and red markings of a Parthos Chieftain on his green scaled skin. "Meet Lorgarn, Chief of the Parthos people. What you see here is the marriage celebration between himself and the Vankihi princess, Alerin. He has forged alliances with the leaders of the Onglopol and Mendganac tribes, but the Vankihi, the strongest of the four, had resisted his bid to unite, until now." Smiling, her words dripping with sugared sarcasm, Verena concluded. "When we are attacked by Lorgarn, and make no mistake about it he is uniting them against us, will we not need all the experienced fighters possible to defend our nation? Or will you be able to train the farmers, merchants, business-men, and other common folk in time?"

The tension in the room was profound. The Auldian counselors who had been present when Amiel executed his coup d'état turned from the damning evidence before their eyes to look at their king. Verena con-tinued to stare into Amiel's eyes, peripherally aware of their audience. He leaned over in his chair so that their faces where merely inches apart.

"Well done," it was a whisper. Only she heard the words and a blush of pride stole across her cheeks. Then she berated herself. She shouldn't care for his approval. He moved away from her then.

"Use the aen worms," he said to the others. "Flush the Dravidians out of the caves and into the Valley of Garpeth. There we can surround them and force a surrender."

"Aen worms?" she had no clue what those were.

"Beautiful carnivorous creatures," Amiel smiled cruelly.

"Waste of men," she said derisively.

"Perhaps," Amiel said. "But not all will die, certainly none of mine. We will still be able to count with some of yours after their surrender."

"You could count with all of them if you sent a messenger and brokered a truce instead," she pressed her point.

"Where is the fun in that?" It was delivered with such flippancy; a shudder ran down her spine.

Could he really be so callous to care so little for the lives of brave men? Many had their families with them, women, children, elderly. It was shocking, but only served to reconfirm in her mind what she had known of him since she'd been sixteen; he was a monster.

"We can release the worms on the southern side," the Duke of Aul suggested as he changed the image, replacing her evidence with a holo-map of Dravidia. He zoomed in on the caves the senord had indicated were the rebels' hideout.

"I thought the point of the marriage was to put an end to the bloodshed and unite against the true enemy," Verena tried again to bring reason to bear. "We have allowed misdirection, a poorly conducted investigation, and wanton desire for the humiliation of others to leave us weakened and divided. The betrayal perpetrated here, in this very room, drove these men to arms once more. If we send an emissary to treat with them, they will return. The Dravidians that remained have been treated well since that debacle. It could serve to show a new kingdom worth defending is here for them. We can have a united Vidden as was the plan from the start."

"Lord Uld, how many aen will we need to do the job?" Amiel asked, as if Verena had not spoken. The younger lords snickered, enjoying crushing the nation that had long overshadowed them. Verena was only slightly comforted to note the elder nobles did not engage in this conduct.

"Well, let me see now," Lord Uld responded. "There appears to be..."

Amiel leaned close to her again while his advisors' attention was concentrated on Lord Uld and the holomap.

"If you had wanted to prevent bloodshed you would not have run off as you did," his whisper was a harsh accusation.

"My mistake has already cost many lives, including that of my father," she whispered back, her voice almost breaking at the mention of her papa. She would not think of him now. She had to concentrate on the present situation. "An innocent old man remains locked in his jail cell, denied justice or a speedy trial. You could bring about peace, unite the land if you truly wanted to while still giving them their victory. You promised to let them live if I accepted your rule, which I did."

"I accepted letting them go out of the castle rather than be slaughtered in the bailey courtyard. I never said that if they continued to rebel I would let them."

"They are confused and uncertain how to proceed. No doubt they feel my proclamation accepting you as king was under duress. If we send them word that we are united, we can end this without further problems. How much more pain and blood will your wounded pride require?"

They stared into each other's eyes. She hoped her look was confident and disdainful. His was completely unreadable.

"Don't know really," he threw at her nonchalantly. "I suppose we'll find out."

"...I think ten should be enough," Lord Uld concluded. All eyes focused on the thrones and their warring occupants once more.

Amiel stood up and stretched as if the whole conversation had simply bored him to death.

"Proceed with it then," he commanded. "Let's adjourn for the day, shall we?" He strode out of the chamber without a backward glance.

Verena remained seated as the councilors began to depart. Looking down at her hands, she pondered what he could be thinking to play into these lordlings hands, giving in to their pettiness. The sound of the chamber door closing made her look up. She was not alone. The Earl of Ydarb stood hesitantly before her.

"Excellency?"

"He is doing what he must—"

"No, My Lord," Verena's voice filled with the righteous indignation that raged within her. "There is no need for more death. A truce could be had, we could rebuild and strengthen... his... whatever is driving him, it will leave us at the mercy of a foe that will not show any. He will destroy us all."

The gentleman shifted nervously. He seemed to want to say more, but then opted to simply exit. *Fools! Couldn't they see the truth?* She sagged into the chair. Unwilling to continue thinking, unable to keep herself from doing so.

"Why, Deni?" Verena asked, shaking her head in disbelief as she sat before her vanity later that evening.

Attired in her nightgown, the queen stared at her clearly haggard-looking self in the mirror. The swish of the brush as Mrs. Denip ran it through Verena's long auburn tresses failed to relax her as it would have done in the past.

"Why would he set us up like that? I can't understand. Perhaps, I was right in going away. I'm not very good at this political thing."

The queen sighed recalling the emotional conversation with Amiel in the forest, the tense bordering on incivility of his public treatment of her, and the flirty almost loving way he spoke with her in private. What most bothered her was how he allowed and even encouraged his nobles to treat her with mocking disrespect in the council chamber. The exhausting dinner, only an hour ago, with the Auldian courtiers mocking her and her people while he sat quiet, broke her heart. She had endured the evening beside him in silence as well. *What was there to say?* With Amiel everything seemed to be hot or cold, no in between. One moment they seemed to be reaching an understanding, the next they were at war again.

Now, Mrs. Denip's voice stirred her from the morose recollections of the hopeless situation she found herself in.

"Speaking frankly, Majesty—"

"Nothing ever stopped you from doing that and scolding me to boot," Verena gave her beloved nurse a warm smile, thankful for at least one ally in the castle.

"Well, it seems to me that your father, God rest his noble soul, did wrong in keeping you in the dark. But, in all fairness, I don't think you're doing too horribly."

"Thanks." Verena laughed with chagrin. "Let's hope I get better fast. I fear when the Gortives arrive on our shores we will be divided and fighting against each other. I thought this marriage was supposed to bring about a truce and a new nation."

"Well, begging your pardon, Majesty." Mrs. Denip looked at her with sad eyes. "Perhaps it would have, had it taken place in the right moment and not now, when Dravidia has been taken by war."

Verena knew she spoke the truth. Her fear of Amiel and her ignorance of the true situation on Jorn had led her to make the worst mistake of all. She understood it would be an uphill battle, but somehow, she must make these stubborn victors see union was the key to the survival of them all.

At least, Amiel continued to allow her to move about freely, well, with her new armed escorts. She was aware he had placed her confiscated ginmra in her father's vault. But Verena would get it back soon enough with the master code.

"You may go, Mrs. Denip," Amiel's command startled the two ladies, as they had not heard him enter. He stood in the doorway of the bathroom, bare chested with just loose pajama pants and a long silk robe.

"Of course, Sire." Denip gave him a quick curtsey, and exited the room via the servants' door. Verena caught her worried glance in the mirror and shot her a quick reassuring smile.

"Why are you here?" She turned in the bench stool and locked eyes with him.

He leaned into the frame of the door, his eyes sweeping over her body before returning her gaze.

"You are my wife." The statement hit her like a bucket of ice shards. Was he seriously thinking she would...? Could she after all that had happened?

"I don't want to be."

His cool composure slipped for a moment, revealing a tinge of... pain, anger? It was too fleeting a moment.

"I'm sorry you feel that way. I have never wanted anything other than to be your husband." He shifted, walking to the side of the sunken whirlpool tub in the middle of the room, he sat on its edge. "I can't remember a time I didn't wish to spend my life with you."

"This is exhausting."

"What is?"

"This game of cat and mouse you play. One moment hurting me with your hatred, the next proclaiming your affection," Verena let out a sigh. Her voice sinking into a whisper, "Why don't you just try being real for once?"

"I think the problem is you can't distinguish our political life from our private life." He ran a hand through his jet-black hair. "There was a war, Rennie. Aulden won. We can't just hit a reset button and pretend nothing happened. What I'm doing now is necessary for our political survival. Tomorrow, the land grants will be issued as per the Earl of Sarnac's advice. And we will see what happens..." His voice trailed off and his gaze moved to the floor.

She wasn't sure what he thought would occur, but it clearly worried him. "What do you fear will—"

"I don't want to talk politics." His clear blue eyes sought hers. The intensity in them sent a shiver down her spine. "I want you to understand all of *that*," he extended his hand toward the door, "doesn't matter in here." He swung his arm toward her, his hand open. "In here we are just two people, not rulers. Do you get it?"

Verena's breath quickened at the longing in his voice and eyes. Her mind churned his words. Just then she understood. It was like an act, in public; he was acting a part, maneuvering, like her father had. But privately, he was this.

"I think I do," her voice almost a whisper. "But if you really care for me, Amiel, then I am going to ask you to promise not to belittle me in public ever again." She held up a hand as he was about to say something. "I know that you're playing your political games, and maybe you think that is the way to go. But if we are life partners, then we need to show respect to each other always, public and private. We need to have a united front, as my parents always had, as yours did. That's the only way *we* can succeed."

"All right." He slid off the tub's edge and knelt on the rug in front of her. His hands enveloped hers. "Try not to challenge me so brazenly then." A wry smile curled up his lips, a gleam in his eyes.

"It would help if you told me what the plan is... I wouldn't feel like I had to—"

"Not now. Not tonight."

Dropping hers, his hands cupped her face. His lips took hers. She felt herself sway softly as his mouth claimed hers.

Verena resisted. Turning her head, she pressed, "I need to be a part of these decisions. That's how we can hold the land united, bring—"

"Yes."

"Yes what?"

"Yes, we will make this work."

He rose up to bury his face in her neck, trailing kisses on her skin.

"Amiel—"

"Please..."

Then he kissed her mouth hungrily. Her heart beat quickened and Verena let her lips part, returning his kiss. With a fluid motion, he rose, swooping her up into his arms.

He deposited her on the bed, coming to lie beside her. As his hands worked to undo her robe, Verena's emotions tumbled. She enjoyed his touch, but after everything that had happened, should she let him have her? He was right. She was his wife. Intimacy was a duty owed him, she supposed.

His mouth trailed kisses down her neck. Frustrated by the knot, he lifted up on his knees. Taking both robe and nightgown in his hands he pulled them up. She shifted allowing him to remove them over her head.

His eyes took her naked body in, the hunger in them brought a flush of heat to her cheeks. Verena's heart raced. She wanted him. Yet, she shouldn't let him. But she had to have the glorious release he provided. Gazing up at his muscled body, Verena felt warmth pool in her abdomen. He was as much hers as she was his. Why not let herself enjoy it, enjoy him?

Amiel repositioned himself, letting his mouth find her breasts. Verena's body responded as he suckled her nipples in turns, his hand reaching between her legs. She placed her hands on his shoulders, letting her fingers feel his skin, her body a live wire in his hands.

She let herself relax and enjoy his touch. Soon she was lost in him, in the waves of passion their intimacy elicited. As he thrust into her and they came together, Verena admitted to herself, she had missed this.

Later, when he'd left, Verena hoped that perhaps the open dialogue between them that evening might bring better relations moving forward. Yet, her heart felt heavy with the certainty she was fooling herself.

CHAPTER 23

LADY VIVELDA

A MONTH LATER, Verena found herself, yet again, in another unpleasant discussion in the Council of Peers chamber. Amiel had caved in and given the lands of the nobles in rebellion to Lord Uld's pack of frivolous lords. Verena's pleas to reach out to the men of Dravidia and bring peace went, as always, unheeded. Now, she brought the result of this decision to everyone's attention.

"There are many reports, across the nation, of the new lords of these lands using public funds for personal purposes."

"These false allegations are put forth by Dravidian rebels to rally people to their cause." Lord Uld fixed her with a derisive glare. "They escaped from us in the Parthiak Mountains, but we will soon crush their rebellion."

"The queen is correct, Lord Uld," the Duke of Aul commented. Verena threw him a grateful glance. "There is some evidence of the misuse of money by a handful of lords. This does not help to create good will among the people of the towns that have been assigned to them."

Verena watched as Amiel considered the matter. She had suggested that they issue a proclamation making it a priority to use all public funds for the rebuilding of defenses and accompany the edict with hefty fines for violators of the public trust.

"It is important, now with these lands in Auldian hands, that the lords assigned to them act responsibly," the Earl of Ydarb spoke up. "We are entering wauger. The Gortive will surely not attack during this period. They fear water above all things. Ara's rays have already begun heating up our atmosphere causing the deluge of rains and the melting of the snows. Jorn will soon resemble a water world. This will keep them at bay, hidden in the tall mountain peaks, at least for the next three months. But we must be ready when they come."

"Not to mention that the burning of the town walls damaged the force shields that protect the villages from the flooding. It is imperative we rebuild those now, before the rains become heavier and the real melting starts," Verena pressed the point with which she had opened.

Amiel's brow furrowed. After their resumed intimacy, he had shown her more respect in public. Yet, he refused to share his thoughts or decisions with her. She didn't know if he would back her or not, but she had to try. These lords, particularly the one given the Barony of Gar and the one granted the lands of the Torsgeld, where plundering and killing and destroying instead of ruling justly. They were a blight to his rule. Surely, he understood that. How would her people survive the floods with storage houses emptied and burned down and the force shields inactive?

"It is the victor's prerogative to enjoy the spoils." Lord Uld's petulance grated on Verena's nerves. "You gave them these lands, theirs to do with as they please."

"Wrong!" Amiel spoke for the first time. "These lands, as indeed all lands, belong to the crown, to me. The lords hold and administer them at my pleasure." He paused letting his words sink in. "Before we issue proclamations and fines, let's send out an informal command to begin work on these matters immediately and to cease any looting. The war is over, now it is time to think of the future."

Verena felt a bit disappointed, but at least he had not completely disregarded the matter. Perhaps his informal missive would halt them. She hoped so for the good of all their nation.

"Returning to the matter of the rebels, Sire," Lord Uld's tone as he pronounced the title felt incredibly disrespectful to Verena's ears, but she noted Amiel's countenance gave no sign of concern. "Not all of their lands have been assigned. There are still many of us that have not received any—"

"Lord Uld, I will not bestow further lands for war time deeds. Only the most valiant warriors, those who showed superior valor, were rewarded with lands to rule. The rest of you have been amply paid for your participation."

"Then what will happen with—"

"We will first bring an end to the rebellion, then we will worry about those lands."

"I hate to make this suggestion," Verena said, feeling her cheeks grow warm. "But as these parts of the kingdom are in rebellion, we should withhold crown funding that would normally be given for public works. They will need to protect their lands on their own, if they want to be against us."

The surprise in Amiel's eyes was clearly evident. That she would advise something that was not completely in favor of her own people was obviously a shock to all those gathered there. The councilors murmured approvingly.

"It seems just to me as well." Amiel turned back to the council. "Let it be so. Do we know where they may be hiding now?"

"We have launched the senords, but, with the heavy rains starting, we will need to recall them," the Duke of Aul informed them. "No sign of a new encampment at this time."

"Keep searching."

Soon after, the meeting adjourned. Rising from her chair, Verena noticed Amiel stood looking at her.

"Yes?"

"Your suggestion to withhold funds from the towns whose lords are in rebellion... It was—"

"It's what makes sense." Verena straightened her shoulders and kept her eyes on his. "Perhaps, if they feel the pain of no longer being under royal protection, they will seek a peace. Or we could do so knowing they will be more motivated to accept?"

He looked away for a moment, *considering? Maybe?* Verena still couldn't be sure what Amiel really thought. Even after their truce, and the intimacy they shared nightly, Verena felt there was a side of him that she couldn't quite comprehend or reach.

"How do you come by all this data?" Amiel asked after a moment's silence. "I have secured the castle with new passwords several times now and yet you just—"

"I love technology." She beamed at him mischievously and relished the frustration on his face. "There is no password I cannot break."

"All these years I've known you, and I am learning so much about you now."

"As am I," Verena said. "About you... and myself."

"I'll see you at dinner."

They had just walked out of the council chamber, when a liveried hudroid approached. Verena frowned noticing the servant's synthetic skin had been returned to the original white paleness of the factory settings. Gone was the lovely bronze she'd ordered years ago.

"Majesties." The servant bowed. "A rajin ship has requested permission to dock."

Verena saw Amiel tense. "Allow it to do so and we will welcome their emissaries in the throne room," she commanded before Amiel could speak. He furrowed his brow but didn't contradict her. "Shall we head there together?" she asked, turning to him once the hudroid had gone off to relay the command.

"Of course." He offered her his arm.

As they made their way to the throne room at the front of the castle's first floor, Verena noticed all the changes he'd made. Servants now wore the livery of Aulden, with the shell and coronet crest in black and silver. The Garinquel maids, who'd overseen baseboards and other hard to get places, were nowhere to be found. Her heart ached and the silent procession through her home began to feel like a death march.

The Duke of Aul already stood before the throne dais when they entered. His expression struck Verena. He always seemed serene, in control of his emotions. Now, he fidgeted and his face was marred by a grimace. She noted a silent message pass between Amiel and Figor. *Why would the arrival of a rajin shake them up so much?*

They had only just taken their places, when the Lord Chamberlain's voice announcing the visitors boomed from the doorway. "Rajin Master Lady Vivelda the Bountiful, Filear Rajin Dormas Helvan, and Filear Rajin Elina ra Sareg."

Lady Vivelda swept in attired in skin-tight gold metallic-like pants, a matching blouse cinched at her waist by a golden belt with multiple pouches, and gold-toned leather boots. Her knee-length cascade of golden hair swirled as she strode forward, blue eyes fixed upon Verena. Behind her, the two apprentice rajin followed dressed in matching yellow and white utilitarian pantsuits girded with a golden belt like that worn by their master.

"Majesty," Vivelda's musical voice filled the chamber as she bowed before Verena. "I have been sent by the Rajin Conclave to investigate the attack on Sanctal." Her eyes hardened as she glanced derisively at Amiel, then softened again as they fixed once more upon Verena. "A formal complaint has been launched before the Intergalactic Council."

Before Amiel could say anything, Verena took the lead. "Master Vivelda, you are very welcome here. The rajin tower and suite of offices in the north wing are at your disposal as is the library and anything else that might aide you in your quest."

Amiel's body, already tense, stiffened further.

"Thank you, Majesty." Vivelda bowed, preparing to exit, but Amiel spoke then.

"Have you had word from Master Horsef?"

Verena noticed the sudden clenching of the rajin's fists. The chamber seemed to fill with a chill as frosty as the worst of winter's blizzards. Slowly, Vivelda turned toward Amiel. Her eyes skewered him with a hate-filled glare.

"We have not had a chance to visit Sanctal, claim the bodies of our dead, nor give them proper burials." The words cut like shards of glass. "Did you bother doing anything for the innocent men and women of learning and faith you and those..." She swallowed, and Verena had to admire the way Master Vivelda, drawing deep breaths, gathered her composure. "We are neutral, yet you struck... you slaughtered them with forbidden powers that darken the soul."

Amiel's face bore a mask of unconcerned boredom, but Verena noticed the throbbing vein at his temple. "I declared war as required by law. The rajin would have—"

"On Dravidia!" Vivelda's tone rose, then quickly she calmed herself. "YOU kill without conscious. I remember the Sehy. The council failed to curb your darkness then, using your grief of your parent's death as an excuse, but now..." She turned and quit the room without further word.

Amiel sat still and followed the rajin master with his eyes. She saw a look pass once more between Figor and Amiel, but she wasn't sure what it meant. The room returned to its normal temperature and the tension eased as the door closed behind Lady Vivelda and her apprentices.

"Sehy?" she asked tentatively, seeking to open a potential conversation that might shed light on Amiel. Verena knew, of course, about the situation, but perhaps in this moment she might glean something deeper than just common knowledge.

"The blue fish people that killed my parents." Amiel's words came from between his clenched teeth.

"Oh, yes I recall something about that." Verena reached her hand to touch his fisted one. "Why does she mention forbidden, dark powers?"

"It doesn't concern you." He stared ahead. She felt his seething ire. He yanked his hand away, feeling for the pendant he wore beneath his shirt.

"Well, I'll be off to the library then." Verena rose, anxious to leave his presence. The rage, mingled with something else she couldn't name, scared her. "I'll see you at dinner."

He grunted his ascent as she quickly exited followed by the ladies in waiting and guards that were her constant shadows.

Verena sighed as she reached the doors to the library and her entire retinue followed her in. At first, she had managed to shake the ladies off at least during her daily reading time. But now they had simply taken to joining her there, too. The first time they accompanied her for her quiet time, Verena had been harsh on them when they attempted to converse, chiding them for making noise in a library. That, sadly, had not dissuaded them from pestering her with their presence.

Entering the marble sanctuary perfumed by books and the fragrant blackwood bookcases, she grabbed a set of nodes and curled up in her favorite spot. Over the past few weeks, she had researched the Shrang LaRoo liquids. Finally having a name for the special bottle's content, Verena felt certain she would soon figure out the purpose of the perplexing gift from her mother. But it had turned out to be much tougher than she thought. There were very few references, even under legends, for the mystic element.

With Vivelda's arrival a new approach presented itself. The rajin were a factor in the liquid's use, that much had been confirmed. Accessing her private holonet account, she opened a convo box and invited Vivelda. Moments later, the rajin master accepted, sending her a reply.

<How can I be of help, Majesty?>

<Are you settling in all right?> Verena typed back.

<Yes, Majesty.>

Without further preamble, Verena launched into the inquiry. <I have been searching for information on a rajin. Perhaps you can tell me about him? Rajin Shrang LaRoo?>

There was a pause and Verena feared Vivelda had gone off-line. Her icon showed green, but then sometimes people got busy and didn't look in on the net. Then another message popped up on the screen.

<Tell me, Majesty, what information do you seek?> Vivelda's response bolstered Verena's courage.

<Is he alive?>

<I'm afraid not. He is one of only three members of the order to ever attain the title of Bravura Rajin, the Highest title the order can bestow. Those of us who have reached great standing are blessed with longer lives, but I'm sorry to say, Bravura Rajin Master Lord Shrang LaRoo has been dead these past 300 years. In fact, he is buried in the crypt at Sanctal.> A pause followed this statement, then quickly she added, <If those hollowed grounds have not been destroyed.>

<What do you know of the liquids of Shrang LaRoo?> Verena's heart pounded as she awaited a response. It seemed forever before the Lady answered.

Finally, Vivelda's message came through. <The liquid's power can only be accessed by the blood of the women in your family line. Do you have it? If you do, you MUST NOT LET AMIEL KNOW OF IT!>

<I doubt it would be meaningful to him anyway. He scoffs at such things.> Verena stated, adding quickly, <But, of course, I will keep it a secret. I hope to find out how they might help me get my country back on track. Maybe they can defeat the Gortive?>

The vehemence of the rajin's response seemed extreme, but then, Lady Vivelda's words about a dark power used by Amiel in the Battle at Sanctal returned to her mind. *What did the rajin refer to?* Aulden had never kept any faith, though members of the royal family had become rajin from time to time.

<The elmalin are helping him kill his enemies and any that stand in his way. He denies it and those heretics deny it, but if they got ahold of the power in the liquids, there's no telling what they might do!>

<From what I have discovered, a rajin must help access the power and only I can use it. I will be careful, but I'd like to know what they do and how they might help?>

Minutes ticked by. Then Vivelda responded, <You need the crystal dagger of LaRoo. It may be at Sanctal. And you need Horsef.>

Verena read the words and felt a deep pang of disappointment. Horsef could well be dead by all accounts.

<Amiel asked about Master Horsef. I believe he may be alive.> Vivelda's message encouraged Verena.

<We must find him.>

<That's why I'm here. But the dagger will be harder to locate. It could be buried with Bravura Rajin LaRoo or elsewhere. Maybe not even on Jorn.>

<Could you find it for me?> Verena asked.

<I have my own mission, Majesty. I cannot divert from it. Though the outcome may assist you in yours.>

Verena let the rejection slide. The Rajin Order was a neutral and independent organization. As men and women of faith, they counseled and assisted but always with justice and fairness. Verena knew, from the interactions in the throne room, that Lady Vivelda had come to gather evidence to present before the council against Amiel. *What would happen if Lady Vivelda could prove he had used some illegal means to destroy the rajin? Would the council sanction him? Dravidia? The whole planet?*

Shaking her head from these conundrums, she responded, <I understand.>

<May the Great I Am grant you strength and wisdom. The Intergalactic Council may rule against Amiel and that might be a blessing for you. But given the status quo proclivities of that body, you might be forced to deal with him yourself. You'll always have our support and advice as much as we can offer to you.>

<Thank you. I will send a petition to the Rajin Conclave for a formal Rajin Consul to be named to our court. I trust Sanctal will be rebuilt.>

<Its future is part of my mission, yes, Majesty.>

<Excellent. Thank you for your help, Master Vivelda.>

<It is my pleasure to serve you, Majesty.>

Verena logged off and removed the nodes. Stretching her legs, she looked around at the ladies. The older ones had fallen asleep. A couple of the younger were huddled on the other side chatting up a storm in hushed whispers.

The queen knew then the only way she could possibly find this crystal dagger and maybe Rajin Horsef, if he was yet alive, would be to have someone locate them for her. There was no way she could leave the castle on a long quest. Amiel's threat to kill all of Dravidian noble blood if she left him again haunted her. If she was to learn what power her mother's special liquid held, a quest would be essential. She could not risk his wrath upon her people by going herself. She needed someone she could trust.

Her gaze fell upon Sir Andross. His bored expression told her everything she needed to know. He was a man of action relegated to watching over women. Verena felt certain she could coax him into going on the mission. She had three months to work on him. No one could venture out during wauger. But come the beginning of spring, Verena vowed to have Sir Andross's help for the quest.

CHAPTER 24

POSSIBILITIES

"ARREST HER!" Amiel commanded, barging into Verena's private study with five guards hard at his heels a few weeks later.

"What is the meaning of this?" Verena demanded rising from her desk chair and positioning herself between Mrs. Denip, who had been sorting recipes for her, and the guards that had moved to seize her hudroid.

"She is a traitor," Amiel stated bluntly. "She must be decommissioned. Stand away from her."

"What specifically has she done? Where is your proof?" the queen challenged, standing her ground.

"She has been sneaking messages to the Dravidian resistance," Amiel stepped forward and stood in front of Verena. "I suspected it was her, but now I have definitive proof. I hope she has been acting alone of her own accord and not at anyone's direction."

They glared at each other, tension growing between them as the veiled threat to Verena's person hung in the air.

"Where is the proof?" she asked again.

"Here!" Amiel drew out a leather envelope and threw it in her face. The item slapped her right cheek, the alleged evidence falling to the floor with a thud.

"Amiel," Verena's voice was a tense whisper as she closed the gap between them further. "If you ever strike me again, in any way, you will live to regret it. I *can* fight and you have to sleep sometime."

"You dare—"

"You've insinuated I would on many occasions. I will not allow you to physically—"

"I'm sorry. I didn't intend to hurt you." Something in his eyes wavered. His gaze took in the slight redness on her skin the missive had caused.

"I went too far. I am sorry, Rennie," his tone as he spoke the nickname he had given her years ago held a strange note that Verena could not quite describe. "But the evidence is clear."

The queen backed away from him, shocked by his apology and the indecipherable look in his eyes.

"Take her away," Amiel commanded his guards. He placed his hand gently on Verena's arm and moved her out of the way. He bent to pick up the pouch and placed it into her hand, holding her eyes with his.

"Please," she whispered the words, her heart breaking. "Have mercy on her."

"Mercy is for the weak." He turned and followed his guards.

Verena felt as if she was going to fall apart.

"Majesty," a young woman in Auldian livery curtsied before her. "I am Andena. His Majesty said I was to attend to you now, ma'am."

"Thank you," Verena said with quiet composure. "Please finish sorting the documents that Mrs. Denip was working on. The categories should be clear."

"Yes, ma'am," the young maid hudroid got to work quickly and efficiently.

Verena returned to her desk. She looked at the pouch. Opening it, she unfurled a letter, a warning. Mrs. Denip had tried to get a message through to the Dravidians. Verena clutched the evidence to her chest and took in deep breaths.

She held on to her stoic composure, even when left alone with her new lady's maid. It was only later, when she found herself completely alone in her bedchamber that she succumbed to a fit of crying that left her prostrated and doubled over from grief. She was alone, completely alone. The last connection to her mother was gone forever.

"Master Vivelda, how is your investigation proceeding?"

Verena glanced up from the book of Aulden Royal Ancestry she'd been pouring over. The Duke of Aul stood respectfully near the rajin master as the lady reviewed pictodes with media and surveillance videos of the attack on Sanctal. Verena watched as the beautiful rajin tossed her cascading hair aside, lifting her exquisite countenance to Figor.

"Are you here trying to let your king know how the evidence gathering against him is proceeding?"

Figor shook his head. "King Amiel did nothing wrong. The Rajin of Sanctal were a vital part of Dravidia's defenses and—"

"Do not try to justify your slaughter to me!" The horrible pain that marred the lady's beauty broke Verena's heart.

The queen knew why Vivelda was so fixated on this investigation; why she'd come personally rather than send an Inspector Rajin. Vivelda and Horsel's love affair spanned millennia. The rajin was here to find the man she loved, either dead or alive, and do justice upon the person who'd attacked him.

"I just feel that your personal emotions—"

A bright burst of light covered Figor, then dissipated. The startled duke blinked rapidly. Verena gasped in amazement, but quickly stifled it.

"Maybe you and your king believe your own lies, but I will find the truth." Vivelda shut down the pictode, rising with fluid grace. "And don't worry, your sight will return shortly."

Verena watched the grieving master exit the library. Shutting her book, Verena approached the duke. "Your Grace," she said, touching his arm.

He jolted but recognized her voice.

"I can't see!" Panic tainted his voice.

"Lady Vivelda said it will pass. You need to give her space," Verena admonished. "Lady Vivelda will find that the attack on Sanctal, though ruthless, was in fact legal."

The duke froze. He'd been shaking his head and rubbing his eyes as if that would help. Now, he turned his sightless gaze toward the sound of her voice.

"You believe Amiel?"

"I know the law." Verena made her voice as matter of fact as possible, placing a hand on his arm. "The rajin helped Dravidian forces on many occasions. They could have been considered an essential element of Dravidia's defense and as such the council will rule in favor of Aulden."

"Amiel is fortunate to have you."

Something in how the duke said those words made Verena uncomfortable. She withdrew her hand from his arm self-consciously. Seeking to deflect the awkward moment, she said, "What is strange to me is the elmalin. Why would they help Amiel? If it was them, it seems... odd."

A flicker of emotion crossed the duke's unguarded face. Verena couldn't name it, but within her understanding dawned. Some other group was helping Amiel. The strange hooded man in the council chamber came to her mind. *What has Amiel gotten involved with?* Master Vivelda's words echoed in her thoughts: "*forbidden powers that darken the soul.*"

"Are you all right?" Figor's question made Verena realize he could see the emotion on her face.

"I'm fine." The queen turned and left the library.

As she headed to her chambers, trailed by the startled retinue of ladies and guards, she pondered the clues. The elmalin might not be the only new order. Another powerful group, one that used darker energies, might be taking shape. The queen recalled the strange sensations she'd felt when she'd touched the jewel Amiel wore. Uncertain why, Verena had the sudden conviction she had to get the amulet off Amiel. It had to be connected to the evil man she'd seen. She determined to find a way.

Verena sat in her favorite garden bench under the wide forest green canopied trellis. The metal swing with its plant print cushions had a smooth glide. Winter's blanket of lavender-hued snow had melted into a slushy mush by the time the energy field was activated. Now, Verena swung her legs idly in her pink galoshes sloshing the remnants about. Wrapped in the warmth of her minoxit fur coat, she relished in its red-gold softness.

Usually, the Wauger Festival was a time of great excitement with parties and celebrations leading up to the New Year hand off. A great fair would be held here in the castle's backyard with games and vendors. The noble families of the realm would join them and spend the season with the Royal Family. Smaller fairs would entertain the various villages and towns. Cosplay was a fun part of the festivities. But with the war and the uncertain start to the new king and queen's reign, Verena had noted the lack of carnivals and fairs across the kingdom.

Just as well, Verena thought. The year 2950 TGW loomed on the horizon and would focus on defenses, military buildup, and war. There wasn't much to celebrate and even less to come if they weren't ready to fight off the savagery of the Gortive offensive. Verena glanced up at the energy field. Emitted by the castle's outer wall, it protected them from the deluge of rain during the three months of wauger. The honrol center of the stone walls kept the rising flood waters out, as the snows melting, combined with torrential rain, turned Jorn into a water world. The splatter of the rain on the energy bubble created an almost continual spark of blue and green in what had always seemed a fantastic light show to Verena.

A box of nodes sat cradled on her lap. Pulling her gaze from the weather outside, and the beauty it created, she placed the silver discs on her temples and accessed the quantum net. With her father's code, she programmed the satellite probe to gaze down on Gar City. The informal command Amiel had issued to use public funds for rebuilding of walls and energy conduits in preparation for wauger had been obeyed by all his nobles, except, of course, Lord Uld's clique of followers. The worst offender was Falno Dlu, the new Baron of Gar, who had used the time and money to redecorate and fortify Gar Keep, completely neglecting the wall of the city itself.

Verena zoomed in and her heart ached. Gar had become a literal lake. The waters of the deluge coupled with the snow melt had all the single-story buildings completely submerged. Homes with second floors and buildings with multiple levels now housed the refugee citizens of the flooded areas. Verena watched as a flat barge docked at several buildings delivering food and other supplies as well as tending to the wounded or ill. Its energy field protected the heroes in a neon blue transparent umbrella. They bore the flag of the Knights Salvant, a charitable order Verena's great-grandfather had established.

She zoomed over to the store houses. Damaged by the battle fought before the city's walls, the burned stone melted like wax had left what food supplies had not been destroyed in the war open to the elements. All that had once been within lay destroyed either by fire or rain.

Then she saw Gar Keep. Its walls fully rebuilt and its energy shield bright with the splatter of rain. The new Lord Gar was hosting a feast. Verena watched the reveling lords chasing scantily clad ladies from the pleasure houses around the beautifully landscaped gardens. Her mind recalled her last conversation with Lady Gar. The garrulous plump wife of the true Baron of Gar had gushed about the wonderfulness of having a queen. Tears spilled down Verena's cheeks. She'd failed her people. War, destruction, pillaging, that was her legacy. Lord and Lady Gar dead. So many dead. While the Auldian victors chased whores, her people battled the elements just to survive.

And then there were the Dravidian nobles who were rebelling so they could make her their queen without Amiel. Their lands, some whose energy fields were damaged, were suffering the same fate as Gar, though for different reasons. Cast out and in exile, the rebels had sought shelter in the caves on the slopes of the Verludian mountains. She'd gotten word to the earl, using her special access code on the quantum back channel, that Amiel would be attacking the Parthiak tunnels. That missive had elicited a response at last, and just in time. Verena shuddered at the thought of what her husband might do if he learned of her treason.

A deep pain filled her. Mrs. Denip, faithful hudroid to generations of her family, had tried to get word of the attack to the earl and been caught. She'd nursed the babes of House Drav for almost two centuries. Now, she was gone, off to a scrap metal processor.

Plucking the nodes from her head, she tossed them back in their box. Verena wiped her face of tears. Looking toward the promontory cliff, the oceans water had risen to almost eye level with the steep drop. Finding Horsef and locating the crystal dagger was paramount. If those special Shrang LaRoo liquids could help correct this mess she'd made, she had to try.

She'd already begun building up her friendship with Sir Andross. Verena was sure he had a good heart, but he was beholden to Amiel. Revealing the truth and asking him to go on the quest was a huge risk. *But who else can I trust?*

Verena recognized the first sign that spring was around the corner when the rains stopped. One day it was pouring. The next, Ara was out and shining his warm rays upon the land. Then the winds started. The water from the rivers and lakes would recede and the land would dry up in a matter of weeks, as the planet's rotation took it away from Ara's embrace.

She knew that the time had come to approach the idea of the quest with Sir Andross. During the past months, while Amiel and the Council of Peers worked out a way to incorporate Aulden's lands into the centralized government of Dravidia, and a variety of plans were developed for the possible Gortive attack on them, Verena had spent the bulk of her time chatting up her rescuer.

"Sir Andross, I would like to know more about you." Verena said the next day, after listening to the weather report that told of the first green grass showing already in the higher elevations. She had begged a migraine and sent away the ladies from her rooms. Her guards remained, of course.

"What would your Majesty like to know?" He asked from the corner of the room he stood watch over.

"You mentioned that you were brought up on a farm, but you sought the life of a soldier when the war broke. Why?" She turned her face to look at him to gauge his reaction as she lay on her couch in the sitting room of her suite. She made sure to make her voice sound a bit weak, as if truly suffering.

"To be truthful, I never wanted to be a farmer," he looked in her eyes. "I wanted to be a lawyer, but we did not have the money for such expensive education. My father's farm had been in the family for several generations and as his only son, I have three sisters but no brothers, my father just expected me to take over the business. I am not complaining. He was an excellent father, but farming just wasn't me."

"A lawyer." Verena pondered this glimpse into him. "And what kind of law would you have wanted to practice?"

"I always admired the public defenders." He flashed her a sheepish smile. "I know it sounds strange, but some of the cases they would defend in my village, you must understand it is a very small village, made me think how amazing it would be to be able to help people. Aulden is not like Dravidia. The laws are harsh and the punishments harsher. The king is a good man, but sometimes the powerful get away with hurting those who don't have the capacity to protect themselves." Realizing he might have given offense, he quickly added, "Oh, I..."

Ignoring his discomfort, Verena pressed, "And you see Dravidia as being different?"

He considered her question in silence before responding. "Well, yes, Majesty. I have a friend that married a Dravidian lady. She often talks of the fair laws and just courts, of how low the crime-rate always was compared to Aulden's. It made me wonder..."

"Wonder what?"

"What it would have been like to be a farmer's son in your country, not that I am saying Aulden was bad or anything... I just..."

"Don't fret," Verena gave him a reassuring smile, though she noted the other guards had harsh expressions on their faces. "You are not betraying anyone by noting that things are different between our nations.

Hopefully we will be able to take the best of both and forge a new one that will bring us great prosperity and peace."

She allowed the room to return to silence. Verena thought about what this conversation revealed. He seemed an earnest person who truly desired to do good. But, he owed his status as a knight to Amiel and now, he had been ascended to a knight of the castle guard by the king. Still he noticed the inequities of his land and the good of hers. *Maybe...*

Verena waited until the weather permitted her to ride in the forest once more before pursuing the matter of the quest with Sir Andross. The reaction of the other guards to their conversation made her more reserved in their presence, not wishing to cause the knight complications. And the mission would require secrecy.

"I have a proposition that I wish to put before you, Sir Knight," she broached the subject of the search for the rajin once they were deep into the Oldey Forest and her other guards had lagged behind as was the custom she had established. Sir Andross rode beside her at her request.

"Oh."

"You see, I must find someone, but I cannot embark on the search myself. Perhaps, you might help me?"

"Of course, I would love to help your Majesty in any way I can." He sounded hesitant and wary.

"Well, you see, the Gortive are expected to attack us soon. As you know, with the war and now the wauger season, well we just aren't ready for them." She noticed how his face became more concerned for the wellbeing of the land and plowed on. "If I could find the Master Rajin, Horsef the Great, and the crystal dagger that Rajin Shrang LaRoo owned, I think I could safe guard the kingdom."

"How?"

She hesitated, but there was no one else. "You see, my mother, when she died, bequeathed me a special gold liquid prepared for our family by Rajin LaRoo back when we still lived on planet Drulin it seems. This has power, but I was too young and she never told me what they could do. Only a rajin can help me figure out how to use them to protect our kingdom."

"Like in the legend. That's why your Majesty was so interested in it."

"Yes. At the time, when you shared it with me, I didn't have a name for the liquids. Now, thanks to you, I know what they are. With the help of Master Vivelda, I was able to discover that the crystal dagger may be in the tomb of Rajin Shrang LaRoo and that we need Lord Horsef."

She gifted him with her warmest smile and sweetest gaze. They rode a time in silence, the only sound that of the horses' glop-glopping as they lifted their feet from the soaked and muddy ground. He pondered her words for some time. As the silence dragged on the queen's impatience grew.

"Will you help me, sir?" She pressed him.

"How can I, Majesty?" He responded, averting his eyes from hers. "Would the king not become offended I leave after his generosity to me?"

"Well... of course not," she adopted the most convincing tone she could muster. "I will tell him that I have sent you on this mission and he will approve I am sure of it for it will be for the good of the land."

Verena resisted the urge to bat her eyes, trying instead for the queenliest demeanor; as though her sending a guard on a quest of her own accord was the most natural thing. As he considered again her request, Verena realized that slowly Amiel had purged the castle of practically all Dravidian staff.

"I shall do as you instruct, Majesty," Sir Andross's vow brought her out of her reverie. "But, where shall I start?"

"I have been giving it some thought. The rajin studied and lived in a monastery located at the confluence of the Tarsus and Vongo rivers. The building was known as Sanctal. In the crypt, according to Lady Vivelda, lies the tomb of Lord Shrang LaRoo. The dagger might be there. And perhaps if you search their former headquarters, you may find a clue as to where Lord Horsef may have gone into hiding."

"Well, it is as good a place as any to start."

CHAPTER 25

THE QUEST BEGINS

THE QUEEN HAD ADMONISHED HIM, as they returned to the castle, that he should allow her to broach the subject with the king.

"Once I have his acceptance of the plan," she had said. "I will let you know. I will set up an account for expenses—"

"No need, Majesty, I have an account," he'd informed her. Lord Uld had created it when forced to give Sir Andross money upon his knighting.

"Excellent, send the information to my com, and I will make sure to transfer an initial amount for the expenses you itemized me just now."

"Yes, Majesty."

She had headed into the castle with a dainty spring in her step. He was almost certain she had no intention of telling the king about her scheme. Granted, Sir Andross was relatively new at this knighthood thing, but it felt wrong to keep a secret from his sovereign.

Growing up on his father's small, but lucrative, farm the knight had never bothered much about the politics of his world. He had just graduated from the Institute of Agriculture and Husbandry, resigned himself to inheriting and running the family farm, and finding one of the local girls to marry, when the war had started.

Sir Andross, as a youngster, had loved the ideals of knighthood. The war allowed him to escape the farm and seek his fortune as a soldier. He knew his highest hopes would be to become an officer someday. *The dubbing had been a stroke of luck!*

After taking the horses to the stables, a duty the other guards had assigned to him as an expression of their resentment that the queen held a special regard for him, Sir Andross had sought out the Duke of Aul and requested an audience with the king.

Now, as he waited to see King Amiel, the grateful knight felt he had to reveal the queen's plans. He owed everything to the king. Deep inside, Sir Andross hoped his monarch would feel the queen's objective of getting help for the coming war with the Gortive worthy. *Surely the king would wish that too, right?* He yearned for it to work out well, he did not cherish betraying the queen. *What if the king becomes angry with her?* Sir Andross had personally seen his liege lord's harsh punishments upon members of the small community of Dran who broke the law. What if by telling him, the knight was placing the queen in danger? How had he ended up in this quandary?

The door to the king's office opened and an old man in a midnight-blue cape exited followed by the duke. A chill filled the small ante-chamber, and Sir Andross shivered at the sudden temperature drop. The thunderous look on the weathered face of the stranger bespoke the man's anger.

"Be patient, Godar," the Duke of Aul said, a concerned look written upon his classical features.

"The deal was..." the man's voice trailed away, locking eyes with Sir Andross.

The knight felt an icy grip on his heart as those dark-amber eyes fell upon him. They held such a glare of hate, Sir Andross wondered what could cause such a deep and terrible emotion.

"He better keep his end," the man said, poking a crooked finger at the duke.

"He will," the duke assured. "Give him time."

With an animalistic grunt of shear frustration, the man stomped away. The duke turned to Sir Andross. As the door shut behind the visitor, the room's temperature returned to normal. The knight had been in the presence of only a few rajin during his lifetime and wondered now at their immense power.

An apologetic smile spread on the duke's face as he ushered the knight into King Amiel's private office. The king sat behind a massive blackwood desk with intricately carved inlay paneling of contrasting honeywood. His sovereign was leaning back in his chair, relaxed and at ease. *He doesn't look like an unreasonable man,* the knight thought optimistically.

"Please, Sir Andross, come in and take a seat." The king gestured to one of the black leather-hide chairs positioned before his desk. "His Grace tells me you want a word with me."

"Majesty, you have done so much for me... and I am very grateful... for the opportunity to serve here... and..." Sir Andross began awkwardly, unsure how to tell his liege about the queen's request.

"No need, Sir Knight," the king waved away his gratitude. "You earned what has been given you through valor and deeds. I feel greatly relieved to know my queen is in your care."

"It is about the queen I wanted to speak to you, Sire," Sir Andross began again, even more nervously than before. He wrung his hands together on his lap and swallowed hard. "You see, her Majesty has asked me to go on a... quest... mission... of sorts."

"Quest?" The king sat straighter in his chair. Sir Andross noted the confused look on his face.

"Yes... well, it seems, Sire, she needs to find the Rajin, Lord Horsef the Great."

"I see," the king was pensive for a few moments. "Did the queen say why she needed to find Lord Horsef? After all, we have the great Lady Vivelda here now."

"Her Majesty mentioned some liquid with special powers that only he could show her how to operate. The queen hopes it might provide a way to defeat the Gortive and maybe finally bring peace to the kingdom."

"Those are equally my goals." King Amiel had an earnest look in his eyes as he leaned forward toward the nervous knight. "I am assuming she has asked you to perform this service secretly? Yes... I can see that is the case. I am gratified and honored by the loyalty you have demonstrated in coming to me. You need not fear, you have not placed the queen in any danger. I would never harm her."

"She did mention she would speak to you."

"I'm sure she will."

The king stood and came around the desk. Sir Andross rose quickly as well. The knight followed as King Amiel walked toward the doors of the study. As they made their way, Sir Andross glanced down and noticed the royal-purple carpet with the emblem of Dravidia on it. *This is really the queen's realm*, he thought. Reaching the threshold, the king turned back and looked at him.

"Let me talk with the queen, and I will let you know how to proceed."

"Of course, Sire."

That night, back in the knights' barracks, Sir Andross lay on his assigned bunk and worried. *Have I done the wrong thing? Will the queen pay a horrible price for having trusted me?* He tossed about sleeplessly. *Being a knight sure has turned out to be a lot more complicated than the stories made it out to be!*

Sir Andross rode out of Castle Dravidia eight days later and headed south through the Oldey Forest. The queen had provided a jorse A-105 for the journey from the castle's vehicles. It looked and felt like a real horse, but it was an AI machine. Sir Andross had seen some during the battles, but never hoped to be able to use such an expensive conveyance. He'd had a bit of a time learning to operate it, too. Sir Eriq had helped him key it to his fingerprints and retina to avoid anyone being able to steal it.

The legendary warrior had sent Sir Andross on his way. "If you betray her, you will answer to me." The words were spoken in a matter-of-fact tone.

"I'm certain this mission will help us all," Sir Andross had stated, feeling his cheeks burn at the thought that he'd already kind of betrayed her to the king. "I will do my best to achieve its success."

"See that you do." Sir Eriq had moved off then and gone back into the castle.

It hadn't surprised Sir Andross that Sir Eriq was helping the queen. He wondered briefly if the king knew of the Lord High Marshal's involvement. Heading out, Sir Andross decided not to inform the king. After all, if the mission was a success and it helped the entire kingdom it wouldn't matter.

As he sat comfortably within the seat, using the steering wheel and protected by the energy field of the jorse's cockpit, Sir Andross set off at an easy pace of thirty miles per hour and thought about the quest. The king had summoned him the afternoon following Sir Andross's revelation and had given his blessing to the endeavor.

"To be honest, as you have been with me, Sir Andross," the king had told him. "I decided not to mention it to the queen. I think she may be worried that the liquid might prove worthless and doesn't wish me to think ill of her for believing in such things. Rennie has always been a bit shy like that, who would believe a woman of such immense beauty could have insecurities, but it seems they plague us all."

"Should I go on the mission then?"

"Yes. Keep me informed, but let her think I don't know. She will tell me when she's ready. You will inform me first the moment you find Horsef. If this liquid can help us then by all means we must do what we can to figure out its use."

Sir Andross had left feeling relieved. After all, the fact that the king and queen had known each other since childhood was common knowledge. Their marriage might not be on the best of terms right now, but surely they would work it all out. All marriages were rocky at times, but the king really seemed to be in love with the queen. Then again what man wouldn't want to be married to a sexy little minx like her. It was probably hugely disrespectful of him to think that way about the queen, another man's wife, but Sir Andross had always been a sucker for the ladies. He smiled cockily to himself.

Now, here he was on his way, alone. The Rajin Master Lady Vivelda had set out to Sanctal days ago. The queen had told him she hoped he reached the rajin temple while the lady was still there and could help. Nevertheless, the queen had provided Lady Vivelda's contact information should Sir Andross need the rajin's help.

He had decided to make his first stop Dravidia City. He had reached out to his old friend, Ven Sans. They had grown up together before Ven's recruitment into the Nedlua, Aulden's intelligence gathering service. Sir Andross was not sure if Ven had really quit to manage his father-in-law's inn or if he was still working undercover. Anyway, his old boyhood friend might be a valuable source of information.

He reached the war-scarred metropolis as Ara reached its zenith. Despite the war and subsequent insurgence, the bustling city continued with business as usual. As he made his way through the city, Sir Andross considered purchasing a hovercraft for the quest. A hover craft would make the mission easier with more space in the trunk for supplies. Erivor, as the AI he'd been given was named, had limited storage capacity. On the other hand, the jorse had military capabilities and came equipped with a nice stock of ammunition. Both hovercraft and jorse ran on dark energy engines, which gave them a significant advantage over more primitive methods of travel.

Sir Andross had learned a thing or two about dark energy engines during his time at university. Bigger farms used machines for labor that used such devices. This clean and self-sustaining energy source meant no harmful emissions and no need for re-fueling for the five years of its lifespan.

The problem with purchasing a hovercraft, of course, was the expense. The queen had limited the funds for the quest's original supply purchases. Sir Andross suspected this was due to her having to hide the mission from the king. *Such a shame; could I appeal to the king?* No way could he lie to the queen about where he got that much money. *Oh, well, jorseback it would have to be.*

"Andy," Ven Sans' boisterous greeting rang out, snapping Sir Andross from his reverie. "Long time no see, my friend. What brings you this far north?"

"Ven," Sir Andross returned the greeting. He activated the stairs for dismounting from the cabin seat as he drew to a stop in front of his friend's inn. Small and quaint, it was nestled in a quiet neighborhood that bordered the wholesale purchasing district. "Actually, I'm heading south."

"Come on in. I've set up a table for us to have lunch," Ven invited. "We have much to catch up on."

Sir Andross handed the valet control of his jorse to a groom. Ven led him to a table overlooking the garden in the inn's dining room.

"Now," Ven said once their meal had been ordered. "What have you been up to? I see you are wearing the livery of an Auldian castle knight. Congratulations, I hope."

"Started off doing mercenary work round the continent, but got lucky and ended up working at the castle."

"Merc work's not the nicest of jobs and not really your style, my friend. Is that what brought you north and now takes you south? Or is this a castle job?"

"Castle job. Happily, I'm out of the mercenary business. I'm looking for someone, a master rajin named Horsef the Great."

"You're on a fool's errand," Ven exclaimed in surprise. "The rajin of Jorn are all dead or gone off planet."

"There are rumors that some may be in hiding here. Perhaps your old Nedlua contacts might know something?"

"I'll ask around and keep my ears open for news. I doubt you'll find the rajin though. Those guys are powerful and if they don't want to be found... well."

"I will do what I can, and I sure appreciate any bits of information you can find for me."

"How'd you get to be a knight of the royal house?"

"Got lucky. Saved Lord Uld's worthless son. Then, I happened to be at the right time to save the queen from a runaway horse."

"She is a beauty. You always were a sucker for the ladies!"

"Beyond beautiful," Sir Andross's overwarm exclamation embarrassed him. He quickly turned the subject. "You sure have a sweet set up here. Your lady love's inn seems to be surviving the war."

"Yeah," Ven answered looking around proudly at his modest, but profitable business. "Ebusa had a rough time convincing her dad to let us marry, my being Auldian and all, but since the wedding we have been working the inn for him and he has been able to retire. We are expecting our first child soon."

"Congratulations!" Sir Andross was genuinely glad to hear that his friend was doing well. "Where is Ebusa?"

"She is at home. The pregnancy has been rough on her and the doctor ordered bed rest. If we were rich we could afford to have her go through incubation birthing. Our inn is doing well but not that well I'm afraid. The war isn't making things easy and now news from Parthia is that there may be more fighting ahead."

"I am sure we will all come out of this all right," Sir Andross said, digging in to the succulent meat pie the cute waitress had just placed before him. "Anyway, natural birthing is better I think. I mean, cutting the baby out and having it continue development in the artificial womb just seems... unnatural."

"Yes," Ven agreed. "But would be easier for her body and less weight gain. Not that I'm saying she's getting fat."

Sir Andross lifted his glass, and they toasted to the coming addition of a healthy baby boy to Ven's family.

Tenuous rays of green and purple adorned the sky, as Sir Andross loaded up the supplies two days later. He had purchased a used palfrey jorse from Ven's stables to do the hauling while he rode Erivor. The pack AI would be able to keep up with most of the destrier-styled jorse's speeds and his friend had given him a great deal.

Heading southeast toward Eporue City, he held a steady pace. By noon, he had left the Oldey Forest behind and was well into the Dravidian prairie lands. He passed through the tall burnt orange grasses, trampling them briefly only to watch them spring back up around him. The sweet fragrance they gave filled the spring breeze. Soon they would begin to flower and the air would be filled with the purple pollen they released. He was glad to be coming this way now when they were not yet germinating. His allergies would not survive that. He slipped on his ear pieces and clicked on his personal music device. The PMD's holo-home screen floated before him. Selecting his favorite Auldian band from his collection, he relaxed and enjoyed the journey.

Having set off at the break of dawn, the day passed uneventfully. The horizon was a blaze of bright orange, pink, and red as Ara began to set. Sir Andross quickened his pace, arriving at Eporue's gates just before the auto-shut down for the night. He need not have worried, as the gates, along with large chunks of wall, were nonexistent. The charred remains of what little was left gave the city a melancholy feel.

He made his way through the city's potholed streets, passing more ruined buildings than those standing. Major fighting had taken place here and the city evidenced having a rough go recouping. The deluge of wauger had not helped. There was cut out carpets and destroyed furniture along with bags of personal items that the waters had ruined lining every street he passed. The scent of molding wood permeated the air.

Sir Andross sought lodgings, but most hotels where closed for renovations. He was about to give up and sleep in the open prairie when he came upon the Wildflower Inn. The simple yet prosperous establishment had survived intact thanks to its own energy shields. It was unusual for individual business owners to spend on such luxuries. Almost all relied on the crown to provide the protection needed.

Settling into his room, the knight headed down to the large dining room. It housed twelve rows of long tables, which travelers shared. It was an old style, but pleasant as one could gather stories from ones' diner companions.

Taking a seat close to the hearth, Sir Andross commented, "Looks like the city got hit hard with the war."

Furtive glances from nearby patrons flitted his way, no doubt taking in his castle armor and its Auldian crest. Sir Andross felt heat rush to his face as he considered his ill-conceived topic.

"Things ain't got much better now we have that Auldian prick Lord over us," a fellow lodger complained to Sir Andross. He sat in front of the knight, a pint of savok in his chubby hand.

"King Amiel is not as bad as you may think," Sir Andross defended his monarch. "And the queen has great ideas for getting us back to stability."

"Kings and queens," the disgruntled guest spat on the floor to show his disgust. The robosweep beeped indignantly as it rushed over to clean the spot and sanitize it. The offender completely ignored the little robot's ire. "They's too far away to see how that Baron Sreg has been pilfering this city. He ain't done nothin' to fix it up and get things back to hows it was before the war. All our homes flooded. He never bothered a fixin' the force shield. Worst wauger ever! The Lord Epo, God rest his noble soul, never would'a left us in this mess."

"Hush man," his dinner companion chided, elbowing his comrade. "Don't you mind him none, Sir Knight, he's already drank too much of the savok, and it's gone to his head it has. He doesn't mean no harm."

"Do not worry yourselves about me," Sir Andross tried to reassure them, seeing the concerned look in the second man's eyes. "I serve our queen and if something untoward is going on here then I am sure our sovereign will want to know and do something about it."

"Queen's a traitor," the first man spoke in slurred tones. "Abandoned us she did, left us to rot with war and usurpers." He spat again to show his displeasure, earning himself more irate beeping from the ever vigilant robosweep.

"It's late," his companion said. "Come man, we should get home 'fore the wives get antsy on us." He grabbed his friend and lifted him bodily from the bench, shoving him toward the door.

"But I's haven't finished me dinner yet!" the inebriated man grumbled as his friend pushed him along, dragging him out of the inn.

Sir Andross finished his meal alone after that. Other guests left the seats around the knight empty. A reaction that the knight knew was due to his armor and the insignia it bore. Not to mention his own stupidity at opening the conversation with the war.

The realization that all the knights of the castle wore Aulden's crest popped into his mind. The only one who had armor with the new united symbol was actually Sir Eriq. How did the queen feel about that, Sir Andross wondered. *Did Sir Eriq try to get the others to have a united emblem, too? Was the king purposefully not making the change?*

Retiring to his room, he took out the black box of nodes. Positioning the small silver discs on his temples, he accessed the virtual home screen that sprang up. Connecting to the holosite for the queen, he reported his progress so far and what he had learned from his dinner companions.

"Send me some pictures of the state of the city walls and other areas so I can address the issue as soon as possible," she had requested.

He sent a second message to King Amiel. The king seemed bored with the whole thing. He didn't bother to comment on the situation in the city. As Sir Andross readied for bed, he hoped his sovereigns could help the good people of Eporue, though he felt disappointment at the king's lack of interest in the matter.

CHAPTER 26

SANCTAL

HE WAS UP WITH THE SUN and on his way bright and early the next morning. He headed due east across the prairie to the river crossing at Sus Tar, arriving in time to catch the noon ferry. His fellow travelers stayed well clear of him and even the waitress of the on-board deli restaurant served him with curtness.

Once he arrived on the other side, he followed the Tarsus River road south. The Tarsus was the only river that slashed across the entire continent of Vidden, running north to south, and the old road that followed it had not been given proper maintenance during the war. Sir Andross was glad he had not opted for the wagon that Ven had offered. It would have made the journey harder with all the holes on the path. The jorses' legs could go around with minimal effort. *Of course, a hovercraft would have been even better,* he sighed longingly.

There were no major cities between Sus Tar and the rajin's former home. No matter what he found there, Sir Andross intended to stop at the nearest city to store his castle armor. The Auldian crest brought too much attention and hostility. Thankfully, he had thought to bring his old set, which he had bought used when King Amiel knighted him. He hoped to fare better in his unadorned, beat-up mail during the rest of the journey.

It was late afternoon when he first spied the towering spires of the great rajin monastery, Sanctal. The building seemed to glow in the fiery rays of the setting sun. Sir Andross was taken aback to note that it seemed unscathed by war. Made from multi-toned yellow limestone from the quarries of the Perthiark Mountains, it stood eight stories tall. Its beveled glass windows glittered and shimmered in greeting to travelers on the road. The two northern towers seemed to twist and twirl as they stretched up to the sky. In actuality, they were straight. The expert use by its masons of the various shades of yellow stone created the optical illusion.

How could the building have survived unmarred? Sir Andross wondered to himself. He had been present when the attack on the temple took place. Positioned with the infantry, he'd watched fire engulf the structure. His fellow soldiers whispered of dark magic, but the news had reported a new weapon, the flurn bomb. The knight had watched the edifice burn. He'd been spared the task of finalizing the deaths of the wounded survivors. A special group of knights had been sent in once the fires had subsided for that gruesome task.

Sir Andross followed the road as it curved away from the river. It would circle the wall surrounding the property before leading back to its great gates from the southern side. It was when he turned the bend that Sir Andross saw the battle damage.

From that side, Sanctal was charred black. The wall and gates, leading to the entrance of the main building, were in ruins and its windows were blown out. The jagged shards of glass on their sills gave the impression of teeth in the gaping black holes. Here the monastery's towers looked like lopsided dripping candles, the stone seeming to have run in a molten state thanks to the heat of the flurn bombs. The structure's once massive honeywood doors hung on by a single hinge on either side, their wood blackened, leaving the entrance wide open.

He rode up the drive and around the twisted remains of the great iron sculpture that had once been a working miniature of Thyrein's Galactic Wall with all its planets and stars. A smaller version sat in the center of Dravidia City's downtown square. Sir Andross had ridden by it when he first arrived in that part of the kingdom. The scale of this piece was double that one. *It would have been amazing to see it turn,* Sir Andross thought regretfully. Dismounting, he left his jorses near the now ruined masterpiece's entangled beams.

Entering the great hall, his eyes were greeted by further devastation. The golden honeywood floors sported blackened holes where something had exploded. He walked through the war-tarnished halls and blood-splattered rooms looking he-knew-not-for-what and a great sadness began to descend upon him. The rajin were men and women of learning and good, and while they did train in the fighting arts, they were, at heart, proponents of peace. The attack, which at first Sir Andross had considered a brilliant move on the part of King Amiel, now reeked of an evil ruthlessness that saddened the honorable knight.

Every room had been pilfered. Cabinets and drawers were open and bare. The floors, littered with paper and strewn with books, had the marks of battle scraped and burned into them. The deeper he went, the heavier the atmosphere became. A deep melancholy hung in the air and clung to Sir Andross. The weight of the gloom made the tall, broad shouldered knight walk in a drooping slouch. The fragrance of frankincense and myrrh served to mask the scent of rot that permeated the building. The incense had clearly been burned recently, not but two days at most. He wondered if it had been Lady Vivelda and her filear who'd used it. *Had they found the dead bodies of their comrades unburied and decaying? Had the great lady been the one to entomb her brothers and sister in the order?* His heart ached thinking of the burial of his own friends after the various battles.

He came upon a room filled with consoles for holonodes. Sir Andross attempted to activate the first node to access the rajin's servers. His spirits lifted for a few seconds at the possibility of finding a clue to a potential hiding place for the master. They were quickly dashed; there was no power. Sir Andross remembered how his quick glance at the ruined roof had shown the Araal panels destroyed. There seemed to be no juice left in the solar power conserver unit. *He wondered if Lady Vivelda had been able to access anything. Being able to wield energy, she might have found clues.* He'd have to contact her and ask if Horsef had been among the dead. He swallowed hard at the thought of such a painful conversation. The love between the two most powerful rajin alive was legendary. *Her anguish at not knowing must be horrible.*

Returning to the first floor, he noticed a large open-air inner courtyard and was amazed to find its natural beauty untouched. No signs of battle marred the space. Verdant grass with brightly colored flowers formed a geometric pattern of greenery around an oval shaped pond. The sullied walls and arched doorways of the ravished building surrounding it seemed to lean back away from the one place of light that stood against their gloom. *Is this Vivelda's handiwork? Perhaps one of her apprentices?*

The weariness of his journey, the latent hostility of the people he had come across, and the blanket of sorrow that suffocated the monastery began to take a toll on the knight. Exhausted and overcome by a grief he couldn't explain, he sat down and rested his back against a flowering judas tree. He inhaled the sweet fragrance of its pink flowers. Their scent mingled with that of the other blooms of assorted colors that thrived in the garden beds. He relaxed and, before he knew it, he had dozed off into a deep, melancholy slumber. He had not napped for long, when he heard a soft gentle voice whisper his name. Waking he shook his head and wondered if he had dreamed the voice. Then he heard his name spoken once more.

Jumping to his feet, he turned to face the building, his back to the garden and pond, looking to see who had arrived.

"Who's there?" he called out.

"Why do you offend me, sir?" the beautiful voice asked in a peevish tone. "By addressing me with your back?"

Sir Andross spun around and stood breathless as he gazed out into the middle of the man-made pool. Floating over its still waters was a beautiful lady with long silvery hair that hung down well below her waist. She was dressed in a flowing blue silken gown, much like a toga, with a belt of silver water droplets girding her waist. Her clear blue eyes and almost translucent skin gave her an ethereal appearance.

"Are you mute? Can you not speak?" she demanded.

"My Lady," the stunned knight responded recovering his composure. "I have never seen a woman as lovely as you, and I was surprised by your sudden appearance."

She came toward him, gliding over the water without causing even a single ripple upon its peaceful surface. She stopped at the edge and, tilting her head to one side, she pinned him with a penetrating stare.

"Pray tell, Sir Andross, what brings you to this desolate place of grief?"

"I am Sir Andross Draneg, knight of the royal house of..." he paused, did he belong to Dravidia or Aulden? he wondered.

"Do not worry, sir," she spoke as though reading his mind. "Soon the kingdom will be one and all shall call it by its new name, Auldivia."

"How can you know this? Who are you, my Lady?"

"I am Elmalin Lady Darlia."

An elmalin! Sir Andross had never met one before. "How come you to be here, Lady Darlia?" Sir Andross asked, bowing deeply to her.

"Oh, I visited the rajin often. I was once one of them, before becoming an elmalin, and I enjoyed debating with them. I was passing by, saw you sleeping here, and wondered at your presence."

"I was overcome with despair and exhaustion. It has been a long journey. I fell asleep."

"The rajin are powerful beings. Their needless massacre left this once peaceful and joyous sanctuary impregnated with the negative energy of pain and deep sorrow," she explained. Stepping out of the pond and walking around the garden, though Sir Andross felt it was more like she hovered as her bare feet never seemed to actually touch the ground, she said "When I came, after the battle, this beautiful place was marred by blood and the decomposing dead. My friends and I buried them. Then we cleansed this small part of the heaviness. We are the keepers of the natural world you know. Still, you can feel how the oppressiveness of the rest of the halls tries to seep through."

She came back to where he stood and looked up at him. She was very petite and her eyes gleamed softly in the dimming evening light. Sir Andross felt a tug as if he could fall in and swim in their cool waters.

"So, what brings you here? Which was my question, sir, as I already know who you are," the peevish tone was back, he noted dimly.

"I am on a quest, Lady Darlia," Sir Andross answered.

"A quest! For what, sir?"

"I seek the Great Master Rajin Lord Horsef. He will be able to help the queen know how to use the liquid Rajin LaRoo gave her family. Do you know where I may find him? Was he among the dead you buried?"

"No. He was not among the dead. But I am afraid I have lost contact with the rajin that survived. I believe they headed to Tarmal. It is one of their larger temples located on the Intergalactic Council moon of Eskopock."

"He is not there. Lady Vivelda arrived on Jorn searching for him. Did you see her when she came here to Sanctal?"

Something flickered in the elmalin's eyes, but it was gone too soon for Sir Andross to name. "I did not have the pleasure." There was no hint of emotion in her tone. But her eyes remained fixed on his.

"Do you know where the master might have sought refuge?" he pressed.

After a moment's consideration, she said, "I know that Rajin Horsef was a good friend of the Prophet Orloff. Perhaps Horsef confided in the prophet where he was intending to go?"

Fern Brady

"Where might I find Orloff?"

"He resides in a cave on the eastern side of Mount Tarsus," she responded, a mischievous twinkle in her eyes.

"My Lady, your help has been invaluable. Thank you."

"No need for thanks," the elmalin said. "I do so love quests!"

And then she was gone, dissolving into a blue mist that seemed to merge back into the pond's waters. Noting that the sky had darkened considerably, Sir Andross made camp in the garden for the night.

The next morning, Sir Andross went down into the crypts. He still had the crystal dagger to find and Lady Vivelda had told the queen it might lie entombed with Rajin Shrang LaRoo. He'd decided, given how dark it would be with no electricity, to wait for daylight. Not that he was scared of rummaging around among the dead at night, not that it would be any less dark down there in the morning. It would just be safer with daylight, he reasoned.

Now, with a torch, the light's beam illuminating the marble chamber, he searched for the resting place of Rajin Shrang LaRoo. The first five floors of tombs yielded a lot of rajin names, but not the one he was looking for. It was at the deepest level, on the tenth floor down, that he found the marble coffin. The air was stale, the ventilation having shut off when the electricity of the solar energy conserver unit gave out.

Verifying the name on the plaque one more time, Sir Andross hung his torch in a nearby sconce, and struggled to open the heavy lid. It wouldn't budge. He pushed and pushed, but it held secure. Exhausted he wiped his brow and looked about the marble coffin in hopes that maybe the dagger might be around it rather than in it. *No such luck.* But he did note the hinges on the back. Lifting the thick piece of marble with immense difficulty, Sir Andross was shoved back as a mass of thick black dreadlock hair exploded out of the coffin, spilling in all directions.

"What the—" Sir Andross pushed through the dreads, releasing a woodsy scent into the stuffy air of the crypt.

Peering into the coffin, a thick web of coiled hair barred access to the body. The shock of seeing the phenomena hit him. This was not scientifically possible. Yet somehow the master's death had not halted the hair's growth. Had it been growing for nearly 300 years? What would Sir Andross find if he pushed it aside to reach the body?

A chill of horror ran through the intrepid knight, but there was

244

nothing for it. To find the blasted dagger the queen needed, he had to search this sarcophagus. Taking a deep shuddering breath, he dug in with trembling hands. After removing enough hair from its tight net-like thickness, his startled eyes fell upon the body of Bravura Rajin Shrang LaRoo, the Great Mystic. The yellow skin of his face was smooth and supple and his countenance held a serenity Sir Andross couldn't even fathom. His slit-like eyes, denoting his original Asprienese heritage, looked like they might open at any moment. Clad in the formal brown attire of the Mystic Rajin branch with the scarlet ceremonial robe pushed aside, Sir Andross was amazed at the extreme thinness of the dead master's body. The knight recalled Lord Sabred and his weak-looking body, which much resembled the one before him now. Though the dragon slayer was not a rajin, many believed his uncle, Rajin Zegan, had taught the legendary hero much about the use of power in the universe.

Another shudder of terror slithered down Sir Andross as he beheld Rajin Shrang LaRoo's hands. They had been placed one upon the other over his chest. The nails had grown creating a thick, twisting, gray vice-like chain around the corpse's body. In some places, they had dug into the flesh and come back out on the other side. Sir Andross closed his eyes and tried to calm himself. He drew in deep breaths of fresh forest scent and began to feel a little less lightheaded than just moments before. He thought of his beautiful queen and the need of their nation.

Shaking, the knight began to search the pockets of the rajin for the dagger, which was clearly not grasped in his hands, thank the Great I Am. He found nothing. Carefully he rolled the body to one side, searching the thick mass of hair there. Nothing. He rolled LaRoo to the other side. Nothing. Carefully he lifted the hands just enough to wiggle his own to search the chest area further. Nothing. As he drew his hand back, a sharp edge of the dead rajin's nail scratched him. He yelped in pain. A jolt of electric current spread through Sir Andross, knocking him back onto the cushion of hair on the crypt's cold marble floor.

With a terrified whine, he rose and slammed the lid down. A ton of hair remained outside the coffin. Sir Andross pushed his way out of the tangle of dreadlocks and took the stairs up to the ground floor at a run. Maintaining his urgent pace, he dashed through the empty building, reaching the front courtyard. Out of breath, he heaved, taking in the fresh spring air. Bent over, his hands on his knees, he closed his eyes to calm himself. When at length he opened them again, his gaze fell upon his scratched hand. His ebony skin was smooth, no open wound, no blood.

"What the—"

Sir Andross moved to his jorses and settled his bags, keeping his mind from dwelling on the experience he'd had. Mounting up into the comfortable seat, he steered his jorse back onto the road, with the cargo palfrey in tow.

CHAPTER 27
PREPARATIONS FOR WAR

"Have you seen Sir Andross?"

"He has gone with Lady Vivelda."

Verena looked up from the vegetable soup before her and into Amiel's guarded blue eyes as she spoke the lie. It had been several days since the knight had departed on the quest.

"Who gave him permission?"

"I sent him with her, of course." She returned her attention to her meal as if that were the end of the conversation.

"Why?"

"Why not?"

"The rajin asked for assistance?"

"No," Verena said, putting her spoon down and returning her eyes to his. "I sent him with her. If she finds Lord Horsef, I want to be the first to know."

"I didn't realize you were that interested in Horsef," Amiel's tone was too matter of fact. He clearly didn't like this development.

Does he suspect something? Why would he? She picked up her spoon and dove into the soup once more. Time stretched between them.

"What do you seek with Horsef?" Amiel pressed, turning his statement into a full question when she remained silent.

"Nothing specific. He was always a great help to my father. His counsel on the coming Gortive situation would be welcome. Don't you think?"

Verena lifted her gaze once more and motioned a hudroid to take her bowl away. Her eyes drifted to Amiel at the other end of the table. He shrugged.

Silence settled on them once more as the second course plates were set before them, and they continued their meal. Verena had nearly finished her steak when Amiel broached the subject again.

"So you just want to know about Horsef to get his advice?"

Verena sensed he didn't believe the simple explanation and wanted to know her true purpose.

With a smug smile on her face, she answered him, "I realize you don't believe in the rajin, perhaps not even in the Great I Am, but I do and yes, I do want the great master's support and input."

"You should have cleared it with me," his tone of condescension showed his irritation. It grated on her nerves.

"They are my guards. If I want to send one somewhere, why shouldn't I?" Verena watched his face redden.

"In future, you would do well to get my approval before directing my knights on missions."

"I command my guards, and I felt it prudent to have one accompany Lady Vivelda. This will ensure our nation will know first if Horsef is alive."

"Our nation?" he asked cryptically.

"Yes, Amiel," she let her voice drip with the patronizing tone he so often applied to her, "our nation. You asked about him yourself. Do you not want to know?"

"Of course, I do. I just wonder for which nation you seek his help?"

"*Our* nation," Verena responded firmly. "You should start thinking in terms of *Our* as well."

Rising, he ended the conversation with a frustrated, "Do not send out other knights without consulting me first."

He exited the room before she could reply. Her stomach tightened into knots. Amiel's inquiry hadn't felt normal, though really what could she consider normal for him? Was there more to it or did he simply dislike her taking actions without his permission? Unable to keep eating, Verena thanked her hudroids and retired to her chambers.

"As you can see, my Lords and Ladies, the defenses of Eporue have not been rebuilt." Verena gestured to the holoimages floating above the council table. She had carefully edited them to ensure Sir Andross was not visible in any reflective surfaces. He had sent her the footage during his report on what he had learned at Sanctal. "Indeed, the citizens suffered greatly as the waters of wauger flooded many homes due to the force shield only being activated around Epo Keep."

"Lies!" Lord Uld stated. "If this were true, there would have been reports of it in the news media, not to mention, requests for assistance. Clearly, this is an attempt to discredit the new Baron."

"Where do you think I got this footage?" Verena challenged, letting them infer that she might have retrieved it from a news channel.

"Why hasn't it been seen by others?" Uld called her bluff with an arrogant sneer.

"The queen has presented us with information that she found on news channels," Amiel spoke in a calm voice. "Are you really going to disrespect my wife by calling her a liar?"

Lord Uld hesitated, his eyes flitting about the room for some support, but finding none. "Of course, I did not mean she was a liar. I meant that the reports are lies. I—"

"The source is reliable." Verena met Lord Uld's hateful stare. Her eyes challenging him, confident in Amiel's new support of her. "I myself witnessed it using the satellites to check the country's situation during wauger."

"Baron Epo will be sent for to answer these allegations," Amiel stated, putting an end to the discussion. "Your Grace," he addressed the Duke of Aul. "Send a request to the Council of Vassal's for aid to the people of Eporue. We must get those defenses repaired and ready without further delay."

"Right away, Sire."

"Also," Verena added. "Have the Royal Engineer Corps mobilized to rebuild this city's walls as soon as possible."

"Yes, of course," the duke responded, casting a glance at the king for confirmation. Verena was pleased when Amiel gave a nod of ascent.

"Perhaps a proclamation now about the importance of using public funds—"

"I sent word to all informally. The fact that one lord failed to comply doesn't mean the others haven't." Amiel's eyes met hers and Verena knew she best not press further. "Let us send some of the engineer corps officers to make a tour of the various cities, of primary priority the ones most affected by the war and to the north and east of our continent," he spoke to the duke, who jotted down the command.

"The rebels have taken Fort Iark and are holed up there," Lord Uld commented.

"Bring up Iark," Amiel commanded.

The Earl of Ydarb accessed the maps and soon the images of Eporue where replaced with the great Fort of Iark. The imposing square keep filled the space above the council table.

Verena had only ever visited there once, but she remembered the fortress as a dark and musty place. Built in the times of colonization, the windows were narrow slits and the masonry was reinforced with honrol. It had been from Iark that the Gortive had finally been defeated all those centuries ago.

On the holomap, the image of the mighty stronghold, sitting atop the plateau of Perth's edge and overlooking the Valley of Garpeth, flew the flag of Dravidia from its battlements.

"One thing we know about the Gortive, they don't like to sail." Lord Ydarb's brown eyes met Verena's as he continued, "It is most likely, when they attack, they will come at us from across the frozen lands of the North or South. If from the north, Iark will be crucial in keeping them from invading the rest of the continent."

"An attack from the north is not as likely as from the south," Amiel stated. Using his chair's control panel, he zoomed down the map of the continent to the southern shores. "The Strait of Dralden is shorter and its waters are calmer. They could land their forces across the shores of the Torsgeld to the west of the Aulden Mountains and in the Udeep to the east. They wouldn't have to scale a plateau in the south as they would be forced to in the north." He zoomed back to the Perth Plateau with its sheer drop cliff. "A northern attack would mean a longer boat ride for them plus scaling tall cliffs to gain access. I don't feel they would take that route."

"Then we should prepare our strongest defenses in the south," Verena said, considering what Amiel had explained.

"Yes," Amiel concurred. "As to the Dravidians, we will need to launch a siege, until they surrender."

"Couldn't we just send a missive asking them to come here and accept the new government?" Verena asked, hoping still to avoid bloodshed.

"They were given that chance months ago, when you accepted." Amiel's eyes were hooded as he stared into hers.

"Not really. When I accepted, they no doubt felt it was under duress, which would make them even more intent on rebelling. Things were heated and confused, plus then they were attacked in the Parthiark tunnels. That escalation made things worse," Verena pressed. "During the deluge months, things have been at an impasse. We've had time to cool down, as have they. They weathered wauger in Iark, surely aware of the progress we have made on merging the laws of Aulden and Dravidia. I feel certain, with the news of the legislative changes, they will have seen that progress toward a united continent is going well. Asking can't hurt."

"Giving rebels a chance to come and stage a coup d'état here in the castle would be ridiculous," Lord Uld's venom dripped across the room. "They would take the opportunity to attempt yet another assassination of our king." .

"It was never proven it was them in the first case." Verena struggled to keep a cool tone to her statement. All these months, she had felt the great injustice of the events that had set aside the betrothal agreement. "Count Tor has been held without due process this entire time. When will he be given his day in court? His attorney has petitioned several times for his release, but to no avail. What is the hold up?"

"The evidence is clear—" Lord Uld began.

Amiel broke in, silencing the brash Lordling. "Send the ninth fleet to surround the Perth Peninsula and position a regiment near Iark, but keep it well out of range of their turrets. Iark is at the edge of the plateau and they will have an advantage over land forces, but with the navy blockading the water escape, a siege might be plausible." Amiel's voice was cool and collected. "Draft a note offering them mercy if they surrender and swear allegiance to me as sole sovereign, like their queen did." He turned his gaze to her as he finished. "We shall see if they have indeed become reasonable."

"May I draft the missive?" Verena's voice was full of hope, and she chided herself to refrain from showing emotions. "The wording will be important."

"My wording won't appeal to them, you think?" Amiel smiled at her. It wasn't mocking, but rather a reflection of actual amusement.

"I think my way of saying it may be... better... in this instance."

"Very well," Amiel acquiesced. "But I will proof it and make changes if I feel they are needed."

"Of course. And what of Count Tor?" Verena pressed.

"Lord Baraven, as head of our Judiciary Oversight Committee, look into the status of this situation and ensure it moves forward in the proper manner according to our laws." Amiel stood and stretched, signaling the end of the council session.

He left via the back door near the thrones that led to their private sitting area behind the chamber. She remained, as had become her custom. Verena found the quiet of the room after the discussions soothing for some reason. Now, she watched as the nobles filed out. The older, wiser ones, bowed their head slightly to her in reverence to her position as they exited. *Perhaps I am earning their respect, maybe?*

"Are you sure you want to make that move?" Amiel asked, his eyes glinting with a predatory look.

Verena's hand stilled over the gameboard. Her fingers held her playing piece over the space she had been about to deposit it on. Her eyes took in the status of the game, her mind a whirl with all the potential moves and countermoves. Satisfied that her choice would not leave her open for a win by Amiel, she let the piece drop into place.

"I think so."

Her eyes lifted to his from their battle of sovereign. The game's hexagonal board and its complexity of maneuvers had always been her downfall. This time she was sure she had him.

The door to the private salon slammed open, startling Verena. Lord Uld and a handful of his friends stormed in.

"What is the meaning of this?" Amiel's voice held anger at the disrespectful intrusion into their personal time.

"After all we have done to support your cause," Lord Uld spat, "you're offering the rebels their lands back, a full pardon. What kind of man are you?" The lordling's face almost glowed red with his anger. "Those lands should be given to YOUR people not back to hers!"

A tense silence blanketed the chamber. Verena secretly clicked the button next to her chair, which summoned Sir Eriq. The guards who stood in the periphery of the room had taken a few steps closer to Amiel and their hands were on their weapons. Uld and his companions blocked the doorway, seething like feral dogs.

"You forget yourself and to whom you speak," Amiel stated with a calmness that awed Verena. Placing the cup of brandy he'd been enjoying down on the table beside his armchair, he rose. Coming to stand in front of her, he faced the insolent nobles and blocked her view. "What I choose to do is my prerogative, not yours. You are hereby removed from the Council of Peers and you will leave my castle, now. Sir Eriq, see to it."

Verena peered past Amiel's side and noted the Lord High Marshal had arrived with more guards. They stood behind the impudent lordlings, ready to take action.

"We gave you this nation." Lord Uld sneered in Amiel's face. "We can take it from you."

"Out with you!" Sir Eriq spoke, pushing aside the nobles and clasping strong hands upon Lord Uld.

He and the guards soon removed the mutinous nobles, escorting them out of the castle and tossing their belongings out with them.

Verena felt relief at having Uld and his cohort far from them. The lord's unpleasantness every time they crossed paths was increasingly belligerent. She shuddered recalling the one time he'd bumped into her in the hall before her guards had caught up with her quick pace. If they had not rounded the corner, Verena was almost certain the ridiculous boy would have taken liberties with her body. Amiel's giving in to their demands after their attempt on his life had clearly emboldened them.

The worried look on Amiel's face as he settled back into his chair and took a long drink from the amber liquor told her he felt as she did, that they had not seen the last of this bunch. Soon, they would have something unpleasant from them to deal with. Verena sighed and gave Amiel a reassuring smile.

She let her eyes enjoy his body as he leaned over the gameboard, calculating his next move. His shirt was open, his chest hair peeking out, making her hands yearn to touch him.

"You aren't wearing the jewel." The observation slipped out of her, and she felt her cheeks heat up.

He looked up, his eyes taking her in. "It's supposed to be for protection. I... guess I really don't feel unsafe here... with you." He smiled. "I win, I believe."

Verena glanced at the gameboard. "Foluc!"

CHAPTER 28

A NIJAR AND HIS KING

GODAR HAD CHOSEN FOR HIS ROOMS the lowest level of the prison housed beneath Dravidia Castle. Though the palace was a rectangular series of buildings interspersed with open-air courtyards above ground, the jail levels were shaped like a pin-wheel within the box of honrol walls buried deep beneath the earth. Each level had at its heart a monitoring station for the guards. Corridors of cells ran from the center out ending in small cafeterias and interrogation rooms. The cells themselves had full bathrooms installed in one corner and each inmate was individually housed; isolation was the key component to the punishment system. The nijar found it amusing. Being left alone delighted him.

He enjoyed his new abode far more than the catacombs beneath Auld Palace. These spaces he'd designed for himself. When he went up to the main building, he cloaked himself in his Viscount Pembra persona, but here, in his domain, he could be in his natural form. He detested the Council of Peers meetings, yet he had to play his role, advising King Amiel. Soon, however, the nijar would reign and all these pathetic humans would be dealt with.

At the nijar's request, the twentieth level of the castle's underground prison had been cleared of guards. The consoles of the center monitoring station had been removed. The cells cleared away and all doors taken off, the rooms now contained tables with assorted scientific equipment as well as bookcases filled to capacity.

The honrol floor and walls had been stained jet black. On the south side, the long passageway had been modified into a bedroom suite with a small sitting room. His young apprentice had a smaller set of rooms for himself on the other end of the level. Godar had taken the boy on when the father, one of his informants, failed. He'd dealt with the mother and the father, but something about the boy had caught Godar's interest. He was irritatingly slow, yet willing to serve.

The light flow, which in all other levels simulated sunlight, on Godar's floor had been changed to a red tone. The scarlet light gave the proper glow and set the mood for his rituals. Only in his small greenhouse for herbs and other necessary items of the like was the light bright. His apprentice had proven useful there at least.

In the center, where the monitoring station had been, there was now a large blood red circle painted on the floor. Within it a square and a triangle intersected. Tall candelabras of red ionized-honrol stood at each point where the geometric shapes touched the main circle. Black candles with orange flames combined with the red flow made for the perfect ambiance of the chamber as far as Godar was concerned.

The nijar stood in the center of the symbol of his order, pouring water into a maroon marble basin. Clad in his midnight-blue robe, he tossed the empty pitcher to his assistant, and waved the boy away. He pulled the hood tighter around his pale face and stared into the container. His eyes glowed amber in the dim light of the black candles. The nijar positioned his hands on the edges of the water, running his fingers smoothly across the glistening surface, the restlessness that had plagued him for many months now eating away at him.

What's making me feel this... this... uncertainty... discomfort... I can't pin-point the root. Godar had been so pleased with the outcome of the war. The rajin of Jorn extinguished, the Auldians in power over the whole continent, Amiel married to the Verena bitch after all, and Parthia soon to be conquered, for he knew Amiel was a great military genius. The nijar were about to set the entire planet firmly in the hands of the royal house that had long supported their secret order.

Still, Godar's stomach churned with the disturbing suspicion that something was wrong. He felt his hold on matters shifting, but could not understand why. Amiel was firmly in his control. The boy consulted him on everything and Godar felt sure the amulet was having its effect. Yet... Vivelda's arrival was a bad omen. The nijar had been clear that by no means must the rajin be allowed on the planet again. The duke swore all was in hand. *Chump! She is here and maybe Horsef as well.*

The water rippled. Godar stepped back to allow the portal to open. A blue mist rose and the shape of a beautiful woman formed.

"Master," Darlia, the water elmalin in his service, greeted him.

"What news do you bring?"

"I met a knight from the castle guard. He was on the ferry at Sus Tar. I followed him as he made his way to the rajin monastery."

"He sought the rajin? There are none left." Godar's heart filled with pride as he recalled how the nijar had destroyed those ridiculous idiots. Soon, they would all be crushed and the Galactic Wall purged of their weak religion.

"Yes, Master," the elmalin continued. "At the behest of the queen, he is seeking Horsef the Great."

"Great! Ha! The dead, more like," Godar's voice dripped with hate. "Why does the queen seek the rajin?"

"The knight says she has some liquid, made by a Rajin LaRoo. She—"

"Shrang LaRoo! Could the legends be true then?" The nijar began to pace around the basin, muttering to himself. If Verena had actual liquid, then their powers were real. And she had them in her possession. Godar clenched his fists at the thought of Verena. "Boy!" he hollered.

"Yes, master," his apprentice scurried back into the room.

"Fetch me The Chronicles of Time!" He watched as the young kid ran from the room to do his bidding. Turning to Darlia, he pressed her for information. The compliant elemental answered all she knew from the conversation with Sir Andross.

"The book you asked for, my Master." The boy presented the leather-bound volume.

Godar held the tome. The title stood out against the golden cover. The boy stood there, gaping at the curvaceous elmalin.

"Am I supposed to hold the book while I read?" Godar asked with annoyance. When the boy continued to stare at the lady, he hollered, "Fetch the book stand, you worthless idiot!"

The boy mobilized. Godar wondered if the child was mentally challenged. His father had been pretty stupid, though the mother had been useful at times. As the stand was placed before him, Godar set the book on it. The nijar flipped through its pages until he found the information he sought. Silence filled the chamber while Godar read.

"Where is the knight now?" he flung the question at Darlia, his eyes aflame.

"I sent him to Mt Tarsus, to the cave of the rego, Eldan," Darlia giggled triumphantly.

"You sent him WHERE?" Godar's voice became almost shrill as his displeasure flashed in his amber eyes.

"I... thought you would wish him to fail, Master." The look of fright that entered the elmalin's eyes pleased Godar, but her idiocy did not.

"Try not to think for yourself in the future, child," the nijar spat out, his voice dripping with condescension and malice. "Leave that to those who know better."

Reaching into the water with his left index finger, he watched with satisfaction as the simpering elmalin cried out in pain, the electrical shocks rippling through her water-based connection. She writhed in agony, begging his forgiveness, until, at last, she doubled over, spewing blood into the clear water. She didn't try to break the connection or close the portal, as she had in previous times; she was learning, he thought with glee. Attempting escape would be futile. Godar's thin lips curved with delight as he watched the basin's contents swirl with the scarlet streaks.

"Find out what has become of him. Ensure his survival and you will guarantee your own. The quest must succeed." He dismissed her with a disgusted wave of his hand, watching with satisfaction as she slowly slinked into the mist. "Boy, summon our king to me!"

Godar's ire was palpable. His whole body shook from the violence of the anger that roiled through him. He sat, awaiting the king's pleasure in the antechamber of the sovereign. The insolent boy had refused to come to him, as he had always done before. Instead, this "king" had summoned him, Godar the Powerful, to grovel for an audience. Worse, the impudent child was making him wait.

The door to Amiel's private study opened and the Duke of Aul came forward.

"You must understand, Godar," the duke addressed him with a placating bow and smooth words. "He is young and his victory over Dravidia may have gone a bit to his head. He is still our boy though. You can be sure of that."

Godar graced the duke with silence. His eyes glaring at the indignity he was being forced to suffer. Of course, he was here. *What choice do I have?* Powerful though he might be, the nijar was no fool. He would bide his time and take his vengeance for this insult.

"You... may go in," the duke stated, swallowing hard, averting his eyes from Godar's cruel gaze.

Rising with deliberate coolness, the nijar made his way into the king's study. Amiel sat behind his desk busy shuffling papers. The king neither rose nor acknowledged Godar's presence. It was not until the nijar lord had stood for a full minute before the desk that the arrogant boy bade him to take a seat.

"You asked to see me. How can I be of service?" Amiel's voice held a note of indifference not lost upon the nijar.

"It is I who am here to serve you, Sire, as I served your father before you," Godar's voice crackled with the effort to contain the wrath flowing through him.

He had whispered the incantation that shielded his eyes and turned them a dark brown. He would not let the boy see the agitation he was causing. Silence ensued, which only augmented the aggrieved nijar's darkening mood.

"I have discovered a plot to harm you, Sire," Godar proclaimed, breaking the tension.

"Oh?"

"It would seem your wife has hired a knight for the purpose of locating Rajin Horsef. No doubt, she hopes to use him to overthrow you."

"Is that so?"

Silence reigned again. The king's eyes became hooded. *The ridiculous besotted fool! He is truly in love with that little wench of his.* Godar's face broke into a wide, satisfied smile.

"You must know she never wanted you. Now, she seeks to find a way to be rid of you forever." The nijar shook his gray-haired head, as if he felt sympathy for the arrogant prick's plight. "But I have set my people to the task of seeing to it she does not succeed. You can trust me, Amiel. I have ever sought the good of your royal house."

"I'm afraid I must command you not to interfere with our quest."

"Your quest?" Godar's face rippled from the shock of Amiel's revelation.

The boy knew. The roiling undefined emotion that plagued him intensified. *Is my hold over Amiel waning? Can a woman exert that kind of power? No, it could not be.*

Bringing himself under control, he asked, "What do you need the rajin for? Has the loyal service of the nijar displeased your Majesty?"

"It seems you do not have all the facts." Amiel's smug expression grated on the nijar's already overwrought nerves. "Let me explain. My wife has the Shrang LaRoo liquid in her possession. Sadly, she doesn't know how to work it. So, we seek the Rajin, Horsef the Great. Only a rajin can teach her. Unless..." the king leaned forward across the desk. "Can you show her their use?"

"I am afraid I cannot, Majesty," Godar's confession came out through clenched teeth. "Do you know what the liquids do?"

Amiel's hesitation gave the nijar his advantage.

"Allow me to enlighten you, Majesty," Godar's voice dripped condescension. "They were created by a rajin on planet Drulin, who was in service to the House of Drav there. It is said that the women of the line are the only ones that can use the liquid. The rajin who made them taught the first Countess Drav, and she taught her daughter, and so forth."

"Verena's mother died when she was very young. She probably did not teach Verena the secrets of it, so now my lovely wife must seek a rajin for help."

"The liquid, when activated, can transport a person anywhere, across space and time, through to any of the fourteen dimensions of the universe."

"Why do you suppose the rajin limited their use to the females of the line?"

"No doubt they felt a woman was less likely to misuse their power, though really, they didn't understand women very well, now, did they?" Godar gave a snorty laugh. He noticed the boy's genuine interest in the subject. *Good, you should remember who rules you little king.*

"You are not powerful enough to use them?" Amiel asked just then, gracing Godar with one of his most arrogant stares. *The insolent pup!*

Godar leaned forward, his eyes scanning Amiel's neck. The chain that held the amulet was not there. Why did he not wear it? Where had his control mechanism gone? He would need to find out.

"The rajin did not write that knowledge down, which is strange considering their love for writing books," Godar defended, throwing Amiel a nasty look. "But once they are unlocked, we should be able to use them as we wish. You own her, and when the rajin teach her, we will have the power."

"I will have the power," Amiel corrected the nijar. "She is mine after all."

"Be wary, Majesty," Godar said, feigning concern. "You have a soft spot for her, and she clearly seeks to go against you. Perhaps she wishes to rule on her own. She never did want to marry you, did she?" The nijar's eyes gleamed with delight at the wounded look that flickered briefly in the boy's eyes.

"We must see to it that Sir Andross succeeds," Amiel asserted covering his pain quickly, though Godar knew the boy suffered his unrequited love. The nijar smiled malevolently as Amiel continued, "Get one of your informants to help the knight. If Verena is already funding this expedition no point in wasting money on another one for the same purpose, don't you think?"

"She is funding it?" Godar struck home. "I thought you were together on this with her."

"She doesn't know I am aware of the mission she sent Sir Andross on," Amiel's tone showed he didn't like having to confess this fact.

"Well, then," Godar said rising. "We shall play her game against her and ensure your success." As he made his way toward the door, he asked casually, "Where is the gem I gave you?"

"It bothers me, so I put it away."

Turning before exiting, Godar counseled, "These are perilous times. You should have it on always, for your protection, Sire."

He didn't wait to hear a response.

Foolish little king! Godar rushed through the hallways toward the lift, his mind turning over various plans to ruin the boy who dared play deceitful games with him. The nijar was certain Amiel planned on allowing the rajin to return. The Elemental Darlia had given Godar the news of the Abloir's imminent arrival. The tri-un leadership of the Elementals would seek to establish a foothold on Jorn. They'd been most disappointed when Verena had disappeared. Now, they would seek to strengthen her rule, against the ridiculous king. Amiel had given his word to rid the planet of all these orders and establish the nijar openly. With the rajin and elementals against him, his wife would soon overthrow his short-lived reign, Godar was sure of this.

Now, Amiel played with powers he couldn't possibly understand and went against those who'd helped raise his house from an insignificant principality with no seat on the Intergalactic Council to the status of king of one of the most powerful planets in Thyrein's Galactic Wall. *He'll pay for this betrayal, if it's the last thing...*

The tinkling laughter brought him up short. The beautiful sound came from the main hall, just around the corner. Moving stealthily, Godar took a look. And there she stood. Fiery red hair cascaded down her elegant back as she tilted her graceful neck with laughter. Delicious pink lips, luscious breasts, and a cinched waist that flared to well-proportioned hips, ended in curvy legs displayed in skin-tight pants. Creamy skin glowing with health and emerald eyes twinkling with mirth completed the woman that stood out among the other wenches. These paled in comparison to the beauty in their midst. Verena, the woman whose power warred with Godar's hold on Amiel, was scrumptious.

No wonder the boy is besotted, Godar thought. Of course, he'd known she was considered by many to be the most beautiful woman on Jorn, perhaps, some asserted, in all the universe, but Godar had never bothered to *really* look at her. In the council chamber, he kept his head down, listening to the power struggle; reserving his words for Amiel in private. He'd never worried enough to glance at her for long. What use had he for the pathetic woman too rebellious to do her father's bidding? *None.*

But now, his mind brought forth an opportunity.

Whispering softly, the nijar spoke the incantation transforming his features into those of his youth. His old, wrinkly skin, became a smooth bronze and his graying hair changed into full brown curls. Once ready, Godar made his way to her.

Coming near, he bowed. "Majesty," his voice a rich tenor.

Godar's eyes were captivated by the look in Verena's as she turned to him. Her emerald gaze was filled with a sweet innocence and beguiling glimmer that left him speechless. The nijar realized he was gawking at her like a love-sick school boy. Yet he couldn't seem to take his eyes off her full luscious lips and the silkiness of her hair.

She gave him her hand. He felt the fire the moment he touched her soft skin. It was as if he had been set ablaze. His mind's eye filled with tantalizing visions of this beautiful creature spread out naked upon his bed. Lust, unlike any he had ever felt before, caused an erection that throbbed in his loins.

"Oh... are you a rajin?" the queen was speaking to him. His befuddled mind tried to focus on the words she was saying.

"No," his voice came out hoarse as his vocal cords took on the deep timber of his youth. "I'm just your humble servant, Majesty."

Godar gave her a deep bow, taking her hand, which he continued to hold, gallantly to his lips. The baby softness of her skin on his mouth made a groan of desire rumble in his throat.

"I'm sorry?" Verena gave him a confused look. "Your robes... I thought maybe..." A flustered crimson graced her cheeks.

"I am Viscount Pembra," the nijar explained, using the title given to him by Amiel so he could openly stand at his side.

"Of course! I am sorry I did not recognize you, Viscount."

"Why would your Majesty bother with a lowly noble like myself," Godar's flirty smile elicited another delicious blush. *She is truly magnificent. No wonder Amiel has been enchanted by her.* "I'm here only to serve. On my way to the library to do some research on the king's behalf now, as a matter of fact."

"I, too, am headed that way."

"Well, then, would your Majesty do me the honor of allowing me to escort you there?" he asked gallantly.

"Of course, Viscount." She allowed him to guide them toward the lift.

A malicious gleam came into the nijar's eyes, as they walked, though he made sure to hide it from her whenever she turned to look his way. Godar knew exactly how he would teach the impudent cur of a king a well-deserved lesson. *Who knew, maybe he would take the kingdom as well?*

CHAPTER 29

MOUNT TARSUS

SIR ANDROSS CROSSED THE EAST VONGO RIVER and rode south toward the Tarsidian Mountain Range, of which Mount Tarsus, was the highest peak. The Vale of Tars consisted of mostly farmlands and ranches, with very small villages interspersed in between. Using his nodes, Sir Andross accessed the holonet and looked up Mount Tarsus as his AI continued on the clear path to their destination.

He discovered that the mighty volcano, which rose well over 8,000 feet, had once fertilized the Sarnac River Valley, the Vale of Tars, and the Torsgeld plains but was now dormant. Though it had not erupted in more than four generations, the rumbling from within its belly gave proof that it was not yet extinct. Sir Andross hoped that it would not suddenly decide to blow when he was climbing it. *Of course, a prophet wouldn't make his home there if it was dangerous, right?*

Sir Andross reached Tars City a few days later. It was the seat of the Count of Tarsin, a Dravidian nobleman who, Sir Andross learned, had chosen to accept the queen's proclamation and swear allegiance to King Amiel the second time. The city buzzed with activity. Everywhere he looked, the knight noted rebuilding and fortification work.

The Pelinal, a small inn located near the south gate, had storage lockers for rent. Sir Andross decided to purchase one and leave his castle gear, putting on his old beat-up and somewhat ill-fitting former armor. It was remarkable how much nicer people treated him in his non-crest-bearing attire. That evening, after a delicious meal in the inn's restaurant, Sir Andross made contact with the queen over the holonet account she had set up for them.

"Have you found the prophet, Sir Andross?" the queen asked by way of greeting.

"I have just arrived at Tars City, Majesty," the knight reported. "It is quite a difference from Eporue."

"Oh, how so?" The queen's tone gave away her disappointment that he had not yet reached his objective.

"The count is rebuilding all the city's defenses, and from what I have shared with you, your Majesty will be pleased to see that the city is in great shape."

"That is good to hear. Contact me once you find Orloff."

It was natural, of course, that she would be eager for news of the quest, but Sir Andross couldn't help but feel disappointed she was not more excited to learn this part of the realm was doing well. Once he signed off with her, he logged on to report to the king.

"I've reached Tars City, Majesty," Sir Andross began. "The situation here is very good. The defenses are being—"

"Sir Andross, I appreciate your sending me updates on the progress of the rebuilding and the status of the cities you cross, however, it is unnecessary," the king's tone was curt. "Contact me once you have found the rajin or when something of importance is discovered. I have others that report about the defenses and city status. And, I will ask you not to send images of your travels to the queen!"

"Of course, Majesty, I should have known—"

"No need to apologize," the king cut him off. "I'll await news of the quest."

Left with a blank screen, Sir Andross signed off and removed his nodes. As he prepared for the evening, Sir Andross wondered if he would succeed. So much depended on him. First, he had to make it up the mountain. The knight could only pray he was fit enough for the endeavor. Settling in for a comfortable sleep in the inn's bed, Sir Andross hoped his body could take the rigor of the coming days.

The following morning, Sir Andross arrived at the foot of the volcano. He noticed that although the left side of the mountain sloped gently, the eastern face was extremely steep. It would not be an easy ascent. Undaunted by this, or by the mountains incredible height, Sir Andross prepared to hike in search of the cave where Lord Orloff might live. The day was unusually warm for that time of year. Jorn's springs tended to be mild, easing into summer's heat. But the day of the climb dawned with temperatures akin to those of Geldenbur, Jorn's hottest summer month. The fearless knight removed his old heavy armor and put on the lightweight hiker's suit he'd purchased in Tars City. It was black, reinforced cloth, and included an oxygen generating unit, much smaller and compact than the one in the armor.

He secured his jorses in a thicket of lletel brush. The hardy dark-purple plant with bright orange flowers common to the area around the Tarsidian Mountains would hide them from the view of passersby. Turning to the mountain, he began his task.

It was rough going. As the day progressed the sun became hotter and hotter. The shirt of his suit was completely drenched in sweat by the time Ara had reached his zenith in the sky. The knight worked steadily, hooking his harness and equipment securely to the smooth blue rock of the mountain's side. Twice he almost plummeted to his death. As the day wore on, he began to despair of finding this cave, for the entire mountain seemed hewn of a single solid piece. Seldom did he find even a small crack that might serve as a foot hold.

By the time evening began to descend, Sir Andross's strained muscles quavered from the rigor of the exercise. He looked up and saw he still had a good way to go to the top. He leaned back as far as he could and scanned the area just ahead of him, as he had been doing periodically; there was still no sign of a gap that might indicate a cave. However, he spied a small ledge jutting out that seemed just big enough for him to rest on.

As he pulled himself onto its flat surface, he was glad he had chosen to stop. His body was in complete exhaustion. He could hear his blood pounding past his ears. Sir Andross was a young man. His time out on the farm and his participation in numerous battles meant that he was in excellent physical condition. Yet, he felt completely drained of all his strength after the day's arduous climb. So, he just lay there on the cold, hard stone of the ledge to rest, just for a moment.

He didn't know when he fell asleep, but he woke up shivering in the night. A chill had settled over the mountaintop and his sweat-soaked shirt augmented the coldness of the evening. He opened his pack and took out the portable heater. The small square, no bigger than his palm, would keep him warm. He activated it and an energy shield extended out ten feet round the unit. Immediately the air around him in the bubble grew warm. Retrieving his sleeping bag, he settled down again and slept once more.

When dawn came, Sir Andross had his breakfast, the pickled eggs tasted heavenly. He realized he had skipped dinner entirely the night before, fatigue getting the better of him. Finding his strength somewhat renewed, the knight began his climb again. Four hours later, he noticed the mouth of a cave just to the right of where he was.

Soon he was able to pull himself over the edge and stood at its gaping, black entrance. It seemed to be deep and narrow. Instinctively, his hand drew forth his honrol solun, a Kest, from its holster. Sir Andross wished he could afford a solg, for they were made of liog, which withstood heat from the electric pulse bullets better than the more conducive honrol alloy. Of course, Sir Andross thought wistfully, now that he served the castle, he might earn his very own ginmra someday. For now, he bore his honrol sword in its sheath on his back and a short dagger hidden in his boot.

Thus armed, he entered the cave cautiously and was momentarily blinded by the darkness. As his eyes adjusted he realized that he was in a kind of tunnel that tilted downward toward an even thicker, deeper blackness. He drew out his newly purchased torch; its beam of light illuminated a few feet in front of him. He'd abandoned his old one in the crypt at Sanctal. Sir Andross followed carefully using the wall as a guide. Soon, he was deep within the mountain. He was beginning to wonder if he had entered the wrong cave, when he saw a colorful brightness shining at the edge of a turn in the passageway just ahead.

When he rounded the bend, a wide cavern of brightly colored crystals jutting up haphazardly from the rock floor and ceiling was, as far as he could tell, his dead-end destination. Colored beams of light playfully danced about the cavern walls and reflected off the clear waters of a small thermal spring at its center. He switched off his torch and tucked it back into his pack. Looking round the room, the knight was disappointed to note there was no sign of anyone living there. All his exertion had so far been for naught. With a shrug, he slid his Kest back into its underarm holster.

Perhaps there was another cave further up. Sir Andross was extremely thirsty by this time, so he rushed to the pool to drink deeply of its sweet waters. As he drank, he heard the sound of rushing water and scanned the stone edges of the fount. His eyes came to rest on a small opening at the far right, where water seemed to flow into an underground river beneath the cavern's floor and through the mountain. He examined the spot closely. It was almost like a water slide, big enough for two full-grown men, and it spilled into a seemingly endless cavity.

Glancing up, Sir Andross decided to explore the back of the cave. It might hold another passage. Walking across the length of its smooth surface, he avoided the jagged crystals. Then he saw it, a gem embedded into the rock face. He might have disregarded it entirely as there were several crystal encrusted into the rock. Its shape, however, caught his attention. The gleaming, almost transparent, quartz looked like a dagger, with a blade and hilt all forged from a single piece.

Nearing the unique object, Sir Andross ran a tentative hand over the cool, glowing surface. This had to be the crystal dagger he sought. Excited that all his effort had yielded at last some success, Sir Andross carefully plucked the crystal from its snug home in the rock.

It was the size of his palm. The radiant glow from its faceted essence held Sir Andross's gaze. The knight was dimly aware of the sound of rock sliding, but the gurgle from the spring muffled it. He wondered if a chunk of outer rock had avalanched. Mesmerized by the magnificent blade in his palm, any fear of the cave opening being affected quickly dissipated.

Setting his pack on the ground, the knight knelt down to carefully place the treasure in a secure pocket. Tucking the crystal in and swinging his pack up on his back, Sir Andross prepared to climb back down the mountain.

But he was no longer alone. He was picked up and hurled across the cave. He hit the cold, stone wall and fell face down on the floor, nearly impaled on a jagged blue crystal. Rising quickly, Sir Andross looked around for his opponent. There was no one, nothing.

A strong, something, hit him in the chest and sent him crashing back once more. Thankfully he landed in the clear area around the spring. Unsheathing his sword, he scampered to his feet. Moving rapidly toward the entrance, he continued looking around. But still, there was nothing.

Then he felt a fist hit his jaw, and he was thrown backward, crashing through a series of razor-edged crystals, which cut into his pack, mercifully sparing the flesh of his back. His bottom lip was bleeding where he had bit into it from the unexpected blow. He felt disoriented and shocked. Looking about as he regained his feet he still saw nothing.

Sir Andross held his sword in front of him and swung it about thrashing the empty air. He began to retreat to the far side of the room, keeping his sword arm moving in front of him in a blind attempt to defend himself from the invisible threat. As a warrior, he knew that being backed up against a solid rock barrier was not the most strategic of positions, but what other course of action did he have against an enemy he could not see?

As he moved backward toward the wall's dubious protection, he stumbled over a small green crystal and tripped. His left hand shot out to break the fall and his palm was pierced through by a yellow crystal, whose light became an eerie orange hue as Sir Andross's blood covered it. Pain flashed up his arm. He felt something jab at his right shoulder and turned his body quickly, ignoring the agony in his left hand. Rolling away, he came to his feet as soon as he could. Sir Andross sliced with his sword in the direction of whatever was trying to kill him. When he pulled it back, the blade was covered in a green gooey substance. *The enemy's blood?* Sir Andross wondered.

A petrifying roar of agony rumbled through the cavern and echoed through the recesses of the tunnel. Something flickered; a shape began to materialize before his astounded eyes. In all his twenty odd years, Sir Andross Draneg had never seen such a horribly terrifying sight. He was paralyzed from fear. Cold sweat ran down his spine and his heart beat raced, thumping against his chest as though it would push right through it. His mind went numb, unable to form a coherent thought.

The eight-foot "thing" roared again and grasped at its wounded arm, if indeed that part of it could be called an arm, where Sir Andross's sword had left a gash in the creature's gray-green flesh. Its red eyes pinned the now fear-struck knight with a glare of shear hatred. It rushed forward in fury. Sir Andross could not move. He thought for sure this would be his end.

Chapter 30

A Prophet of Ressord

"HE'LL BE FINE, don't fret so much!" a woman's gravelly voice was saying.

"I hope you're right," a man replied.

"Shall I fetch more water?" a younger woman's voice asked, lyrical and gentle.

"Yes, dear," the older woman spoke again.

Sir Andross hovered on the border of consciousness. The triad of voices reached him, though he couldn't place them. He felt a firm hand on his ribs. *Where am I?* He struggled to wake, willing himself to open his eyes. His heavy lids refused to budge. Tired from the effort, he let himself sink back into the beckoning blackness.

Sir Andross awoke in a small, comfortable bed and could not remember where he was. He tried to sit up, groaning in agony. His whole body felt sore and the sharp pain in his right rib section almost made him lose consciousness once more.

A cool hand came to rest on his forehead and a lovely, heart-shaped face surrounded by a riot of soft blonde curls leaned over him. Big blue eyes, which held a sweet expression of concern and comfort, examined him.

He tried to speak, but the angel tending to him pressed a glass of cool water to his lips, cutting him off.

"Do not tax yourself, Sir Knight," the beautiful vision spoke. "Rest now, recover your strength. The time for explanations will come later."

He drank greedily of the refreshing offering, and, before he could say a word, he felt himself drift off once more.

Waking again, Sir Andross struggled to sit up. He looked around the room. It was small with simple wood furnishings. He looked down at his body and saw that he was bandaged. He leaned back and closed his eyes. He wondered how he had gotten here and how long he had been unconscious. Slowly, images of the fierce fight with the "thing" started coming back to him.

He remembered "it" rushing at him and how he had managed to move just in time. He had fought with all his might, slashing at it with his sword. He recalled how he had been the one enduring most of the blows while inflicting precious few on his powerful opponent.

Fear, Sir Andross realized, had been his real enemy. It had gripped him and had made it impossible for him to think clearly. Despite his usually strategic mind, he had been blinded by fear and unable to defend himself well.

Now, with his mind clearer, he thought of a number of alternatives he could have tried in the battle. He remembered how proud he had always been of his reputation as a fearless warrior after the Battle of Eporue. Now, the knight's heart filled with shame at his defeat.

He wondered again how he had gotten here. He focused on his last memories. He recollected a terrible blow on his head from the thing and then a sudden rush of warm water engulfing him.

"Of course," Sir Andross exclaimed aloud, opening his eyes. He thought it most likely he had fallen into the pool and been swept into the thermal river that ran under the cavern's floor. He wondered where he had come out, and who the lovely lady was that had obviously been tending to his wounds.

Just then the door opened and a chubby, red-faced man entered followed by the angel who had been there when Sir Andross had awoken earlier. The man had a cheerful countenance; the only signs of his advanced age were the scattered patches of gray hair at the temples mixed in among his natural black hair.

"I told you I heard him wake, papa," Sir Andross's angel addressed the man.

"Yes," the girl's father answered her in a deep, rumbling voice. The knight remembered hearing it at some point. "So I see." The man approached the bed. "How do you feel, sir?" he asked kindly.

"I feel," Sir Andross responded, attempting to sit up further before a rush of pain stopped his movement. "Like I got run down by a herd of stampeding elhrin." He gave the two strangers, who were looking at him with warm concern, a winning smile.

The man chuckled softly and pulled up the small wooden chair. Setting it by the bed, the unfortunate piece of furniture creaked as the portly gentleman's weight descended on it. The girl stood shyly by the door.

"I've been wondering a few things, sir," Sir Andross began.

"You would like to know how you came to be here," the kind man said, smiling. "Perhaps you want to know where you are, how long you've been here, and who we are."

"Yes, sir."

"Well, I am Armond Orloff. This is one of my daughters, Favila."

"Orloff!" Sir Andross became so excited he forgot his injuries. They were brought back to his remembrance when pain so strong he almost lost consciousness again shot through him.

"Now, now, you must not excite yourself," Lord Orloff chided gently.

"Are you the Prophet Orloff? If not, are you related to him? Might you know where I can find him? I must find him!" Sir Andross fired away at the kind man.

"Settle down, son. Yes, I am he whom you seek."

Lord Orloff turned to his daughter and asked her to begin preparations for dinner, which made Sir Andross realize it was dark outside. When she left, the prophet turned back to the knight and proceeded to explain his presence there.

"I live to the north, in the Valley of Soane, many miles from here and not far from the Oldey Forest," Lord Orloff began. "One afternoon, I was praying and studying the Word when I was overcome by the spirit and a vision came to me. I saw you as you spoke with the evil Elemental Darlia. I heard you tell her of your quest and watched as she misdirected you to the cave of the dreaded rego."

"But," Sir Andross interrupted, his voice tinged with disappointment. "The lady said she was—"

"Friend of the rajin?" Lord Orloff said. "Yes, well, the elmalin for the most part are aligned to the rajin. They splintered from the great order not so long ago, about ten years or so. They focus on studying the elements, which the majority of the rajin feel can lead to a darker use of

power. Sadly, some of their members may have already aligned themselves with evil. I believe a new order is rising, a sect focused on a darker
path. Yet, it is unclear who they are or where they are based out of.
Darlia, I know, serves the one who resides on Jorn. That much I'm sure
of. No doubt she thought to ingratiate herself to her master by leading
you to your death."

"She was toying with me then?"

"Oh, 'tis more than a game with Darlia, my dear boy. Her hypnotic
stare can make anyone reveal all they know, and she quickly carries all
information to her evil master, whoever he may be."

"Forgive me, Lord Orloff, but how can you be certain of a new order?"

"A prophecy was given to me some years back, which has been
confirmed across the Prophets of Ressord and was recorded before the
Intergalactic Council as a GenWord. It foretold the split of the elmalin,
and it tells of a dark power that will rise. Since then, I've noticed the use
of forbidden powers that bring a hardening of the heart by King Amiel.
The rajin thought the acts against the Sehy were done by elmalin. They
believe the elementals are the dark evil foretold. But I fear Amiel may
be under the influence of the new sect and allowing himself to be led by
these misusers of the energy of the universe." Lord Orloff shook his
head in sadness. "Which does not bode well for the future of Dravidia,
or Vidden, for that matter."

"If this is so, then truly I have betrayed the queen, perhaps even
placed her in great peril!"

"Do not worry," Lord Orloff said placing a comforting hand on his
arm. "As soon as I knew of your encounter with Darlia, I sent my assistant,
Javern, to her Majesty, with instructions for safeguarding the liquid and
the queen. He has successfully been employed at the castle at his last
communiqué and the queen is aware of the situation."

"You don't understand. If there is a new order and the king is being
advised by them then the king cannot be trusted."

"Quite so."

"You see... when the queen offered the quest I..." Sir Andross couldn't
finish, guilt lay like a heavy stone in the pit of his stomach. He looked
down at his bandaged hand avoiding the prophet's earnest gaze.

"You told the king?"

"Yes... I owe him my knighthood... my place as a castle guard... I owe
him my allegiance as an Auldian. I couldn't go behind his back... I just

couldn't." The knight's horror at his error brought heat to his ebony cheeks. Yet, how could he have known? He believed he was acting nobly by being loyal to the man who'd given him opportunities Sir Andross had never even dreamed of.

"And he approved your mission?" Lord Orloff asked.

"Yes."

"Interesting." Lord Orloff sat back in his chair considering the situation.

The silence stretched uncomfortably. Sir Andross wondered what the prophet was thinking. He felt sure the king would do the queen no harm. It was apparent to the knight that his monarch was seriously in love. Sir Andross had noticed the way the king's eyes looked upon the queen and the way the king was always worried about her, though he worked hard not to show it in front of the Auldian courtiers.

"They need the queen, for only she can work the liquid. She'll be allowed to hold on to it until the moment the quest meets success. We must be cautious in how we proceed."

"We should let her know that the king is aware," Sir Andross suggested, though the thought of making that confession had his stomach twisting in knots. *How can she trust me after this? What will she think of me?*

"Yes. It is best she know the truth, so she can be on her guard. I'm sure she'll understand your motives for telling the king." Sir Orloff patted the knight's hand reassuringly.

"I hope so. But you still have not told me how you found me."

"Oh, oh, yes, well... when we knew of your interview with the elmalin, my daughter and I set out immediately for Mount Tarsus to intercept you. But we had some trouble along the way and were unable to reach you in time," Lord Orloff explained apologetically. "Favila and I were yet some leagues from here following the Tarsus River road, when once again the spirit took me and I saw you fighting the rego. I must congratulate you on a most valiant battle, Sir Knight, though I feared we would lose you. The rego's most powerful weapon is inflicting its prey with a fear so intense it paralyzes anyone and anything. It is amazing you had the strength to fight him off as you did. You have a strong and courageous heart. Then I saw you fall into the internal river. We went quickly to the spring it empties into in the Tars Forest where we found you practically half-dead. Naturally, once we got you to safety, we sent to fetch your jorses." He gave Sir Andross a fatherly smile. "We had to tow them since you were unavailable to turn them on, and I fear the valet key may have been swept away. We couldn't find it."

"Thankfully, they brought you here to me, Sir Knight," the words were spoken by an elderly woman whose youthful beauty had not yet faded though a few wrinkles here and there gave away her age along with a spattering of gray hairs among her dark black tresses.

"Allow me to introduce to you my dear sister, Lady Newog," Lord Orloff said, smiling affectionately at his sibling. "She is a great healer. She has agreed to teach Favila, who seems to have a talent for the healing arts."

"The old arts?" Sir Andross asked.

"Yes," Lady Newog confirmed as she checked his bandages. "The use of modern medical technology is good, of course, but cannot, at least in my old mind, replace the natural cures. I believe them to be healthier for the body overall than the medicines made synthetically."

"I agree, my Lady," Sir Andross reassured her. "My mother was a healer of sorts, and she taught me a little. It has served me well after many a battle."

Favila entered with a dinner tray for Sir Andross and then left again, returning with food for her father. When Lady Newog had finished refreshing the poultice and bandages on Sir Andross's wounds, she and Favila left the gentlemen to their dinner and conversation.

"Well, Lord Orloff," Sir Andross took up the subject of the quest after they had both finished their meal in companionable silence. "I must find Rajin Horsef. Do you know where he might be?"

"Alas, I'm afraid I do not. When I knew of your mission I spent many hours in prayer seeking guidance as to the rajin's location. I have not seen Horsef since well before the battle at Sanctal."

"Were your prayers answered?" Sir Andross inquired. He was not a particularly religious man, but if the prophet had been given a lead he would gladly accept the help.

"Well, like most things with the Great I Am, the prayer was not answered with a vision," Lord Orloff explained. "Those are for very pressing matters. However, I felt it come to my heart that Horsef often spoke of the Lady Viona de Varnipas."

"Who?"

"Lady Viona is a great writer of love stories. She lives in the town of Gar in the Valley of Garpeth, just north of the Jornian Desert," Lord

Orloff explained. "She and Horsef were great friends. Perhaps she may be able to shed some light as to his current whereabouts."

"At least we have a new starting point. My Lord, would it be possible for me to send the queen the crystal dagger through you? I believe I may have found it in the cave, and it should hopefully be in my pack."

"The crystal dagger," Lord Orloff's voice took on a reverent tone.

Rising, the portly man fetched the knight's pack, placing it on the bed. Sir Andross drew forth the radiant blade. Taking it in his hands, the Prophet's eyes seemed mesmerized by its gleaming beauty.

"It seems the Great I Am does indeed turn all things for our good. The elmalin intended your death, but the Great I Am used her to help you find this most important artifact."

Uncomfortable with the religious turn the conversation had taken, Sir Andross replied, "Is it safe for me to communicate with the queen via her holosite? Do you think the evil one might have it monitored?" If he were truthful, Sir Andross would confess he did not want to see the look on the queen's gorgeous face nor hear her lovely voice after telling her of his betrayal, coward that he was. *A letter would be good, surely.*

"I will be heading to her Majesty on the morrow," Lord Orloff said. "Horsef gifted me, and the other prophets in my order, with special encryptors. I will place one in your holonode and will deliver the other to her Majesty. That way you will be able to communicate without fear of being overheard. The encryptor will ensure a secure line."

"Can you be certain this evil sect does not have this technology?"

"Absolutely certain," Lord Orloff asserted. "The rajin did not share this invention with anyone except the Sisters of the Geldian Heights and the Prophets of Ressord."

"It will be good to have the queen surrounded with people friendly to her cause." Sir Andross remembered the sad look that often pervaded the queen's emerald eyes. Those poignant windows that he now wished to avoid looking into, fearful he would see disgust for him or worse, hurt!

"Naturally, you realize it will be at least a week before you can travel. Those wounds are no small matter. If I begin my journey as I plan to tomorrow, I may be able to catch up to you when you reach Rafargar on the north side of the desert, which is very good for me as I do not envy you your road." Lord Orloff smiled widely and Sir Andross understood, for the Jornian desert was not an inviting place and was filled with dangers.

"I will be grateful for your continued help."

"No need, my son. We must help our queen safeguard the continent from the Gortives." He rose to leave. "Who knows, perhaps we can finally break the curse of the Auldian royal lineage. King Amiel may be saved in the process."

The next morning, Sir Andross attempted to stand and see Lord Orloff depart. He hoped that his strength might have returned enough to set out as well, for he was loath to delay the quest when there was so much at stake.

"You must recuperate fully," Lady Newog reprimanded him, as she helped him back into bed after finding him strewn on the floor in pain. "Now see what you have done. One of the wounds has re-opened. If you insist on leaving when you are not ready you will die either from infected wounds or bleeding out."

Lord Orloff drew near to shake the knight's hand. "I will be at Castle Dravidia within the week," Lord Orloff promised as he said his good-byes. "Heal up. I will see you soon on the other side of the desert."

"Godspeed to you, my Lord," Sir Andross bid the prophet goodbye.

"And a fast recovery for you, son," Lord Orloff prophesied touching the knight's head with both his hands, and saying a whispered prayer.

"Now, you rest," Lady Newog ordered. "Favila will be in to clean and redress that wound in a moment. We must ensure the poison is fully drawn out of your system." Seeing the look that came into Sir Andross's eyes at the mention of the lovely Favila, she added "Behave yourself, sir. Remember you are a knight sworn to a life of honor."

Sir Andross relaxed back on his pillows and waited for the angel to return and help heal him. Of course, he was a man of honor, but a little flirtation with a beautiful woman was not a sin, right?

CHAPTER 31

ELMALIN ABLOIR

ONE WEEK LATER, Verena sat upon her throne. She'd been summoned when the elmalin delegation requested an audience. It had surprised Verena that Amiel had actually sent for her. After allowing Rajin Vivelda access to the castle, Verena had thought he would have kept her out of this meeting. Instead they sat side-by-side as the Lord Chamberlain announced their visitors in his baritone voice.

"Dova Elmalin, Lady Jafra of Gelderant. Misrim Elmalin, Lady Nomri of Fratern, and Misrim Elmalin, Lady Andiera of Fridgia, your Majesties."

Verena's eyebrows lifted in surprise. The three leaders of the Elmalin Abloir, their high council, sought an audience with them. She noticed the confident way they entered, heads held high, their clothing of the utmost elegance and quality. Dova Master, Lady Jafra, came first, being the highest ranking. She was clad in black leather from head to foot, her fiery red hair pulled back in a tight bun at her nape. She was master of space, Verena recalled, and her attire reflected this. Behind her, Misrim Lady Nomri flanked her right side, clad in a light blue and silver dress that flowed down to the floor. The lady's eyes locked with Verena and the queen remembered their conversation on the occasion of her coming-of-age birthday. *Had they come to make good on Verena's promise to have them set up a Cleyior on Jorn?*

On the left side of the Dova Elmalin, was Misrim Lady Andiera. She wore a gold dress that shimmered as she walked. Her jet-black hair and ebony skin seemed to glisten with a light golden dusting of powder. Verena knew that, unlike the rajin, the gold of the elmalin signified mastery of the element of time.

The queen almost gasped as her mind swirled with the realization that the Shrang LaRoo liquid was golden. Could the legend Sir Andross had relayed about the power of this mystery element be true? Might this elmalin be able to help her discover it if Horsef was not found? The elmalin trio came to a stop before the thrones and curtsied deeply, bringing Verena's attention back to the moment at hand.

"How can we be of service?" Amiel asked their visitors, adopting the phrase her father had always used when someone requested an audience.

"We are public servants, kura; don't ever forget that," his words echoed in her mind. "We exist to serve as much as to lead." She stole a sideways glance at Amiel wondering if he understood why King Dekkyle spoke that or if he just mimicked the King of Dravidia's style.

Dova Lady Jafra spoke, her voice deep and filled with a sense of authority. "Majesty, it is we who have come to be of service to you." She paused for effect, then continued. "A member of our order has found evidence that will shed light upon the true culprits of the assassination attempt on your life. The events that arose from the fabricated 'evidence' need to be set right."

Verena noticed the Duke of Aul tense at the elmalin's pronouncement. Beside her, however, Amiel's body remained relaxed. A look of actual interest came over his handsome face.

"We will be glad to see this new evidence you bring us, though we were not aware you were investigating," he spoke. "Please, show us."

The dova elmalin extended a pictode. "Our order has been accused of many things. We are not an enemy. It is our wish to be allowed to serve, as the rajin do."

Activating the pictode in the palm of her hand, the dova elmalin adjusted the size to its largest level so that it would be clear to them from the distance of their thrones. Footage, obviously taken stealthily, of Lord Uld, Lord Dran, and various other Auldian lords projected holographically. The gathered lordlings were laughing and tossing back and forth to each other a ring.

Verena took in a deep breath, recognizing it as the signet of the House of Tor.

"Now with this, we'll force Amiel out of his stupidity." Lord Uld's mocking tone filled the throne room.

"She is extremely fuckable, but really, is he so in heat he can't think?" Lord Banjee cackled.

"Blood's gone from his head to the other head!" Lord Dran laughed, holding the signet ring bearing the crest of House Tor.

Verena's fists clenched, and she felt the heat rise to her cheeks. She'd known they had nothing but contempt for her, but hearing them speak of her as though she were nothing more than a common whore sparked her ire. *Thank the Great I Am they had been thrown out for their impudence.*

"She wore their family flower all over her when she changed!" Uld's face twisted into a sneer. "He'll think she did it. Maybe he'll kill her with the others."

"Not until he gets his fill of her cunt," another lord off camera chimed in.

"Enough!" Amiel's tone was sharp. "Turn it off."

The dova elmalin complied. Walking up the three steps to the thrones, she knelt holding out the pictode. Verena rose quickly and took it from the head elmalin's palm.

"Thank you," Verena said, locking eyes with Lady Jafra, who'd lifted her face. "How can we repay you for this great gift that will finally set our nation on the right course?"

The dova elmalin rose. Face to face with Verena, she answered, "You offered our order an opportunity to have a Cleyior in Auldivia. We would like to be here, available to help your Majesties." She turned her eyes to Amiel, including him. Carefully, she backed down the steps to stand with her leadership.

Amiel rose and came to stand beside Verena. His voice was tight, controlled, as he spoke, "You are welcome to have your Cleyoir."

"There are some lands the crown owns just northeast of Anco City on the western shore of the Bay of Perth. You may build there," Verena offered, remembering the land with its beach grass and beautiful golden sands leading to the water's edge.

She turned to Amiel, and he bowed his head in agreement.

"Thank you, Majesties." All three elmalin bowed in a low curtsy.

"We shall have the land grant issued and in your hands within the week," Amiel said. "Will you honor us by remaining in the castle?"

"It would be our honor to do so, Majesty," the Dova replied.

"Have a set of chambers assigned for use by the Elmalin Order whenever they choose to visit us. Perhaps in the wing opposite the rajin suite?" Verena glanced at the Duke of Aul.

"Of course," he acknowledged after a brief pause.

"What shall you call your Cleyior?" Verena asked out of curiosity.

"We shall call it Cleyior Elireth, Majesty," Dova Lady Jafra responded. "It means Victory in Geldish."

The elmalin followed the Duke of Aul out, no doubt the castle Steward and Lord Chamberlain would get everything organized quickly for the ladies. Verena smiled knowing the efficiency of the castle staff had not diminished with the change to Auldian livery.

Alone in the chamber, Verena turned to look at Amiel, who now stood beside her.

"You always knew the truth, but you chose to turn a blind eye and give these bastards free rein to pillage my people." Verena's fist clenched over the pictode, cheeks burning with her indignation.

"The evidence we had—"

"Don't even try to justify yourself. You knew, but preferred to let arrogance and hate rule the day. An innocent man yet wallows in a cell he should never have set foot in. Other innocent lives destroyed by your pride in setting aside an agreement under false pretense. Even more lives ruined by wanton looting of public coffers and refusal to rebuild necessary protections for wauger." Verena's words came sharp and curt. Her body shook with the impotence and injustice of it all.

Amiel glanced down at his com. He tapped it, then met her gaze.

"I did what I believed to be right."

"NO, you did what yielded you more power than you deserve, as obviously you aren't able to rule justly, nor protect ALL the people of this continent."

"Yes, Majesties," Sir Eriq Seller entered the throne room.

Amiel turned his gaze away from her and addressed the Lord High Marshal. "Draft warrants for Lord Uld, Lord Dran, Lord Banjee, and Count Dukette for treason and the attempted assassination of their king."

Shock registered on Sir Eriq's face.

"And let's not forget Count Tor is yet imprisoned." Verena watched Amiel as she spoke.

"Release him at once, Sir Eriq," Amiel commanded.

With a quick glance to Verena, Sir Eriq responded, "Right away, Majesties."

"These men have done a lot of damage," Amiel said, facing Verena once the High Marshal had left the room.

She'd turned to watch Sir Eriq go to free the innocent count and the bile of disgust kept her from looking at him. Nausea hit her, but she swallowed hard.

"I'll set things right." His voice was little more than a whisper.

"And how do you plan to do that?"

"Write to the Dravidians again, let them know of the new evidence. I'll have the duke draw up full pardons and we will send them with the letter. They can all come home. Have all their former positions back. We can start again."

Without a further word or glance at him, Verena stepped down from the dais and left the room. Her body shook from the stupidity of all the death and destruction.

Two days later, Amiel came to stand in front of Verena as she sat on the garden bench near the promontory's edge. She looked up at him.

"I have been thinking about what you said. I believe you are right about the proclamation that public funds must be used only for the rebuilding, and any misuses will be met with a hefty fine besides the reimbursement of the original amount. We need to unite. There are new reports from Parthia that suggest Lorgarn will be ready to attack us perhaps as early as this fall or sooner. Though I have yet to see evidence of these ships he is supposedly building."

"Dravidia and Aulden have lived in peace for many years," Verena said softly. She ran her hands across the book's hardcover. "I don't understand why your people have such hatred for mine."

"Your breaking the betrothal and leaving Jorn when the wedding was just four days away was a great slight to us," Amiel's tone sounded barely contained.

"I..." she looked up again and into his eyes. The coolness of his countenance seemed at odds with the hint of pain his voice had held. "I didn't intend to create this kind of resentment and anger. I was afraid of..." Her voice trailed off, and she averted her eyes, looking out toward the promontory cliff and the glistening green waters of the ocean beyond.

"Of me. Yes, you mentioned it before. But—"

"You beat Helen," she looked him in the eyes now, hoping against hope to hear the truth. "I saw you myself. And you never denied having beaten that prostitute... killing her?" the last words were a whispered exhale.

"Helen?" For a moment he looked confused, then recollection sprang in his eyes. "You are too soft-hearted, Rennie. You seem to care about all kinds of beings that really don't matter."

"Everyone matters, Amiel. Everyone. Can't you see that? All people, no matter where they come from or what their station in life, deserve respect, because they are human. Even, even the Gortive are worthy of respect."

"They're technically not human," Amiel corrected her, a small smile on the edge of his lips.

"They are living beings," she countered. "They are intelligent enough to become a threat to us without our realizing it."

"Too soft for your own good," Amiel shook his head. "I thought you would want to know I have issued the proclamation. Now, if we could get those last Dravidian renegades to surrender." Her heart felt a pang at his smooth turning of the subject.

He had not denied the charges; he had justified himself. *Had he killed that woman? Would he, one day, run out of patience, or whatever grace and favor he felt for Verena, and beat and kill her, too?*

"I gave you the letter I wrote this morning," she reminded him, looking at her hands again. "We are one nation now," she said rising from the seat. As Verena turned to walk away, she threw at him, "If we stop talking in terms of yours and mine and we begin thinking in terms of ours, maybe we may have a hope of becoming a truly great nation."

She strode to the castle, her back straight, her head held high, intensely aware of his eyes following her every step.

They didn't have to wait long for the next unpleasantness from Lord Uld and his clique. Just four days after the issuance of the warrants, Verena sat in the Council of Peers listening to the Earl of Ydarb detail a security strategy the generals had developed.

"The key to the defense of the Tor delta—"

"Majesties," Eriq Seller, Lord Marshal, entered the chamber without knocking. "The Vale of Soane is under attack."

"Bring up satellite imaging from that sector," Amiel commanded.

"By who?" Verena asked, perplexed. "Are the Gortive on our shores already?"

"No, Majesty," the Lord Marshal responded, just as the holoimages from satellite 4-5 showing the forces in the Vale appeared over the table. "It is Lord Uld and several of the nobility that followed him."

Verena turned to look at Amiel. His eyes had turned glacial. His strong jaw clenched, his face holding tight to its composure. She could see the throbbing vein that was the tell-tale sign he was holding back his anger. He stared at the images of the Vale. The Auldian lords and their retinue of soldiers had encamped around Anco, the capital of Soane.

"Lord Soane will have activated the defenses of the city," Verena stated confidently. "He no doubt will take steps to secure the banks." For a moment, the sad sight of old and dignified Lady Soane, dead in this very chamber, murdered, flashed in Verena's mind.

After that tragic day, her grandson had reluctantly accepted to swear loyalty to the new government. Verena recalled the messages they had exchanged right after she had awoken from the ginmra sleep. She had sent him a private message that he should not rebel as the others had done.

<If you rebel you will leave your lands open to be filled by Amiel with his own people.> She had typed. <We must hold the banks.>

<They murdered by grandmother and all her household servants in your castle. I can't just fold my hands and do nothing! Unlike you, we stand and fight. We don't run or give up.>

Shaking off the insult, which she understood had some basis, Verena had pressed her point.

<I made a mistake in running. If you join the rebellion, you will be making a worse one. Leaving the money in the hands of the Auldian lord Amiel appoints will not help Dravidia one bit. Your family have been the stewards of the banking system of Dravidia and of the Royal Treasury. Will you abandon that trust now?>

She'd waited tense moments, but his response had soon followed that he understood, and she had a point. He would do as she asked.

Amiel's words brought her back to the moment at hand. "We must act quickly to deal with this treachery."

Amiel rose from his seat, striding out of the chamber with a gesture that the Lord Marshal and the other lords should follow. Verena rushed to do the same. Catching up with him in the hall, she heard him telling them to muster their retinues. They would ride to Anco within the hour.

"What are you doing here?" he asked, as he passed her heading to his rooms to change for battle.

"I can fight." She was already making a mental note of what she would need. Passing a footman, she threw at the liveried hudroid, "Let them know to make ready my jorse."

"No. Stay where you are," Amiel countered the order. The hudroid stood waiting. He waved it away. Focusing on her, he continued, "You are not going to war. You are staying here where you're safe."

"You've seen me fight. I can—"

"Yes, and you end up in a coma for who knows how long afterwards. Is that really what you want?" Amiel stated, irritation at the delay the conversation was causing evident in his tone. When she didn't reply, he continued, "Please, follow orders. For once in your life."

He turned and headed down the hall once more, entering his rooms without a backward glance.

Verena stood, uncertain what to do. The ginmra sleep was his reason for not letting her fight. For a second, the thought of her father, refusing to let her go to war, entered her mind. Had the coma-like slumber been his reason as well? Tears threatened to overflow as the grief of her loss hit her. Shaking away the pain, she concentrated on the situation.

The Vale of Soane was critical. Verena knew Lord Soane and the banks at Anco had to be safe guarded. There was no physical money in Thyrein's Galactic Wall. Funds were transferred digitally. The banks received and kept records of deposits and debits. If Lord Uld and his cohort were able to get control...

Amiel reemerged from his room. He was dressed in his honrol-coneb blend armor. The pommel of his ginmra hung from the leather belt at his waist.

"Are you going to obey?" He asked, pausing on his way. "I need you here."

"I can fight," Verena answered. "Why—"

A look of earnestness entered his gaze as he looked down upon her. "If they see me leave, there may be a group ready to ambush the castle. You need to be here to protect our home. The work of the Council of Peers will be in your hands. Will you obey?"

A tingle of joy at his leaving her in charge warred against the rising irritation over his use of the word "obey." Verena swallowed hard as she responded, "I suppose so."

"Good." He started off once more.

She followed him through the castle to the outer bailey where the others had gathered. His black destrier jorse awaited him. Swinging up into the seat as if it were a real horse, he glanced down at her as she came to stand by his side.

"I'll see you soon," his tone fully confident, a smug smile across his face. He bent down and kissed her lips, there, in the public view of all. "Miss me." Then, he steered his jorse, speeding off, and the group of his men followed suit.

CHAPTER 32

THE LITTLE THIEF

THE DAY STARTED WITH SIR ANDROSS'S CALL to the queen on the holonet. Dread of what she would say about his betrayal of her secrets to the king plagued him.

"Has the Prophet Orloff arrived at the castle, Majesty," Sir Andross asked, hoping that the seer had already relayed the tale; wishing maybe she still didn't know and yet liked him; anguishing over having to tell her now.

"He has not, but he sent Javern to me. He managed to get himself employed as King Amiel's valet. Javern told me that you were sent to that cave with the intent that you should lose your life. I'm glad to see you are well and that Lord Orloff made it to you in time." Looking earnestly into the cam, she asked, "Is he coming?"

"Yes, Majesty." Sir Andross swallowed hard. "But he actually didn't get to me in time. Not exactly, Majesty." Sir Andross explained all that had transpired. His fight with the rego, his finding of the dagger, the rescue by the prophet, and the convalescence at Lady Newog's home. Gulping down his shame, he prepared to launch into his confession. "I—" he had started.

"How are your wounds, Sir Andross? I trust you are recovering. You look well."

"Yes, I am well. I will be able to continue the quest on the morrow. If, of course, Your Majesty still wishes me to after—"

"Why wouldn't I?" The confusion on that beautiful face made his heart ache.

"I have to confess, Majesty, that before leaving on the expedition, I told the king about the mission. I felt I had to. I couldn't go behind his back," Sir Andross paused, then seeing the confusion turn to hurt, he plowed on, "I know now, after speaking with the Prophet Orloff, that King Amiel is not to be trusted, but... I... I must apologize to you for having spoken to the king about..." his voice trailed off watching a variety of emotions pass across the queen's face.

After a moment, the queen, spoke. "No need for apologies." Looking earnestly at him, she continued, "I am upset, but I do understand. It was naïve of me to expect you to go behind Amiel's back when you owe him so much... perhaps it was even wrong of me to have asked it of you."

"Majesty, you did nothing wrong!" Sir Andross's eagerness to reassure her filled his voice. He hated seeing the sadness that filled that beautiful countenance. "It is I who betrayed you and that act was not one of honor, indeed—"

"No, you did what was right. Your honor is untainted. The question now is... who are you going on this quest for? Are you with Amiel, or with me? You must be honest now and decide. I will hold no rancor if your allegiance is with your king, but the matter must be clarified."

Sir Andross gazed into those eyes, so open. The prophet had said the king could be saved, but right now he was not to be trusted. The king was surrounded by an evil force whose power should be broken from the house of Aulden. That much was clear to the knight as he considered the attempt to end the quest by having him killed by the rego. The more he had dwelt on this while convalescing the more the knight realized the success of the queen's mission could be the hope for a more just kingdom for the people of Aulden.

"I see now, Majesty, that the power of whatever evil is lurking behind all this must be removed from Aulden. It seems that this quest might be the very way to establish a fair and just kingdom across both nations. If you will let me, I would like to finish this mission for you."

"You will be playing a very dangerous game, Sir Andross," the queen's voice became solemn. "You will need to continue checking in with the king, but he cannot know when we have found Horsef. He must not learn what we find out about the liquids' powers and how we decide to use them."

"Do you intend to harm him?" Sir Andross shocked himself with his own boldness. He had to ask. There was no way he could help her kill his king.

"I could never harm him... but he needs our help in ridding himself of the evil that influences him." She gave him a shy smile. "Though he doesn't think he needs anybody. And we have the Gortive matter to consider as well. This liquid could help us put an end to that threat, maybe before the bloodshed begins."

"Then I will help you, Majesty."

Once he had signed off with the queen, he sought out his angel. He found Favila seated on the porch, watching the wild ducks as they swam in the pond. Their quacks echoed in the stillness of the day, as he sat beside her on the comfortable bench.

For a moment, Sir Andross watched her. The wisps of blonde hair that had escaped the wide-brimmed hat she wore flitted about her delicate oval face. The simple sheath dress in a dark brown she wore framed her petite body loosely, making him long to hold her in his arms, to feel the shapely woman beneath the folds. A pert nose and soft bow-shaped lips beckoned to him to shower them with kisses. With a sigh, he walked over and sat beside her.

"I've packed you a bag with some first aid gear and a few helpful salves for your travels, Sir Andross," Favila said with her sweet musical voice.

"Thank you, Favi. If I had more time... but I don't... I have to go and do what I can to help our kingdom," Sir Andross reached in his pocket and drew out a small ring he had fashioned out of a piece of metal. "I know it is inadequate, but would you do me the honor of bearing this ring and waiting for my return?"

"Sir Andross, I—"

"In Aulden, a man gives the woman he wishes to formally court a plain ring. If she accepts, it signals they are committed to pursuing the relationship." Sir Andross explained, unsure if in Dravidia the giving of a ring meant the same thing as in Aulden.

"I don't know if I am ready to accept that kind of commitment." Favila crushed him. "It isn't that I don't like you... I do... but..." She trailed off. The beseeching look in her eyes did nothing to soften the blow of her rejection.

"I understand... I do," he said, pocketing the pathetic ring quickly. "We hardly know each other. Well, I will go pack." He rose to get away from the humiliating situation.

"Wait, Sir Andross," Favila's soft hand touched his arm and he froze, hope springing in his heart. "Perhaps, when all this is over, you might seek me out again."

"I will."

An hour later, Sir Andross rode north, to the gateway city of Agrifar. The retinal scan had given him access to the AI beast. He'd have to figure out how to get a new valet key somehow.

As spring got firmly underway, the blossoming orchards and vineyards of the Vale of Tars perfumed the warm breezes. The beauty of the flowers, the fragrance of the ripening fruit, and the lush green landscape of the farmlands he passed failed to bring his spirits up. Gazing on the agricultural steads, he wondered if he might not have been better off remaining on his father's thriving farm and forgoing a life of adventure.

Several days later, Sir Andross crossed the East Vongo River and made his way through the grasslands that flanked the southern edge of the Jornian desert. As he traveled, the cities became fewer. Small nomadic tent dwellings dotted the landscape with increased frequency. The people of the area were goard herders.

These hardy little animals' milk was famed throughout Thyrein's Galactic Wall for its sweetness and medicinal qualities. Sir Andross decided to buy some and have it sent to Lady Newog and Favila for their work. He also purchased a wool cover, made of the goard's special purple coat, for the cold nights in the desert.

Holding to the ancient code of hospitality, the nomads extended shelter for the night to Sir Andross. He enjoyed the evenings listening to their folktales and legends, many of which told of the fabled desert stallion, which rescued travelers in distress. Sir Andross's resolve to someday write a book with all the wonderful stories he was collecting on the journey strengthened.

He arrived at Agrifar just as spring was giving way to the first days of heat of the summer season. The city walls had but one gate, and Sir Andross had to wait for hours under the hot sun to enter. Once inside, the streets of the city were full of people selling all manner of things. It was a bazaar day and anything and everything could be bought at a bargain prize, or so the merchants hollered as visitors passed the multicolored stalls.

Sir Andross made his way through the homes and business buildings, built of the pastel colored clay-like adobe that was unique to the desert area. Mingled in with the stench of sweaty people and animals was the paradoxical array of sweet fragrances from perfume and spice merchants, and the mouthwatering aromas of the food vendors.

The knight trudged along steadily through the sluggish throngs to an inexpensive inn Lady Newog had recommended. With his jorses stabled and after a good meal, Sir Andross found himself on the holonet talking with the king. The queen was right, he'd have to play double agent for a time. If he stopped communicating with the king, his liege lord would realize something was wrong. Sir Andross didn't know what might result from that, but for now, it was safer for all concerned that the king believe nothing had changed.

"How goes everything?" the king asked.

"Well, I have a new lead and am making my way north again to pursue it." Sir Andross made his statements vague hoping the king would not notice.

"I thought you were looking for Lord Orloff?"

"I found him, and he clued me in to the possible connection between Horsef and a lady around the Garpeth Valley area." Sir Andross ran sweaty palms on his trousers. *How much to say, how much to keep from the king; this was nerve wracking.*

"Ah..." Something flickered in the king's eyes. *Suspicion probably.*

"Yes. Lord Orloff will be arriving at the castle soon, I think. He said he was going there to use the library's resources to see if he can trace other connections that the master rajin might have had," Sir Andross said, words flowing quickly in his nervous state. "That's what he said anyway."

"Hmmm... I will keep my eye on him." The king looked at Sir Andross with a sharp gaze. "I want to know right away if you find the rajin. Understand?"

"Of course, Sire," Sir Andross said. "I will contact you immediately if that happens."

"Good."

Sir Andross found it hard to sleep that night. This was a dangerous game, as the queen had said. If the king found out that the knight was no longer being completely truthful to him, what would he do? The punishments in Aulden were harsh and often cruel. *This could be bad for me, very bad.*

The next morning, resolved to see things through no matter the cost, Sir Andross made his way to the local Soane Bank. Digital payment methods in the desert were unreliable. Lady Newog, who often came for spices and other elements for her salves, had informed him he would need to carry physical funds. She had patiently explained how the sands of the Jornian desert, heavily saturated with minerals and ores, caused major electrical interference, even with only slight breezes, to the digital payers. Thus, while the vast portion of the intergalactic system used only virtual funds, pockets of areas still required physical money, and he would be traversing one such zone.

"We don't have olg coins, but I can fill your request in ronver," the teller said.

"That's fine." Sir Andross accepted the heavy purse she handed him. Olg would have been lighter and less coinage. Still, this would do for now.

Reemerging from the coolness of the bank into the hot summer day, Sir Andross proceeded to purchase his supplies for the treacherous journey across the desert. He bartered a great exchange for the palfrey he'd bought from Ven back at the start of his journey in Dravidia City. He gained two jadels for the worthy horse. The desert animals had large humps that held water for months, making them ideal for the crossing. Sir Andross's final purchase was a huchive, which Lady Newog had advised he carry with him for the occasional sand storms.

Evening fell, and the air began to cool. After a delicious meal at a local eatery, Sir Andross made his way back to his inn. He had not gone far when he felt someone push past him, and saw a small figure running away into an alley. He felt for his bag of money, and, sure enough, it was gone. Sir Andross set off after the little thief. He ran fast enough to keep the fleeing silhouette within sight. Soon he was catching up, and then the thief entered a dead-end alley, and Sir Andross knew he would catch him.

Making the turn, the knight saw the cornered thief cowering against the stone wall, which had thwarted his escape. The knight approached with caution, aware that the little guy might jump at him with a weapon. But the thief extended his hand, and offered the knight back the bag of coins he had so unsuccessfully snatched. Surprised, Sir Andross took the purse, and put it away. Then he looked at the thief.

"Step into the light, boy," Sir Andross commanded the huddled form.

"Please, sir," the thief begged, doing as he was told. "Please, sir, don't call the police. The Lord Governor will cut my hand off."

In the dim streetlight, Sir Andross saw tears rolling down the sun-kissed cheeks of a young boy. He couldn't be older than ten, max twelve, Sir

Andross guesstimated. He was thin and grimy, and the scanty rags he bore barely covered his frail body.

"I will not turn you in, boy," the knight said with kindness. "What is your name and where do you live?"

"My name is Rafgin," the boy answered, an impish smile lighting up his face.

"Where are your parents?" Sir Andross asked.

"I don't have parents... well, not anymore," Rafgin explained. "They died several years ago."

"I see," the knight considered the visibly emaciated boy. "Come on, let's go in this open-air bistro over here and get you some food."

"Sir?"

"Well, come on."

Sir Andross led the way. The ragamuffin boy followed. Despite the look of concern from the restaurants' staff, the knight sat watching Rafgin voraciously consume the meal.

"Why don't I take you to one of the local orphanages, so you can be looked after?" Sir Andross suggested after paying for the food.

"No way!" Rafgin shook his filthy head of dark-brown curls with vehemence. "Those places are hell."

"It's better than being out here on the street, risking the loss of your hand." Sir Andross pressed, hoping to persuade the youth.

"You're a knight. You have no idea what those places are like, or what they do to you there." The look in the boy's chocolate eyes told of harrowing experiences.

"Well, then I bid you farewell, Rafgin. There is nothing more I can do for you." Sir Andross pressed a couple coins into the boy's hand, and made his way back to his inn.

The knight was aware of the small figure following him. When he reached his lodgings, Sir Andross noticed that the boy settled himself in the doorway across the street. He knew Rafgin would spend the cold night there.

Some time later, in the middle of the night, Sir Andross knelt over the small body curled up on the cold stone steps and placed the warm goard blanket over him.

The next day dawned and Sir Andross was up bright and early. He had planned on setting out right away, but had to make additional purchases for the journey. Exiting his inn, Sir Andross found himself staring across the way to where the boy had spent the night. Sure enough, the urchin sat there, the blanket neatly folded by his side.

"Sir Andross!" The boy exclaimed waving excitedly to the knight. Rising the boy hurried across to him. "Thank you for the blanket," Rafgin said, handing it over to the knight. "Can I help you find what you need today?"

Sir Andross considered the boy as he took the blanket. "Perhaps you can, Rafgin. I need to buy some supplies. Can you help me avoid the merchants that deal treacherously?"

"Yes, sir, I can help." The eagerness in that face brought a smile to the knight.

"Very well." Leaving the blanket back in his room, Sir Andross set off with his helper.

Rafgin proved a savvy haggler and once again Sir Andross invited the boy to dine with him. He learned a lot about the cruelty of the orphanages that the boy had escaped from. Three in the span of just a year, the boy enlightened him with pride.

"Look, tomorrow I head out across the desert. The journey I'm on is not safe for a young boy such as yourself," Sir Andross's voice was stern as he tried to make the situation clear to Rafgin. "I can only spare these coins, but they should be enough to get you some decent clothing and give you a chance to find a job with one or another of the caravans." He pressed the coins into the boy's hand.

"Thank you, Sir Andross, but I would like to come with you. I can help you."

The hopeful gaze in the boy's eyes broke Sir Andross's heart. "That can't be, son. It's not safe. I'm sorry."

Night came and went, and in the morning Sir Andross, dressed in the special coneb outfit for desert travel, prepared all the gear and got the real animals and his AI jorse loaded up for departure. He was aware of Rafgin, who followed him as he made his way through the city to the gate that led into the desert. Several caravans of traders were setting off at that same hour. Sir Andross caught word that one in particular was headed to Rafargar City. By keeping it in sight and using the desert compass he had purchased and the map of the oasis roads, Sir Andross hoped to make it across in two weeks' time. Lord Orloff had promised to meet him on the other side and the prophet might have news gleaned from his time at the castle.

He'd not gone far, when he heard the cries of pain from behind him. Turning back, he saw Rafgin, running, his bare feet no doubt in major pain from the sands' heat. The boy caught up to him and Sir Andross reached a hand down to swing him up into the jorse's back seat.

"Just what do you think you are doing?" the irritated knight asked.

"You are a knight," the boy replied, a cheeky grin flashing through his tears. "Every knight needs a squire, sir."

Sir Andross could not contain his laughter at the boy's gumption. When his mirth died down, he inspected the boy with a critical eye. Bringing one of the jadels up to them, he transferred the boy to the animal, then took out some clean clothes and shoes from one of the satchel packs.

"Here," Sir Andross extended the garments to Rafgin. "I figured I wouldn't be alone on this journey. I hope I got the right size."

Rafgin took the coneb outfit in his hands with reverence. "I have not had new clothes in a long time."

"I can tell."

"Thank you, Sir Andross, thank you."

"No need to thank me, Rafgin." Sir Andross looked out toward where the caravan he'd hoped to follow was slowly disappearing into the horizon. "A squire is a knight in training, and the work will be grueling. You will train hard and learn discipline. I hope you are prepared for that."

"I won't fail you, sir," Rafgin's voice held such earnestness, Sir Andross couldn't help but smile at the boy.

"Well, come on, we mustn't get lost on day one." Sir Andross got his jorse moving, the second jadel tied to it. With Rafgin following, the knight made his way into the Jornian desert lands.

Chapter 33

A New Quest Opens

The summer sun shone blisteringly hot as Sir Andross and his new squire traversed the Jornian desert. As they rode, day after day, Sir Andross taught his young apprentice the basics of a knight's life as he understood them. He'd not been born one, but he'd read plenty about knights and followed his favorite ones during Thyrein's Galactic Tournament. It took place every four years and knights from all corners of the alliance competed for the title of First Knight.

"Remember, Rafgin," Sir Andross extolled one day. "A knight's most important possession is his honor. Without honor, there is nothing. Never give your word unless you are committed to keeping it. Never back out once you are involved in a cause. And never engage in behavior that might bring disgrace upon your reputation, the house you serve, or your nation."

Sir Andross gazed across the horizon. They had lost sight of the caravan he'd hoped to follow almost from the outset, but Sir Andross was sure they were heading in the right direction. The ocean of gleaming sand lay before them.

Returning to what he was saying, Sir Andross continued, "Beyond honor, is loyalty and justice. Never betray a friend. Never commit yourself to an unjust cause. And always champion the need of those who seek justice."

Turning to look at his companion's rapt attention, the earnestness of the boy's expression filled Sir Andross with the realization of his responsibility. He was accountable for this young person and the knight took the matter very seriously. Smiling, he reached over and ruffled the boy's hair.

"Enough serious talk," the knight said lightly. "Tell me more of your mischievous escapades, Rafgin."

The squire was just about to speak when the jadels started pulling at the ropes. The nervous animals halted and tried to turn around. Looking up into the sky toward the western horizon, Sir Andross realized a sandstorm was coming. Already he could see the electrical currents it generated crackling. Sir Andross had researched the desert before arriving at Agrifar. He'd never had occasion to traverse this part of the continent before. The sands of the Jornian desert consisted of iron and mineral ore particles, which were highly conducive for electricity. When strong winds blew, the desert sands swirled and their friction created electrical charges in the air.

It was hard to know how long it would take the storm to reach them, but Sir Andross knew he had no time to lose. Dismounting quickly, he took out the huchive he had purchased.

"Here," he commanded Rafgin, "put these blindfolds on the jadels and hold them steady. Try and calm them."

Putting the jorse in stop mode, the knight moved quickly, setting up the eight metal spikes in an octagon formation around the animals, leaving plenty of room for himself and Rafgin. When he was sure he had them in just the right places, Sir Andross activated the mechanism, which embedded all eight securely ten feet deep into the hard ground below the sand. Then he switched the huchive on and the energy force field surrounded them and kept them safe from the storm.

The winds, which had been mounting steadily, were cut off, and the roaring sound of the storm, which would soon have become a deafening howl, was silenced. Sir Andross noted that the tempest seemed to be traveling with great speed.

The wild electrical discharges crackled outside in a myriad of shades of yellow, white, and orange. The swirling sands blocked out Ara's light, and only the greenish glow of the energy field allowed them to see.

"Don't worry," Sir Andross reassured his squire, whom he noted was standing in fearful awe. "We are perfectly safe here."

Sir Andross's jorse went into sleep mode to conserve energy. Together, the knight and Rafgin set up their sleeping bags to wait out the storm.

The sandstorm took a week to run its course. Though it traveled quickly it was very wide. Meanwhile, Sir Andross and Rafgin exchanged stories. The knight shared with his squire the folktales and legends he had heard during his travels, as well as tales of the battles he had been in during the war. Rafgin told Sir Andross of his time in various orphanages and of his life on the streets.

When at last they continued their journey, their progress was delayed by the sudden running of a wall of fire. Sir Andross learned quickly to identify this danger's onset by looking for the tell-tale sign of greenish-red sparks that hovered on the sand and indicated the rise and direction the wall would take. These fire walls could rise up to twenty feet into the air and spread like slithering serpents for up to eighty miles in a matter of seconds. They would usually burn for two or three hours, then subside, leaving the air tinged with a burned metallic scent.

As they traveled through a desert valley surrounded on two sides by towering sand dunes, Sir Andross heard the noise of horse's bridles jingling. He stopped and listened intently, silencing his young companion's current story. Taking out the farlens, he spied a line of ten riders on the rim of the sand dune to their right. He realized they were bandits.

Quickly, he spurred the jadels and his jorse into a wild gallop, hoping to cross the valley and escape into the populated oasis of Pung that his map indicated was near. He couldn't floor the jorse, as the poor jadel attached would surely perish. There was no way she could keep up with the AI. The wild cries of the bandits echoed as the group charged at them, like vultures on a dead carcass. As their animals reached the base of the dune that they had to cross over to reach safety, Sir Andross realized the bandits would gain on them before they could do so. The loaded down jadels were slowing their progress.

Bringing his jorse up to the jadel Rafgin rode, he managed to unhook the satchel with the most essential supplies and hooked it to his jorse. The knight grabbed the boy and pulled him into the back seat. Released, the jadel began to slow its pace. Sir Andross instructed Rafgin to grab from the second jadel the satchel with the water supply and then unhooked the animal from his jorse. Rafgin complied quickly.

Sir Andross slipped his jorse into full speed. In no time the AI reached eighty miles an hour. With the jadels behind them, the knight hoped the bandits would be happy to ransack and gain the two animals and less desirous of following the escaping pair over the dune to a populated area. Sure enough, his gamble paid off.

That night, they enjoyed the hospitality of the Cliek of Garpun, who was encamped at the oasis on his own journey to his home in the desert.

"We are in trouble, Sir Andross," Rafgin commented, as the pair settled onto the comfortable cushioned bedding their host had provided them.

"Yes," Sir Andross responded, lying on his back. "We lost a lot of supplies back there. But, we aren't too far from our destination now. We may well make it in the next few days."

"It is amazing that such bandits still conduct raids. King Dekkyle created a special force to deal with them and travel was much safer," Rafgin commented. "I remember hearing many caravan owners praising the king's efforts and the work of the Intertribal Clieks Council that cooperated to make it happen."

"No doubt you overhead all that while trying to steal from them." Sir Andross threw his squire a look he hoped was stern.

"Yes, well..." The boy's face reddened with embarrassment. "I didn't have you then."

Sir Andross smiled. "The war must have given the bandits the chance they needed to resume their work. No doubt the forces that had been assigned here were moved to fight against Prince Amiel."

"Hmm..."

Sir Andross watched as the boy's eyes closed. Returning his gaze to the tent's ceiling he lifted a prayer for the quick and incident free passage for the short journey left.

The next two days passed quickly. The pair made excellent time with just the jorse to ride. With no live animals to consider, Sir Andross let the AI go at its top speed of 120 miles per hour. Soon, they were before the gate leading to the city of Rafargar. The pair spent the last of the day restocking their supplies, enjoying a great meal and taking a shower in the Paldour Inn.

A knock at their bedchamber door, woke them the following morning. Rising with a languid stretch, Sir Andross inquired, "Who is it?"

"It's me, Ven. Open up, Andy."

Springing to the door, Sir Andross opened it, ushering his friend in.

Hope surged in the knight at the thought of Ven's contacts in the Auldian spy network his friend used to work for might have paid off. Perhaps he'd brought important information on the whereabouts of the rajin master.

"I am sure glad to see you. How did you find where I was?" Sir Andross asked.

"You aren't as hard to find as you think, old pal."

"I hope for regular folk it is. You don't count," Sir Andross said. "I've picked up a squire." The knight gestured to Rafgin. Ven gave the boy a calculating look over. "Rafgin, this is my old friend, Ven."

"Well, I don't know about the old part," the former Nedula spy said with a self-deprecating smile. "Come, boy, let's have a look at you." Rafgin approached warily. Ven's brow furrowed. "Well, come on, son. I won't bite you."

Standing before Ven, the ragamuffin boy fidgeted. Sir Andross ruffled the boy's hair and went to take a seat on the small window's ledge. He watched his squire as the former spy turned innkeeper gave him a thorough inspection. The boy genuinely seemed petrified.

"You look like you could use a few more good meals. We could take care of that back at my inn in Dravidia City, hey Andy," Ven smiled, before dismissing the boy and heading over to Sir Andross. Taking a seat in a nearby chair, he commented, "So you know that information you asked me to be on the lookout for."

"Yes. Have you discovered where the rajin master went?"

Ven sent a warning look over to Rafgin, who had taken a seat across the room out of respect.

"Don't worry about Rafgin. He's my squire, and I trust him fully."

With a final assessing glance at the boy, Ven began, "I guess. Well, my intel has Horsef at Lady Viona's house. He's been there since the attack on Sanctal. According to my source, he's been communicating with Rajin Bral."

"Bral! I don't remember if he was on Jorn when the war started."

"He wasn't. Apparently, King Dekkyle had sent him to talk to the Gortive, see if some peace could be forged before anything nasty got started."

"It makes sense to send a rajin master. After all, even the natives must respect their power."

"That seems to be what King Dekkyle believed as well. But, from what I discovered, Bral never met with the Gortive."

"What?"

"Yeah." Ven glanced once more to the boy, shrugged, and continued. "He must have uncovered something that took him off world. Anyway, Horsef and Bral have been communicating and, if my informant is correct, they are gathering, the three masters, at Lady V's."

"That's excellent." Sir Andross thought about the end of his quest. It was both exhilarating knowing he would soon be able to let the queen know they had found the rajin, and depressing thinking of returning to the life of royal bodyguard. Still... it was good to be successful. "Are you sure your source is accurate?"

"Of course!" Ven gave him a wide satisfied smile.

"You could have sent word digitally, my friend. Why put yourself out like this? I mean your wife... Is she okay? Has she delivered your baby?"

"I am the proud father of a healthy baby boy!" Ven's expression showed his joy.

"Congratulations!" Sir Andross stretched out a hand. "Not that I don't appreciate the information, but shouldn't you be home, with her?"

"I should, but my boy sure can wail like a banshee. I needed to get away!"

"It's a baby. What did you expect?" Sir Andross shook his head at his friend's reason.

"I know," Ven said, a sheepish look on his face. "It's selfish of me, but, hey, I came through with your intel, right?"

"And I sure appreciate it, Ven, thank you." Sir Andross rose. Turning to Rafgin, he instructed. "Get our things packed. We should set out at once... maybe after a good breakfast. Will you join us?" he asked Ven.

"Just for the meal." Ven stood, clapping a hand on Sir Andross shoulder. "After that it's back to baby duty."

"I'll send word to Lord Orloff. He's on his way to Dravidia Castle, but promised to head out and join me here as soon as he finished his business there."

"Orloff? The prophet?" Ven asked, his brows rising in surprise.

"He is helping with the quest," Sir Andross informed him.

"Makes sense, I suppose." Ven had never been particularly religious and his tone showed his dubiousness at the holy man's involvement. "Come on, let's get food into this young man. He needs it as bad as I do." He tapped his wide belly as he spoke.

"Ven, my friend, married life has proved good to you, what with the inn's kitchens at your disposal."

The laughing trio made their way to the inn's restaurant.

Sir Andross and Rafgin set off before mid-day for Ludan, the city where Ven had confirmed Lady Viona resided. The knight purchased a used, older model palfrey jorse for Rafgin. He hoped this would make travel easier. With both beasts being mechanical, they could go faster on their way back to the castle, Sir Andross hoped.

They arrived in Ludan just as the city gates were closing. It was a sprawling metropolis with towering skyscrapers and thriving businesses. Its night life was no less vibrant and the streets were congested with people seeking fun times. Gradually, they made their way to the high-rise building where Lady Viona's penthouse condo was located.

The concierge scrutinized them, but once Lady Viona sent word they were indeed expected, he let them in. The lift opened on the penthouse floor and Sir Andross's jaw dropped. Lady Viona's home was pure glass. The floor-to-ceiling windows that made up the entire perimeter of walls looked on to a spectacular view of the Verperth Cluster of Mountains. The furniture was glass, leather, and steel. Everything seemed to gleam and sparkle.

"Welcome to my home, Sir Andross," a throaty voice boomed. A chubby lady dressed in white flowing robes, came toward them. Her golden hair tumbled over her shoulders and her blue eyes twinkled.

"Thank you, my Lady," Sir Andross responded. "May I introduce you to my squire, Rafgin."

"Welcome, young knight in training," the lady turned her smile on the boy, whose face now glowed crimson at the attention. "Come. This way is what you seek."

They followed the lady through the open living room space, through a gleaming white kitchen, and past a wall of frosted glass into a private den. There, standing before the white marble fireplace, were Rajin Master Lady Vivelda the Bountiful and Rajin Master Lord Horsef the Great. Or at least, Sir Andross hoped that's who they were. A feeling of intense power emanated from them, and they seemed to have a glow about their persons.

Lady Vivelda was speaking. "I have sent my filear back to Sanctal. The main temple supply ship should arrive soon. It must be ready..." She let her words trail away when Lady Viona announced Sir Andross and his squire.

"Sir Andross," Lord Horsef's gruff voice startled the knight. "I hear you have been searching for me."

"Indeed, my Lord," Sir Andross said, taking the seat that Lady Viona indicated for him. "Queen Verena needs your help."

"More than she knows, I fear." The cryptic words surprised the knight. "She has the—"

"Liquid of Shrang LaRoo and the crystal dagger as well, thanks to you," he interrupted. "Good work on finding that artifact. No one has ever survived a rego, that I know of."

"Thank you, sir. It was really accidental."

Sir Andross took the preferred cup of tea from his host and watched as Rafgin partook surreptitiously of some cucumber sandwiches.

"So, will you return to Castle Dravidia, Lord Horsef?" Sir Andross asked, as the rest of the gathering took a seat around the room and sipped tea.

"I'm afraid not right away."

Sir Andross nearly sputtered out the beverage he'd just taken into his mouth. Lady Viona's brow, the knight noticed, furrowed at the rajin's response.

"We must help—" the lady began.

The rajin master put up a placating hand. "Yes. We shall help. It is clear now, that there is a new order in the universe, and they are known as the nijar. I have been tracking them, and, thanks to Bral, I believe we now know where their main headquarter is located."

"Oh?" Sir Andross was intrigued. All this time Rajin Horsef had been undercover investigating. He supposed that was what rajin did, after all.

"As soon as Bral is able to join us, we will head to planet Magdezb."

"What planet?" Lady Viona enquired. "I don't recall such a world."

"It is just outside of Thyrein's Galactic Wall."

"No one can travel beyond the wall." Sir Andross glanced about the room as he made his comment. "The space between walls is dead. There are no quantum streams to make a jump."

"You don't need a quantum stream, Sir Knight," Lady Vivelda spoke, her musical voice a caress to his ears, "when you can access the forces of the universe itself."

"Don't worry, Sir Andross." Rajin Horsef smiled broadly. "This adventure is one you will never forget. We shall go into the wall next to ours and seek Magdezb. There, we will find the source of our current dilemma. Then, when we have uncovered the full plans of our enemies, we will return and ensure Thyrein's Galactic Wall and our Queen Verena succeed in thwarting them."

"So we're off on another quest then?" Sir Andross asked.

"It would seem so, Sir Knight." Lady Viona took out her com device. "I will let Lord Orloff know. He should be reaching Dravidia Castle soon."

CHAPTER 34
REBELLION

AMIEL HAD LEFT HER IN CHARGE, as his queen, while he was at war. This pleased Verena greatly. Her first action had been to send word to Lord Soane of their imminent arrival to end the siege of his city. She followed that by contacting the Earl of Sarnac and the others at Fort Iark. Informing them of this critical moment, she asked them to aid King Amiel in bringing to heel these rebelling nobles. The earl's response saddened her.

<Majesty, this could be the perfect moment to attack him ourselves, retake the realm.>

<Excellency,> Verena had typed back, measuring out her words. <This is a chance to show your allegiance and earn the pardon he has already given you. We need him. We can make this work together. Will you help?>

There had been a long pause. Verena guessed he and his followers were conferring on the situation. Eventually, he had responded they would go to Amiel's aide.

<We will cut across the Verludian Mountain pass and reach Anco from the northeastern side. If King Amiel rides north, he can attack the besiegers from the south side and they would no doubt attempt to escape northward. We can arrive in time to end any further resistance and crush these lordlings.> A short pause and then he added, <For you.>

<Thank you, and Godspeed.>

That evening, alone in Amiel's office, which had once been her father's, Verena reached for her com. She connected to the holonet using the nodes in the beautiful box. Her heart felt heavy as she realized these were the same ones her father would have used. Verena hoped a time for grieving would come, but she had to push back her feelings now. Things were starting to right themselves.

On the net, Verena scanned to see if Amiel was logged on. She saw his digi right away. Composing a convo box, she sent it marked urgent.

<The Dravidians at Fort Iark have responded. They have accepted the pardon and are ready to swear allegiance to us. I can have them return to the castle now, or have them wait for your return.>

She waited, hoping he would respond, unwilling to jump right in and tell him she'd convinced her people to go fight for him. He must be encamped en route to the Vale. Perhaps he was planning an attack with his generals and her convo box would blink in a corner unheeded. Seconds ticked by, and she was starting to get restless. As she waited, she scanned the private net her father had set up. She saw his journals all carefully dated. Verena had just tapped on the one that comprised his thoughts during the betrothal period, when Amiel responded.

<I would prefer you await my return.>

<Ok. Do you want them to help you fight? I can ask them to. They could come round from the north of Anco and seal Uld's fate.>

No response. He was no doubt considering the idea. Perhaps the others around him were arguing against it. What if the Dravidians took the advantage to over throw him at a critical moment? Was no doubt what they were saying. She wished she could be there to counter their arguments.

<If you are sure they will be loyal to us both, then yes, I could use their surprise assistance if they come from behind. They will have to cross the Verludian Mountains. Do you think they would make it in time?>

<Yes. They can use the pass of Verld. They are loyal.>

<I'm trusting you.>

<Yes.>

She saw his digi go red indicating he was no longer there. This was a huge step for them. If the earl and his men reached Amiel and helped him, then the kingdom could be united at last. Amiel's final words warmed her. "*I'm trusting you.*" A new hope buoyed her heart.

The first two days following Amiel's departure, she spent communicating with each of the noble houses of the realm to ascertain the status of their defenses. Sitting in Amiel's office with the Earl of Ydarb, who served as Chief Peer in the Duke of Aul's absence, she assigned monies as needed from the funds appropriated by the Council of Vassals for securing the kingdom.

"All these will need to be ratified by the full Council of Peers and the king," the Earl of Ydarb informed her, as they finalized the round of calls on the second day.

He had been drafting each disbursement on his holopad, and she watched as he compiled all the forms into a single request document.

"Send the funds now, and we will ask for ratification after," Verena's voice held the tone of authority she had often observed her father use.

The Earl of Ydarb's face showed his concern. "But—"

"Excellency, we cannot know just how soon the Gortive might launch their attack." Verena explained with as much patience as she could muster. "Delaying assistance for bureaucratic approvals may cost us the kingdom."

"I will do as you direct, Majesty." the Earl of Ydarb held out the device to her with the screen requiring the sovereign's authorization. "If you will sign for them here."

Verena took the device from him. Placing her palm upon it, she waited for it to accept and process the documents. A red screen flashed the word "Unauthorized." Verena tapped the button to override. Entering her father's master code, she tapped "Submit again." The system accepted her authority.

"There you are." She returned the holopad to the Earl of Ydarb. "That will be all."

His face showed his consternation at the system's acceptance of her authority. For a moment, he looked like he might inquire, then he clearly thought better of it and took his cue to leave.

Alone, Verena fidgeted. She ran through the various papers on Amiel's desk. Her eyes fell upon a notepad with a list on it. Taking it in her hands, she read it, a smile forming on her face. It was Amiel's to-do list. Most of the items had been crossed off. Turning the page, she found one circled. "Make sure Verena goes to Dr. Koll for follow-up."

She realized this was from almost five months back, when she had awoken from the ginmra effect. With all that had followed, Verena had completely forgotten she was supposed to go in for further testing. She marveled that Dr. Koll had not pressed the issue. Perhaps she had and Amiel simply didn't relay the messages. It was probably superfluous now, but going would provide her an excuse to visit Dravidia City.

"It is unbelievable," the doctor's voice was a whispered exhale. "Your Majesty, in my forty years as a physician I have never seen anything like this."

"Is something wrong with me?" Verena sat up from the scanning table.

"There is nothing wrong with you, Majesty," Dr. Koll announced. "As you know, the nodes that activate the ginmra are implanted in the very center of the cerebrum and connected to the brain by six very delicate synthetic nerve synapsis, which allows for the brain-to-ginmra link. Usually these synapses are covered over by scar tissue and sometimes the node itself is enveloped in brain matter tissue that forms around it over time. In your brain, however, the neurons have extended dendrites and are forming their own contacts to the node."

"What?"

"Here, Majesty, take a look." The doctor tapped on the holopad to which the scanner bed had sent the images, transferring them to the large monitor mounted on the wall. Walking to it, Dr. Koll zoomed in on the brain section explaining, "Here is the node. These are the six axon-styled cells that connect it to your brain. See how all these dendrites are extending from your brain to the node? Your brain has forged its own networks to the technology we implanted. This explains a lot."

"What does this mean?" Verena asked with trepidation.

"For one thing, it explains why your Majesty has the long coma-like restoration time after ginmra use instead of just a small recuperation like most others. Your brain creates new dendrites and strengthens those already there and needs deeper slumber to do this." Turning toward her, the doctor continued, "It also explains why you're so fast and strong in combat. Without the ginmra, fighting with other weapons, your Majesty is good, but with the ginmra, your strength is doubled and your reflexes quicken."

"So... this is a good thing?" Verena struggled to fully understand the implications as she stared at the scan of her brain's dendrites covering the node like a spider's intricate web.

"A very good thing, Majesty," Dr. Koll confirmed beaming.

"Why is this happening with me and not with others?"

"I can't say." Dr Koll walked over to the counter where a syringe lay.

"I'm hoping to be able to get a better understanding once we do blood work. If I may, I would like to have a sampling of the castle's guards' blood as well to compare yours to other ginmra users. May I return with you to the castle to collect these?"

"Yes." Verena extended her arm so that Dr. Koll could proceed. Master Rajin Horsef must have known what was happening. He had prevented her father from removing the node when King Dekkyle had become alarmed at the coma-like sleep the ginmra induced. Verena made a mental note to ask the rajin about this situation if Sir Andross was successful in finding him.

Verena sat in her rooms, the nodes on her temples, watching in horrified silence as the news outlets reported on the Battle for Anco. The Auldian insurgents had surrounded the city, whose defenses, thankfully, had not been damaged in the war. As Soane lay to the north of Castle Dravidia, Amiel had never attacked that part of the continent.

Now, Verena watched as Amiel's warriors formed a line across the edge of the Soa plateau. Overlooking the Valley of Soane with the besieged Anco City at the bottom of the gentle slope, their army held the perfect spot from which to attack. Elite knights on jorse were flanked by infantry soldiers.

The steal beasts and weapons shone in the sun's rays while the black pennants with the united crest of their kingdom flapped in the wind. As she scanned the line of men, Verena noted the Dravidian nobles that stood with Amiel's Auldian men. They were the houses of the northern lands, and it filled her with pride to see them beside their king.

As soon as the army had gathered, Amiel lead the charge toward the rebels below. They moved with speed down the slope to where Lord Uld was quickly reforming his men in response, part of them leaving their attack positions from the city walls to prepare a defense.

As Amiel's men grew close, the Auldian insurgents charged, the enemy's mounted men closing the gap on Amiel. The two groups clashed in a bloody melee. Erows and epulses erupted from weapons; ginmras and regular honrol blades sparked as they met in combat.

Verena's heart raced. Before her eyes, wounded men fell from their jorses. Some recovered to stand and fight on. Others lay dead, their blood soaking into the green land of the valley. The foot soldiers arrived and took to the field.

Hand to hand combat ensued as the battle intensified. The media coverage zoomed in and Verena caught sight of the men of house Diev among the others. They bore a black band on their left arm over their Dravidian armor. As her eyes scanned the scene, Verena noted all of Amiel's men wore a similar marker. *Of course, he'd made sure they knew friend from foe with this simple method.*

She thanked the Great I Am her ladies had not insisted on sitting with her, letting her have solitude. As the holonet flow of the live video footage passed before her eyes, Verena knew her face must show her emotions. She wasn't a hundred percent sure she knew what those feelings were precisely.

Verena had been raised with the certainty that Anco City could not be breached. *But... then again Castle Dravidia's defenses were a replica of those in Anco, magnified by the forest surveillance and security system, and it had fallen to Amiel.*

As the battle continued, Verena tried to find Amiel in the fray. It was hard to keep a line of sight on him, as the news media video tended to scan to and fro, showing the entire battle.

Frustrated, Verena switched off the net and inputted her father's code, accessing the satellites. Re-focusing the one over the northern Dravidian lands, Verena zoomed its lens in on the area. After much searching, her eyes found Amiel. He was fighting hard, dodging blows from three opponents, and occasionally activating his arm force shield to block an erow or epulse from a bow or solun.

She marveled at how Amiel maneuvered seated upon his jorse, the AI animal remaining in sync with him. During battle, it seemed odd to her that men would choose to ride astride as if the machine were a real horse. They would be safer within the seat and energy shield. But even her father liked to battle in the old traditional way.

It did give them excellent maneuverability, though they would be more secure within the cockpit. Verena shook her head. She wouldn't have risked it if she'd been in the fight.

She watched as a man on jorseback rushed Amiel. The opponents blade cut across Amiel's chest. Red seeped onto the white cloth of his shirt, now visible under the honrol armor breastplate.

A gasp escaped her, and she struggled to see how deep the wound might be. It was impossible to tell. Verena saw Amiel turn and thrust the assailant through with his own blade. Ripping the nodes from her temples, she tossed them across her bed, her emotions overwrought. She couldn't think.

If he died, how would she feel? It would be maybe a good thing. Maybe... she would be queen. The Auldians might break away, which she would let them. She had no need of governing the whole continent. She could let them leave her lands and establish her rule in Dravidia.

An emotion tugged at her; an emotion she didn't want to give voice to; an emotion she would rather remained in the dark recesses of her heart. But as she sat, curled up into a ball, rocking back and forth, her arms hugging her knees, Verena couldn't deny it. *I don't want Amiel to die.*

I don't want to be alone... Yes, that's it. She was afraid of being isolated. That's all it was. But, Verena knew better than to lie to herself. She didn't want Amiel to die, because she loved him. *I have always loved him.* Even when he scared the daylights out of her, she loved Amiel ra Aulden.

With a trembling hand, she picked the nodes back up and replaced them on her temples. The images of blood-splattered bodies and smashed up jorses flashed once more before her eyes. She hunted for a sign of him. She couldn't find him in the smoky haze of the battlefield. *Great I Am, he can't die. He has to live.* The prayer, silent yet intense, roiled in her mind.

Then he was there, on his jorse, shouting something she couldn't hear. *There had to be a way to make satellites pick up audio,* her frustrated mind told her. She would see to it that something like that was developed. But for now, all she could do was watch a silent film, in all the gory glory of war. He was rallying the troops as they gave chase to the retreating Auldian insurgents. *Well, of course he won. It was Amiel after all!* She felt rather proud of him just then.

And then Verena saw them. Riding across the northern plains, cutting down the insurgents that had attempted to flee from Amiel's forces. Her people. The Dravidian forces from Iark arrived in perfect timing to help wrap up Amiel's victory.

As the gates of Anco opened, she noticed Amiel hold back the men, led by Lord Soane, who were coming forth to fight now that the city was no longer surrounded. This made her frown, but then she noticed the group lead by the Earl of Sarnac also bore the black band upon their arms. The men of Soane did not. Verena watched Amiel indicate to his own men to hold and secure the city, leaving the insurgents to the Dravidians. *Smart move,* she thought pleased. *This way none of our loyal men will be cut down by accident.*

Soon it was over. The Earl of Sarnac, dragging a tied up Lord Uld behind his jorse, rode up to where Amiel waited at the city gates. Lord Soane sat astride his own jorse beside Amiel. Verena watched as the earl and the other Dravidians showed their respect and allegiance to the new king.

CHAPTER 35

VICTORY

AMIEL, ACCOMPANIED BY HIS MEN and flanked by the Earl of Sarnac and the Duke of Aul, approached Dravidia Castle as it peaked out over the tree tops of the Oldey Forest. As he had traveled, people had come out and lined the streets. The joy of victory flushed through him as he noted the pathway to the castle was equally bordered with rejoicing subjects.

As the entourage approached, the tree line gave way to the castle. The rectangular building with its round corner towers took up the full length and breadth of the promontory that lead to the Green Ocean beyond. *I am home.* A warmth filled him at the thought.

Amiel's breath caught as it had since he was a child at the sight of Dravidia Castle. Strong lavender-hued walls with white stone trim stood proudly in the afternoon sunlight. Pennants featuring the united crest of his kingdom flapped from the parapets and towers as if applauding the victorious army returning. The sound echoed in the clapping and shouting of the people.

Approaching the double entrance, Amiel took in again the beauty of the architecture with its royal-purple ashlar work, and the Dravidian coat of arms above the gate arch. On each side, the two slender watchtowers with semicircular segmented roofs in white stone seemed to gleam. This castle had always seemed such a happy place, a stark contrast to the jet-black stone work of Aulden Palace.

He passed through into the first bailey. It was a small square courtyard space with thick walls ending in gilded parapets with the royal house's crest. Designed only to create a bottleneck during an attack, it was empty of people. Amiel continued under the second portcullis into the inner bailey wondering if Verena would be there to welcome him home. His heart pounded as the anticipation of seeing her again grew. He could still feel her lips on his from when he'd stolen a kiss before riding off to war.

The inner bailey opened wide in a rectangle before the stairs leading up to the main entrance of the castle. Gleaming white walls rose up protecting the stables and armory buildings that flanked the area. Behind him, the men spread out so that the whole entourage filled the space.

Castle servants, guards, and noble subjects welcomed them home with garlands of fragrant flowers. The chant of his name filled his ears.

Then he saw her as she stood there, atop the steps leading up into their home. His heart skipped a beat at the sight of his wife. Her glorious fiery hair was demurely held back at the nape of her neck, flowing down her back to just above her waist. Emerald gems gleamed as her eyes took in their arrival.

A frown creased his forehead as he took in her attire. *Why did she insist on wearing pants all the time?* She looked glorious in her dresses; the sway of their fabric as she walked had always mesmerized him. Yet, as he took her in, the tight fit of her clothing accentuated the curve of her legs and hips. She wore a loose blouse. The soft forest green cloth pressed against her skin as the breeze flowed through the open space.

He longed to dismount, climb those steps, pick her up, and take her off to his bed. A groan of regret escaped him as he glanced at the gathered staff and courtiers who cheered now as they watched the warriors fill the bailey. Making love to Verena would have to wait.

The nobles who'd ridden to war with him flared out around the courtyard. A satisfied smile wreathed Amiel's face as he took in Dravidian and Auldian warriors aligned together. He'd called upon the Dravidian nobles who held lands in the north, and they had responded, fighting alongside him from the start. The arrival of the Earl of Sarnac with his forces had been the final touch. Their victory under his command proved the nation was now one kingdom.

The clatter of the jaihover drew his gaze as he dismounted. This box-like hover craft had clear walls allowing all the world to look upon the humiliated forms of Lord Uld and the other lordlings that had rebelled and been caught alive. His chest filled with pride as he looked upon the men who'd thought they could defeat him.

Amiel turned and took the steps two at a time to where Verena stood. She curtsied to him as he reached her.

"I see you were victorious, my King," she commented, rising and meeting his gaze.

"Of course, we were, my Queen," He smiled down at her, letting his eyes have their fill of her face with its delicate features. The scent of her lavender soap drifted on the breeze, and his hand trembled with the urge to touch her hair, hold her in his arms. "Shall we deal with the traitorous rebels so we can..."

"Yes, of course," she said, taking the arm he proffered.

She moved like silk beside him as he led her to the throne room. They ascended the steps to the throne dais and turned. After settling her on the queen's throne, he took his place beside her.

The victorious nobles brought forth the conquered insurgents. The Duke of Aul, the Earl of Sarnac, the recently released Count Tor along with his son, all the other great men of war stood before them. Amiel waited as they took their places, letting the exhilarating sight of a truly united nation fill him. At last, he was king of their planet as he had been born to be.

An hour later, after having declared the prisoners guilty of treason and sentencing them to death, Amiel led the way once more as they headed to their chambers to clean up and change for the dinner celebration. He longed to skip all that and just spend the evening with Verena in his bed. Still... it was the fate of kings to delay their own pleasure.

"I'll see you in a few moments." He took her hand and lifted her delicate fingers to his lips before they each entered their own chambers.

Amiel made his way through his rooms and found his valet, Javern, waiting for him.

"Welcome home, Sire," the young man greeted, rushing forward to help Amiel out of his armor.

"It is good to be back," Amiel said with a smile.

Retiring his old hudroid valet, he'd decided to have Javern serve him personally rather than place the boy elsewhere in the castle. At fourteen, Javern was orphaned and having to make his way through life on his own. Amiel recalled the pain of losing his parents at that age. Taking the boy under his wing had just felt like the right thing to do when he and his sister had come looking for work in the castle.

"You can go." Verena's voice startled him.

She stood there, a flush of crimson on her cheeks. She'd come into his chamber. Amiel's heart pounded seeing her there, in his room, seeking him out. He always went in to her. She'd never come to him.

"Go," Amiel waved an impatient hand to the boy, snapping Javern to action.

Amiel stood there for a moment. Her emerald eyes filled with an emotion he couldn't name. He wondered what this was about. She moved hesitantly toward him, grabbing his hand and leading him to his bathroom.

"Take off your clothes. I'll get a bath going for you," she instructed.

He cocked an eyebrow, shocked and pleased by her daring. Heat pooled in his loins as he realized she intended to bath him. A smile coiled on his face. Well, if this was her plan, she should do it right.

"If I am going to have to undress myself, why dismiss Javern?" He teased her and enjoyed the deepening of her blush.

She glanced up at him, then quickly averted her eyes. "Well, then I'll do it as soon as I fill this tub."

"Okay." He felt himself smile broadly. The heat within him rose as he stood and waited. Anticipation building, he imagined what was to come.

Amiel followed her every movement with his eyes as she knelt by the tub, turning the water on and checking for the right temperature. Rising, she moved to where he stood. Javern had already removed his upper garments, so all she really needed to do was help him take off his pants.

A mischievous gleam sparkled in his eyes as he thought of what she would uncover. He watched Verena's fingers shake as she undid his belt buckle.

She'd never undressed him before. He always took her clothes off and then his own. Watching her increased his urge to pick her up and carry her off to his bed. His pants became a growing restraint to his desire, but he was enjoying this too much to interrupt her. His heart swelled as he considered the astounding fact that she had sought him.

With her head down, the soft lavender scent of her hair filled his senses. He closed his eyes for a moment breathing her in. Rennie's hands were soft on his thighs as she pulled his pants down. He heard her gasp.

He opened his eyes. "What?" He asked the top of her head, as she refused to meet his gaze.

She had freed his manhood and he wondered if she'd been shocked by its response to her. Had she ever actually looked at him before? He doubted it. The fact that she was seeing her effect on his body sent a thrill through him.

"You don't have any underwear on," she mumbled. Rennie slowly lifted her eyes to his, but couldn't hold the smoldering look of raw desire he must be giving her, because she dropped her head again.

"They're uncomfortable." He kept his voice even, yet he heard in it the husky tone produced by his need.

He noticed her eyes lingered on his erection. Amiel wanted her to tell him how she was affected by what she saw. He wanted her to want him. Yet, he couldn't speak. The scarlet of her face and the trembling of her body told him she was scared, but of what? In this moment, surely not of him, though she'd claimed he frightened her. What was this beautiful woman he loved thinking?

"Shall I get in the tub now?"

"Oh, yes... of course," Verena turned back to the bath and checked the water temperature, shutting off the faucet. "You don't have any bath salts?" She looked about the room.

"Bath salts?" Amiel had slid into the tub and was leaning back in the hot water. "Because I look like a bath salts kind of guy to you, do I?" He smiled at the thought of her bathroom with its myriad crystal containers of assorted who-knew-what stuff.

"Not really, no."

A familiar smile crossed her face as she looked down upon his naked form submerged in the water. His heart skipped a beat. The unguarded warmth and affection that radiated from her face filled him with past joys.

He could almost imagine it was love shining in her eyes. Hope flooded him. He never wanted to share her with anyone else, this was just for him. The niggling thought that he'd done too much for her to actually love him tried to overtake the moment, but he cast it aside.

He made no effort to hide his longing, as he commanded, "Get in."

"Where is your loofa?" she deflected, breaking eye contact.

"My what?" Irritation crept into his voice.

"The sponge you bathe with, silly," she said, her smile light and playful.

"I use a soap bar to bathe with." He'd buy a damned loofa if she wanted him to, if she planned on using it on him often. His eyes caught hers and he held her gaze. "Just get in."

He watched her chest rise and fall. "Okay," Verena's voice was a whisper.

Slowly, she undid the zipper on the side of her pants and let them slide down her supple legs. She kicked her legs free of them at her ankles, then gripped her blouse, pulling it up and over her head. The fabric fluttered to the ground as it landed on top of her discarded pants.

His breath caught as she stood there in her white lace corset, thigh high hose, and lace panties. Her eyes didn't leave his as she removed each stocking, uncovering her gorgeous legs. Then she loosened with deliberate care the satin laces on her corset, gently sliding it down her body to the floor. Finally, Verena slipped her fingers under the elastic of her panties. She stood there, naked before him.

His hands itched to touch every inch of her. The heat of his gaze was matched by the crimson of her blush, bringing a satisfied smile to his face.

Lowering herself down into the tub at the other end, her body slipped beneath the water. Amiel grabbed her arm and pulled her on top of him, splashing water everywhere.

"Amiel!"

She struggled to regain her balance and ended up straddling him. Her hands splayed across his chest for a moment. Then her fingers traced the red welt of the scar that slashed across it. Her eyes grew wide at the sight of the battle wound.

"Would it have mattered to you if I had died?"

The question slipped out of him unbidden. He wanted to know the answer, but the question revealed his fear. He held his breath.

The look on her face told him she was unsure how to answer. His mind willed her to tell him... that she loved him... could he ever hope to hear those words? Did he have a right to? After all that had happened between them?

"As a matter of fact, yes, it would have mattered to me."

His eyes grew hooded as he asked, "How so? I thought maybe you might be glad to be rid of me."

"I don't want you dead."

Verena reached for the bar of soap. Her bare breasts brushing against his shoulder. The touch of her pert nipples on his flesh sent a tingle through his body. He held her hips firmly, helping her balance, which brought his loins in contact with hers.

"I need you alive." She ran the soap over his neck and shoulders.

His heart pounded at the tenderness in her touch. A blaze of joy filled him at the thought that she didn't want him dead.

"You should get a sponge you know." Her words were delivered in the girly tone he remembered from their childhood.

The innateness of the conversation made him impatient. She had not wished him to fall in battle, but why? Did she care for him?

"Why?" He needed to know.

"Because a sponge will help exfo—"

"No, why do you need me alive?"

"Because..."

She continued to lather him up in soap, the silence stretching. Amiel let his eyes take in the woman he loved as she sat, naked, in his lap. Her face glistened from the steam of the water. Her full breasts floated on the surface, their rosy nipples beckoning to him. His throat tightened as he realized she didn't mean to answer.

Her hands made their way from his neck down to his chest. She let her fingers linger in the thick hair, tracing the reddened scar once more. The excitement of her touch warred with his need to hear an answer.

"Tell me why? Why do you need me alive?" His words were a whispered plea and he chided himself for giving her this power, the chance to wound him.

"I..." She looked into his eyes.

He could see her fighting an internal battle, and he longed to know what thoughts filled her. Was the answer to his question that difficult? He steeled himself against the possibility of... he wasn't sure what.

Then her eyes shone with the decision. What would she respond?

"I'm pregnant."

Amiel's heart stopped. His eyes grew wide as his mind swirled with the words she had spoken. She carried his child, his heir. They had made a baby. He straightened, wrapping his arms around her, his face inches from hers. Her breasts rubbed on his chest as he held her, secure in his arms.

"Are you sure?"

"Yes. Dr. Koll confirmed it when she took blood work a few days ago."

Her eyes locked with his. In them Amiel could see emotions that he couldn't name. The tension he'd felt in her body as he'd pressed for an answer relaxed.

"You're perfect," he said.

Every fiber of his being thrilled at the knowledge that she would be the mother of his child. A baby, a new life, a combination of the two of them merged into one. His Rennie would give birth to their baby.

"Wha—"

He swallowed up whatever she was to say, his mouth claiming hers. His arms, wrapped around her, crushed her to his chest. Her breasts pressed into him.

A jolt of pleasure filled him as she kissed him back, matching the hunger of his mouth. He felt her arms slip around him, her fingers sinking into the moistened hair at the nape of his neck. Her mouth tasted him, daringly, and he let her, returning passion for passion. The passive, timid woman who let him enjoy her was gone.

He moved down her neck, tasting the salty-sweetness of her skin, nibbling on her slender shoulder. Amiel kept his arms around her, sliding her back slightly to gain access to her breasts. He took the rosied tip of one into his mouth, feeling it roll on his tongue, he suckled it until he heard her moan.

She nibbled on his earlobe, letting her hands run down his arms that held her securely in his lap. He thrilled at her touch, at her new-found audacity. Amiel delighted at the thought of her taking a more active part in their lovemaking. He took in one breast, then switched to the other. Her body arched to let him get his fill.

His manhood throbbed as he lifted her up, settling her on the edge of the bathtub. Kneeling between her legs, he held her secure as he pushed himself gently into her body. He felt her passage expand at his invasion, her warmth contracting around him. Bracing his legs, he began to thrust in slow, pulsing rhythm. His hands caressed her back as he enjoyed her breasts.

Her body trembled with the rising pleasure, and he lowered his hands to her hips, helping her rub on his pelvis as he filled her over and over again. Raising his head, his eyes locked with hers. His mind whirled as he fell into their green depths. *I love you Verena Elidena Destavi. I've always loved you.*

She dug her nails into the flesh of his back as she sought to press him tighter into her. Rennie took his rhythm and matched it with her hips, seeking the release. He adjusted himself so she could come. He held his eyes with hers as the orgasm rolled through her. With breathless pleasure, he watched her let herself go, riding him, enjoying the fulfillment of his touch.

As her orgasm pulsed through her body, he quickened his thrusts. He kept his eyes locked with hers as his body shook with the satisfaction of his release. He spasmed, filling her with his seed. A smile wreathed his face as he thought about the baby within her, casting away the niggling worry that this might not be good for it. Surely, that was not so. He'd have to ask the doctor about it, but he'd be damned if he would stop having her now. Maybe that worry was later in the pregnancy?

She sagged in his arms, her forehead touching his. Amiel kissed her nose, her cheeks, then took her lips in a long, sweet exploration.

Adjusting them, he came to a squatting position. He grabbed her thighs and helped her wrap her legs around him. His chest against hers, his face burrowed into her neck, for a moment Amiel held her there, wrapped up in her body. Then he rose to his feet, taking her with him. She gasped but held on to him. With care, he got out of the tub and headed to his bed.

"I've always known you would be mine." The huskiness of his voice was muffled against her neck. "Always." The possessiveness of his words matched his taking of her body. Lifting his gaze to hers, he added, "Verena Elidena Destavi, you are mine."

He watched her as he spoke the words, laying her down, her arms still wrapped about him, her strong legs holding him tight. There it was, a flicker of dissention in the green depths. He smiled cheekily as he imagined her thoughts. "I am not an object to be owned, Amiel ra Aulden." He could hear her saying it with her hands on her hips and her eyes flashing angrily. His chuckle at the image turned into a possessive groan.

Oh but you are mine. You were born to be mine, and I will never let you go, Rennie.

He straightened, pulling away from the warmth of her to fix their position on the bed. A groan of reluctance escaped her as he left her embrace. She sought to hold him in place. The thrill of her desire for him shot through him. Whatever she might or might not feel for him, Verena wanted him in her bed.

Amiel looked at her there, her beautiful body open to him, her eyes demanding he come to her. She wanted him. Desire spread over her, and the thought brought a surge of happiness to him.

Joining her on the bed, he adjusted them so that his body covered her. He nibbled her neck, stopping at the base, where a small pulse made her extra sensitive. He heard her sigh and felt her push her head back at his touch. He continued his perusal of her, making his way down to feed on her breasts, cupping them, teasing her nipples to attention.

She arched, giving them fully to him, and he took them into his mouth, tasting the sweetness of her body.

As he kissed his way down her abdomen, he placed soft, tender pecks where her womb was, his heart full of pride and joy at the thought of the babe within.

"You have an amazing mother, little one," he whispered to his child. "She's smart, funny, fierce, and beautiful. You're going to love her. I do."

"Are you saying something?" Verena asked, her voice glazed with passion.

He raised his head to look at her. Leaning on one arm to support his weight, he ran his other hand along the beautiful smooth curve of her leg, pushing out and onto the bed, opening her up, giving himself access to her secrets. His fingers explored as his mouth tasted her. The fiery red hairs tickled his cheeks.

Amiel felt her body shake with waves of pleasure, which drove his fingers deeper as his mouth took on a greater urgency. He made her burst with delight as many times as he could coax her to it. Then he was ready to bury himself inside her again. He rode her hard. Her body surrendering to his hunger and need with equal passion. Verena tightened around him, driving him over the edge as he exploded within her once more. Amiel didn't care about anything then. The world could disappear as far as he was concerned. As long as he could be here, inside Rennie, possessing her, extracting her passion, nothing mattered.

Sometime later, Amiel lay with Verena, her back to him, swallowed up by his strong arms holding her close. The lavender scent of her perfume mingled with that of their lovemaking as he began to drift into sleep.

Thoughts of his heir, growing within her, filled his mind. He would keep them safe from the threats that loomed in their future. Determination and confidence filled him as he thought of his new life, the woman he loved beside him, their children playing about them, and their kingdom flourishing under their rule. Smiling with satisfaction, he fell into a deep and restful sleep.

CHAPTER 36

A NEW NATION

VERENA SAT BESIDE AMIEL as he greeted the prophet. She longed to get the holy man alone to discover what news he brought about the quest and Sir Andross.

"You are welcome to use the library and remain with us here in the castle, Lord Orloff," Amiel was saying.

The request for access had been presented to them and Verena now sat watching the portly gentleman bow in reverence and head out to settle into his assigned chambers.

"A prophet in the castle, perhaps he can give us guidance on the coming situation with the Gortive." She turned to look at Amiel as she spoke. Verena noticed the veiled look in his eyes.

"Perhaps," his tone seemed guarded. Turning to her, he excused himself, "I'll see you at dinner."

Verena quickly dismissed her ladies, which now included Lady Geld and Baronness Perth again along with the Lady Ydarb, Duchess of Aul, and Countess Udeep of Aulden. Nataya, Countess of Udeep, was by far Verena's favorite. Married to Lord Sabred, the dragon slayer, she had the best stories and was less frivolous than all the other ladies having been a kaper, as the members of the Intergalactic Alliance Peace-keeping Corps were called.

As she made her way to the library, Verena wondered why such a strong and capable woman would willingly leave her position as a lieutenant. She supposed her love for Lord Sabred had been the cause of the sacrifice of her career. The Countess of Cartul, the earl's daughter, had not yet rejoined them, having been sent to planet Drulin by her father as a precaution after the events of the Council of Peers chamber.

Entering her favorite part of the castle, Verena inquired after the Prophet from Mr. Nairbil, who told her Lord Orloff was in the private study room on the tenth floor.

Verena burst out as she entered the cozy chamber equipped with a chair, desk, comfortable sofa, and long table for spreading out maps and charts. "What news do you have, Lord Orloff, of Sir Andross, I mean?"

Lord Orloff rose and bowed to her, "He was badly wounded in the battle with the rego, but he has mended quickly and has reached Lady Viona."

Settling onto the sofa and gesturing for him to regain his seat, Verena pressed him for information, "Lord Orloff, this quest, how do you find it proceeding? Do you think it folly? Should we—"

"My apologies for interrupting, Majesty, but no I do not feel the quest to be folly at all." His eyes filled with concern as he leaned forward. "Are you aware of Godar, Majesty?"

"No, who is he?"

"When Sir Andross reached Lady Viona, he found Lord Horsef who informed us of the existence of these nijar. They are a new sect of energy wielders that have used their knowledge and power for evil."

"Is Godar their leader?" Verena asked, wondering at the sudden rise of yet another group. *What was happening with the rajin that so many seemed to be forming new orders rather than join them?*

"I am uncertain of his position within the order. From what I have discovered and what Lord Horsef and Lady Vivelda have shared, however, he serves Amiel and is his primary counselor."

"I thought the Duke of Aul was Amiel's main advisor."

"On the outside, yes, but in private, Amiel meets with Godar for advice." Lord Orloff's voice took on a sober tone. "Arwace, Clicktess of Fragma, has uncovered some circumstantial connections between this Godar and the House of Aulden that may go back to King Amiel's father, possibly even to his great-grandfather." The seer sighed deeply.

Gazing at her with hope in his eyes, he continued, "I have heard of the peace with the Dravidians and the conquest of the Auldian insurgency as I traveled here. I am aware things seem to be stabilizing, and I am pleased that your Majesty is doing so well in uniting the land. However, I feel it wise to continue the quest under Rajin Horsef's direction, now that he has been found. I can't shake the idea that things are not completely as they seem."

"I was glad to see the realm starting to come together at last. Amiel seems to be much more open and willing to establish a rule that includes us both in the decision making."

"Has he told you that he knows of the quest and the liquid?"

"No, but Sir Andross told me that he is and has been aware since the beginning." Verena's heart ached. There was yet this secret lingering between them. Maybe there were even more. "Does the Nijar Godar know of the liquid?" Verena asked, her voice devoid of feeling.

"Yes, undoubtedly so. If the king had not told him, which he probably did, then the Elmalin Darlia, whom Sir Andross met at Sanctal and who tricked him into going to the cave of the rego, must have done so by now."

"I see."

"Majesty, this liquid is very potent, but only Rajin Horsef can access it and only you can wield it. Rajin LaRoo gave its secrets to no one else, trusting only Horsef with this power." Lord Orloff dared to reach out and place his hand on hers. The fatherly gesture comforted her, but her mind seemed to have gone numb. "We must be very cautious now."

"Yes. Are the elmalin in league with this new dark sect?" Verena hoped the answer was no. She rather liked the idea of an all-female group of energy wielders.

"No," the Prophet said with a smile. "It is uncertain who might be in this new group, but not all the elmalin will have turned from the true path. I feel certain that there may even be rajin involved with the rise of this nijar sect."

"Really!"

"Yes, Majesty." The prophet turned and reached into the folds of his voluminous cloak. "This is the crystal dagger. You must guard it and the liquid well until Horsef returns."

Taking the glittering artifact with reverent care, Verena asked, "Where is Lord Horsef going? Is he not coming here?"

"No, Majesty. The rajin, with the help of Sir Andross and myself, will head out to investigate the true origins and purposes of these nijar. We will return once we have answers that can safeguard the alliance."

"You are going as well? When? Why is Sir Andross going?" Verena's mind swirled with questions about this turn of events.

"Lord Horsef feels Sir Andross will be important in the coming quest. I go to seek answers to the schisms in the faith. But we will not leave you alone. Javern is here and will help you. I hope the Great I Am will guide us and we will return very soon."

"I trust your judgment and that of the rajin masters, of course. I will do what I can here to keep the planet safe." Verena gifted him a wan smile before continuing, "I will leave you to your study... I need some time alone."

Verena didn't wait for an answer.

Covering the dagger with her sweater, she rushed through the corridors. Once in her room, she placed the valuable crystal in what had been her mother's vault and hid it in a secret compartment below the various jewels.

Settling onto her bed, she thought again about how Amiel actually knew everything. How he'd feigned surprise at finding Sir Andross gone. *He sure is a good actor.* All those moments when she thought for certain he might really care for her could all be just more of the same. She sat there, on her bed, rocking back and forth, wondering just how much of an idiot she really was to have fallen in love with Amiel ra Aulden as tears made their way down her cheeks.

That afternoon, Verena sat before the Council of Peers. The joint members from both nations were the same as when the marriage had taken place. Except for those who had perished, of course. Verena looked at Lord Soane, young and solemn in his role as Royal Treasurer, replacing his mother, the late Lady Soane. It still ached that people died needlessly over a lie.

"Lords and Ladies," Amiel began, "we must review the allocations—"

"Before we commence, there is the matter of the betrothal agreement," Verena's voice, full of confidence surprised them all.

"We already—"

"The betrothal agreement was set aside under false accusations and based on faulty, contrived evidence." Verena took joy in interrupting him. "A situation was created that led to the acceptance of King Amiel as sole sovereign taking my rights away as Queen of Dravidia, but it was based on falsehoods. The betrothal agreement was illegally set aside and should now be reinstated in view of the truth."

The council members murmured and the tension in the room escalated.

Amiel shot her a dark look at her blindside. *He deserved it. He had done the same to her but without merit.*

"The queen is correct," the Duke of Aul said. Gasps of surprise echoed in the chamber. "In truth, my King, the betrothal agreement along with the land grants that the Earl of Sarnac and I worked out before the situation the queen mentioned, should be honored. The basis of accusation for the House of Tor has been proven completely false."

"I will second the queen's motion to reinstate the betrothal agreement," Viscount Pembra spoke up. He would be marrying the earl's daughter soon and become Count of Cartul. Verena had mixed feelings about him, his attentions to her a bit too familiar for her liking. Still, he seemed to be honorable.

Silence fell. All eyes were on Amiel. Verena watched him adjust in his seat. She knew he was angry, but she didn't care. *What he'd done was wrong and he'd pledged to set it right, hadn't he?*

Leaning close to him, she whispered, "You pledged to make things right."

His eyes locked with hers. A blue gaze made of ice. "The betrothal agreement will be honored." His voice shook.

"Now," Verena said, sitting back in her white leather chair, "let's discuss the allocations for defenses."

The councilors suggested critical areas. Verena only superficially participated. A great sense of righteousness filled her as she noticed Amiel struggle to seem unaffected by the development. She would now have final say in all matters that affected what had been the independent nation of Dravidia. He preserved final decision-making power over Aulden. But somehow, they would both need to come to an agreement on matters that affected the whole realm. This arrangement had been created by her father, and she would find a way to make it work, for his memory and her people's future.

That evening, Verena sat in the throne room. The silver cloth from the train of her ball gown's skirt pooled around the floor to her left. The room was filled with nobles from both nations. The flags of those whose houses were now allied to the new rulers hung from the ceiling in a lineless map of their continent. The proclamation of the creation of the unified kingdom of Auldivia had been made over the media channels and now the celebration would begin. In the end, they had all settled on the name her father and Amiel had originally agreed upon.

The castle had been quickly decorated with flowers and ribbons. The musicians brought in for the royal ball. The room glittered with bejeweled noble men and ladies. Her people mingled among Amiel's. It all seemed wonderful. But that was on the surface, for below it all a restlessness lingered.

At first, Verena had thought it was knowing that Amiel's affection was nothing more than a ploy to earn her trust so that he could gain access to the liquids. But it went deeper than that. She couldn't put her finger on just what it was that seemed off somehow, but it was there in the back of her mind.

Still, she smiled as the noble houses of the realm stepped forward to curtsey before them. Amiel looked dashing in his military regalia uniform. It had been decided that they would merge the colors of their houses, her royal purple with his black and use silver as the third color. Thus, the new uniform pants were black while the coat was royal purple.

The merged crest depicting Thyrein's legendary sword, Marama, with outspread dragon wings sprouting from the hilt piercing the principality's coronet in silver on a field of royal purple was now on every guard and liveried servants' outfit, whether human or droid. There had been heated discussion about the background color. Some argued it should be half black and half purple, but the look didn't feel right. In the end, her colors had won out. Verena's lips curved into a smile at the chagrin in Amiel at the final coat of arms.

The silver trumpets sounded as the last of the nobles made their bow. Amiel rose, extending his hand to her. She took it and stood by his side.

"Tonight, we celebrate the birth of a new nation," his voice resounded in the silent room. "We have put an end to war and have come together at last. It gives me great pleasure to announce on this momentous occasion, that the new kingdom of Auldivia will be welcoming a royal heir in five months' time."

The gasps of surprise were quickly followed by exuberant applause. Verena felt her cheeks grow hot and knew she was blushing. Her gaze met with the Earl of Sarnac, who stood to the left of the platform. Verena noted the somber look. Perhaps he felt it too. Something was being overlooked.

Verena went through the motions of receiving the congratulations of their guests. The delicious dinner proceeded without incident. Soon, they all adjourned to the ballroom for the dancing.

"Shall we?" Amiel asked, as they entered the room arm in arm.

"Yes."

She allowed him to lead her to the center of the dance floor. His arm wrapped around her waist, bringing her in close to him. The scent of his cologne filled her, and she felt herself follow as the music began. As always, they were in perfect harmony on the dance floor; as always, something lay between them.

"You don't seem very happy." His whispered comment startled her, making her miss a step.

She felt him sweep her around, covering the error smoothly. "I feel like something is not completely right... Like we are missing something."

"I can't imagine what it could be," his tone implied she was clearly being silly. "Lord Uld and his followers will be executed on the morrow. Count Tor's signet was found among his things, did you know that?"

"No. I had not been told." Verena had suspected it was Uld and his group that were responsible for the assassination attempt from the start. The video the elmalin presented had shown them in possession of it. Yet, she couldn't shake the unease. "You know, it might go deeper. There may be others that were in on it who chose not to follow the rash course of out and out war."

"Rennie, I do believe you have become a bit paranoid." Amiel's arrogance stung her.

"I don't like things that are wrapped up so neatly."

"With the betrothal agreement, you have regained your power to rule. You should be jubilant."

"I am glad we will be able to rule *together*." She emphasized the word, though she had to admit making him go back to the agreement had filled her with a sense of justice.

They finished the rest of the dance in silence. Allowing him to lead her to the thrones, Verena stepped up and took her seat. He chose to head back out to mingle with the guests.

"May I approach, Majesty?" The Earl of Sarnac asked.

"Of course." She gestured to him. "I am glad to have you back. There is much to be done, much yet to be considered."

"Yes." He stood before her, his face marred by the worries of recent events. "I wanted to ask for an audience with you. As we were on the run, I pondered some words that your father said, before his death. I would like to share them with you, perhaps you might make sense of them."

"You know, I came across his journals. He encrypted the last one, and I can't seem to access it." Verena commented. "Come, let's go out to the gardens. Some fresh air might help us think better."

Rising, she took his arm and allowed him to lead the way through the glass doors out into the warm summer night. The moon's silver beams illuminated the rose flower beds. They made their way down the stone steps, stopping after a time near one of the fountains.

"What did my father say?"

"During the betrothal period, we had several REIS teams hunting down information about what initiated the interest of the Gortive in coming together. King Dekkyle believed that someone beyond just Lorgan was behind their sudden advancements in technology."

"Indeed, that makes sense." Verena understood now why he had been away all those months. *If only he had said something to me then, but no time to worry about that now.* "Did he find something, some clue?"

"I believe he may have, but he kept it to himself," the earl, who had been gazing out across the garden to the sea beyond the promontory, turned to look at her now. "Right before he died, he was feverish. He said many things that made little sense, but he mentioned the Calvernsin repeatedly. For a time, I thought he was referring to his youth, when he fought the Calvernsin alongside the other intergalactic forces during the annexation of the Bralyer system."

"But you think his reference to them could be related to the Gortive?"

"Amiel fought for Fratern recently when they fended off an attempt by the Calvernsin to take over the Fraternish colonies on Galdegov. I did some digging, and it turns out that one of the fighter craft Amiel destroyed was captained by Prince Z'Pau'z."

"The son of General Z'Tro'z!" Verena had been forced to study the military strategies of this famous Calvernsin hero. Rajin Molent had stressed the importance of always knowing your enemies, and the Calvernsin would forever be at war with the intergalactic planetary system in Thyrein's Galactic Wall. As a child, she had gone with her mother to handle a dispute and met the general and the prince. Verena remembered how much she had liked both of them.

"I think the Calvernsin may be helping the Gortive," the earl explained. "It could be a new strategy for overcoming our council's protection over the planets. Or maybe a search for vengeance on Amiel for the death of Z'Pau'z. When we were on Laitera, King Dekkyle set up a meeting with a man who claimed to have proof that the Calvernsin had given the Gortive the information on building sailing vessels and were training them to make ocean voyages, but he didn't show to produce the data. Later, on Fridgia, we had a rendezvous set for very much the same purpose, but the informant was killed before we could speak with him. We recovered a chip, but when we returned for the wedding everything fell apart. I don't know what became of that chip or what information it may have contained."

"Tomorrow we must bring this up in council," Verena spoke confidently. "We must focus our attention on discovering the Gortive's plans and the truth behind who is helping them and why."

"Yes, of course," the earl's voice sounded relieved to have delivered to her the information. "I wanted you to know first."

Verena smiled up at him. She was glad to know he was hers at heart. It had not been so when she first returned. She remembered how he'd confided in Amiel instead. Perhaps all this mess had made her a bit better at this ruling thing. Good enough to have at least this man's respect. He'd been Chief Peer for her father, his closest confidant, and wisest advisor. She'd almost lost him to Amiel. A sense of relief came over her at the thought of moving forward with his renewed trust in her leadership.

"Can you help me find Telion?"

"Who, Majesty?"

"Telion was my father's favorite tech specialist. Papa always said Telion understood digital technologies better than anyone else in the galactic wall. The journal that is encrypted, it must have been done by Telion. My father didn't have the experience for that kind of sophisticated work. If we can get him back here, we can unlock the notes papa made. Those may shed light on this matter." Verena sighed. "Maybe Telion knows where the chip is. If it is in my father's former office, well, Amiel may find it."

"I will locate this Telion and have him report to you, Majesty." The earl nodded his head almost imperceptibly toward the gaiety of the ballroom. "Our absence has been noted. We should rejoin the party?"

"Indeed."

Verena allowed him to lead her back. She could see on the patio several nobles, among them Amiel. As they made their way up the steps to the ballroom again, Verena flashed her husband a smile.

"Taking the night air?" he commented as she reached him.

"It is refreshing."

"I will head back in, Majesty," the earl bowed to her and to Amiel before returning to the party.

"Your Majesty looks stunning this evening," the Duchess of Aul commented.

"Thank you, your Grace."

Viscount Pembra stepped forward. Bowing deeply, he asked, "May I have this dance, Majesty."

"It would be my pleasure, my Lord." Verena allowed him to lead her back into the ballroom and onto the dance floor.

"Your Majesty is ravishing and rightly so upon such a glorious occasion," he gushed as he twirled her around the room.

"Well, I certainly am glad that we seem to have finally made real progress." She smiled politely, feeling her cheeks flush. His attentiveness and the look in his eyes when he saw her always made her feel uncomfortable, though she did appreciate his support in the council chamber today.

"King Amiel reigns as sovereign over the whole continent with you by his side with full powers to help him. There is peace, and who knows, if the Gortive do attack and we win, why, he could be king over the whole planet."

Verena chose not to reply. The mocking tone, as if Amiel were unworthy of ruling, irritated her. As the music prolonged itself, Verena regretted having said yes to dancing with the Viscount. In the past months, he had been a fervent ally in the Council of Peers and for that she was grateful. But he made her uneasy.

"I for one am glad to have you as our queen," he said as the music finally ended. Bowing, he added, "I look forward to being by your side to help you in all I can for many years to come, Majesty."

"Thank you, Viscount." Verena walked away with him following. Making her way to Amiel, she stood by her husband's side.

Verena released her breath, which she hadn't realized she'd been holding once the earl finished his remarks. The Earl of Sarnac had delivered the information about the Calvernsin connection to the Council of Peers. Verena hoped this time, the members would be stable. She liked that the earl was given back his position of honor as Chief Peer with the Duke of Aul as Assistant Chief.

The chamber fell into a thoughtful silence.

"The earl has shared with us critical information, which we should have been aware of long ago if we had not had all that unpleas—" she began.

"But we know now and that is important." Amiel cut her off. "The Calvernsin are a dangerous group. Their empire has become stronger since Z'Yvot'z became their supreme ruler. While they continue to be a planet-less space people, they are becoming bolder in taking over natural resources on the free planets within Thyrein's Galactic Wall."

"The REIS teams have been on standby with no new direct instructions," the Earl of Sarnac mentioned. "Your Majesties may wish to debrief the teams and perhaps send them out once more. We should have men on the ground to bring back reliable intelligence on the Gortive progress."

"During the war, mining production on Parthia came to a virtual standstill," the Duke of Aul commented. "Many of the companies that had mining operations there have expressed a desire for protection as their men return to their posts. They wish to resume their work in order to forestall further loss of profits."

"The troops that are standing down, for now, from active duty, should be offered as security for the companies," the Earl of Ydarb suggested.

"We could send REIS members among those to spy out the continent and bring us information on Gortive developments and movements," the Earl of Sarnac added.

"Proceed with that plan," Amiel acquiesced. "We will have the teams that were working on the issue debrief with us alongside the Nedula teams. We in Aulden had set our own intelligence gathering services to the task of understanding what the Gortive were up to. With information from both, we should be able to get a handle on where we stand."

Verena felt exhilarated at the thought of finally digging into the real threat to their nation. She had wanted to bring up the fact that the assassination attempt still had loose ends, but decided against it.

"I would like to share some interesting satellite images that may be of use here," she commented instead. "As you can see, the Gortive have some kind of compound here at the Bay of Parthos, and another here at the Bay of Parong, and a larger one at the Gulf of Vankgort."

The three images hovered over the council table. They showed large hangers built to house whatever it was the Gortive were building. Gortive clansmen from all four of the usually warring tribes could be seen working with surprising diligence.

"We should get eyes on what is within these hangers," Viscount Pembra urged. "We have been going on the assumption that they are building sailing ships, but, if the Calvernsin are involved, they could have given the natives space technology."

"I doubt they would be so reckless," Amiel said dismissively. "They are not that foolish."

Verena noticed Viscount Pembra's face redden at the slight. She felt bad for him, having his comment shot down like that. Verena had noticed now a few instances where the Viscount ventured to speak, which were not many, and Amiel treated his words with complete disdain. Something strange was going on between her husband and the Viscount. Verena wondered what it could be.

"Revenge is something that often blinds people to what would be wise," the Viscount commented. "If the Calvernsin are not all behind this, but just General Z'Tro'z, then it could be that he might give them whatever he felt it would take to get back at you... my King."

Verena caught the pause before the respectful address with Amiel's title. By the way he stiffened in his chair beside her, she guessed Amiel had noted it too.

"Maybe," Amiel conceded grudgingly. "But he is smarter than that." He lifted a hand forestalling the Viscount's next comment. "Yes, revenge and all, it might be."

"Then we might send reconnaissance units to these places to investigate further?" The Duke of Aul inquired.

"Send Nedula agents to investigate," Amiel commanded.

As the members began to leave, Verena saw the Earl of Sarnac block Viscount Pembra's path to her.

"I have sent for my daughter, Viscount," the earl said, putting a fatherly hand on the nobleman's shoulder.

Pembra jerked away quickly, surprising both the earl and Verena. "My apologies. I was wounded, and it still hurts." Looking at the earl, he said, "I look forward to meeting my bride soon then." Bowing, he turned and left.

The look on the earl's face showed concern. "Don't worry, Excellency," Verena said, trying to reassure him. "I'm sure the countess can handle him."

Chapter 37
United Vidden

Verena stared out the window of her bedchamber. The garden courtyard below was ablaze with color, the myriad flower beds and their beautiful denizens swayed in the dying embers of the day's sun. Summer would soon turn to the coolness of autumn and the blooms would fade away. As she contemplated the turning of the seasons, Verena's heart ached. Amiel's affections seemed to change with just about the same frequency.

A pair of arms surrounded her, and she stiffened as Amiel said in her ear, "I missed you."

"Your time in Dravidia was productive I trust," she said in response, a terseness in her tone.

"I don't want to talk about the kingdom or our work." He turned her toward him and dropped her gaze down, averting her face. "This is our private time. Time for us to be together. Let's talk about us." He let his lips rest on her hair as he brought her forehead to his chest, enveloping her fully in his arms.

"Is there an us?" she asked, her heartbeat quickening as his hands ran up and down her back in soothing strokes.

"Of course," his voice held a note of surprise at her question. "We are husband and wife, rulers of this planet, we are having our first child, there is a very definite us and that is what we need to develop now."

Verena pulled away from his embrace. He didn't try to stop her. She walked around him and out to the sitting room portion of her chambers. She settled on her favorite sofa and curled herself tight into her light blue robe. He followed her and sat in the seat in front of her. When she let her gaze lift to his face, she found his eyes guarded.

"How do we develop us?" she asked.

He leaned forward, resting his hands on his knees and interlocking his palms. His head dropped and he stared at the floor for a second. Verena was surprised that he didn't have a quick answer. He always seemed so sure of everything he did.

"Rennie." The nickname came out in a whispered plea. "I just wish we could..." His voice trailed away.

"I wish we could treat each other with respect, work as equals toward a prosperous future. But you don't really trust my judgment." Verena realized she was picking a fight.

Now that the kingdom was indeed united, they had begun to forge a balanced relationship, at least as far as their rulership was concerned. Yet, she couldn't shake the feeling that, if given a chance, he would rip her power from her once more. After all, that was what Amiel loved more than anything else in the universe... power.

He took a deep breath and sat back, crossing his legs. "We will always have different ideas and, yes, I do feel you are very naïve in many areas." He ran a frustrated hand through his thick black hair. "But... I wouldn't be trying to build a relationship with you if I didn't care. I am here, sitting with you, talking with you. Do you think if I didn't respect and care about a future with you that I would do this?"

Verena looked down at her hands, avoiding the earnestness in his eyes. She knew he was right.

"What is this really about?" he asked as if he'd read her mind. "This isn't about the ruling part. You know we've done well so far and will continue to build our kingdom up together. Your help bringing our people to a united victory and a united Vidden shows that we can make this work." He rose and came to sit beside her. He leaned in close, taking her chin in his hand and lifting her face to his. "It isn't our governing that holds you back, now. Tell me, talk to me."

"You didn't want to reinstate the betrothal agreement. You want all the power." Verena gazed at him, challenging him to deny it.

"Yes. I would rather continue being sole sovereign," he confessed. "I don't trust you, not fully. But I am willing to move forward and make it work. For us and for our child."

His head leaned in to kiss her lips. Warmth pooled in her abdomen. Her mind flooded with the experiences of his touch on her body, and she responded to him. His arm wrapped around her, pulling her to him. He held her close and let his hand drop from her chin, caressing her throat as he made his way to cup her breast. She arching her back at his touch, resting her head on his shoulder as his mouth became more insistent and hungrier.

He left her lips and trailed down to the sweet spot on her throat.

"Rennie." He looked up, locking eyes with her.

Emboldened, she pushed him back so she could sit straddling him. He wrapped his hands around her and pulled her into him, burying his face in her neck, trailing kisses on her skin.

She ran her hands through his thick wavy hair and let the flood of love fill her being. Then a doubt hit her. Recalling her ladies' words about men and their need for other women, Verena shuddered. She wouldn't share Amiel. He was hers.

With trembling hands, she grasped his face, pulling it up so she could look in his eyes.

"I don't want to share you... not ever."

"What are you talking about?" His eyes showed his confusion.

"I... if you are with me, then you can't be with any other woman..." She felt awkward even saying it. Heat invaded her cheeks at her daring.

"I have the most beautiful woman in the universe as my wife. I have no need for anyone else." He smiled at her as he added, "You shouldn't listen to gossip, Rennie. Those hateful biddies and their tongues are not good for you. So, you want me all to yourself, do you?"

The teasing statement caught her off guard. "Well, I mean..." She ran her hand over his chest through the open shirt of his sleep ware, enjoying the feel of his skin and hair. Verena noticed he wasn't wearing the blood-red jewel. She remembered how he wore it less and less. *Had he worn it to war?* She didn't think so.

"Yes. I do want you to myself. I don't want to share you with any other woman." Gazing at him she noted the shine of mirth in his eyes. "I mean it Amiel ra Aulden. You said to me that I was yours some nights ago. Well, I'm telling you now... you are mine."

"You have my word. You're the only woman I've ever wanted and you will never have to share me."

"Good."

A sexy smile spread on his handsome face as he slowly brought her in for a kiss. As his lips touched hers, his words brushed them. "I always have been yours, Verena Elidena Destavi, and always will be."

She wanted desperately to believe him. His mouth locked with hers, he lifted her with him as he rose, carrying her wrapped around him to the bed.

Hours later, Verena lay satiated, a deep contentment enveloped her. As her eyes grew heavy, the glint of something peaking from Amiel's discarded jacket pocket caught her attention. Rising carefully so as not to wake him, she reached the spot where his clothing lay strewn upon the floor. Her hand trembled as she drew out a small silver holochip. Could this be the data her father's informant had been killed over? Had Amiel found it in her father's office?

Verena quickly hid it in her desk drawer. She would share it with the Earl of Sarnac in the morning. Returning to bed, she nestled into the warmth of the covers. Thoughts swirled in her mind. They had a new kingdom, Auldivia; they knew what needed to be done next to defend against the Gortive strike; and soon Rajin Horsef and his group would find the most important answer of all, the origin and plan of this new order.

A united Vidden had risen and would become stronger as they finally worked together. If only she could trust Amiel. As much as she loved him, Verena knew he was dangerous and always would be.

About the Author

Fern Brady is the founder and CEO of Inklings Publishing. She holds multiple Masters degrees and several certifications. She began her professional life as a foreign correspondent, taught for 15 years in Alief ISD, and is a full-time Realtor in Houston. She has published numerous short stories, two children's picture books, a couple of poems, and is excited about the upcoming release of her debut novel, United Vidden, which will be book one in her Thyrein's Galactic Wall Series. She is an active member of the Houston Writers Guild, with whom she served as CEO for four years, and currently serves on the board of Authorology, a non-profit organization which helps authors in a variety of ways. She is also a member of Authors Marketing Guild as well as of Blood Over Texas and Romance Writers of America. Follow Fern's writing at: www.fernbrady.com

You can contact her at:
fernbrady@inklingspublishing.com

Printed in Great Britain
by Amazon